B-BOY TO MAN

Corey Lamar Tanksley

B-BOY TO MAN

Volume 1.0

FRESHMEN

LEG
Lady Esquire Group, LLC
Publishing & Management Firm

SILVERBACC BROTHERS, LLC | Montgomery County, MD

Boy to Man should be read solely as a work of fiction. Names, characters, places and incidents are the product of the author's imagination or are used fictitiously. Any resemblance to actual events, locales or persons, living or dead, is entirely coincidental

FOR

Velma Tanksley
Josephine "Moine" Tanksley
Gwendolyn Evans

FRESHMEN
1958-1993

"Perspective and the ability to reason are the pillars of maturity…"

Professor Archibald King

1 May 26, 1989

Camara Truth could not take her eyes off her royal plum, taffeta, multi-tiered prom dress. The poof sleeves made her think immediately of Cinderella and Prince Charming. She was certainly pretty enough to be anyone's princess. Her goddess mother must have dipped her twice in the river Chocolate, ankles included. She was a shade lighter than Pepsi-Cola. Her burnt bronze-tinted eyes were luxurious even without makeup. They lured men in like almond-shaped Sirens signing. The boys in her high school classes would often get lost in them like wayward sailors until she freed them with a slight turn of the head or a rapid blink.

Camara's figure would have gotten her banished to a small deserted island by a jealous goddess had she existed during Zeus's rule. Tiny waist, full breast, protruding backside and ample hips—her body was as puzzling as the proverbial ship in the bottle. It forced women without African genes to consider the merits of augmentation and silicone.

Although barely eighteen, Camara had a remarkably mature perspective when it came to her looks. She was keenly aware that her beauty was by happenstance and not a skill. Humility and congeniality balanced her physicality. More importantly, her intelligence allowed her to 'nerd it out' with the math and chess club geeks whenever the mood hit. These dimensions gave her popularity, likability and a high probability of being voted prom queen.

The dress was spread across Camara's bed among ten colorful teddy bears. She adored teddy bears of all sizes, shapes, and colors. She had another five on her dresser and eight on her desk. Good music was her other passion. Posters of Big Daddy Kane, Queen Latifah, Bobby Brown, Jodie Watley, and Kwame adorned her walls. Her favorite artist KRS-ONE was reserved for the space on her wall directly above her headboard. She loved the intelligent but streetwise nature of his music.

She was listening to Soul II Soul's 'Keep on Moving' when the telephone in her room rang. It was her boyfriend of eighteen months and prom date Harold, who was more excited about the possibility of what might happen after the prom than the actual prom itself.

"Hello, can I speak to Camara please?" Harold asked politely.

"Harold, we've been going together for a year and a half, and you still don't know my telephone voice?" asked Camara slightly annoyed. Part of her understood why he didn't know her telephone voice well. Camara was not a telephone person at all. She basically used it to get important information and that's it. She wasn't gossipy nor could she be painted with the stereotypes often brushed across young women. She and Harold talked on the phone once or twice a week and never longer than ten or fifteen minutes.

"Well, the last time I thought it was you, it wasn't. It was your mom, and I was pretty embarrassed."

"What time are you picking me up tonight?" asked Camara in a just-the-facts-ma'am kind of way.

"Well, the limo is supposed to be here at six. So I figure I can get to your house around six-thirty or so. We will be at the prom by seven," Harold stated as if struggling with a math problem.

"That's cool, see you then," Camara responded quickly before Harold could talk about their after-prom plans. Camara wanted to focus on the music, the fun, and the possibility of being prom queen. She knew that Harold wanted something more valuable. Camara was proud of the fact that she was a virgin while so many of her classmates were not. Although she had plenty of opportunities from the young and old to 'help' her with that issue, she remained pure.

Chastity aside, Camara was curious about sex. She and Harold were affectionate towards each other but did not know each other in the biblical sense. As far she knew Harold had only had sex twice in his life and had been celibate for the duration of their relationship. Part of her felt like she owed Harold because he never begged, guilt-tripped, or made having sex a condition of their relationship. He did bring it up on occasion and prom night was a big occasion.

"Camara! Did Harold take care of everything he was supposed to?" grilled Brenda Truth, Camara's semi-overprotective mother, from the bottom of the stairs.

"Did he confirm the limousine? Pick up his tuxedo? Did he get the right kind of corsage—white?" She was bent on making sure everything was right for her only child. Sensing it was a sore subject with her mother, Camara barely asked questions about her father. The ice cold fact was that she never laid eyes on him. He could be Harold's father for all she knew.

"Yes, Mama Truth," Camara answered in a playfully sarcastic tone to the machine gun line of inquiry.

"Good. I'm working an extended shift tonight, so I won't be home till about three-thirty. For just this, once you can stay out past your 11 p.m. curfew. You have till 2 a.m., Cinderella, and not a minute later, you understand me?" asked Mama Truth sternly.

"Yes mother dear, 2 a.m. it is," said Camara. She was pleasantly surprised that her mom would willingly let her stay out so late.

"One minute later and you'll turn into a sweet potato and you know I make a mean sweet potato pie," Mama Truth half-joked.

"Yes, sweet potato pie. Very clever…old biddy," Camara responded making sure the last word was inaudible. Even though her mother was a smidgeon over forty, the discipline and sacrifice she often displayed made her seem much older. She often appeared immune to enthusiasm and celebration.

But this was Camara's night to celebrate. She was a 4.0 student and had her pick of colleges from around the country on scholarship. She whittled down her options to Georgetown, NYU or Columbia but her mother gently forced her at the last minute to enroll at McNair University, less than a half hour drive away. Her mother was attracted to how close McNair was, the small class sizes, and the quality of the professors. Camara agreed because she was a bit nervous about living far away from her mother anyway. But tonight was all about womanhood and liberation. She was five hours away from the arrival of Harold, the limo, her white corsage and perhaps a bit more.

■

The school colors, maroon, and silver adorned the lavish ballroom of the downtown Ritz-Carlton. School security guards and more than a few helicopter parents now doubled as chaperones. 'Every Little Step' by Bobby Brown was the theme song of Greece High School Academy's 1989 Senior Prom. It was supposed to represent every little step that the senior class took to get to this point in their lives—the cusp of adulthood.

Unfortunately for Camara, every little step she took, Harold was right there doing a fabulous puppy dog imitation. When she got up to get some punch he followed her. When she wanted to dance he was behind her. When she had to go powder her nose he waited outside the bathroom door. When she got up to mingle with other friends he was at her side in her peripheral view at all times. Winning prom queen only seemed to intensify Harold's desire to violate her personal space. Camara felt powerful but slightly annoyed.

For Harold, it was truly like seeing her for the first time. He could not believe that this beautiful specimen was his girlfriend. The prospect that he might have sex with her was a dream straight out of the deepest crack pipe. Doing his best to not look so obvious, Harold stood by the speaker watching Camara intensely. Harold was tall and husky with a medium brown complexion. His thick glasses did nothing to help his overall appearance. For Camara, his kindness and intelligence more than made up for his lack of savoir-faire.

Entouch's 'Two Steps to the Right' poured from the speakers into the ears of the crowd which was visibly becoming all estrogen and testosterone. Heavy petting and grinding had replaced the MC Hammer impersonations that dominated the dance floor just 30 minutes ago. Camara curled her index fingers making the come here motion and Harold responded like a doting puppy.

"It's 11:00. I'm ready to leave," Camara whispered as she moved her body into his. She had moved in too quickly for Harold to hide the fact that he was fully aroused.

Slightly embarrassed Harold looked for comfort in clarification, "You mean take you home?"

"No, retard. I mean come home with me. Meet me in the limo in five," Camara backed up slowly and made a beeline towards her friends.

Harold's beatific grimace said it all.

■

Standing in Camara's bedroom smelling soft vanilla and perfume, Harold was struggling to break the ice. The R&B group Ready for the World moaned in the background. *Oh, Oh, Oh, Oh, girl tonight.*

"Camara, did I tell you how beautiful you look tonight?" asked Harold while fiddling with his white tuxedo bow-tie.

"Thank you. Yes, about thirteen times," she responded.

An uncomfortable silence followed. Milliseconds seemed like minutes. Camara allowed Harold to torture himself in his own awkward nervousness. She watched him shift his weight from left to right as he scanned the posters on the wall. Left hand on her left hip she followed his eyes and decided it was time to rescue him from a complete and epic fail. She walked up to him and kissed him with ferocity. A surge of energy and foreign power permeated her body. She liked the feeling and began to wield that power over him, suddenly stopping then starting to kiss him again at her discretion. Harold was shaking like a pair of maracas. When he felt she had stopped kissing him for good, Harold felt the next move was his. Empowered, he swept the stuffed animals off the bed aggressively.

Harold looked as if he was prepared to cannibalize her. Nervous doubts began their assault on Camara's courage. She realized what was about to happen, and more importantly who it was about to happen with. Before she could mount a sufficient defense, Harold lifted her off her feet and placed her semi-gently on the bed. He quickly began removing his clothes as if the current window of opportunity would close in precious seconds.

Upon seeing Harold as naked as Adam before eating that wretched apple, Camara nearly bolted from her room. *You went this far don't be scared, it's time to know what sex actually feels like.* As Camara prayed to herself for strength, Harold helped remove her dress. Only a pair of thong panties and lace bra stood between her and her maiden voyage.

Camara laid back, slowly removed her panties and opened up her shivering legs. Watching eagerly Harold rolled a condom on for just the third time in his life and approached. Camara felt like she was in the doctor's office waiting for that dreaded shot and instinctively held her breath. Harold struggled through his inexperience and finally found his way. He roughly pushed himself inside of her – or so it felt that way to Camara as her brain was now full of hyperbole.

Oh my God! It feels like someone is shoving a camel through the eye of a needle. Wait. That's a biblical reference...nothing biblical about this. Get it together girl! The pain began as excruciating, then went to tolerable, and ended as a numb buzzing that wouldn't quite go away. To keep her mind off the pain Camara began to sing with the song playing on her radio.

"Sunny days everybody loves them, tell me baby can you stand the rain. Storms will come, I know, I know all the days won't be perfect. This we know for but tell me can you stand it can you stand the rain?" Camara sang softly.

The unintended consequence of Camara melody was that it drove Harold crazy. Turned up to 10, he began racing toward the finish line. He screamed her name in ecstasy over and over before falling limp on top of her. A thought, fleeting but strong, ran through Camara's head, *Never ever again.* Four minutes of curiosity clearly had its price. *Nigga get off me.*

2 June 15, 1989

"You're a dirtbag man - straight up fuckin' sicko!" Will yelled as he laughed almost uncontrollably at the musings of his best friend Chase Douglass. Prince readjusted the rear-view mirror inside the dusty blue 1988 Chevrolet Nova hatchback to get a good look at Chase and shook his head in disbelief.

The glistening and rain-soaked streets of Rochester, New York welcomed the rotating wheels of the adolescent chariot bound for mischief. Early that night the trio had graduated from Malcolm X High School. As a graduation gift, Will's uncle allowed them to use the Chevy until sunup. They had about three more hours left.

The late night drizzle plopped and pinged rhythmically against the windows to the sounds of Kool G. Rap's 'Truly Yours'. As the melody blared from the sub-standard stereo system, the banter between comrades continued. Will—lanky, dark-skinned and handsome—sat shotgun with his sneaker-clad feet resting on dashboard looking skeptically at Chase in the back seat. He was still in the process of getting his mind around what Chase was trying to explain to them.

"Chase, homeboy, you're Chester the molester from Rochester. You're a diaper sniper dog! Darren's sister just turned thirteen last week. She probably ain't even bleeding yet, and you talking 'bout she gonna have some good pussy when she grows up!"

"Sure did. I said it," Chase responded unmoved by Will's lecture. "You heard it here first. She shall have that good-good when she grows up."

"Wait until she grows up, and then comment on her pussy. Sick bastard," yelled Will.

"But wait Will. Didn't you just knock Tiffany's boots on Monday? Prince asked Will sounding genuinely confused. "She's fifteen, I think."

"Naw, man, she's sixteen. Well, that's what she told me. And we not talking about me, we talking about Kinko the Clown sitting back there," Will answered as he continued to laugh. Confident that he was free from hypocrisy, he waited for Chase to expound upon his pussy forecast.

Chase was known throughout the neighborhood for his advanced sexual appetite. His caramel complexion fused with his pretty boy features made him a prime time attraction for females. He was skilled with his tongue and made women feel simultaneously relaxed yet frisky with well-timed compliments, braggadocio, and promises. He was wise beyond his years when it came to seducing women. Chase brushed off the left knee of his stonewashed jeans and with his thumb and forefinger, slightly squeezed his bottom lip, took a deep breath and proceeded to clarify.

"I ain't sick, I'm just scientific bout things. It's called projecting. I take her current body mass, weight, looks, and sex appeal, and I project her vagina power forward. And I project that Darren's little sister is going to have some snapping-turtle-good-ass-pussy! Now I didn't fuck her, she's way too young, and I ain't bout to go to jail. But she got ass and tits like a grown woman, right or wrong?

"So?" Will asked, not fully grasping the line of inquiry.

"My point being, that she got the equipment of a grown woman. Now, I'm not gonna tap that ass yet, but I know somebody is going to if they haven't already. So in a few years when she done worked all the little kinks out of her sex game, I'll be right there giving her grown man lessons. I'mma let that pussy marinate for a few years then tax it! Straight up!" Chase said while looking out the window.

"You sound like a low-life pimp sizing up a toddler. Tell you what. When you return in a few years, make sure to bring the baby wipes for clean-up duty," Will said while hand slapping Prince who had just made an ill-advised left turn, failing to yield the right-of-way to dump truck. Despite the near collision, the vehicle's occupants seemed unconcerned.

"Fuck both of y'all. She's a toddler, huh? Well, she can sit on daddy's face like a potty."

Prince lost control of the wheel as uncontrollable laughter erupted from each of them. Prince haphazardly pulled the Chevy to the curb. No one could speak through the laughter although each tried. Chase was a real jokester. He often exaggerated his intentions and the depths of his depravity for effect and cheap laughs. Nothing—no topic, no person—was off limits. Still, this latest statement was too much even for him to say with a straight face. Will could barely breathe and attempts to speak made it worse.

When control was reestablished, Chase was the first to form a complete sentence. Stoking the deep waves in his brush cut he abruptly changed course, "Damn, we are college men now. We can do what we want, how we want when we want."

Will nodded and thought about his soon to be college home, Cornell University. He visited the prestigious university and fell in love with the campus and the women. Upon his return home, he urged Chase to think about going to college, namely for the scores of beautiful, intelligent women in the student body. Because a dedicated and thoughtful teacher named Alvin Dance pulled a few strings, Chase was accepted at McNair University. Prince was happy to be playing basketball at the local community junior college as he remedied his Proposition 48 problems. While Will was the equivalent of *summa cum laude*, both Chase and Prince were graduating *thank the lordy*.

Prince spotted an older black woman wearing a gray knit wool cap and matching gray mini-skirt approaching the Chevy. She looked as if she'd seen better days but was still attractive.

"Bingo!" Prince exclaimed as he pointed.

Will was unsure whether bingo was the appropriate word. "Prince, she might be a crack head. That's all you baby."

She flashed a toothy smile when she got close enough and said, "Hey y'all. What's up? I'm trying to get into something."

She looked and smelled decent but was clearly very intoxicated. Chase realized that they were parked a few blocks away from a popular strip joint called Club Cheetah.

"Listen here, Miss Lady, we just graduated tonight, and want to treat my man here to blow-job," Chase said referring to Prince. Prince was not shy about his use of prostitutes. He'd screw anything that moved. If it didn't move, he'd kick it into motion and then hump it to dust. Prince made sure to poke his head into a position to make eye contact with the seasoned vixen.

"Ten dollars...if you want it, it's yours. If not, have a nice evening no hard feelings, Miss Lady," Prince said.

"Uh uh, no you didn't," she responded placing her hand on her hip. "I strip–I lap dance for ten dollars but I don't fuck or suck for that," she said with a drunken slur.

"But you do suck, correct?" Chase took over. "One nut ten dollars and my man Prince will be very quick."

As if exposed, she broke eye contact and reached to open the back door. A game of musical chairs ensued, which started with the prostitute entering the rear passenger side of the vehicle and ended with Chase in the driver seat and Prince behind him. The maroon, potato chip, and engine oil-stained cloth seats were sparsely littered with cigarette butts, ashes, and empty Big Mac boxes. Prince cleaned the seats enough to get comfortable with his new date as Chase hit the gas and maneuvered the vehicle behind an abandoned building a few blocks way.

Will lowered the volume on the car stereo to avoid attracting attention. Will was the most ambitious of the trio. He excelled in school, played sports and more importantly worked part-time. As his buddies were typically broke he often paid for everything. Will dug into his pockets and handed the prostitute a raggedy ten dollar bill.

"Now you understand, we are paying you for the nut, not your time. So the faster Prince busts, then the quicker you can get gone and be on your way. So are we clear?" Chase asked.

The answer came twenty seconds later in the form of a sloppy sucking sound. It was loud enough that anyone standing on the corner of Jefferson Ave and Bartlett Street could have heard it. It made Will uneasy and he fought not to turn the music up.

"Damn, did they give you too much penicillin as a baby? You're big as hell. It's like a fishing pole!" she exclaimed while taking care of business.

Prince felt like the man as he high-fived Chase. After about ten minutes he realized that he could not finish with company in such close proximity to him. Plus, he noticed Chase sneaking peeks in the rear-view mirror.

"Okay, I'm done. I can't do it," Prince said frustrated.

Chase reminded the prostitute that they paid for one orgasm. "Well, let me try the tall dude then," she said as if enjoying the challenge.

With a little coaxing from Chase, Will got out of the passenger side and got into the back seat. After unbuckling his belt he leaned back as far as he could go in the small car and folded his hands behind his head.

"How you want me to do it baby, my mouth, my hand, slow, fast how you want me to do it?" she asked.

"To tell you the truth I really don't care what you do to it, just get that nut up outta there, Miss Lady," Will said while exhaling trying to play it cool.

After about five minutes, Will, like Prince, concluded that he could not concentrate. The laughter coming from the front seats did not help. Feeling like he'd lost a manhood competition Will complained, "I can't nut either man! Keep the money, we're done."

"Shiiiitttt!" yelled Chase drawing out the word so it lasted a full four seconds. "I bet I can nut! I can do it with my mama looking me square in the eyes if I had to! Let me show you amateurs how Chase Douglass gets down."

Miss Lady applauded and let out a joyous cheer, "Woo, Wooo, Wooo!"

Chase and Will switched positions in the vehicle quickly before the prostitute realized she was getting a bum deal. By Will's calculation, if Chase got serviced, they would be paying three dollars and thirty-three cents a head.

Not only was she not upset with the low wage, she was pleased as cherry punch.

Getting the hurry up sign from Will, Chase quickly dropped his pants. "Don't worry this won't take long at all."

As Miss Lady sloppily engaged her new client, Will and Prince decided they would distract Chase so they would all end the night on an even keel. Prince turned and attempted to have a conversation with Chase about Detroit sweeping the Lakers for the NBA championship. While too uneasy to try and make eye contact as Prince did, Will turned up the music slightly and began his best Bizmarkie impression. These antics were all for naught as Chase was not the least bit discomforted.

"Yeah, yeah, yeah, yeah, yeah, yeeeaaahhh, that's the lick!" Chase screamed as he reached his climax. "Clean your plate, yeah, yeah. Good girl!"

Prince and Will looked at each other in amazement. Two minutes flat. They were not exactly comfortable with hearing him orgasm but were impressed by the remarkable performance under pressure. Miss Lady began clapping again, proud of her work and Chase's performance.

"Okay ho, that's enough. This ain't amateur night at the Apollo," Prince said mostly out of disappointment that he could not match the pornstar focus of Chase. "Kick rocks, Miss Lady!"

Will was kind enough to wave farewell as she exited as happily and drunk as she arrived. Will was very interested in his best friend's ability to focus on the matters at hand despite obvious distractions. Thinking it through, he surmised that sex was a little bit different for Chase. It had always been. Shrugging off a latent feeling of concern he watched Miss Lady cut through a nearby yard. Turning to Prince he said, "Drive my brother—Nick Tahoe's. Let's get Ron Jeremy Jr. back there a garbage plate. I need a white hot and home fries my damn self."

The ignition fired as the prostitute faded into the black night. By the time the vehicle turned toward the main street, Chase finally recovered. He looked on the floorboard and saw Miss Lady's gray skull knit cap. He picked it up, used to wipe the residue from his manly parts and then tossed it out the window.

As they headed downtown Chase thought, *This is going to be a wild, wild summer then McNair University, here I come.*

3 August 28, 1989

"Batman was good, but I just think it could've been better. The Batmobile and Jack Nicholson was really all I went to see it for—and I mean it was average. I just wish Batman was more—I don't know—just more. You know what I'm sayin'?" asked Harold.

Camara was barely paying attention to the conversation as she had more pressing matters to attend to this morning. In fact, she was in the middle of packing when Harold decided to call for the second time in as many hours.

"Yeah, more," Camara responded sleepily trying hard to suppress her latest yawn. Harold's conversation pieces progressively bored her and she tuned everything out except when he begged for a response. She might as well have been talking with Charlie Brown's teacher. *Wah whaa wah wah whaa, Wah Wah Wah, Whaa.* The very sound of his voice was beginning to irritate her. As Harold droned on, Camara placed an imaginary .357 pistol to her temple and pulled the trigger. As she caught oozing brains in her left hand, guilt about her behavior and attitude toward Harold brought her back into focus.

After their first and only sexual encounter, Harold began calling Camara on a more frequent basis in hopes that they would drive down the road together to carnal wisdom again. Harold was a good guy and he certainly meant no harm but she felt impoverished by any form of contact with him. In conversation after conversation, she desperately searched for openings to express her need to end the relationship before they went off to college. She knew Harold was high school and you can't stay in high school forever. She wanted to be free, clear, and unattached entering college. Not wanting to hurt Harold, Camara could never muster the courage to broach the issue. Consequently, she had let the matter go down to the wire. It was the two-minute warning and now she needed to be curt.

"Harold, listen for a second ok? I need to tell you something. You are such a sweet guy it's kinda hard for me to say this. I think that you can do better than me. Matter of fact I know you can. With both of us going to—with college coming up and all, I know it's going to be hard to keep in contact," Camara said in a manner meant to soften the gut punch she just landed.

"Camara, wait…umm, Syracuse University is about two hours away, I'll be getting a car soon, I can't do better than you. Why are you trying to breakup with me? I don't want to breakup, please," pleaded Harold. He began to sob uncontrollably as the realization that their relationship had reached the terminal point began to set in. He was confused.

"Harold, oh my God, are you crying? Wow. You gotta stop that. Please, I'm feeling bad about this already and now I'm feeling weird. Please, Harold, stop crying."

"I need you. I love you. You're everything to me," Harold cried.

"All right all right, we can still stay together for now. Bye! I gotta get ready to go," Camara said as she hung the phone up abruptly. Her head started to pound from the thought of continuing the one-way relationship. *I'll deal with this later.*

On cue, Mama Truth yelled upstairs to give Camara a time check. Back on task, she began to box up her favorite books, photos, and teddy bears. Camara carefully selected six of her prized teddy bears into a black treasure chest. Rusty, Frenchie, Ronnie, Dazzle, Rose, and her favorite, Mr. Fizzy all made the cut. The rest were tasked with watching her room and guarding against an incursion from Mama Truth until Thanksgiving.

"Well guys, I hope you're ready for McNair University. I most certainly am. No crying, we're big boys and girls now. Ok, keep tight till we reach campus," Camara said as she closed and locked the chest. Her mind raced, running through the alternative futures college might offer. She was nervous but she was prepared.

■

The drive to McNair University was not a long one and before she knew it, her mother was pulling up in front of her dormitory building. From time to time she passed McNair University but never once thought she would be attending the school one day. After helping Camara unload her belongings, Mama Truth gave her daughter some very simple instructions, "Keep them books open and keep your legs closed. I love you."

Not knowing how to take the very simple and straightforward advice, she replied by giving her mother a warm hug and soft kiss. With the confidence of young warrior she slung her book bag onto her back, grabbed her two suitcases and walked into her new home, Morgan Hall.

Camara was met by the resident assistant who gave her some literature on campus life and the keys to the main entrance, her mailbox, and her room. She attached them to her class of 1989 gold key ring and walked up the stairs to her second floor room. When she opened the door she discovered that her new living space was two bedrooms and a suite.

Within a half hour of moving in, Camara was warmly joined by her suitemate, Rhonda Wheatley. Rhonda was a pretty and portly, brown-skinned young woman with short braided extensions in her hair. Her engaging smile revealed a gap in between her two front teeth that added to her sweet character.

"Hello, girlfriend. I'm Rhonda Wheatley from Buffalo," she said as she dropped her suitcases and extended her thick and well-manicured hand.

"Hi, I'm Camara Truth and I'm from Rochester. How are you doing?" Camara asked.

"I'm fine. Just anxious to see what college life is all about that's all. Wow, you are so pretty!" Rhonda exclaimed genuinely.

"Thank you so much! So are you. I plan to major in business, what about you?" Camara asked.

"Sociology," Rhonda shot back.

"You know, I thought we would just have a room, but we got this extra space out here. Maybe we could all pool together and maybe get a sofa and a TV, you know?" Camara said while walking to the window.

"I think that's a real good idea, Camara, I could even call my—"

Before Rhonda could finish her sentence a human explosion came through the door. Four rambunctious young women entered laughing and screaming about something or the other. They walked around the suite, entered both bedrooms, and continued to jump loudly from one conversation to next. The discussions were difficult to follow because they all seemed to be talking at once for large chunks of time. The group totally ignored Camara and Rhonda. Camara realized her hand was frozen in a hand wave. She dropped her hand quickly in embarrassment and looked at Rhonda in mild disbelief.

The four ladies were dressed fashionably and wore heavy makeup. The tallest one of the bunch was attractive but had a look on her face like she had not gone to the bathroom in months. From the parts of conversation they were able to follow, Camara and Rhonda were able to figure out a few things: her name was Brandi; she was Rhonda's roommate, and she was from the New York City area.

"It's so country—tired and country up here! All the dudes here got Jheri curls and shit. I'm counting down the days until I go back to Brooklyn. Bed-Stuy, do or die!" Brandi said as she turned and tapped fingers with her friends. Rhonda surmised—based on many visits with her family spread across five boroughs—that the accent was not entirely genuine.

"You right Brandi, it's so corny. I can't wait for Thanksgiving break either," one of the other girls said.

"The only reason I'm here is because mom dukes forced me. Otherwise, I would've gone to Pace or NYU or someplace in the city, you know what I'm saying?" Brandi asked as the crew exited the suite without so much as a farewell or a peace sign.

"How was the weather in Poughkeepsie, or Schenectady?" Rhonda yelled as the ladies exited. "If she's from Bedford-Stuyvesant, I'm the Queen of England."

Camara let out a little chuckle even though the fraudulent accent went over her head. She had only explored New York City via rap lyrics and couldn't tell Hoboken from Long Island. The suitemates stood in silence for a few moments gazing at the door Brandi had just exited, adding a few head shakes for good measure. Without the luxury of knowing Rhonda for more than five minutes, Camara knew they were both thinking the same thing. *We've just been assaulted by the roommate from hell.*

4 September 1, 1989

Chase awoke with literal fire in his lions. He knew the time had come to seek professional help when he nearly passed out from the excruciating displeasure of everyday normal routines like urination. He walked to the bathroom as if he was mummified. The pain from his throbbing manhood barely allowed him to walk. He slowly pulled down his white and tight, Fruit of the Lomb underwear that stuck to his pus-filled member like Velcro. Chase clinched his teeth and breathed sporadically as he attempted to urinate. To Chase, it felt like his penis had decided to give birth to a bastard child with a razor-back and medieval sickles for hands.

Chase knew a visit to the clinic was overdue. He could not continue like this. His trademark ravenous sex drive had been parked in the garage for the last two and half weeks. Ironically for how brazen and unabashed he was sexually, the thought of being seen at a clinic because of that same shameless behavior by someone he knew frightened him to his soul. He remembered Will laughing and calling him stupid for not getting checked out two weeks ago. Whenever they talked he would ask how the Tuskegee Syphilis experiment was going. Either that or he'd rap select phrases from Kool Moe Dee's 'Go See the Doctor', "*Don't blame me if it turns into a foot, extending from the middle of your body!*"

Worse, Will also advised him against having raw sex with Tracey, the girl who scorched him during the pool party. According to Will, every Tom, Donte and Hakeem on the Westside was hitting Tracey like uncontested layups. There was a reason why they called her 'Dick Tracey'. She then brought her trifling ass across the Clarissa Street Bridge and passed herself off as goody-two-shoes. Chase took the bait and the rest was history, pain, and pus.

Chase took the painful walk back upstairs to his bedroom, located in the attic of his grandparents' home. It was sparsely furnished with a television, a boom box, a dresser, and a twin size bed. He was nonchalant about beginning his new life as a college man today although his two suitcases had been packed for a full week. Now he was carrying a venereal disease to McNair University with the rest of his luggage. He knew he ought to listen to his best friend more often—especially since Will was the type to rehash judgment errors over and over with the worse told-you-so attitude in New York State.

Later that day Chase's grandfather drove him to McNair University. The trip was uneventful and expectedly quiet. Chase did not have a bad relationship with his grandparents; it was simply a quiet relationship. They rarely spoke more than what was absolutely necessary. Small talk was not a part of the Douglass household.

By the time they reached campus, the pain in Chase's nether regions had become unbearable. Once they located Chase's dormitory, Gordon Hall, he asked his grandfather to put his belongings in his room and bid him farewell. Chase was on a mission to go see the doctor. He saw two campus safety officers posted outside of Morgan Hall, directly across from his dorm. Upon seeing them he walked as quickly and as painlessly as he could towards them.

"Hello, officers. I was hoping you guys could tell me exactly where the campus hospital is located," Chase said while adjusting his fire-breathing penis by placing one hand in his pocket and gently pulling it to the side.

"Well young man it's not a hospital it's a clinic. What's wrong son, you ate something that didn't agree with you?" The officer asked.

"In a matter of speaking, umm… you can say that. Can you tell me where the clinic is please?"

"Sure, it's called the Drew Campus Clinic and if you hang a quick right past the Student Union right there and walk about ten minutes, it will be on the left side of the yard, you can't miss it," the officer said politely as Chase made a beeline to the clinic.

■

Chase walked into the campus clinic and immediately went to the receptionist. She was a fair-skinned Latina with sensuous eyes and plump lips that were smeared with red lipstick. The low-cut V-neck red t-shirt she wore hugged and pushed her sizable breast forward and up.

"Hello may I help you?" the receptionist asked in a low and slow sexy voice.

"Absolutely, I'd like to see a doctor. Just to check out some things is all. You know what I mean?" Chase asked with a sly smile.

"That's what we're here for—to check you out," she said with a light giggle. "I'm going to need for you to fill out this form. Don't worry it's confidential. Then bring it back up to me and someone will be with you shortly after, ok?" she asked.

"Sounds peachy to me…umm," Chase said trying to correctly read and then pronounce the name on her name tag. It also gave Chase another reason to look in the direction of her breast.

"Estefania, I'm a junior here at McNair. My major is nursing and this is my work-study job," she said with the same light giggle. Chase knew she was ripe for the picking so long as she didn't find out the real reason he was visiting the clinic. Pain shot up through his stomach attempting to blow his smooth cover. He grimaced but quickly recovered.

"Hello, E-stef-an-ia. I'm Chase and I'm a freshman. And I would love it if you were to show me the ropes—you know—the ins and outs of college life. I've heard college can be hard, very hard. So, I need all the nice and easy friendly faces I can find, you know what I mean?" Chase asked while softening his eyes to focus on hers. "I'm living at Gordon Hall, room 204. You should come over and see me next week. Not this week. Next week. I wanna make sure I get a solid start on the academics."

"Sure, I'll give you a week to get your feet wet, Chase."

Give me a week to extinguish this goddamn fire in my drawers Chase thought.

Estefania wrote down her number and handed it to him with a smile. Chase sat down and momentarily forgot why he was at the clinic in the first place. Then the painful knot in his groin area reminded him why. Being ten minutes away from tetracycline restored Chase's libido. As he watched Estefania go about her daily duties, he began to get an erection. The pain had never been more intense but it did not stop him from fantasizing about the pleasure he was sure to experience with Estefania.

"Douglass? Chase Douglass? The doctor will see you now."

September 5, 1989

A regime change was coming. Dr. Archibald Moses King II surveyed the new land that he believed he was destined to conquer. He understood that land had to be toiled, work put in, hours given, and heads taken. His rule would bring forth new villagers; villagers who have historically been peasants, slaves, and thieves and otherwise ignorant to the fact that they have access. Some of these villagers will be intellectual royalty and it was up to Archibald to alert them to their majestic bloodlines. He, along with his allies, would raise a new flag that would stand for education and a real opportunity for those who meticulously and bravely sought it out. Obtaining sovereignty in the world of academia would be a long and difficult passage but this was his calling. Archibald King always kept his mother's favorite saying in the forefront of his mind: *The longest journey begins with the smallest step.*

His small step began when he accepted the position as an assistant professor at McNair University earlier that summer. Although he was born in Rochester, New York, he spent a great deal of time down south. He earned his PhD. in Black Literature from Morehouse College in 1980. His only ties now to Rochester were a few stray family members and a handful of ex-girlfriends, friends, and enemies.

Before attending Morehouse, Archie did a short stretch in the Monroe County correctional facility for menacing. The menacing charge could be seen as either a high misdemeanor or a low felony. The judge in his case viewed it as the latter rather than the former. That black mark on his record likely explained why it had taken him so long to land a full-time teaching position.

Archie looked more like a linebacker coach than a scholar. His hulking 6 foot 4 inch, 275-pound frame supported muscles everywhere except his sizable belly. Dark-skinned with black horn-rimmed glasses, he could be as serious or jovial as the situation required. A voracious reading appetite developed in jail helped to focus Archibald and ultimately led him to make teaching and research his vocation. He simply wanted to educate young people. And, he wanted to do that near his hometown. At the tender age of 40, he was finally getting his chance.

Professor King stood across from the Student Union and looked south towards the various lecture halls and administration buildings and shook his head in disbelief as it hit him that he was now a member of the faculty. As he walked the campus, he greeted several students by nodding his head and smiling. His blue-knit wool sweater, a white shirt, and a blue and gray striped tie helped to offset his imposing stature. He also smiled as a way to let the students know that he did not pose a threat to them physically—mentally, however, was another matter altogether.

Before his first class, he had a meeting with the English department chair, Dr. Seth Fellner. Dr. Fellner, an openly gay man and a staunch believer in diversity was instrumental in helping Professor King land the position. He felt as long as you are competent and you loved to educate, you were deserving of at least the opportunity to either succeed or fail. He could sense Archibald would approach the job with humility and seriousness.

Professor King walked into the office and was greeted by a pleasant and eager secretary who told him that Dr. Fellner was expecting him. He slipped into Dr. Fellner's large-sized office. It was carpeted and painted a warm red. Ironically, there were far more potted flower plants in his office than books.

"Dr. King, welcome. Please have a seat. I know what you're thinking. Where are all the books? I'm the head of the English Department so I'm required to have at minimum a thousand books in my office, right? Books don't smell as good as flowers."

"You have a point there, sir."

"So, are you nervous about teaching your first ever class?" Dr. Fellner asked while sitting down at his desk grabbing his cup of coffee with both hands and crossing his legs.

"With all due respect sir, I'd prefer to be called Professor King. I know I have a Ph.D., and that affords me the title, but I am a professor first and foremost. And am I nervous? To be quite honest with you, absolutely not!" he lied as both men chuckled. "I think you well know I'm as nervous as Jimmy Swaggart in a room full of hookers."

"I totally understand, Professor King. Just remember to rely on your intelligence, your research, your preparation, your common sense, and most importantly your manners. You can tell the Queen of England to go screw herself and get away with it if you do it with manners. Good manners will go a long way. Because trust me, some of these kids you're going to come across here will test your patience. Trust in yourself and I promise you that you will excel. Do we have your schedule all worked out?" Dr. Fellner asked with a slight lilt to voice.

"Yes, sir. I do believe I'm good to go," Archibald answered cleaning his glasses.

Dr. Fellner who dressed casually comfortable in a short sleeved striped shirt, faded Levi jeans, and socks and flip flops, adjusted his thick glasses and leaned back in his leather chair.

"Ok, but for housekeeping purposes, I have to inform you that you must report any students that violate our academic integrity standards. Also, McNair University has a strict policy against faculty having any kind of sexual relationship with students in their classes. It would behoove you to consider all students off limits even if they are not enrolled in your class. If a consensual relationship develops between you and a student you must report it immediately to me. Such relationships may have unintended consequences and lead to conflicts of interest down the road. So, I would encourage you to steer clear of the co-ed snatch. Not that I would have to worry about any of that with you, but it is my job to explicitly communicate university policy. Capisce?"

"Understood... and, again I appreciate the opportunity," Professor King said while extending his hand to shake Dr. Fellner's.

"I didn't give you anything Professor King. You earned it. Frankly, you are a brilliant man. I was truly surprised that another university didn't already snatch you up. Your dissertation was borderline genius," said Dr. Fellner.

"I appreciate the compliment, I truly do."

"Doc—Professor King, with all due respect, I rarely compliment people and I'm certainly not complementing you. I am merely speaking the truth about your work, period. No need to thank me, Capisce?" asked Dr. Fellner once again.

While Professor King was humbled by Dr. Fellner's words, deep down King knew that all the accolades in the world did not amount to a block of government issued cheese if he could not connect with his students. He looked at the attendance lists for his Black Literature class due to begin in ten minutes, counted forty-eight students, and smiled. No time like your first time. No time like the present.

6 September 14, 1989

Free will can be a dangerous thing. Chase was exercising his free will by waking up around noon every day since arriving at McNair. He approached class as if it were merely one of many options. Reading and problem sets were alternatives to be weighed against other competing priorities. Chase had been keeping very late hours by studying the mating patterns of the female species that inhabited the university. Keg parties and fraternity smokers were a few of the functions that Chase frequented to gain working knowledge of the habits of these lovely creatures.

This particular morning, Chase woke up expectedly hungry from a night of co-ed decadence. He decided to take the leisurely ten-minute stroll to the Student Union cafeteria which had a potpourri of high cholesterol but extremely tasty choices to soothe his hunger pangs.

In front of the Student Union's entrance were scores of students, some stretched out on the grass studying, some playing hacky sack, some smoking cigarettes. As he approached the entrance to the Student Union, Chase looked to his left and noticed a steep set of stairs and railings. There he saw his roommate Brad skateboarding with a few of his buddies. He had been meaning to have a proper sit down with his roommate since he had arrived but they kept missing each other. Chase walked over and was immediately impressed by the various moves the group performed with their skateboards. Brad was the best of the bunch, successfully pulling off tricks such as the 'Impossible', the 'Kickflip', and the 'Ollie'.

What impressed Chase the most was the black boom box with the chrome trim that looked as if it was standing post for the skateboarders. As Chase walked closer the sounds of Public Enemy's 'Black Steel in the Hour of Chaos' got aggressively louder. When Brad finished his run, he walked over to greet him.

"Hey, what's up man? You're real fly with that skateboard man. Word up! But, my question is whose boom box is that and why is it pumping P.E.? No disrespect but I know none of y'all know anything about Public Enemy," Chase said with a wide and friendly smile on his face.

"P.E. is the best. They're fucking mint. Chuck D is dope. The Bomb Squad's production is ill, and Flavor Flav, well Flav is just crazy!" Brad said while standing his skateboard straight up like a walking cane and leaning on it slightly.

Chase looked at Brad dumbfounded. He looked him up and down again and still couldn't believe he even heard of rap music—especially Public Enemy. His tanned white skin, large mop of dirty brown hair, extra baggy burnt orange shorts, plaid button up shirts, and lounge type sneakers that were apparently scored from the old man section of Sear's department store, did not exactly scream Hip Hop. But to Chase, his love of the music seemed genuine.

"Elvis was a hero to most? But he didn't mean shit to me? Straight up racist, the sucka was simple and plain? Fuck him and John Wayne?" Chase asked in stutter step manner meant to assess whether his roommate was cool with Chuck D's analysis.

"Dude I love Hip Hop! It's the best music in the world to skate to. The vibe and energy is fantastic!"

"Kool G. Rap is my favorite. Just-Ice is dope too," Chase said.

"Rakim is my favorite. He is absolutely incredible. When I heard 'Check Out My Melody' for the first time I got goosebumps, literally. Caught up in the moment Brad began to rap. "I take seven MC's put 'em in a line, and add seven more brothers—"

"—who think they can rhyme, well it'll take seven more before I go for mine," Chase jumped in to help Brad finish the impromptu rhyme.

"And now that's twenty-one MC's ate up at the same time!'" They both rapped while slapping each other five, laughing, and shaking hands all at the same time. As far as Chase was concerned he hit the jackpot for roommates.

"Hey, Chase, you see that cassette case over there? I got about 50 tapes in it. G-Rap, De la Soul, Beastie Boys, EPMD, you name it…I probably got it. Whenever you want to listen to something or dub something, by all means, man, go right ahead. We're roommates, bro," Brad said.

"Where are you from Brad?" Asked Chase with an even more confused look on his face.

"Rockland County…Downstate. It's about twenty miles or so from the City," Brad answered.

"Are all the white boys Downstate as cool as you? Cause the white boys, I come across in the Roc that claim they love rap only say that cause they want us to think they're tough or down or some other bullshit like that— nothing but wannabes. Shit, we could give a goddamn what type of music you listen to, especially if you were cool," Chase said.

The two roommates exchanged a few more pleasantries and promised to meet up for Sunday brunch. Chase, still famished, walked back to the Student Union. As he walked into the building he approached the right quarter of the Student Union where most of the Black and Latino students were congregating. McNair University was a majority white institution with about 17 percent of the population consisting of black and Latino students. Extremely boisterous, the masses exchanged opinions on the topic of the day.

"Yusef Hawkins and his boy were slippin', walking around in white ass, Italian Mob, Benson-Hurst! What the hell did he expect? I mean I feel for his family but hey, you gotta know where you can and where you can't go in NYC," said a tall, muscular boy with pretty features. The others in the immediate circle around him referred to him as Squeeze. He had hazel eyes and thought he was cuter than the women trying to date him.

"Squeeze, you got a point man. Why go chill in Benson-Hurst anyway?" said a gentleman almost as pretty as Squeeze.

"Mira, mira! Listen, they weren't just chillin. He was about to buy a car so get your facts right, Squeeze," blurted out a very spirited Puerto-Rican student. "Even if they were—so what? I'm Spanish Harlem, born and raised, and as long as I'm in NYC I will go to each and every spot in each and every borough because it's my right—Fort Greene, Howard Beach, Lefrak, Sugar Hill, Stapleton, Coney Island, the Village. I should be able to go anywhere and expect to go back home that night...especially if I ain't wildin' out or robbing, knowwhatimsaying?"

Chase heard about the murder of a young African-American man who happened to be in the wrong neighborhood at the wrong time but really didn't bother to think deeply about it until he heard this conversation. Although he had been exposed to harsh situations, this was the first time that he began to look at the world from a slightly different perspective. He wasn't quite sure why or what he was thinking but he knew that it was wrong that the young man was killed, no matter what a clown named Squeeze said. Injustice is injustice. You don't get a second chance to make a first impression and Squeeze left a sour taste in Chase's mouth. He needed a burger and a ginger ale to repair his taste buds.

7 October 13, 1989

"I hope this party ain't as tired as the last one! I swear these Rochester and Buffalo people don't know how to party. They need some NYC up in here! Word! We used to wild out at The Devil's Nest and Roseland, Friday and Saturday nights," said Brandi who was looking at her mirror touching up her blond-dyed, shoulder-blade-length hair. Her blood red scarf wrapped around her forehead matched her full body spandex catsuit. Gold doorknocker earrings, white sneakers, white leather jacket with red and yellow trimmings completed her ensemble for the evening. "Shit, I'll take the Palladium over any club in country-ass Rochester. It's so dead up here. If I wasn't so bored I wouldn't even be going to this Homecoming Jam or whateva they calling it."

Brandi's similarly dressed friends were currently hogging up both the bathroom and common area in preparation for the Homecoming Jam. The area smelled of an unholy alliance between burnt hair, perfumes, spray-on deodorant, and Vidal Sassoon hairspray.

Camara and Rhonda who began as suite-mates, but were now roommates, were also getting ready for the Homecoming Jam. Thankfully, Camara's assigned roommate never showed up. Sensing the tension between the polar opposites Brandi and Rhonda, Camara suggested that Rhonda move in the room with her. It made perfect sense given their natural affinity for each other and strong mutual dislike for Brandi.

For the most part, Camara and Rhonda kept to each other and stayed in their room, while leaving the suite and the other bedroom to sun Brandi and her three minions who consistently orbited her. They routinely took over the suite, and this night was no different.

To drown out the blather coming from Brandi and her friends, Camara blasted EPMD's 'Unfinished Business' and focused on putting on her lip gloss and eye-liner. Rhonda was all dolled up as well and was all ready to go but wanted to use the bathroom before they left. Camara was just about finished and was bopping her head to 'So What You Sayin?' when she heard raised voices coming from the bathroom.

"Listen here whatever your name is. This is not your place of residence. I asked you nicely to please leave the bathroom so that I could use it. There are two mirrors in the suite and two in Brandi's room. You could've easily used either one of those. But you got the nerve to scan me up and down and tell me to wait till you're done?! Are you outta your mind? You can let this friendly face fool you if you want to, but trust me if you want it tramp, I'm definitely open for business!" Rhonda said while knuckling up in a southpaw stance.

Camara could not believe what she was witnessing. The last time she saw two people actually fight in person was in the fourth grade, and she herself never had a fist fight. What shocked her most was the speed of the transformation of her friend and roommate Rhonda. For the little time that she had known her, Rhonda was always sweet, mild mannered, and even-tempered. But the transformed Rhonda was ferocious, raw, and aggressive. Somehow Camara's instincts took over to help suppress the growing and ugly situation.

"You fat little bitch, I'll-"

Before Brandi's friend Bonnie could finish her statement, Camara stepped right in between the both of them while yelling to Brandi to come and save her friend from an ass whipping.

"Shit, you better get *your* friend. I live here too. They are my company. So as long as I'm here, they can be here. And here includes the bathroom. Rhonda could've waited a few more minutes. We're getting ready to leave anyway and y'all will not get a fair one if shit jumps off," Brandi said while walking towards them theatrically.

"Brandi, I'm from Buffalo—Bailey and Warwick Ave—and I don't care about what you know or don't know about Ruff-Buff or the Roc for that matter. I could give a rat's ass that your skeezoid friends are from the City. And, notice that I didn't say you, 'cause your background is sketchy. Where you from don't mean shit. It's where you at and you are Upstate now. So if you and these trash bag bitches ever make the mistake of even plotting on me or Camara, I'll have a posse up here quick, fast and in a hurry," Rhonda yelled as Brandi took two steps back.

"Okay, let's all take a deep breath," said the smartest of Brandi's friends.

Rhonda responded quickly, "I'm breathing bitch. Come on, Camara, let's jet before somebody gets straight fucked up and stops breathing."

Camara grabbed her jacket from the closet to the surprising quiet that Rhonda's tirade had engendered. When the door closed behind Rhonda, one of Brandi's slower friends finally broke the silence, "How y'all like my hair?"

■

Bass pounding booms. Drum loops and snare kicks. Mixing and scratching of vinyl against a needle. The semi-lit faces that could be barely made out in the off-black darkness of the Student Union Ballroom were moving in unison to the syncopating rhythmic chanting voices blending seamlessly into the accompanying music. The DJ screamed for vocal approval. Chase was nearly in a trance as he watched a group of young ladies move their bodies like snakes dancing in cursive. The constant flickering of the strobe lights added to the pulsating vibe throughout the room. Chase had his eyes on a few honeys.

Being an avid Hip Hop music video watcher helped Chase to master almost all of the latest dances. From moves by Kid n Play and MC Hammer to every other dance in between, Chase could pretty much pull it off. What he wanted to pull off now was the bra and panties of a thick and beautiful redbone girl wearing a spandex suit who was dancing in front of him. She was square in the middle of about seven girls and Chase's eyeballs were glued to her. He got close enough to her to hear her talk to her girls and her New York City accent gave him an instant erection. She was a walking billboard for great sex thought, Chase. *She was built for fucking.*

"Rhonda, come here. I wanna show you something," Camara said as she pointed towards Brandi and her crew who were in the middle of the dance floor.

"I know you didn't call me over here to look at Brandi hoe-ass dancing nasty with a dude, Camara," said Rhonda.

"Hell to the no! You already know I couldn't give a damn about some Brandi! It's the guy she's dancing with. He's in my Black Lit class—when he actually comes. He is so sexy!"

The usually reserved Camara could hardly believe her own ears. The way he looked and carried himself fascinated her in ways she was unaccustomed to. The fact that he was dancing with Brandi did not make her jealous in the least bit. *Brandi could never have what's mine especially if I truly want it. A woman of her caliber could never add up to me,* Camara said to herself. Her newfound cockiness urged Camara to walk up to the guy, mush Brandi and cut in.

Camara had no opportunity to act on her instincts however because while Camara was focused on her prey, she was being sized up. The stalker made himself known, walking directly behind her and swiping his middle finger down her arm all the way to the tip of her ring finger.

"How are you tonight gorgeous? Please allow me to introduce myself. My name is Steven but my friends and family call me Squeeze."

Camara having had older men approach her was familiar with the friendly gentleman pick-up line. What she wasn't familiar with was the fact that it was coming from such a young man about her age. It did impress her.

"I'm Camara, nice meeting you, Steven. Can I ask you where or who came up with the name Squeeze?" asked Camara.

"Well, Steve is short for Steven. My baby brother couldn't quite say Steve and it sounded like he was saying Squeeze when he was calling me. It stuck and everybody started calling me Squeeze when I was around ten years old," he said while taking in her beauty.

Camara's eyes drank Squeeze and definitely liked the taste. He was tall, light-skinned and extremely handsome.

"Can we dance?" Squeeze asked as a parade of Alpha Phi Alpha members, all lined up behind one another, passed using their trademarked steps and fraternal calls and responses.

"Sure, why not," Camara said. Three songs later she had all but forgotten about the other cute guy from her Black Lit 101 class.

8 October 17, 1989

Professor King was starting to learn the important differences between lecturing versus teaching. To be an effective educator you had to have both in your repertoire. When you lecture students the communication process goes one way—from the professor's mouth to the student's ears. Teaching involves speaking as well as listening, call as well as response. Wearing his signature black horn-rimmed glasses and black knit sweater, Professor King was in a lecturing mood. Moving between his desk and his lectern, the packed lecture hall could feel it in the air. He stood at the base of the lecture hall as he looked up and outward into the faces of his students.

"Ok, esteemed students. It is good to see all of your lovely faces once again. You all should be pretty much done with the assigned reading, *Imperium in Imperio*, a fairly straightforward book that you could've polished off in a good toilet-sitting or two. Next week, October 24th your five to seven-page analysis of the book is due. But remember, it is not a book report. You did book reports for your seventh-grade teacher.

For the record, let me tell you what I don't want and don't need. I do not want a synopsis or a retelling of the book. I have read the book. I know what happens in the book from beginning to end, therefore, I do not want or need a recap. That is lazy, esteemed students, and far too easy for such intellectual giants as yourselves. In other words, that's high school and you are in college. That's bush league when you're batting cleanup for the Yankees. Most of you are freshmen and some of you have horrible study and work habits that must be eliminated.

Now for the million dollar question, what will get you an A on your first major college paper? Learn from your mistakes. I know it's cliché and a bit trite but at its roots, it is a fundamental truth that will allow you to maintain an A in this course. You all handed in a paper a few weeks ago. I gave you the assignment to see how you all write and how you all think. Writing is a skill that is closely associated with critical thinking and basic common sense.

In other words, if you can write well you can usually think well. I gave each and every one of you suggestions on how to write better and develop your critical thinking skills. Leverage those suggestions.

The grades on those papers will not count...provided that you improve by at least a letter grade on the assignment due next week. Are we crystal? Any questions so far? It is not where you start it is how you finish.

Now, esteemed students back to how do you get an A on this particular paper. I need you to take a stance on a chapter, a page, a paragraph or a single sentence in the book and expound upon it. Meaning to inflate it or give me another angle to it—in a systematic fashion. Back up your stance with the work of peer-reviewed scholars. Analyze all of the information, come up with a thesis statement, and back up what you're saying with evidence, facts. Dazzle me with the brilliance you possess. Make me say, wow...I never thought of it like that. Research, work hard and use your brain and imagination. I want to give you an A, but I cannot give you an A. You earn an A in my class and you take it from me! And if you can do that I will, in the immortal words of Ice Cube, indeed give it up smooth."

Professor King scanned and probed his captive audience to gauge whether or not his soliloquy was effective. Looking back at him was a hodge-podge of young, mostly white, attentive faces with a splattering of black students—seven to be exact. Most of the students were taking Black Lit 101 because it either was part of their major or because it satisfied the general education requirements for graduation. However, Chase, who managed to make it this morning, was taking the course because he promised Alvin Dance that he would. He did not know why Mr. Dance made him promise that he would take the course but he was on his way to flunking it with flying colors.

"Ok, esteemed students, right now I'd like to talk about the book a bit. I want to help you brainstorm ideas for your paper. I'd like a volunteer to begin the discussion please," Professor King said.

Camara looked around the lecture hall to see if anyone would raise their hand. She thoroughly enjoyed Professor King's class and was in awe of his preparation and knowledge. He was intense and a tad intimidating but she sensed profound warmth inside of him. In a weird way, she felt a deep intimate connection with him.

After a few seconds of tense silence, she raised her hand. "Well to me, the character of Bernard Belgrade represents power and sacrifice and what one would do to gain power and what he would sacrifice in the process... even under the guise of helping the larger community. He is a fascinating contradiction," said Camara who was genuinely fascinated with the novel and not looking for brownie points.

"Well put Miss...?" asked Professor King.

"Truth, my name is Camara Truth," she said.

"Well put, Ms. Truth. I like the angle of duality, very well. Now see, that could be the topic of her paper, and she can use the text to illustrate instances of duality. Ok, how about you sir. Way in the back trying very hard to not be noticed and called upon. Yes sir, you with the white Nike sweatshirt. Mr. Chase Douglass, I believe. Please either expound upon Ms. Truth's notion of duality or tell us about something in the book that grabbed your attention," said Professor King.

Dumbfounded as to how the professor knew his name, especially since he'd missed three classes this semester already, Chase did not exactly know what to say. Then he remembered that Alvin Dance and his connection to the university. Pretending to shuffle through his notebook Chase cleared his throat and tried to save face.

"Aaa...Professor, I've been a bit under the weather, so umm... I haven't been able to keep up with the readings. But, umm...I do plan on catching up and umm...getting the paper done that's due next week," Chase said.

"So you were under the weather, Mr. Douglass? Can I ask you a question, sir? Can you tell me where that phrase under the weather originated, and what does under the weather really mean?" Professor King asked while walking up the lecture hall stairs toward where Chase was sitting.

"Umm, it's just a saying. It's just words. I don't where it came from. I wasn't feeling well, Professor, that's all," Chase said fidgeting in his chair.

"Mr. Douglass, you need to understand the power of words. The term 'under the weather' dates back to the late 1820's. Sailors used to use it. You heard of the ship's deck right, Mr. Douglass? Well, when you are on the open sea that's where most of the weather takes place, on the deck. Well directly under the deck is where the quarters were. It was where the sailors slept. So let's say that you are sick like you claim you were. Well, you most certainly wouldn't want to be sick on the deck. If you vomited and a strong gust of wind came by at the same time, it could get messy. So the ship's captain would tell you to go under the weather or under the deck. Makes sense right, Mr. Douglass?"

"Yea, it makes sense to me sir," Chase said sheepishly.

"Well, what if I told you I just made all that up off of the top of my head, the youngsters today would call it freestyling. What if I told you some perfectly prepared bullshit in order to make myself look good at your expense and make you appear dumb? Mr. Douglass, the next time you feel the need to freestyle some lies about not doing the work, at the very least make me think there is a possibility you may be telling the truth. You see, your words told me you weren't being truthful. The words you use, and how you use them tell a lot about you, Mr. Douglass," Professor King said stopping just short of Chase.

Camara did not know whether or not to laugh or feel sorry Chase who was severely outmatched. He was as handsome as ever even as he was mentally and verbally defenseless. His vulnerability spoke to her. Part of her wanted to go over and physically console him even though she did not know him from Adam. For the rest of the class, she found herself looking at Chase and thinking about that dance that they never had.

9 October 19, 1989

Whenever Camara had some time to kill she figured she would kill it by doing something productive like studying her lecture notes. It helped her to reinforce the highlights of the past learning session. She preferred to kill time in the student lounge located directly upstairs from the Student Union cafeteria where she was meeting Squeeze for their first date. She was nervous but fairly excited at the same time. This was after all her first date as a college woman. Just as she was beginning to lose herself in the world of her Black Literature 101 lecture notes, she was pleasantly interrupted by the warm but loud voice of her roommate Rhonda.

"Hey girl, how was class?" asked Rhonda who took off her jacket and sat her book bag in the chair next to Camara.

"It was good and interesting. Remember the dude dancing with Brandi at Homecoming? Well, he is in my Black Lit class and the professor ate him alive for falling behind the syllabus. I felt kinda sorry for him," said Camara. She thought about him a lot since first seeing him at the dance and had spotted him a couple times across from her Dorm. She was too shy to actually approach him.

"You supposed to be hooking up with Squeeze today, right? Aren't you nervous?" Asked Rhonda.

Camara just smiled. She was still thinking about Chase.

"I would be. Damn, he's fine! That butter yellow skin tone, that naturally, curly high-top fade…damn!" Rhonda did a body shiver.

"Well he does look good, it's no denying that," Camara said.

"Tall and I heard he got money too. That's what you come to college for. To get your degree and get you a fine ass man with a degree and a future."

"Hmm, hmm," Camara agreed with her, chin in both her hands.

"He could be related to Al B. Sure. He's from the City, right? Ask him. Shit, you never know," Rhonda said.

"I'll ask him a lot of stuff. I want to see where his head is. I want more than just looks and a degree Rhonda. There has to be something else there. I don't know how to explain it, but I guess I'm saying it has to be something that connects us beyond the physical. Does that make any sense? Or am I being too dramatic?" Camara asked sincerely.

"No, not at all. Some men you play with because all they want to do is play with you. As long as nobody gets serious and there is full disclosure and agreement then that's fine. But some men in life you come across you keep at all costs," Rhonda said in a serious tone that made Camara put down her notes and pay even more close attention to her.

The information that she was receiving from Rhonda about men and all the different ways to interact with them was intriguing to Camara for the simple fact that she rarely spoke with her mother about the intricacies of dating. Her mother did not rush to volunteer some of her own experiences either.

Rhonda continued, "You build something, not necessarily for the person they are at that time, but because you sense something great in them and you know they're going to become that real man, that great man, your man. My Grandmother told me that and it always stuck with me. My Granddad was a provider, who took care of my grandmother and their kids, but coming up he was a stone cold dog. He was a dark-skinned, tall, pretty boy and women were all over him. He slipped up and my grandmother caught him more than a few times early in the relationship. But she stayed with him because she knew he was becoming. She knew that he was the man for her. They were connected spiritually, regardless of what he did physically with another woman."

"Well, my high school boyfriend…my ex-Harold…well technically he made me promise not to break up with him…but trust me, we are most definitely not a couple. Anyway, we didn't have that connection that your grandparents had. He was just a real nice guy and I knew I couldn't be with him and feel complete. I was barely even attracted to him like that. I guess it was just something to do. I know there is more to a relationship than what Harold and I had," Camara said pensively while looking down in her lap remembering how awful her first sexual episode was.

Sensing the downshift in Camara's mood, Rhonda reflected the attention back to herself. "Girl, we all done did things with dudes, or called ourselves going out with dudes that in the end was purely a waste of time. But you learn and you grow.

"I gave him something special, girl. I should have saved it for…for someone special," Camara said staring off into space.

"I'm sorry I didn't mean to go that deep on you and trigger decision regret. Look all I'm saying is have fun with Squeeze. You are young, beautiful, gifted and going places. If you think he is the one and you feel that connection then build with him. But if he isn't, it's not the end of the world. Have fun with him, spend his money, and fuck him like it's 1999 if you want to."

Rhonda gave Camara a warm hug. Over the next hour, the roommates alternated seamlessly from ideal chatter to studying to man-watching back to studying. It was closing in on high noon.

◼

Camara thought the transition from high school to college would be a lot tougher. As she sat in the cafeteria waiting for Squeeze, she realized that almost two months had passed and she had adapted to college life with relative ease. There was no culture shock of suddenly being around a whole bunch of white people because she grew up around and interacted with them in the suburbs. Her early grades were great, Rhonda had been a godsend of a roommate, and she was really enjoying her classes especially Black Lit 101. The only thing she had left to conquer was the dating scene and she liked her prospects.

Sitting with her back facing the entrance, she did not see Squeeze walk in. She felt the tickle of a single red rose that Squeeze attacked her from behind with. "I would've met you outside but it's drizzling and I heard milk chocolate melts in the rain. And what a shame that would be to have you melt anywhere else but in my mouth," Squeeze whispered.

Camara thought his comments were over-the-top for a first date. Her look betrayed her. Nevertheless, she grabbed the rose, gave it a good whiff and sat it down on the table.

Sensing he was out-of-bounds he added, "I'm sorry, Camara. I'm wilding out, right? My bad. How was class today?"

"Thank you…fine, class was fine. So what's your major?" Camara asked beginning the planned interrogation.

"I'm a psych major. Beautiful minds have always fascinated me. I'm a sophomore. I want to have my own private practice one day where people can come and sit on my couch and blab for $125 dollars an hour. Paid in full! So what's your major?"

"If all goes as plan I'll graduate in four years with Business degree. When I graduate from here I want to get an MBA. I'm pretty good with numbers and I want to learn how to run a business. So I guess you can say I'll be paid in full too," Camara said while looking hard into the eyes of Squeeze to see if they were going to tip her off to his true intent. She found him beguiling but she was not sure if they shared that *connection* because it was way too early to tell.

"So I guess that means once we get married we'll have a fat crib on a hill somewhere living very large, right?"

"Humph. I haven't eaten all day. I thought this was a lunch date," Camara said playfully ignoring the question.

Standing up and reaching for his wallet Squeeze reached inside and pulled out, what was for a college student, a sizable amount of money. "Of course, you're hungry gorgeous. Beating off all them dudes all day must be hard work. Whatever you're eating, it's on me. And don't be too shy to eat around me either," Squeeze said spreading his cash out like a peacock.

"As hungry as I am that's something you don't even have to worry about. I'll take a hot dog with everything, burnt, some fries and a Coke. Please and thank you," Camara said with a smile as Squeeze backpedaled toward the grill. She was beginning to really enjoy the attention.

Camara walked to the bathroom to wash her hands before her meal. As she was leaving the cafeteria she saw the guy from her Black Lit class entering the cafeteria. Slight drops of panicked adrenaline swelled inside her throat. As they walked directly toward each other she wanted badly to say hello to him but could not find the voice or the courage. Chase looked her way and smiled. She forced an awkward smile and walked briskly toward the bathroom.

Upon returning to the cafeteria, she walked into the sectioned area of the cafeteria to see if her classmate was still there. She felt guilty checking for one guy on a date with another. Her guilt level dropped significantly when she saw Squeeze writing what she assumed was his telephone number on a napkin and handing it to a voluptuous woman.

As she made her way back to the booth and remembered the conversation that she had previously with Rhonda. *Why get upset about someone you are playing with. You damn sure can never take him seriously now. He is playing with you. So have fun and play him until you win or get tired of the game. He's not your man and you're not his girl. And, I was just looking for Chase Douglass so I can't be upset.*

When Squeeze came back with their food Camara acted as if nothing happened. With no reason to grill him with questions, she relaxed and enjoyed his company. Ironically she learned more about him by letting him choose what to talk about. Professor King was right. The words he used told her a lot about him: he was self-absorbed and materialistic but very book smart. She could have learned more but out of the corner of her eye, she saw Chase leaving the Student Union and mentally left with him.

10 October 24, 1989

Chase could barely move. He was trapped and forced to stare blankly at the wall. The whole left side of his body, from the top of his shoulders to his ankles, was numb. The twin size bed he was forced to share with a willing but boring sex partner was way too small for the both of them to achieve the requisite comfort for a decent nights' sleep. If he was able to toss and turn he would have.

Chase hated spending the night with a woman after the sex. As soon as the act was complete, Chase began the countdown. If a woman was still around at T+45 minutes, it was because he graciously allowed her shower. He felt creepy lying next to a woman he barely knew after sex. Hypocritically, he viewed them as useless, used up, and nasty like an old gnarled up ear of corn. He wrestled with the notion and asked himself whether a few minutes of carnal pleasure was worth five hours of awkward non-rest. As she snored lightly, Chase tried to remember her name but wasn't quite sure they ever traded that information.

What made the moment even more unpleasant was Brad sleeping in the bunk bed below him. His overnight guest was relatively quiet during sex but between the body slapping and bed squeaking, it was clear they weren't playing checkers. He had no idea how Brad would react. Chase's sexual appetite did not care. It demanded to be fed, hell or high water, and Chase was powerless to resist. Now that his appetite was fed he was less inhibited, more realistic and borderline embarrassed.

Just before seven Chase was finally able to awaken the young nameless co-ed. A few words were spoken and no-name climbed down from the top bunk and headed for the door. Brad was up already and had gone to take a shower. *Here's your skirt, there's the door, goodbye, see you later.* The newly freed Chase stretched out on the bed cracking his back in the process. He felt he needed to say something to Brad once he got out of the shower to ease any potential tension.

"Hey, man, listen. Sorry 'bout last night. I hope we weren't too loud man," Chase said to Brad as soon as he came back into the room.

"Well, to be honest, Chase, it kinda freaked me out a little bit. I mean dude, you know I don't care that you're boning a girl in the room. But I guess I'd just prefer to not be there. Listen, dude, as long as I don't have a huge test or something like that in the morning, I don't mind getting up and stepping out of the room. Hell, I might ask you to do the same for me one night," Brad said while putting on his deodorant.

"You right, homeboy, my bad. It won't happen again man I promise. I'll just take my business elsewhere," Chase said with a laugh.

"How about this dude...if either one of us has female company, we will leave a balled up pair of socks just outside the bedroom door so that we don't disturb each other. And again, if you need me to step out it's no problem, all right dude?"

"I swear you the coolest white boy I know," Chase said as he went to shower the stench of sex from his body. When he finished he briefly debated the merits of attending his 8 a.m. class. He was already late. Still tired from last night's activities, Chase opted to get some rest for his intramural basketball game at *six in the evening*. It seemed to be the rational thing to do.

Three hours later Chase's deep, dreamless sleep was interrupted by the ringing of the telephone. Jolted from his sleep, he sat up, wiped the sleep from his eyes and agilely dropped down from the top bunk.

"Speak," Chase said in his throaty morning voice.

"Hello, how are you doing today?" the pleasant and friendly voice on the other end of the phone said.

"I'm ok."

"That is excellent to hear. May I please speak with Chase Douglass?" the voice asked.

Chase rubbed his head and face again to make sure he was fully awake. "This is Chase may I ask who is calling please?"

"Why of course you may, son. I see that you don't recognize my voice either, it's Mr. Dance. Alvin Dance."

"Oh snap! How you doing, Mr. Dance? Man, I haven't seen you since graduation. What's up?" Chase said while yawning and stretching out the last bit of sleep in him.

"How is the college life treating you so far?" he asked.

Not too good to be honest with you Mr. Dance. College courses are tough, man. I thought I was going to breeze right through it. Now, the people here are cool. It's just that classes here are pretty difficult, that's all," Chase said now speaking in his normal vocal tone.

"By people, I'm assuming you are referring exclusively to the ladies and the special way that only they can welcome you onto a new campus. Real warm and very friendly, correct?" laughed Mr. Dance.

"Yes, sir. Until I get fully acclimated and get the hang of some of these classes, you know I'mma be all up in somebody warm and friendly, know what I mean?"

"I absolutely know what you mean, Chase. I was in college not too long ago and I can see that you're going to fuck your way out of school," Mr. Dance said in a clear and plainspoken tone.

Chase who was blindsided by the statement shot back defensively, "What! Are you serious?"

"Chase, you're reacting as if I insulted you when all I am doing is warning you that flunking out of McNair University is an absolute certainty if you continue along the current trajectory," Mr. Dance said matter-of-factly.

"Like I told you, man, I'm adjusting. Classes are boring and it's hard to focus. And part of being a college student is partying and having sex. Come on Mr. Dance you know that! You know I'm not lying."

"Looks like I gambled on the wrong horse—went to bat for a man determined to squander opportunities. I know how boring some classes are. But, Chase, may I remind you that you are a young black man in America. You don't have the luxury to be bored. The system is setup for you to fail, and you're too busy fucking to understand that you are shaking dice loaded against you. Do you have the slightest clue about the position you are in Chase?" Mr. Dance asked still sounding surprisingly calm.

Chase did not know how to respond. He sat down in the lone love seat in his suite and put his hand to forehead. "I guess I don't," Chase said in a hushed tone.

"Listen, little brother. I see something great in you that you obviously cannot see at this point in time. I can understand that…truly I do understand. But you have to understand your greatness before it's too late. You are on the verge of flunking three of your four courses this semester, and these classes are not really that hard…except for Professor King's class. Son, you can learn an awful lot from that man especially in the field of writing. I know how creative your writing can be. But you must apply yourself or you will be back in your Grandmother's attic…doing nothing but fucking…fucking up opportunities…fucking over the people who called in favors for you and fucking up your life. Grow up, Chase," Mr. Dance said before hanging up the phone.

Chase was stunned. He was not expecting a wake-up call quite like that one. He was not fully applying himself and he knew this. He remembered how much he enjoyed Mr. Dance and the way he taught English class. The assignments he gave out spoke to Chase and Chase responded. Mr. Dance made sure Chase was accepted to McNair University through a frat brother who worked in the admissions office, even though he did not have the grades. *What a way to thank him for sticking his neck out there*, Chase thought. Despite the shame of betraying Mr. Dance, he walked to his room and climbed back into bed.

11 November 16, 1989

Chase woke up around four in the afternoon feeling energized. Once again he made the calculated decision to skip morning and afternoon classes so he would be at peak performance for his intramural playoff game. He packed his sports bag and trotted over to the gym. The moment he hit the locker room and began to prepare for his game, his academic problems vanished from his mind. Playing basketball absorbed Chase almost as much as sex did. The sneakers squeaking up and down the tan hardwood floor was a welcome escape. It didn't matter that the gym was hotter than Panama.

At five foot 10 inches tall, Chase did not resemble the stereotypical basketball player and he made it his duty to punish any opponent who dared to pre-judge him. He spotted today's victim during warm-ups—a light-skinned man whom he overheard discussing the Yusef Hawkins incident two months ago in the Student Union. He was jaw-boning and bragging about his skill set. At tip-off, Chase made sure he was matched up with his pre-selected victim.

A clinic of baby hooks shots, pinpoint passes, floater layups and long jumpers ensued. With Chase controlling the tempo, his team jumped out to an early lead. After a spectacular crossover dribble, followed by a stop-and-pop jump shot that snapped the white net, Chase was feeling like a juggernaut. Chase strolled back arrogantly to the other end of the floor.

"Come on, Squeeze! D him up!" one of the members of the opposing team shouted.

Squeeze…yeah, that's his name. How did that jumper taste, Squeeze? Squeeze was becoming increasingly frustrated and yelled back to his teammate, "Shut the fuck up. Don't coach me! I got this."

At six foot four inches, Squeeze wisely decided to take Chase underneath the basket to take advantage of his six-inch height differential. "Mismatch, mismatch!" he yelled in an attempt to get the point guard to pass him the basketball.

"Mismatch? Yeah, it's a mismatch in reverse, homeboy! I'm bustin' your ass!" said Chase passionately as he used his forearm and knee to push Squeeze out from underneath the basket.

Squeeze received the ball in the post, pump-faked into a textbook drop step and banked a milky turn-around jumper off the glass.

"In ya mouth, Shorty. You couldn't bust my ass if you were my 300-pound cellmate in Sodom and Gomorrah," Squeeze laughed directly in Chase's face.

Outwitted and angry, Chase became furious. "Get the fuck outta my face punk ass bitch!" he yelled as he pushed Squeeze into the referee. Squeeze gathered himself and bum rushed Chase. The two wound up on the ground trying to punch each other as hard as they could at varying angles. The other players and referees quickly pulled them apart before any real damage was done.

"Knock it off now or I'm calling public safety! Leave the court now! The referee screamed while stepping in between them. "Make sure they leave using separate exits. If this occurs again the both of you are banned from using any of our athletic facilities for the remainder of the semester!"

"Damn, Chase! You were rocking homeboy. You let him get in your head that quick—off of one punk-ass shot?' said Chase's teammate, a tall, lanky junior from Compton, California.

"I don't give a fuck about this gym, this school, this punk ass ref, and I especially don't give a fuck about that dick-in-his-booty-loving, half-breed! I'm outside waiting for you bitch ass nigga!" said Chase who was being pushed towards the door by his teammates.

Having eliminated the best player on the court that day, Squeeze was victorious. He calmed down and began politicking the referee to allow him to stay with his team. Chase, on the other hand, was outside looking through the gymnasium Plexiglas hurling insults at Squeeze. Squeeze gave Chase the Little Rascal "hi-sign" followed by a stiff middle finger before sitting on the bench with his teammates. Enraged, Chase began banging on the Plexiglas like a trapped Gorilla. Even his team members were shaking their heads in disbelief.

Realizing he looked like a savage fool, he ceased his gorilla impersonation and took a deep breath. His sweat-filled head steamed in the cool autumn evening. Competitive basketball had a way of bringing the worse out of Chase but this episode was embarrassingly uncharacteristic. He hung his head and headed toward the quad.

The walk across campus did very little to decrease his adrenalin, pulse, or heart rate. Cutting through the Student Union he saw just what he needed—a vending machine housing bottles of Gatorade. Twisting the cap and hearing the 'pop' of the orange top made Chase wish it was Squeeze's neck in his right hand. He poured it down his throat in three swallows. He walked down the Student Union hallway wiping excess Gatorade from his mouth.

"Hey. Why you got that look on your face? Are you going to get a butt whooping when you get home or something?" asked a beautiful, dark-skinned young woman with the most fascinating eyes Chase had ever seen. He didn't know if it was the hue or the shape but they hooked him in and wouldn't let go.

"Excuse me?" Chase asked kindly in a somewhat bewildered tone.

"I said why do you have that look on your face? It's a beautiful world," she said from behind the information desk.

"Frustrating day," Chase answered meekly.

"It will pass. I'm Camara."

"Umm…I'm Chase. Umm…"

Chase, for the first time he could remember, stumbled over his words when meeting a female. She turned to quickly answer the phone and held up her index finger to beg for 'one minute'. As she completed the motion, Chase was floored by the way her hips and buttocks connected and formed a capital letter 'C' in her jeans. Once she finished with the phone call Chase resumed, "My name is Chase. Let me ask you a question. Do you usually ask people who walk by your desk random questions?" Chase asked with a smile.

"Only the homely looking ones," Camara said while trying her best to hold in her laugh.

"Hold up…I'm homely looking? I thought that the word homely was reserved for fat white ladies in their 30's who still live at home with their parents and only wears stuff she knitted herself.

"Aww…you're still kind of cute. But, you can be cute and look homely at the same time. Well, maybe homely isn't the right word. You looked lonely," she said unsure of whether or not she hit a nerve. Camara felt the butterflies recklessly flutter against the lining of her stomach.

"Maybe you're right. I guess I get lonely at times. What about you? You got a boyfriend?" Chase asked.

The butterflies escaped from her stomach via her esophagus and transformed into a large frog. She honestly did not know what her official status was and did not want to start off lying. Chase sensed Camara need a few moments to share something so the silence was comfortable. He stared in her eyes with understanding.

"Well?" he asked gently.

"Well, I broke up with my boyfriend Harold from high school. Let me rephrase that. I tried to breakup with him *again* and he started crying *again*. I felt bad so I took it back but I think he is finally getting the message. He only calls me every other day now."

"You're single," Chase asserted. "Are you talking to anybody up here?"

Immediately Squeeze's face came to her mind. "I've been on a couple dates, but nothing that would stop me from getting to know you better," Camara said while turning her eyes to the business book she was reading before Chase entered her vision.

Chase was awestruck by her beauty and felt remarkably at ease in her presence. He asked, "Where are you from Camara? I'm from the Roc."

"Me too—well the suburbs, Greece. Is English your major?" Camara asked as she closed up her business book and put it in her book bag.

"I'm undeclared but I think I'm leaning towards English. I like words. I enjoy writing. I like creating stuff. How did you guess English?"

"Cause we are in the same class together. Black Lit 101," she said.

Oh, with Professor King right? Ok, but I don't see how I would have missed you, as gorgeous as you are," Chase said while looking her solidly in her eyes.

"Well if you came to class more than three times a semester maybe you would've noticed me," Camara said smartly with a hint of laughter.

"Very funny but true...I see somebody's clocking my attendance. You're right, though, I do need to go to class more. Knowing now that you're gonna be there, count me in. I won't miss another class this semester...I promise," Chase said as he raised his right and hand and crossed his heart with his left index finger. "Listen, Camara, maybe we can go out on a date this weekend. Maybe you could help me cure some of this loneliness I feel."

Camara reached into her book bag and wrote her phone number and her dorm room address down. She then reached underneath her desk and pulled out a black and brown teddy bear. The teddy bear sported a green, forest ranger shirt and hat. Camara folded up the paper with her information on it and put it inside of the shirt pocket of the teddy bear.

"Mr. Fizzy, this is Chase. Chase, this is Mr. Fizzy," she said.

Chase instinctively put his hand out and shook Mr. Fizzy's paw. "Nice to meet you Mr. Fizzy," Chase said feeling silly but happy to be silly.

"Mr. Fizzy, my new friend Chase is a little bit lonely tonight so I need you to keep him company and walk home with him. I'd hate it if something was to happen to him. I can't walk with him and keep him safe because I'm working until nine. And, I know Chase has some work he needs to catch up on so that he can be free for our first date on Saturday. I want you to keep lonely Chase safe until then ok?" Camara asked the teddy bear. He telepathically answered her. "Ok, Mr. Fizzy likes you. See you on Saturday Chase."

"Yes you will, Camara, yes you will." Chase walked out of the Student Union thinking, *What a rollercoaster thirty minutes. Camara, Camara, Camara.* He was so excited he began to sing one of his favorite love songs by the Force MD's as he danced with Mr. Fizzy. "Tender Love...baby I surrender…"

12 July 12, 1958

Little Archie hated to be awakened from a sound sleep, especially since that type of rest was hard to come by in the Hanover Housing Projects. The Hanover, a group of seven hi-rise apartment buildings, was Rochester's solution to the problem of housing a growing working-class Negro population. To properly accommodate and contain them, they were stacked atop each other and crammed side by side in tenement buildings. Each apartment typically consisted of four small rooms: a bathroom, kitchen/living room, and two bedrooms. The bathroom's maximum capacity of two people was constantly being challenged by the nine members of the Hunter and King families who shared one-fifth-floor apartment in the Hanover.

The almost nine-year-old Little Archie and his younger cousins and siblings slept in the slightly smaller of the two bedrooms. They had to share a thin, queen sized, lumpy mattress with no box spring underneath to support it. Rat droppings and hard-backed roaches were hard to distinguish from each other as they littered the floor around the bed. Rat bites from time to time were not uncommon.

The children slept head to foot. Little Archie always slept on the edge of the bed nearest the door with his baby sister sleeping next to him. Little Archie was enjoying an unusually good night's sleep despite the loud teenagers singing "It's Twilight Time" outside, the arguing between a young married couple next door, and the screams of an infant child directly above them. He thought he was dreaming when a felt a warm and wet substance tickle the bottom of his left thigh.

He opened up his eyes to see the dainty feet of his baby sister about an inch away from his nose. He checked her. She was dry with the exception of her pony-tailed hair. As the stench of urine hit his nose, he realized that his Cousin Leroy's weak kidneys were the source of the waterworks. Archie's first instinct was to choke Leroy until his voice changed, but he refrained since the damage was done and he was accustomed to Leroy urinating in the bed episodically. Archie grabbed a brown towel from atop their dresser drawer and placed it carefully underneath him and his baby sister.

Being a particularly muggy night, Little Archie found it difficult to fall back to sleep. He thought some cold water would help usher him back safely into dreamland. He walked cautiously to the bedroom door and slowly and quietly opened it. He did not want to wake up his mother or his aunt who was sleeping in the other bedroom with the rest of the children. The rug-less vinyl floor helped to cool his feet as he scampered to the kitchen. He pulled out a dull blue cup from the kitchen cabinet, reached above the sink and turned the faucet on. While waiting for the water to get cold, Little Archie thought he heard a scratching and scraping noise coming from the front door.

He took a gulp of his water, poured the rest down the sink and walked towards the door. Before he could get in arms reach of the front door it mysteriously popped open. Little Archie froze in his tracks as two men with women's stockings pulled over their faces appeared from the darkness behind the door. He unconsciously let out a yelp before the first intruder cupped his mouth and slammed him to the ground. The other intruder went straight for the only thing of material value in the house, a 16-inch deluxe RCA television. Little Archie who ironically enough was big for his age elbowed his assailant and bit the man's pointer and middle fingers in an effort to free himself.

The crook screamed and immediately got up off the floor and ran behind his partner who had the family's television in his arms. "That's my mama and auntie TV!" Little Archie yelled as he took off behind the two robbers.

By this time his mother heard the commotion and grabbed her 12-gauge Winchester Model 97 from underneath her bed. This particular pump-action shotgun was born in 1908 and had been passed down to Josephine by way of her father, who got it from his father. It was nicknamed the *Klanstopper* because it was once used to clear out a field full of Klansman attempting to lynch a family member. The shotgun was prone to going fully automatic due to slamfire. The defect in the weapon could be turned into a forceful advantage for the initiated. Josephine was past initiated. She was fully vetted and downright righteous with the tool in her hand. She could empty a whole magazine tube with great speed and control if necessary.

Josephine proceeded toward the living room. Since she did not exactly know if the intruders were still inside of their apartment, she thought it would be a good idea to alert her sister as to what was transpiring.

"Ernestine, wake up. Somebody done tried to break in this here house! I'm fixin to go into the chiren's room to see if they all right," Josephine said to her in a loud whisper.

"What! Josephine what in the world is going on? I swear 'fore God I can't take this no more. This place is hell, I swear it is! We moving back to South Carolina," Ernestine whispered while waking up the children and rushing them inside of the closet.

Walking in the dark with the *Klanstopper* as her guide, Josephine crept deliberately slow and easy into the living room. She could see that the front door was not closed all the way and the television was missing. Still walking slowly as she approached the bathroom door, she took a deep breath and walked inside. Finding emptiness only served to accelerate her heartbeat which was now pumping so hard she thought the intruder might hear her coming.

She had a twelve-foot walk from the bathroom to the bedroom where the children were sleeping. She decided to use her ever increasing adrenalin in her favor and she ran as fast as she could and kicked open the bedroom door while still in the firing position. She saw three children still sleeping where there should have been four.

"Mama, they—"

She squeezed the trigger without hesitation. The boom reverberated in the tiny bedroom. The gunfire hit its target in the front right shoulder. Josephine walked up to get a closer view of the man who had the gumption to enter her home without an invitation. Just as she was about to cock the shotgun again she looked on the floor at the bleeding body. It was not a man at all. It was a little boy, her little boy, her Little Archie. Josephine let out a scream literally woke up the dead...starting with her wounded, first born son, Archibald Moses King II.

13 November 18, 1989

For Chase Douglass, thinking about a woman outside of her sexual capabilities for any extended period of time was a foreign concept. Women entering his life would only become relevant when his testosterone commanded he explore and conquer new territory. He could not remember having any romantic-like feelings for a woman other than pure sexual attraction.

But these facts were currently being tested by Camara Truth, who inexplicably would not leave Chase's mind. Her face, body, voice and words were on constant rewind and auto-play in his brain ever since he met her. Naturally, he wanted to have sex with her, but his thoughts were not limited to carnal activities. He truly appreciated their conversation and the way she approached him. He liked the way she laughed and carried herself as a woman. Whenever he looked at Mr. Fizzy who was currently relegated to his gym bag, he thought of Camara. This both excited and scared him.

Chase was looking for a way to burn off some of the nervous energy he built up in anticipation of his first date with Camara. He thought that there might be a possibility of them coming back to his room at some point, so he asked Brad if they could disconnect the bunk beds for easier access—just in case they went all the way. The proposed itinerary for their early afternoon date was a free movie at the Student Union ballroom and an early dinner in town. They both agreed to play it by ear in terms of the length of the date and let the outcome evolve organically.

The movie was scheduled to start at two so by 1 p.m. Chase was ready, adorned in his white and blue pinstriped baseball jersey, New York Yankee cap and loose-fitting Lee blue jeans. Stopping to spray Joop Cologne on his neck, wrist, and shirt he exited his dorm and made his across the yard to Camara's dorm room.

Walking up the steps to her second-floor dorm room, Chase started to feel his chest tighten and his heart beat a touch faster. He took a deep breath, and walked smoothly to her door and knocked.

"How you doing, I'm Chase. I'm here to pick up Camara," Chase said to the pretty girl who answered the door. Chase remembered her as his dance partner from the Homecoming dance.

"Yea, come in. Camara! Your company is here!" Brandi yelled as she walked into her room and slammed the door behind her.

Chase could not help but look at Brandi's assets as she switched and swayed her hips purposely harder than usual. He sat down in the love seat inside the dorm room suite and tried his best to relax. Noticing that some music was coming out of the bedroom to his left, he leaned toward the direction of the music and realized it was Boogie Down Productions' 'I'm Still Number One' playing at a respectable decibel level.

Camara emerged from her room wearing a short and tight white Lycra mini-skirt and three-inch white pumps. To keep from showing her bare legs Camara wore thin white leggings underneath. Rhonda suggested she wear the mini-skirt much to the spirited protest of Camara. The leggings were a compromise and a condition for wearing the sexy outfit. Her wrapped hairstyle covered her forehead and accentuated her slanted caramel colored eyes. Even though she was not exactly comfortable dressing so sexy, she still had to admit that she looked good.

Chase, on the other hand, was floored by her semi-provocative look. "You are breathtaking," Chase said as he walked up to her and gave her a warm body hug.

"Why thank you, Mr. Douglass. You are quite handsome yourself. And you smell good. I like a man that smells good. I'm glad that you're not wearing the face you had on Thursday," Camara said.

"Well, I have you to thank for that. You most definitely put a smile on my face," Chase said as he smiled from ear to ear still amazed with her beauty. Because winter had yet to make its presence felt yet in Western New York, the uncharacteristically warm November day did not call for jackets and ensured that Chase's view of Camara's curvaceous body would be unobstructed.

"Oh! I know what I wanted to ask you. Who was in your room playing BDP? Cause I know you don't know anything about KRS-One," Chase said laughingly and as they both made their way out of the door.

"What? Nah, you're right. I don't know nothing about Boogie Down Productions, KRS-One, Scott LaRock, D-Nice, Ms. Melody, Kenny Parker, or DJ Doc. I don't know nothing about the Teacher. You must be psychic," Camara said while shaking her head.

"I didn't think they sold BDP or any Hip Hop in the suburbs. My bad," Chase said as he laughed aloud.

"Oh, you think you're funny huh? I probably know more about Hip Hop than you."

"Yeah right...I'm all the way live! I'm hip hop through and through baby. And, for the record KRS is definitely dope, but he can't touch my man Kool G Rap," Chase said defiantly.

Almost on cue as soon as they hit outside Camara used her balled up fist as a microphone and started to rap, "Rap is like a set-up, a lot of games, a lot of suckers with colorful names. I'm so and so I'm Chase and I'm that. But ya boy G. Rap is just wick-wick-wack!" Camara stopped and did the universal B-boy sign by cocking her body and head sideways and folding her arms. "You don't want any of this homeboy!"

"Oh, we battling...is that what we're doing? Cool, but don't cry when I hit you below the belt. Check this out...Do me a favor and pick up a pen and pad, and try to write down the number of the men you had. Just remember when you putting someone else in check go to the Wizard of Oz and get some self-respect," Chase answered adding a few pop lock steps.

Camara did the Wop dance to answer Chase's dance moves. Her brain had been running through all of her favorite BDP songs at warp speed so by the time Chase had finished, her mini-verse was already on deck and ready to be fired back instantly. "This is the warning known as the caution, do not attempt to diss 'cause you'll soften. Just like a pillow or better yet a mattress. You can't match this style or attack this. While I'm telling you right on schedule, fuck with Cam-a-ra and I'll bury you!"

"When I die scientist will preserve my brain donate it to science to answer the unexplained. But as long as I inhale and exhale, I'll fuck up the female or the next male. What you hear in your ears all appears to be clear, consider me fear 'cause I share ideas. That sticks to mix more tricks than a 6-6-6 so you better pass the crucifix!" Chase responded. He was secretly enjoying hearing KRS-One's gritty rhymes emitting from such a beautiful vessel as Camara.

"Camara and KRS equals one, I don't burn anymore I just cook till ya done. And when you're done, then I'll serve like alphabet soup letters, words," Camara rapped.

"Ok, ok, homegirl. You know your Hip Hop. I can't front on you. But my boy G. Rap will still eat KRS' breakfast lunch and dinner!" Chase said.

Finding Chase undeserving of a response, Camara raises her hand and waved him off like an elephant to a fly. Realizing they were at the outside entrance of the Student Union ballroom, Camara noted, "Wow. We got here fast, huh?" While enjoying their battle the duo were oblivious to their surroundings and did not realize their destination was so close.

"You right, we did get here fast. But it looks like we made a blank trip," Chase said as he pointed to the sign on the door. Due to technical difficulties, today's free showing of Pet Sematary will be postponed indefinitely. Thank you.

"Wow, that sucks. I would say let's go get something to eat but I'm not really hungry yet. Are you?" Chase asked.

"No, not really. But I'm not letting you off the hook for dinner later on this evening, Mr. Douglass," Camara said as she walked seductively towards Chase.

"You like Monopoly?" Chase asked reaching for her tiny waist.

"Are you kidding? I love monopoly!" Camara quickly responded as she felt Chase's hand make intimate contact with the left side of her body. She felt his gentle but powerful tug as she gave in and connected her body with his. She loved the way his hard muscles felt against her body.

Chase never felt a body so immaculate. He pulled her as close to him as possible and whispered in her ear, "So let's go back to my room and play. The loser pays for dinner, bet?"

"Sounds like a plan, especially since I don't plan on losing," Camara said. She thought Chase had dipped both his hands in endorphins and was rubbing it all over her body. They stood for a few minutes outside the Student Union ballroom hugging each other for dear life.

"Well you might luck up and win cause what I really want to eat for dinner is probably not on the menu," Chase said as he reached for the back of Camara's neck with his fingers placing both of his thumbs on her jawline and kissed her. Her succulent lips tasted of cherries and vanilla courtesy of Camara's favorite lip balm. Chase had never tasted anything so refreshing.

■

Arriving at his dorm room, Chase was thrilled to see that Brad was gone. His stomach was doing cartwheels in anticipation of having sex with Camara. He made up his mind that if they did not have sex he was all right with that. Simply put, he was having a fabulous time just being in her presence.

"So are you and your roommates cool?" Camara asked Chase as she sat down on the edge of his bed.

"Yeah, real cool. White dude named Brad, and you'll never believe me but he loves hip hop like we love hip hop. It bugged me out. I mean he ain't no wannabe or nothing like that. He just loves hip hop. Real cool dude," Said Chase as he searched for the monopoly game he thought he had hidden in the closet.

"Well, my roommate Rhonda is just as cool. She is from Buffalo and is really sweet and down to Earth. My suitemate Brandi, well that's a whole different story. She's from New York City or somewhere around there and swear she's royalty. If she keeps it up Rhonda is going to give her a royal beat down. For the most part, me and Rhonda keep to ourselves," said Camara. She did not know if it was the room, or her late night studying catching up with her, but she could not stop yawning and stretching. She stood up to try to shake it off.

"Yeah, some of the people here are kind of arrogant. I find it usually the weaker types that need to claim a city or a region because on a one-on-one, individual comparison they know they won't measure up to most people," Chase theorized.

"That's deep," Camara said.

"Listen, I think Brad left the Monopoly game in the RA's room. I think they are close to becoming a couple 'cause he's been chilling with her a lot. Let me go and check and see if he left it there. I'll be right back, ok?"

"All right, Mr. Douglass, don't take too long. Don't try to delay this spanking I'm going to give you because you might like it," Camara said enjoying the hint of sexual suggestion.

"Now I know I better hurry up," Chase said as he left the room running. The R.A. in question was five doors down from his room. Chase hurried with the aim of getting back to the flyest girl he'd ever met. He was thinking about sex but worried about the disgusted feeling he often experienced afterward. She seemed special and not the type to devalue a potential relationship with premature sex, so perhaps it was a moot thought. Then again, she was in his room.

Chase retrieved the Monopoly game from the sleep-drunk RA after a few minutes of waiting and headed back to Camara. *Ok, all we're going to do is play Monopoly and have dinner. Whatever happens after that happens. No expectations, no limitations.*

Although he had been gone a little over five minutes, Camara was stretched out on his bed sound asleep. Of all the possibilities, this one never crossed his mind. He thought about waking her up but decided against it. *She must have been really tired or really comfortable for her to fall asleep that fast,* he thought.

Chase took his desk chair and turned it towards Camara and sat down. He watched as she took one deep breath afte the other , paying particular attention to the rise and fall of her flat stomach. She was lying on her side with both hands between her knees. Her lips were opened slightly and her eyebrows twitched every so often but she did not snore. Before Chase knew it a half-hour had passed with him just watching her sleep. He found it extremely peaceful. As many females Chase had been with in his life, this was the first time ever he was able to truly enjoy the feminine presence and bask in it.

Chase felt the urge to be next to her at the very least. He had heard old men in the barbershop speak about waking up sex partners 'the hard way' but that was clearly out of the question in this context. Only a real creep looking for a felony would even attempt it and that was not in Chase's DNA. Chase was a quasi-sex addict but unlike a few of his fellow classmen, a drunk or sleeping woman was completely safe in his presence.

But, he just had to hold her if she was willing. He stood up from his chair, walked over, and got into the bed with her. As he hugged her from behind she moved in a manner that suggested her approval. The duo curled into the 'lovers spoon' and Chase surprisingly fell fast asleep. Miracles happen in the strangest places…

14 November 27, 1989

Dr. Archibald Moses King II loved being a professor even more than he thought he would when he initially took the position. The structure, the prestige of being a professor, the smell of the lecture halls, the quiet but steady struggle between the faculty and the administration, the chance to read and get paid for it, and the solitude of his office were just a few of the things he enjoyed. These things all paled in comparison to reaching and elevating students. Taking a good student and making them great was providence for Professor King.

He enjoyed the college life so much that he secretly dreaded the just recently passed Thanksgiving break. Professor King was such a workaholic that he had almost no work to catch up on during the recess. Thanksgiving break is typically a time when college professors grade mid-term papers, exams and write letters of recommendation. The truly prolific ones also work on grant proposals, books, and articles. And then there were scholars like Professor King who had completed his grading and submitted two articles and book proposal for review by the time recess started.

Being an over-achiever and organized to the letter, left Professor King with some serious free time on his hand that he decided to enjoy with his baby sisters Velma and Gwendolyn in Charleston, South Carolina. He elected to drive given the flexibility of last minute detours it offered. The long drive gave him time to think, which was both a blessing and a curse to a man with a bright future and eventful past.

Professor King usually slept no more than five hours a night, so waking up early was something that he was quite comfortable with. This Monday morning was no exception. His two bedroom apartment was neat and economically decorated. His only true overindulgence was his book collection. By last count, he had 585 of them placed deftly around his humble abode, most of which were hardcover. Making up his bed right after he woke up was a tradition he continued to this day thanks to his beloved mother.

After shaving and brushing his teeth he knelt beside his bed to say his morning prayers. He was a very spiritual man but was weary of organized religion. If a church did not have tutorial programs and other support services for the community he did not find it any more desirable than a liquor store. Walking out of his front door, the gunmetal gray clouds greeted him. He decided that a good walk was in order this morning being that he spent many hours crammed into his blue 1988 Honda Accord driving to and from South Carolina.

He had a 9 a.m. meeting with two of his students. It was not going to be a pleasant meeting either because one of the two students had broken the honor code by copying from the other. Professor King's task was to find out which one. He did not like academic fraud of any kind and he knew he had to confront this violation head-on.

Still, Professor King was in a very upbeat mood. He had a Black Scholars luncheon in Rochester to attend in the evening and was itching to re-read "Native Son" for the third time. The more he read a great book, the clearer the book became. His appointment with Richard Wright and his masterpiece would occur just after supper.

Professor King stopped at the local convenient store on his way to campus to pick up a cup of hot chocolate, a glazed bear claw, and a newspaper. He put the newspaper inside of his black briefcase and gobbled down the donut just before he left the store. Between daring sips of his steaming hot chocolate which threatened to burn his lips and tongue, he inhaled and exhaled the early morning's brisk air. His black horn-rimmed glasses would fog up periodically. Only a baby blue knit sweater separated him from the 40-degree morning.

"Fuck you nigger! Go back to Africa, you gorilla!" screamed a white Townie from a fast moving vehicle passing Professor King.

It took a few seconds for those hateful words to register in Professor King's brain. *Fuck you nigger...go back to Africa you gorilla?* Even when the outburst was fully processed he remained frozen, not knowing whether to ignore the hick or to go chasing after the car. He looked around and up and down both sides of the street to see if anyone else was witness to the diseased request. When he realized he was the only person in earshot of the insult he shook his head trying his best to hold back his oncoming rage.

He could not fully grasp why someone would say something like that to another human being. He then began to feel foolish for questioning what he knew the answer to. *Why would I think that being a college professor would shield me from the ignorance of small-minded people? Why would I ever think that being a college professor would transform me from the only thing they will ever see...a big black nigger?* The day was ruined. He started out as calm as Lake Placid but now he was Beirut, Lebanon with Syrian tanks and Palestinian suicide bombers.

■

Those seven words ran rough-shot through Professor King's mind. He fidgeted at his desk wishing that the memory of the incident would just fade away into oblivion. To help this process he decided to focus on the two mid-term exams which were sprawled across his desk. One test belonged to James Augustine, the other to Camara Truth, who sat next to him. James was a non-descript, white student who usually piggybacked off of what other students had already said when he was called upon to give his opinion on a subject. And when he did know something about a topic he generally used flowery over-the-top words to make him seem smarter than he actually was. Camara, on the other hand, was a clear 'A' student—intelligent, articulate, and focused.

Still, he had to give both students the benefit of the doubt. The mid-term exam consisted of fifty multiple choice questions. Both of exams had the same two answers wrong, question number's 14 and 22. Professor King thought he knew who copied off of whom, but needed concrete evidence to substantiate his presumption. He heard a knock on his office door. Looking at his watch, he knew it was show time. Professor King took off his glasses and squeezed his temples until his fingers got to his eyeballs before he gave his eyes a generous rub. Putting his glasses back on, he stood up and walked to the door and welcomed his two pupils.

"Miss Truth and Mr. Augustine, please have a seat. I will dispense with the pleasantries and go straight to the meat. Both of your mid-term exams from a week and a half ago are identical. I'm not a mathematician but I'd dare to say that is highly improbable. And if you couple that with the fact that you two sit next to each other...something is rotten in Denmark. If one of you would like to fess up to the crime now, you will not fail the course. You will simply get an F on the mid-term. I will average it into your current and future grades. It will be put on your record, but if you have no other similar incidents, it will be expunged. However, if you force me to use my considerable, deductive reasoning abilities and I discover on my own who cheated, then you will pay me for my time in spades. Starting with you failing my course, then you will be subject to a permanent expulsion from McNair

University pending a review from the Honesty Board. This will go on your record and it will stay on there like funk on feces. Are there any questions?"

Camara looked at Professor King in bewilderment as he grappled with the charges leveled at her. She then turned to James with searing anger, "Look, whoever you are, you know I didn't copy off you. I have no reason to. Professor King, I love your class. I don't have to cheat."

"Well, I didn't cheat either! All I did was sit down and take the test. I can't help it if she copied off of me" James said smartly.

"Cheat off you! P-lease! Check my record, I never cheated or copied off anybody's test answers. Now I know you did it. All you have to do is admit it. If you were smart you would've at least marked a couple of answers different from mine genius," Camara scolded.

"No, no, that's where you're wrong. I'm not the genius, you're the genius. The course is Black Lit, right? Well, you're certainly black enough. Professor, you can't prove I did anything wrong. You know it and I know it. So my advice—" James said before he was cut off by a now standing up and visibly angry Camara.

"What you mean I'm black enough? Are you trying to be funny? Are you trying to get me thrown out of school? I am not going down with you. And make one more remark about my color white boy and see what happens!" Camara said loudly while standing up and pointing her manicured finger in the face of James who for the most part was remarkably calm.

"There you go, making it a black and white thing. All I meant was that because you're black, you have a natural advantage over me on the subject of black literature that's all. Sounds like common knowledge to me. Boy, you people can be so uptight and sensitive sometimes."

Both Professor King and Camara knew that James meant much more than he professed and his explanation made no sense. They also both knew how it felt to be ridiculed for their darker skin tone. Camara would receive backhanded compliments like 'You're pretty for a dark-skinned girl' all too often. Professor King as a youth was called 'King Kong' and 'Nigga Gorilla'. More often than not the authors of those ill-conceived monikers paid a hefty physical fine administered by Lil Archie.

Professor King felt the strong urge to pick James up by his neck and make him a permanent part of the décor on the wall. Dr. Fellner's warnings against any physical contact with students stopped him from turning his thoughts into action. *However, a point must still be made you pale-faced, impotent little Troglodyte.*

"My, my, my, James, we are sassy and quite opinionated today, aren't we? Can I tell you a quick story? A true story that you might learn a little something from. Did you know that I was incarcerated? Figures, right? A big black guy like me…it's almost mandatory that we spend at least some time in the joint right?" Professor King asked.

James began to squirm a bit in his chair as he for the first time realized how physically big Professor King was. He kept his head perfectly still and followed Professor King only with his eyes as the professor paced back and forth in the small office. He did not know whether to answer him or not. He chose the latter because of his mounting fear of what the consequences were to be if he answered incorrectly.

Professor King continued, "Well, see what happened was I was giving this anti-racism-slash-sexism workshop a few years back and it didn't quite turn out as planned. My techniques and methodology were a touch too progressive and forward-thinking for the time. You see, there were these two rich spoiled white guys around your age—you know the type, the kind that given a 50-yard head start in a race still gets angry when his opponent finally finds his track sneakers that he denied him in the first place. You know the type?" asked Professor King focused on James' eyes.

Camara was somewhat confused about where the story was going but she enjoyed watching James' face go from high pink to blush red in a matter of minutes. She marveled at the way that Professor King told the story.

"So anyway they thought it was cool to take a dump on the front porch of a pretty black woman who refused their advances. I mean they literally pulled down their britches and grew a tail. Wiped their asses and left the tissue for all to see. I mean that's some gross shit, right?" Professor King asked looking as hard as he could into the blue eyes of James who now found it difficult to meet the glare.

"Yeah that's pretty freaking nasty," James agreed in a hushed tone.

"I thought it was too. See what these two gentlemen didn't know is that the porch that they decided to defecate on was my girlfriend's porch. They wanted to have what the French call a ménage a trios with my girl. I guess they thought they were back on the plantation somewhere where they had free reign with black women. They picked the wrong Black woman. Obviously, she said no and that next night we discovered that shit really does steam."

Camara was riveted. She sensed that Professor King was coming to her aid. She kept looking back at James whose face was getting redder and redder after each word Professor King uttered. She was barely able to contain her smile. Professor King stood up and walked over to the students and stood right in front of James.

"Stand up, Jimmy," Professor King requested.

"Excuse me, sir?" asked James who was growing increasingly nervous.

"I know you didn't cheat on your hearing test too. I said stand up and don't make me repeat it. Thank you," Professor King reached to stand James up himself but before he could make contact James stood straight up, six o'clock style.

"See, I had you stand up so that the blood will flow directly to your brain and that will help you to better understand. To make a long story short, Jimmy, I took the two boys on a trip out to the country where shit is king. I kidnapped them. You know they use shit for fertilizer and it helps things grow. I mean they like shit so much I was going to educate them on it. This was how I was going to implement the punishment phase of my program. I knew there was a chance I could get caught but some things are worth going to jail for," Professor King said stopping himself from letting out a laugh.

James just wanted to get out of this tiny little office that had this big and very imposing black man in it. *If I just haul ass to the door right now I might make it out injury free.*

"I had a friend of mine named Chuck with me, real cool, cock-diesel fella. Chuck told me that it was impossible for a man to take a shit without pissing. I said I never really thought about it but I'm quite sure it was possible. Well needless to say we had two lab rats itching to help us with our competing theories that night!"

The last time Camara saw someone shake like this was Harold on top of her. She now had to cover her mouth to keep from laughing at James.

"Professor King, I thought we were here to talk about the exam. Sir, you're making me a little nervous and I really don't understand what two dudes taking a crap on your girl's porch have to do with me," James nervously said to Professor King as he was inching closer and closer to him.

"Don't interrupt me again. So, anyway Chuck and I took them to an outhouse out in Sodus. Chuck told them to drop them drawers and take a shit in a proper place and let us know if they could shit without pissing. One of the crac- I mean white boys was so scared he was shitting as soon as he sat his ass on the outhouse stool. The other one couldn't move his bowels at all. It didn't matter because they were both dipped head first in shit and piss before the night was over. Not to mention how we pounded the hell out of them before they were dipped in, what some country boys call, 'the sauce'.

That's when you can't tell where the shit ends and piss begins and it's all mixed up together. Anyway, we left them there, they walked back home, went to the authorities and I went to the clink for a while. So how does this story relate to you?" Professor King asked.

James was about to pass out any second now from pure fear. He, at that point, realized how reckless he had become in terms of school, his work, and race relations. James realized that for every action someone could react without sorrow or mercy.

"The story is immediately relevant to you because you attempted to move your bowels on dear Camara. Never disrespect a woman in my presence again. I have demonstrated the ability to kill a fly with a shotgun, figuratively speaking of course. I will go out of bounds to make the play and bring you down. When a woman's honor is at stake no journey is too far to travel. Get me?"

"Ye...ye...yes, sir," James stuttered.

"Now did you copy off of Ms. Truth's test? I am giving you one final time to come clean."

It looked to both Camara and Professor King that James was on the verge of tears. James' eyes indeed began to fill with water which spilled onto his rosy cheeks.

"I am not your enemy, James, nor do I want to be your enemy...yet. You don't want me on the other side of you coming full blast with no regard for myself or anyone on your side. I want to be your conduit to a higher way of thinking. So, Mr. Augustine, did you cheat?" asked Professor King standing a mere ten inches from James.

James summoned all the strength he could muster up and nodded his head down then up then down and up again to signify that he did cheat on his mid-term exam.

"I applaud your newfound honesty. Apologize to Ms. Truth for wasting her precious time please."

"Sorry."

Camara responded with a manicured middle finger. She even twisted and rotated it so there was no mistaking her feelings.

Professor King pretended not to see Camara's antics and continued, "You will receive an F but if you work hard you can still pass my course. Thank you, Mr. Augustine, you may leave." He put out his sizable hand for James to shake. At first, James hesitated. But being anxious to leave propelled his hand into the professor's. Professor King squeezed James's hand until he felt the young man's knuckles collide and roll against each other repeatedly, causing excruciating pain to James.

"Now, Mr. Augustine, I hope you don't happen to let the details of how I ran my little anti-racism and sexism workshop out of the bag or about my time in a correctional facility. Those kinds of things are best kept to one's self. I hold no grudges and I'm quite sure Ms. Truth will ultimately forgive you and if nothing like this ever happens again. This incident is already a distant memory. Agreed?" asked Professor King who was still holding James's hand like a vice grip.

James's hand was almost ghost-white and his eyes were beginning to bulge out as he struggled to get away from the professor's clutches.

"Agreed, can I please leave now?" James pleaded.

"There's the door. Have a good day," Professor King noted in a level voice.

Camara who was standing next to the bookcase was astounded by what had just transpired. "Camara, I offer my most humble apologies to you. I knew he copied from you, but I had to have some proof or admission of guilt. You are still an A student and a pleasure to have in my class. You know, Camara, sometimes life calls for you to take matters into your own hands and shape it accordingly."

"Now James knows that philosophy first hand," Camara replied as she busted out laughing. "I do appreciate you not jumping to conclusions and thinking it was me who was the one cheating."

"I would be negligent in my duties as your college professor if I were to do that, Ms. Truth. Please enjoy the rest of your day," Professor King said as he smiled and shook Camara's hand gently.

Relaxed, Professor King methodically straightened up his office. His next meeting was scheduled for 11 a.m. with another troubled student, one Chase Douglass.

15

Chase was unaware of his exact location. He was literally flying up and down South Avenue. Dreams of flight were his absolute favorite kinds of dreams. He would fly and sometimes flutter, looking down over the landscape and peering into familiar buildings from unfamiliar vantage points. So when the obnoxiously loud radio alarm clock sounded at 7 a.m., Chase was jolted from his sleep into a disoriented state of disappointment. Grounded, he accepted reality and began to fight off the sleep that enveloped his body.

For the first time, Chase was making a concerted effort to complete his school work thanks in large part to the gentle but forceful nudges of his new friend Camara. Since their first official date a little over a week ago the two had become inseparable. They connected daily for walks, lunch dates, movies, and library study sessions. When they weren't physically together they connected via telephone.

The most peculiar aspect of the courtship was that there was no sex involved and Chase surprisingly had not made it a priority. He simply enjoyed being around her. She was bringing the gentleman out of Chase but he did not know how long his gentleman's patience would last. She was becoming more and more enticing and irresistible each day.

He marveled at her academic prowess. Watching her study and think actually turned him on. He loved the way her eyes squinted and her lips pursed when she was trying to find the answer to a difficult question. He knew for a fact that he would not have been in the library at eight in the morning reviewing notes and outlining his upcoming paper for Black Lit if it was not for Camara. Once Chase he started reading *The Spook who Sat by the Door* by Sam Greenlee he was immediately engaged. The notes he copied from Camara helped him to better understand the tone and theme of the book, awakening his curiosity.

Again taking advice from Camara he decided to schedule a meeting with Professor King. Chase knew that without a divine miracle he was going to fail the class. He also did not particularly like Professor King who he found arrogant and rude. Still, he understood that he had to at least speak with him about his newfound dedication to Black Lit 101 and college more generally.

Leaving the library at 10:40 virtually ensured that he would be on time for his 11 a.m. meeting. Professor King made it a point to let all of his students know the importance of being on time and making the absolute most of your time. Chase needed to make a good impression and this was a good way to start.

He entered the faculty building and looked for the English department on the black directory board to his immediate right. The block white letters informed him that the English Department was located on the third floor and Professor A. King would be torturing him room 315B. He felt tightness in his chest while riding the elevator to the third floor. Although he had a fear of heights in real life, he knew the thought of sitting down man-to-man with Professor King probably helped to contribute to his nervousness.

The door to Professor King's office was wide open and Chase was not sure if he should walk right in or to knock on the wood paneling outlining the door. Chase did a combination of both announcing himself as well. "How you doing, Professor, it's Chase. I'm here for my 11 a.m. appointment."

"Mr. Douglass, how are you this morning? Excuse me. I was catching up on some pleasurable reading. Have you read *Native Son* by Mr. Richard Wright?" Professor King asked as he turned his leather swivel chair around and held up the book.

"No sir, I have not," Chase answered flatly.

"Bigger Thomas is a transformative character in literature, quite possibly the most. I'm sorry sir, please sit down relax. My passions sometimes sidetrack me. I'm quite sure you can relate to that on some level...correct?" asked Professor King.

"I can relate," Chase said not knowing how much information Alvin Dance had given Professor King about his sexual escapades. He started to regret coming to Professor King's office. The thought of his sex life being the fodder for two grown men's conversation was creepy to Chase. He thought about making an excuse to leave or at the very least to reschedule but suddenly Camara's face popped into his head. He bit his lip, took a deep breath, and tried to change the subject.

"What I wanted to talk to you about was how I can—or better yet—what can I do to pass your course. I've been getting some tutoring as of late and I really want to pass. I know I missed some assignments and a bunch of classes but I am committed to at least trying to improve my grade."

Professor King looked hard at Chase to see if his face would give away his real reason for wanting to talk.

"Well, Mr. Douglass, on one hand, I appreciate the fact that you came down to my office. You are looking me in my eyes and telling me that you want to be a better student and you are seeking help in order to be a better student. That demonstrates humility. I respect humility. However, on the other hand, I have to question your abrupt change of heart. I mean your track record up to this point shows exactly how indifferent you have been in relation to my course. To be quite honest I'm not sure whether to feel inspired or insulted mainly because we have only three weeks left in the semester. Too bad your epiphany did not occur sooner," Professor King said smiling ever so slightly.

"So are you saying I'm trying to get over on you?" Chase asked in a rising confrontational voice.

"I would not waste my time or yours stating or defending an impossibility. All I am doing, Mr. Douglass, is thinking out loud while trying to figure out your true intentions. My apologies, sir, if you misconstrued anything I said as an affront to you. I will give you the benefit of the doubt as I require the same courtesy. I am at your disposal, Mr. Douglass," Professor King said as he grinned even wider.

Normally Professor King would have thrown Chase out as soon as he detected any form of hostility or disrespect. Truthfully speaking Professor King was not fond of anyone who did not have the courage or the discipline required to work hard regularly, and Chase was the poster child. Being lazy was not an option in the world of Professor King. What frustrated the professor, even more, was that he was told by his good friend Alvin Dance that Chase was highly intelligent. Professor King was finding those traits increasingly hard to discover on his own.

"Look, Professor, I'm far from perfect. I guess all I'm saying is that I'm just willing to try harder. It shouldn't matter how I came to the decision, what should matter is that I have decided."

What mattered to Professor King was his promise to Alvin Dance to help Chase Douglass if he came and asked for it. "Mr. Douglass, you are absolutely correct. But in the interest of full disclosure, I have had discussions with Mr. Alvin Dance about your situation. So I more or less have an idea of what we are up against."

Chase sat and pouted as thoughts of what actually Mr. Dance said to Professor King incensed him. He still listened and tried his best to remain calm as Professor King continued to speak.

"I respect Mr. Dance to the fullest and he has a very high opinion of you. He says that you are smart and creative. With that being said, I told him that you are lazy and aloof. I also promised him that if you asked for my help I'd give it to you. My helping you at this stage is based purely on my respect and love for a great friend and colleague. So I will help you in any way I can. But my willingness to continue helping you will depend on how hard you are willing to work. Your problem is not my problem. It is in your best interest to get your degree, not mine. Let me assure you, Mr. Douglass, that I am a man of my word. The most ironic thing about being a man of your word is that it requires of all things…action," said Professor King as he stood up to take a walk around his modest office.

"If I say I'mma do something…I'm gonna do it. But what do you mean my situation? My only situation is I can't pass your class. Anything else is my business unless I choose to share it with you. I don't appreciate Mr. Dance telling strangers strange shit about me. I don't like that shit, man," Chase said as he shook his head back and forth.

Professor King paused. He looked at Chase, turning his head slightly upwards like a canine trying to figure out what exactly he is up against before deciding to attack or retreat. "Mr. Douglass, I am the only one in this office who has the right to use profanity. Besides that, show me some respect! I am old enough to be your father and who knows I probably am. Don't ever curse at me again."

The now seething Chase stood up as if he was going to leave but instead thought better of it. "You're right. My Grandparents taught me better. I apologize."

"Apology accepted. And, about your situation…I would completely understand your anger if I took the juicy tidbits from hours you've spent in young ladies beds and divulged them to the entirety of the student population during one of my lectures…or if I was to publish your sexual trysts in a journal for the world to read. But that's not my style. It would serve no purpose. What I know about you stays with me. Mr. Dance told me because he felt I needed to know in order to understand and help you. Knowledge is power."

Feeling defensive but in safe hands, Chase remained silent for a while before he spoke. He wanted to believe that the two men were sincere in their effort to help him. "Ok, Professor, how do we begin?" he asked.

"Ok, Mr. Douglass, a few points before we begin. First, you can say anything you want to me, as long as you say it and do it with respect. Respect is numero uno. Number two, what we talk about stays with us…Professor

King and Mr. Douglass. If you would like for me to consult with Mr. Dance about something specific we have discussed I'd be happy to do so. If I feel his expertise on a certain matter pertaining to you trumps my own, then I will ask you before I consult with him. Does that meet with your approval, Mr. Douglass?"

"That's cool Professor King. I got no problem with that," said Chase feeling a bit more relaxed.

"We have to define our objectives as well. My number one goal is to make sure you graduate from college, not necessarily my course. Understood?" Professor King asked while sitting back down in his black leather swivel chair.

"Understood and much appreciated," Chase said.

"Due to your numerous absences and low grades, you already have failed my course. According to policy, I can give you an F based simply on you missed classes alone. However, if you complete the remaining assignments and exams with a grade of B or better I will allow you to withdraw from the class without penalty. This way you can withdraw from my course and it will be like it never happened. Do we have a deal? Professor King asked as he put out his huge right hand and waited for Chase to submit to his new destiny.

As Chase shook his meaty claw, Professor King continued, "For now until the end of the semester we will meet the same day and time. Do not miss an appointment unless you are dead. No excuses. All right, Mr. Douglass, we have plenty of work ahead of us, see you in class tomorrow," Professor King said as he stood up and shook Chase's hand once again.

Leaving Professor King's office Chase felt better about being a college student. He still thought Professor King was a cocky bastard but his heart was in the right place. While the issues that truly inhibited Chase from becoming an optimal student were yet to be unearthed, at that moment he felt that both he and Professor King had the tools for the job.

His attention then turned to Camara and their noontime lunch date at the campus pizza parlor. Today's meal was going to be courtesy of Camara because he made it to both the library and his appointment with Professor King. As long as he did both Camara promised lunch was on her. He could taste the garlic pizza and wings dipped in blue cheese already. *No meal like a free meal.*

Looking ahead toward Camara's dorm, his appetite was chased from his body by a toxic combination of anger and jealousy. He could make out Camara at the main entrance chatting and giggling with a tall gentleman. The man seemed to be very touchy-feely. As Chase stepped closer he was to make out Camara's chummy companion. *Squeeze! Let me go see what the fuck is so funny!* Chase picked up his pace.

16

"You been pretty busy lately haven't you, Miss Thang? I almost forgot what you looked like I haven't seen you in *sooooo* long," said Rhonda with a smile and a giggle as she walked into the Morgan Dormitory lounge and plopped herself next to Camara who was lounging lazily on the community couch watching television. "I'm surprised Chase isn't here cuddled up next to you all snuggly. How long has he held you hostage for? What, a couple of weeks? For a minute I thought I was going to have to call Five-O on his ass."

"Did you ever think it was me holding him hostage?" Camara asked slyly.

Unlike the time she spent with Harold where time seemed to have an anchor tied around its neck, days with Chase were fast, fun, and free. Camara adored every millisecond of it.

"Oh, Ok. Let me find out Chase done knocked the dust out of them boots! He must have that Babyface whip appeal going on," said Rhonda as she laughed loudly.

"Well you never know," Camara said as she walked towards the vending machine trying hard to keep a straight face. She hadn't had sex with Chase yet but she liked keeping Rhonda guessing.

Camara had no intention of breaking the 'Three Month Rule' enacted by her mother and aunts for the younger females of the Truth clan to follow. However, in order for her to remain in compliance, she had to build a wall of resistance to Chase's magic. He had been attacking with an assortment of kisses, deep conversations, and sincere compliments and Camara's wall wanted nothing more than be bulldozed and to come tumbling down.

Chase's clean-shaven, brown-skinned face sported a slight but noticeable dimple on the right side. His short black wavy hair always seemed crisp and freshly cut. His bow-legged walk hinted at a dark side that enthralled Camara. She knew there was depth to him and had every intention of riding with Chase down any rabbit hole he might explore.

"Camara, you did you break Chase off yet?" Rhonda whispered in a very serious tone as she got up from the couch and met Camara at the vending machine.

"I see that inquiring minds want to know," Camara said playfully.

"I'm serious, Camara, did y'all do it?"

"No, Rhonda. He is so freaking sexy, I might attack him tonight. But no, I'm going to be a good girl for now. We haven't even made anything official yet. I don't sleep with anyone I'm not in a real relationship with. You know I only had sex once and it was horrible. If and when we become a couple I'd gladly let him be my succulent second. So, there'll be no quick nookie, and no nookie if we are not in a committed, monogamous relationship. Skeezers get no respect and a skeezer I could never be," Camara said as she touched Rhonda playfully on the tip of her nose.

Rhonda loved the fact that there was nothing easy about Camara. This bolstered her pride in her ability to pick great friends. Camara's most prized possession was currently safe. However, Rhonda knew it was merely a matter of time before she gift wrapped and handed it to Chase.

"I know that's right! I have to admit Chase looks good and he is very sexy. You two do make a real cute couple. But..." Rhonda slowed and paused as she wanted to choose her words carefully.

"...you are my friend and I gotta be honest with you. Chase has a reputation on campus. He gets around, girl. Now I'm not saying this to be no cockblocker. I like Chase he seems real cool. And, maybe...you two are meant to be. If so, I'll gladly be the maid of honor at your wedding. But I know of at least five girls he slept with already, and we've only been here for what, three months if that?" Rhonda said in her older sister voice.

Instead of rushing to Chase's defense, Camara thought better of it and decided to listen. Rhonda continued passionately, "Now those are the girls that I know he slept with, it could be double or triple that...who knows. Maybe, he is different once he commits to you. As fine as Chase is once these jealous hoes catch wind that you two are officially a couple, they might start purposely throwing the pussy at him just to spite you. Or worse, just so they can say to your face they fucked your man and you can't do anything about it. Some girls get off on sexing another woman's man. The dude don't start looking good to them until they got a girlfriend, then the nigga becomes Denzel instantly. Bottom line, girl, I don't want you to get hurt. So please be careful."

Although she talked with mother talked about sex and relationships, it seemed more clinical to Camara than anything else. She never felt the warmth or zeal emanating from her mother she was feeling now. She knew she would never find a better friend than Rhonda.

The substance of Rhonda's words weighed heavy on Camara's heart. The thought of Chase having sex with another woman hurt her stomach literally.

Jealousy was a strange new brew that Camara did not like the taste of. So rather than let it upset her stomach or give her heartburn, Camara counteracted the effects by flooding her imagination with future images of relationship bliss.

"I will, girl. I promise. Right after I put it on him!" Camara said as she laughed and she and Rhonda embraced.

"Oh my God...I almost forgot about him!" Rhonda exclaimed.

"About who?" Camara asked.

"Squeeze, that's who," Rhonda said as she pointed to an oncoming Squeeze who was strutting through the Morgan Dormitory lounge.

"Well, well, well, lookee here, lookee here I see my day has just gone beautiful. Hello, Camara, how have you been? I haven't heard from you in a while. You done upped and got married on me?" Squeeze said from a distance.

Squeeze had not crossed her mind in a material way since her first date with Chase. The physical attraction was not strong enough to hold up during Camara's stringent screening process. A scant movie and dinner date here and there was all she would entertain.

"Hi, Squeeze. No, I haven't gotten married...yet. How have you been?" Camara said as he closed in.

"I'm good, I'm good. Just missing you, that's all. Other than that I'm cool."

"Squeeze, what you doing over here in my neck of the woods this early in the day? You know somebody in Morgan?" Camara asked.

"I came looking for you," Squeeze said quickly. In reality, he had just left an all-night sex session.

"Yeah, right. First of all, you know not to come to my room unannounced so I know you're lying. But why lie? We don't go together. Rhonda, I'll see you later I gotta go. Bye, Squeeze," Camara said pleasantly as she exited the lounge and headed towards the door to go meet Chase.

"Hold on, hold on, Camara. You know I'm digging you. Stop playing hard to get. Seriously though I got a homeboy here and we studied all night for this crazy test, word up," Squeeze said as he caught up with Camara right outside of her dorm.

The lie made Camara laugh. She was gifted at detecting a lie, especially when the liar was male. Squeeze was as easy to figure out as a preschooler walking away from a cookie jar. *It's hilarious that he thinks I'm stupid enough to fall for that bullshit. I'm glad I don't have any real feelings for him.*

"What's so funny, Camara?" Squeeze asked seriously.

"You're funny, Squeeze. I appreciate the knowledge, though. I gotta bounce."

"Oh, ok. You got a hot date or something? You got a man now, Camara?"

"No, I don't have a man yet. I'm building, though."

"So that means I still got a chance then huh?" Squeeze asked as he attempted to put his hand on Camara's left hip.

"Not really and please don't touch what's not yours," she requested as she pushed Squeeze's hand away with a smile. "See you later."

Camara walked confidently toward the on-campus eatery. She wanted Chase and Chase alone.

■

Chase's heart pounded against his breastbone as his size 13's pounded the ground towards Camara and Squeeze. For the first time ever Chase felt the emotion of jealousy squirm and wiggle its way through his body from the top of his Adam's apple to the bottom of his belly button. Chase felt physically sick and could not come to terms with how fast this illness befell him. *I don't like this. Hell no!*

Chase was a little less than two football fields away from them. By the time he reached where he initially saw them, Squeeze had disappeared into the Harmon Dormitory building to the left and Camara had just walked into the door of the Off the Tracks eatery.

Still feeling the cold of the early winter winds Camara kept on her thigh-length Shearling coat and the attached flared wool hood. She sat at the first available booth to wait for Chase. Not more than twenty seconds later Chase walked in wearing a black leather full-length MCM coat with gold lettering and a twisted look on his face.

"Hello, Mr. Douglass. How did your meeting go with Professor King?"

"It went. How did your meeting go with Mr. Squeeze?" Chase asked angrily.

"What?" Camara asked completely puzzled by the question.

"You heard me! How did your meeting go with bitch-ass Squeeze?"

"Ok, Chase, listen. I don't know what's wrong with you...or if your meeting with Professor King went poorly...but I'm not used to being yelled at or questioned like this. Please don't take it out on me. If you want to continue on this date you're going to have to calm down," Camara said as she went from sitting across from Chase in the booth to standing up beside the table.

"Ok you're right, I'm wildin' out. I'll lower my voice. Is this better? Now please tell me how you know Squeeze," Chase asked in a sarcastic tone.

"No need to be a smart ass. I didn't know you knew Squeeze. We went out on a couple dates early in the semester," said Camara as she eased back into the booth.

"What you mean a couple dates? What kind of dates?" Chase asked loudly.

"Check your tone. We went to the Chinese restaurant, had lunch one day...and we went to the movies once," Camara started doing a quick mental check for completeness.

"What movie...Pet Sematary?" Chase asked.

Upon hearing Chase's last question Camara could not help but laugh. She realized that Chase was sincerely jealous. Almost immediately her anger subsided.

"I don't remember what we saw, Chase. But if he was that important to me, do you think I'd be here with you? I have zero interest in Squeeze."

Realizing she had a point but not quite, he was ready to stop being mad and continued questioning her in a quieter and less confrontational tone. "How did yall meet?"

"Damn, Chase! However college students attending the same college meet! If you must specifically know, we met at the Homecoming Jam," Camara said somewhat annoyed. To quell the onslaught of questioning she felt she needed to provide Chase some assurances so she slid into the booth with Chase and kissed him softly several times.

"Baby, to tell you the truth since I met you, I don't even think about him," Camara said in the most innocent voice she could muster.

"Well, you aren't available!" Chase said defensively.

"Wait, wait...wait a minute. Are you telling me I'm not available or are you asking will I not be available to anyone else?" Camara asked.

Chase was now beginning to realize what his declarative statement truly meant. He was asking Camara to be his girlfriend. Chase had not had a girlfriend since he was eleven and that did not go well because she caught him kissing her cousin. On one hand, he knew he had real feelings for Camara. He loved being in her presence. But on the other hand, he seriously doubted if he was ready to be in a monogamous relationship. Actually, Chase knew his cock would not let him be with just one woman...no matter how deeply he felt about her. He closed his eyes and took a deep breath before he answered her.

"I want you to be my girlfriend, Camara. I only had one girlfriend my whole life. I'm scared to death. I don't even know if I have what it takes to be somebody's man, to be honest with you. But I'm willing to try. I really, really like you, Camara. I just do," Chase said as he looked into Camara's eyes before he kissed her.

"Chase, I would love to be your girlfriend. I just wish it didn't take you to see me with Squeeze before you officially asked me," Camara confessed.

"You got a point, but it was going to happen regardless, he just speeded it up that's all," said Chase confidently.

"Ok, Chase, I'm yours. But guess what? That makes you mine. And, just how you peppered me with all kinds of questions about how I knew Squeeze and where I met him, if I see you somewhere with someone, you better answer each question I ask you and it better be the truth or I will fuck you up," Camara said with a very quick turning serious face. She pointed her index finger at him to emphasize her main point.

Chase was too dumb to realize the true implications of Camara's statement. He was smiling hard at the idea that he could make her jealous too.

"Oh my God! Where did you get such filthy language from? I know you don't kiss your mother with that mouth! You keep it up I got something to put in there to clean it out!" Chase said as he laughed and tried to dodge the barrage of playful but hard punches Camara rained down on him as payment for his lewd comment.

"Only in your wildest and wettest dreams. The only person I'll ever do that with is my husband. So you got an awfully long wait," Camara said laughing.

The newly united couple kissed, joked, laughed, and ate the afternoon away.

17 December 22, 1989

Although he had been home barely two weeks, Chase was actually missing McNair University more than he ever thought he would. Feet dangling off the side of his bed, he found it difficult to stop gazing at the two pictures he had placed on opposite sides of his dresser mirror.

One was of him and his roommate. They posed in front of Brad's black Chevy Lumina clasping hands, neither one was smiling. Chase who stood to the right adorned a dark turquoise Bugle Boy sweater with a black turtleneck and black parachute pants. Brad wore a grayish white, long-sleeved button-up shirt and a pair of faded Levi Jeans. The only time the pair ever argued was when they were on opposing sides of which M.C. had the 'illest' rhymes.

The other photo was an 8x10 of Chase and Camara taken by Brad who majored in Photographic Arts. Chase was wearing a white Tony Dorsett football jersey. Camara wore a dark charcoal gray oversized Lee Jean jacket, a black shirt, and a pair of tight fitting blue jeans that had two big holes on each thigh that showed white stitching. Chase stood behind Camara holding on to her for dear life. Warm and happy smiles were painted on their faces.

Completely losing himself in the imagery, Chase's nostalgic daydreaming was interrupted by the yelling of his best friend Will Garvey who barged through the attic door.

"College boy! Wake your punk ass up! I bet you didn't get more pussy than me this semester so don't even start lying!" Will said slapping Chase's leg and then moving it so he could have room to sit on the edge of the bed.

"What, Negro? I get more by mistake than you get on purpose! And anyway I'm into quality now not quantity. I had enough pussy in my life for three niggas. I might have to retire the crown homeboy," Chase said as he got up to sit in the lone fold up chair that was in his room.

"How are you gonna abdicate the throne that you never sat on?" Will asked visibly perturbed.

"What? Man you know I'm the all-time pussy getting champ of the Southwedge!" Chase said defiantly.

"Yeah right...we're not counting crackhead pussy, Chase. And, I'm talking real live women!" Will said as he laughed.

"Prince is the trickin' king round here, not me homeboy," Chase said.

Chase was not the type to patronize prostitutes. He thought of it as a cheap way to satisfy your needs. Chase instead would employ his charm and silver tongue to win over the ladies. If he could not get them to bed on his own terms, he did not feel he deserved it. The few times he did indulge it was always on someone else's dime.

"Please, nigga. It's me you're talking to, baby. Will Garvey! And not to change the subject but I love college pussy. High school pussy is ok, but college girls go that extra mile," Will noted.

"That's nonsensical. High school one year will be college the next. It's the same pussy," Chase noted logically.

"No sir, one is aged...advanced pussy. Anyway, I'm starting to prefer head. I'm telling you man college broads will throw a dick in their mouth faster than they'll put one in their chocha. I'm like an executive I just sit back and let them put their work in—especially white girls. I swear, man, I think their mamas be teaching them early how to blow. There's this one white freak who lives on my floor. She knocks on my door at least five nights a week. Once she gets her sample, she leaves like nothing ever happened. No quid pro quo or nothing. Straight sixty-eight and I owe her one. I love college!" Will said as if he found the keys to a brand new world.

"You right about that. I swear I had this Puerto Rican freak early in the semester. Oh my God...she wouldn't leave the dick alone. One night I swear I had to have busted five nuts at least. I think I was coming air. Talk about blue balls. She had me walking like a cowboy that night," Chase said as he slapped five with Will.

Chase was a bit hesitant to tell his best friend about the new love interest in his life. Being known all of his life as a philandering playboy, he was unsure how Will would view him now that he was doing his best to try and settle down with one woman. The last thing that he wanted was to get clowned for being a 'sucka for love'.

"Yo, man, I'm serious about giving up that crown, though. Would you believe I got a girlfriend now? And she is dope! Check her out," Chase said as he walked over to the mirror and pulled loose his picture of him and Camara.

"Damn! Honey is copacetic! She is fine as hell! What is she? West Indian...Jamaican or Dominican or something?" Will asked.

Chase had never asked her about her ethnic makeup. When he took the photograph back and re-examined it again closely he could see why his friend would ask the question. She had a smooth, dark, and exotic look to her that could have been the result of a couple of descendants from the Caribbean Island and the mish-mashing of their DNA. Chase was going to meet the woman responsible for at least half of his girlfriend's genetics, later on, today.

"To tell you the truth I never asked her. I figured she was just black," Chase said plainly.

"Well, whatever she is I can't front on you. This is what it's all about in the long run. What's her name?" Will asked.

"Camara, Camara Truth."

"I know that she got that good-good! No disrespect bro...but if she was mine, I'd eat it like Betty Crocker made it," Will said as he grabbed the picture from Chase's hand and shook his head to let him know how much he approved of his taste.

Chase did not know whether to tell his friend that he had not had sex with Camara yet. This was brand new territory for him. He had not pressed the issue about sex for some strange reason. The question had him thinking that maybe it was time for him and his girlfriend to go all the way. This was the longest time he had ever spent with a woman without witnessing her flesh.

"I ain't hit it yet man," Chase said softly.

"What you talkin' about, Willis?" Will exclaimed doing his best Gary Coleman, 'Different Stokes' impersonation.

Chase had to chuckle. "You heard me, man. I didn't hit it yet."

"Hold on, hold on. You mean you and Camara are officially a couple... boyfriend and girlfriend. You two have been together for how long now?" Will asked.

Chase exhaled in a somewhat frustrated manner and said, "About a month. So what are you trying to say, man?"

"Well, look...that's a sign she's not nasty. At least you won't find out the hard way that Chlamydia ain't a flower. But I know you, Chase. I know you're smashing something on the side," Will asserted.

"Nah...I jerk off. You know, the knuckle shuffle if I get horny," said Chase.

"Dishonorable discharge! Say it ain't so, Chase? Hey, you gotta—" Will stopped midsentence as he spotted a stuffed animal on Chase's bed. Obviously, he'd been sleeping with it.

"What the fuck is that? Is that a teddy bear? She got you whipped and haven't boned yet? I know people say you can meet your wife in college but if love makes cuddle with teddy bears, then they can keep that bullshit."

He attempted to stuff Mr. Fizzy beyond Will's immediate view. Chase knew Will was coming over to let him use his uncle's car for his date with Camara, but because he came early Chase did not have a chance to put Camara's teddy bear in the closet. Chase found Mr. Fizzy very comforting when he was not with Camara. It smelled like Camara's Liz Claiborne perfume and it reminded him of her so he kept him close. Right now the teddy bear was a source of embarrassment.

"Nobody's in love. I told you I'm trying something new. I'm becoming a man! Yo, take your ass downstairs so I can get ready, man. Wait for me in the car," Chase said as pushed Will out of his bedroom and went to take a shower.

"Damn, wait in the car. Not downstairs? In the car...like I'm a stranger picking you up for a first date?" Will said trying to muscle his wiry frame back into the room.

"Whatever's clever homeboy...just get out of here so I can get dressed," Chase said as he won the battle for space and slammed the door in Will's face.

■

Paranoid, sittin' in a deep sweat. Thinkin' I gotta fuck somebody before the week ends. The sight of blood excites me, shoot you in the head, sit down, and watch you bleed to death. The explicit rhymes were accompanied by funky guitar licks and a mesmerizing drum loop inside the Chevy Nova as it moved 25 miles per hour. Chase could not believe his ears as he attempted to make sense of the disturbing but sonically pleasing Hip Hop song.

"Will, what the fuck you got me listening to?"

"Oh yeah. I wanted you to hear these dudes. This is the Geto Boys. I met a dude at school from Texas and he turned me on to them. At first, I was buggin' when I heard them too. But they grew on—"

Chase interrupted his friend Will when he heard the rapper make a reference to rape.

"Is he talking about raping a woman? Man, if you don't take this bullshit out of the cassette deck and throw on some Big Daddy Kane or EPMD I'mma hurt you, man!" Chase said as he reached for the eject button.

Will blocked his hand almost swerving onto oncoming traffic. "Whoa. Whoa. Slow down teddy bear man. Just listen to it. It's more to it than that verse. It is saying it takes a sick person to do it and the song is not all about that. Listen to it from the beginning and give it a chance. Give it the same chance you would give a movie with a grisly murder or assault scene. Now, maybe I flooded you too fast...my bad. Let's start slower with 'Gangster of Love' and 'Life in the Fast Lane' and then come back to this one."

Chase listened to the first two songs and then reluctantly relented and listened to the song called 'Mind of a Lunatic' from the beginning. He could not help but bob his head to the groove of the music and the weird but lethal flow of the rappers. He still could not get past the verse covering necrophilia to give the song a full ringing endorsement.

"Ok, I see. This dude Bushwick thinks he's slick. This is what goes on in the mind of a lunatic, not necessarily his mind. It's an actually kinda clever use of a scapegoat to say some pretty sick shit. But to tell you the truth it's no different than what movies do. But don't you think it dangerous? I mean music is the soundtrack to life," Chase said as he allowed himself to get lost in the music.

"Oh, it is dangerous—dangerous, violent, misogynistic and downright nihilistic. There is no denying that. But don't tell me it's not dope. Anyway, man, you got the whip and now you got some new beats. My uncle has to be to work by midnight. So be here no later than 11:30. Have a good time, and don't let her whip you all the way out!" Will joked as he got out of the car.

Chase turned his attention to the fact that he was going to meet a young lady's mother for the first time. He was too embarrassed to ask anyone for advice on how to deal with the situation. He secretly wished he did not like Camara as much as he did because he was not comfortable meeting mothers or fathers.

Chase decided to focus his mind on how he planned to spend the rest of the day with Camara as he drove to Greece, a suburb of Rochester, to pick her up. The Liberty Pole lighting and some shopping at Midtown Mall downtown were among his plans for burning the brief winter daylight hours away. After that, he was hoping they could burn some body heat at his house. His grandparents were visiting family in Colorado for the holidays so he would have the whole house to himself.

As he pulled into the driveway he was immediately struck as to the size and beauty of her home. He remembered that Camara said that she was an only child. *If that's true why is this house so freakin' big? Damn Camara and her mom got dough.* The house was a four bedroom gray colonial that sat in the middle of a cull-da-sac with an above ground pool perched in the backyard. Chase was impressed.

He took a deep breath before walking up to the door and ringing the doorbell. When no one came to the door after a minute he rang the doorbell again and looked at the address to make sure it was the right one. *18 Timber Oak Drive...yup this is the right address. It's three so I'm on time. I hope her moms' don't trip on me.* The door finally opened with a quiet swoosh.

"Yes. Can I help you?" said a thin light-skinned woman with sandy brown hair who appeared to be in her late 30s.

"Hello, ma'am. I'm Chase. I'm here to pick up Camara," Chase said the last part of his statement as if he were asking her a question.

"Hi. Camara will be down in a minute. Go have a seat in the living room," Ms. Truth said flatly.

Chase followed Ms. Truth through the foyer that boasted a white curled staircase that spilled onto the floor to the living room. The living room featured a roaring fireplace, beige carpeted floors, and a huge beige and white couch which looked as if it could seat five people comfortably. Chase sat down but he also sat straight up. His back did not touch the front of the couch.

"Would you care for something to drink...soda, juice, or water?" Ms. Truth asked equally as flat.

"Ah, no thank you. I'm fine ma'am," Chase said while nervously rubbing his hands up and down his thighs.

Ms. Truth left the room and Chase again surveyed the décor and his mind for a first impression of Camara's mother. *She doesn't look like her mom. I mean she's pretty for an older lady and her body is amazing but they look nothing alike. Maybe she looks like her dad. We never talked about her dad...*

"Hello, Mr. Douglass," Camara said as she came into the living room wearing her shearling coat.

"Hey, what's up? Is all right if I hug you? I don't want your mother coming in from the kitchen with the big black skillet," Chase said in a whispery laugh.

"You're talking about my mama. Don't make me call her back in here. And how did you know about the big black skillet?" Camara said as she pretended to be serious.

"Yo, yall got a fly-ass crib. Why didn't you tell me you was rich?" Chase said as he followed Camara back through the house to the front door.

"It's *were*, Chase, not was...why didn't you tell me you *were* rich? Your grammar is appalling, especially for a college student," Camara whispered just trying to clue him in that Mama Truth was not a fan of butchered English.

"Hold on. Mama Truth, I'm gone!" Camara yelled up the stairs to her mother who was coming down the stairs at the same time.

"Don't miss that curfew. And, young man, make sure to bring my one and only daughter back in the same shape you found her in," Ms. Truth said matter-of-factly from the top of stairs.

The couple went outside and got into the car before they continued their conversation.

"Your mama is mean," Chase said.

"My mama is not mean," Camara said as she hit Chase's right arm. "And by the way, we are not rich. Mama works her fingers to the bone. That makes us working class."

"I doubt that. How about working rich? Y'all got dough. And it's just you two living in that big ass mansion," Chase said excitedly.

"Chase, we are not rich. She has a good job at Rochester Products...been there since she was eighteen...and she has good credit. My mama always taught me if you got a good job, work hard, and you pay your bills on time then you can go far and have plenty of nice things. But, that's far from rich," Camara said wondering whether Chase had enough experience to really know the difference.

"Very true, but you still live in a mansion," Chase laughed and braced himself for another light right hook to his arm.

Downtown they shopped at All Day Sunday, a black-owned business and Record Theater, McCurdy's, and Foot Locker. After splitting a cheesesteak with hot peppers, Boss Sauce, and the usual trimmings they headed to watch the lighting of the Liberty Pole on Main Street.

Neither Chase nor Camara could remember feeling so comfortable with a romantic partner. As the snow began to litter the ground around them, Camara pulled ever closer to Chase. His brain and sex drive began to work at a feverish pitch. He could not take it anymore more. He wanted tonight to be the night that he made her a woman. As they drove back to his grandparent's house, Chase could not remember being as nervous as he was as they picked their way through the traffic.

18

"Besides X, Y, and Z name two of the three consonants that don't begin a state's name?" asked Alex Trebek.

"What are B and J? The other is Q," answered Chase in a nonchalant tone.

"The Baconian Theory expounds this?" asked Alex Trebek.

"That Francis Bacon wrote Shakespeare's plays," answered Chase casually.

"Since the Beadle named his waifs alphabetically, this character came between Swubble and Unwin," asked Alex again.

"Twist. Oliver Twist," Chase answered confidently.

Camara could not believe it. Chase answered all except for five questions correctly and nailed the Final Jeopardy question. Sitting snuggly on the brown loveseat at the home of Chase and his grandparents, Camara was genuinely baffled at the breadth of Chase's knowledge. She enjoyed Jeopardy but could only get a few questions right per show.

"Did you record this?" Camara asked suspecting that Chase was simply using recall.

"Did I record what?" Chase asked while turning towards her.

"Did you record Jeopardy?"

"No, of course not. The only shows I videotape is Yo! MTV Raps and Rap City. Why would you think I'd tape a game show?"

"Cause you got all the damn questions right that's why " Camara blurted.

"Do I detect the smell of envy?" Chase said as grinned pompously.

"Boy, please. How can I be jealous of you when I'm smarter than you, huh? Answer that Jeopardy man," Camara said as she got up from the couch and went into the kitchen.

She walked away switching her substantial hips. When she did not return immediately Chase went in behind her to investigate the holdup.

Camara was in the kitchen at the table going through her small purse looking for something. "You're right you are smarter than me…in everything except Jeopardy," Chase said as smiled once again.

"Seriously, though, Chase, how did you know all those answers?" Camara asked genuinely interested.

She knew Chase was no dummy by the way he expressed himself. Dumb men no matter how sexy they were completely turned her off. Camara refused to settle with anyone who did not possess at least a reasonable amount of intelligence. Stupidity and Camara had nothing in common and stupid men bored her to tears. What fascinated her was finding out previously unknown information about the young man she adored. *Chase is smarter than I gave him credit for. That's a great thing.*

"I don't know. I've always been good at Jeopardy. Weird facts and figures just stick to my brain I guess. But you know what I want to do now?" Chase asked as he pulled Camara up from the kitchen table to and turned her around so that her back was to his front.

"Hold on, Chase. Can I ask you a question? I'm just curious more than anything else. Why do you live with your grandparents?" asked Camara as she turned back around to face him.

The light in Chase's eyes dimmed as he reached mentally to tell his brief life story. Some rooms in his house of memories were dark and he dared not enter. The Cliff Note's version would have to suffice for now.

"Well as far as my dad, well let's say I'm a bastard for real because he was married or involved big time with somebody else when he hooked up with my mother. I've only seen him a couple times in my life as far as I can remember. Fuck him. Moms is cool, she lives on the north side with my sister and two cousins. I got an aunty who is on dope bad. So my mother took her two sons in. To make room I just moved with my grandparents especially since we always kinda just got along. I moved here the summer of my 8th-grade year and been over here ever since." Chase said.

"So you and your mother don't get along?"

"I wouldn't go so far as to say that. I'll say this, though. We get along a whole lot better since we don't live in the same house. Now since we are getting all up in each other's business, what's up with your father? Did your parents get a divorce or something?" asked Chase.

Strangely enough, Camara did not count on Chase asking her a question about her father. She first she fidgeted and then looked downward distantly before she started to answer him.

"Well, I guess that's another thing that we have in common. I haven't seen my dad before either. I do remember my mom saying that he died in the Vietnam War or something like that. But I was real young at the time and whenever I would bring it up when I got older, my mother would just change the subject. So I guess I got the hint and just quit asking her. I was about ten years old...I think...the last time I asked a question about him. As I've gotten older, I do find myself thinking more and more about him. Who is he? Why he chose to ignore my existence when he is the reason why I exist in the first place...stuff like that," Camara said sadly.

All kinds of depressing thoughts about her invisible father hit Camara hard. The fatherly talks, the warm hugs, the warnings about icky boys and the terrible things that they can do were some of the things that she was never privy to growing up.

"I know exactly what you mean. Just know this...I'll never ignore you," Chase said as he turned her back around with her back to him. He as well pondered on what his life would be like had he had his own father there to help guide him.

"You promise?" asked Camara with a serious yet very sensual look on her face.

Chase loved the smell of Camara's hair. It had a green apple peach smell to it. He started to rub his hands up and down her midsection lifting up ever so slightly her shirt. He then repositioned her to the kitchen sink with her back still to his front. Chase slowly unbuttoned her shirt from the bottom to the top.

Camara was breathing heavily as she felt Chase grow and grind her from behind. The rhythmic movement of his pelvis combined with the strength in which he held her forced an unexpected yelp from her and knocked her from her trance. Her panting and moaning raised the intensity level.

He lifted the bottom of her bra up with his left hand and squeezed her right nipple with his wet right fingertips. He then graduated to her whole breast cupping them as best he could. Camara's supple breast would not comply as they were too large for Chase to palm properly.

The half-lit kitchen was unaccustomed to witnessing this type of cooking. Chase felt the heat as he took off his shirt displaying his sinewy arms and pectorals. He then went in like a King Cobra snake and attacked Camara's ears with a fast flickering tongue. The wet and slippery smacking and sucking near and against her lobe and eardrum percussed an infectious melody of seduction. The pleasure she felt almost brought Camara to her knees.

Turning towards him and trying to put her breast back in her bra she begged him to stop the onslaught. "Chase, baby, please...oh my God... baby, I only did it one time before. I'm a little scared because it was so bad...but I want to have sex with you and I swear we will soon. But it's just not the right time."

Being stricken with sudden acute deafness, Chase ignored her and pulled out her breast again and unleashed a savage attack. Waves of delight shot through Camara as Chase sucked, kissed, and gently bit her nipples. Chase got to his knees and gripped her waist and buttocks and continued to orally please Camara's belly button. She was letting out moans back-to-back as Chase picked her up by the back of her thighs and took her into his grandparent's bedroom which conveniently located just off the kitchen. Camara held on to the back of his wavy head for the ride.

After plunking her on the bed, he put his hand on her zipper, garnering an immediate response from Camara. "Chase, wait...please, baby, hold on. I swear I want to give you all of me ...but please can you just wait a little longer. It's just not the right time. But I swear I'm worth the wait."

Naturally, Chase was beyond aroused. Looking at her half naked body and hearing her deep sensual voice smothered invulnerability was pure elation. He pulled his hand away from her and rolled over next to her, exhaling as his back hit the bed.

"Chase, are you mad at me?" Camara asked in a feathery tone. She then turned towards him and rubbed his bare chest.

Chase had a multitude of emotional responses pleading with him to be first out the shoot; frustration, confusion, and white-hot passion were the immediate front runners.

"No, I'm not mad...I'm just horny as hell. I haven't even been pressing you about sex. Which is very surprising for me...trust me. Hasn't it been long enough? I mean we've been together for what a month? That's plenty long for me," Chase said as he shook his head back and forth no.

"Chase, I respect the fact that you haven't been all about just trying to have sex with me. Trust me if you were like that, no matter how sexy you are you would have never gotten this far. Like I said, we are not ready for that yet. Now, on the other hand, I never said we couldn't play around. I was hoping you could do me a favor and help me with something," Camara said as she began to smile.

Chase sat up on the bed and asked suspiciously, "What do you mean do you a favor? I think you done used up all your favors tonight."

"I am forever grateful. But what I want you to help me with may help you too in the process," Camara said.

"Ok, I'm all ears."

Camara who had on only her bra and jeans sat up in the bed began to speak. "Ok listen I am not a freak by any stretch of the imagination."

Chase interrupted her and said "Oh I know that because if you were, you wouldn't have got this far with me," he joked.

"Oh, so you're trying to be funny now?! Forget it I changed my mind," Camara said as she attempted to leave the bed.

"Come on, baby, I'm just playing with you. But seriously if you were some kind of super skeezer I wouldn't be with you. But you're not…that's why were together. Come on tell me what you wanna do. I'm a shut up and listen I promise," Chase said as he put his thumb and index finger in front of his lips and turned it as to mean his lips were locked.

He loved to sit back and just listen to her. The innate intelligence that she possessed always would manifest itself in her speech pattern. This stimulated Chase to his ever-loving surprise.

"Ok, but don't interrupt me again. For some strange reason, I always wanted to…well mutual masturbation. No, contact between us. Just two sexy people enjoying the opportunity to watch each other. Don't judge me and think I'm a freak or something. I watched a couple pornos before and that part kind of turned me on a little bit. So I thought it would be safe and exciting," Camara suggested seductively.

Chase was excited by the fact that she wanted to watch him and he certainly wanted to watch her. Ever since Chase had become sexually active it did not matter to him who was in the room, he could perform without pause. Now that his girlfriend confessed to wanting to watch him do something very specific sexually titillated his mind. "You know what, Camara, you got yourself a deal if you agree to do two things."

"I said no touching and I'm not sucking it so don't even much ask me to do that," Camara protested as her face twisted and she sucked her teeth instead.

"Damn, stop jumping to conclusions and interrupting. I wasn't even going to ask you to do that."

"You're right. I won't interrupt I'm all ears." Camara said.

"Thank you. Ok, you can't hide anything…butt-naked. And you have to get lost in it and make eye contact whenever you can. Deal?"

Camara was starting to wonder if she bit off more than she could swallow but pushed her proverbial chips to the middle of the table, "Deal."

With deal sealed the two entered into unchartered territory to their mutual delight. Camara felt powerful and in control as she learned her body quickly. Chase was as professional as ever and enjoyed watching Camara even more than pleasing himself. It created a pleasure feedback loop that led to primordial screams and a little cheating. Both lovers touched each other, held hands and kissed during the experiment. At the completion, they were satisfied and closer than ever.

19 September 18, 1970

Black Archie was inside of his element. The atmosphere inside of the bar named Palms Gardens on Jefferson Avenue was light and festive. Patrons laughed, talked to each other in animated groups, and danced to the song 'War' by Edwin Star which reverberated throughout the establishment. It was after midnight and the place was almost to capacity. Psychedelic colors like neon green, yellow, orange, purple, and strawberry red swirled and blended with the black and strobe lights to create a stand-in reality. Sitting alone in the burgundy leather half circle booth in the deep corner in the nightclub, Black Archie inhaled his Newport cigarette and then smashed the butt in the small gold plated ashtray conveniently placed on top of his table.

Reaching in his pocket for what he thought was his pack of Newport's netted a wad of folded $50 and $20 dollar bills. He smiled and then put the money back in his pocket. He grabbed a couple toothpicks from off the table and leaned back smoothly. Having a pocket full of money was something new that Black had to get used to. A chance meeting with a member of the Gingello crime family helped to make Black Archie one of the biggest marijuana dealers in Rochester.

Looking up towards the bar he spotted a pretty young blond woman wearing a gold and brown paisley print miniskirt, dark brown fringed buckskin vest and white go-go boots. She sat on a bar stool with her tanned legs crossed smoking a cigarette. Black Archie wanted to try something different.

The fact that Black was not a very handsome man did not keep the ladies away from him. His lean, tall, but naturally muscular figure combined with his deep dark skin and strong features was daunting to many. Confidence, effortless charisma, a silver tongue, and his deep pockets made him somewhat irresistible to the opposite sex. He excused himself from his table, patted his afro, and made his way toward the young women.

"What it is, mama?" Black asked smoothly in his deep baritone.

The young woman turned her head and saw a tall dark-skinned man wearing a six button double breasted suit with a muted yellow tie and gray pocket square. With a toothpick both behind his right ear and between his white teeth, he sat down beside her at the bar.

"Excuse me a moment, mama. Ryan...Ryan, I'll have a Tom Collins and for the lady, she'll have a Singapore Sling. I hope you don't mind my assertiveness, but I can't stand to see a pretty lady without a pretty drink in front of her and a handsome man beside her...so I'd thought I would fill the bill both ways. My name is Black and you are a fox!"

Taken back a bit but certainly not turned off by his boldness the young blond woman replied, "Hello, Black, I'm Ann Marie. Thank you for the drink. It is pretty. What is exactly in a Singapore Sling?"

"It has Gin, Benedictine, pineapple juice, and cherry Heering. I have good taste buds as well as good taste...so I'm confident it will be to your liking," said a smiling Black.

Taking a deep sip out of the tiny red straw stabbing the pinkish drink, Ann Marie agreed. "That is very good. I like a man who takes control and gives a girl exactly what she likes...even if she doesn't know it yet."

Putting his arm around her barstool but slowly moving his hands towards her back he whispered in her ear, "So what brings you to Rochester?"

Looking at him dumbfounded Ann Marie asked, "How did you know I'm not from Rochester?"

"Your style of fashion, your tan, and you accepting a drink from a total stranger says to me you are probably from the west coast somewhere. You are either a hippie or a flower girl. Now why you are here I don't know. Because if I had the choice between the cold-ass winters here and warm sun of California...I'd be in L.A. or San Diego in a flash, dig?"

"Wow. You are starting to freak me out, man. I'm 19. I'm from Hollywood originally. I spent the last year on my own in San Francisco and I decided to come up here with my family to Rochester. My dad got offered a good position at Eastman Kodak last year and I got a little tired of Frisco...it was becoming a drag. So now I'm here. It's pretty copasetic for now," Ann Marie said while playing in her own hair.

Black Archie recognized Ann Marie was on the hunt for a mahogany sexual adventure. *You like being among all these restless black natives. You here to see if you could take a ride on the Negro Express that goes straight to Bliss Ville huh? Well, I'm about to stamp your ticket.*

"Listen, Ann Marie, why don't you finish your drink and slide with me to my pad? I want to show you a part of Rochester that they don't advertise on no postcard or in a brochure," Black Archie said.

"Righteous, man, sounds groovy to me," Ann Marie said as she knocked her Singapore Slingback and grabbed his bulging right bicep and walked out the door.

■

After dropping off his blond surfer girl after her personal tour, Black cruised the highway. He would often jump in his orange and black brand new 1970 Torino, gas up, and drive around the city for hours. He wanted to explore other sides of town, other neighborhoods, and other cities. Black would imagine doing this for hours on end when he was a child living in the Hanover Projects. He was called Lil Archie back then. But as soon as Archie hit high school a fellow classmate called him 'Black' and it stuck.

Black Archie was still called Lil Archie by his mother, aunts, and current girlfriend Sandra Carter who he was on his way to pick up for their dinner date at Eddie's Chop House. Sandra was a caramel-brown skinned beauty who stood about 5 feet tall. She was relatively cool and composed but she was known to show her explosive temper every now and then. Sandra and Black Archie had been together since they both were fifteen. She lived two floors up from him in the Hanover Projects.

Black Archie cruised his way from his bachelor pad on South Avenue to their shared house on Melrose Street. To Sandra it was not a bachelor pad, it was a stash house to hide marijuana, guns, and cash. But word on the street was that Black Archie was using it for more than just illegal business. She loved him ever since he was Lil Archie and she knew he felt the same. However, the two years since he had become involved in the business of selling illegal drugs, Sandra noticed changes in Archie, some slight and some drastic.

Still the perfect gentlemen upon arriving at the house, he graciously opened the passenger side car door for her as she got into the sleek muscle car. Although Sandra always felt sexy riding shotgun in the Torino, she knew that there were women who wanted to replace her and experience that naughty feeling of misbehavior. Insecure feelings had been growing inside of her. Her woman's intuition told her that her boyfriend was not being faithful. The thought made her want to kill.

Being the lady that she was, Sandra did not tear into Archie and accuse him of infidelities because she had no concrete proof. Sandra wanted incontestable evidence before she would sever any ties—and perhaps one of his arteries. So she sat back relaxed and enjoyed the ride to Eddie's Chophouse with her man, Archibald 'Black' King.

The restaurant's color scheme was ruby red and oak. The huge oval shaped bar in the middle of the establishment and all of the tables and chairs were made of oak. The floor was carpeted ruby red, off-black, and lilac. The lighting was dull but sufficient. Some of Rochester's most notorious mobsters were known to frequent Eddie's Chophouse. Feeling like a burgeoning figure in the community, Black was fast becoming a regular at Eddie's.

"Hi, Sal, how you doing tonight?" asked Archie to the envelope-colored waiter.

"I'm doing great there, Mr. Archie. How are you and the Misses?" Sal asked back.

"We are both fine. I tell you what Sal. We are going to go ahead and order if that's ok with you. I got some business to take care of later. We're not in a rush or anything, but we are going to order our dinner now," Archie said nonchalantly.

"Very good, sir, what would you like?"

"Thank you, Sal. Let's see…umm…the lady will have the center cut lamb chops with rice pilaf, and asparagus tips. I'll have the lobster and steak. The 24 ounce New York strip steak well done with sautéed onions and a baked potato. And we will have a bottle of your best red wine," said Black Archie as he looked at Sandra and smiled.

"Archie, tell me how do you know what I want to eat? How do you know I wasn't in the mood for pork chops instead of lamb chops?" Sandra asked sincerely.

"Come on, baby, whenever we come here you are always in the mood for lamb chops just like you are always in the mood for me," Archie said and then reached across the table and kissed her.

"You're right, Archie, I do love their lamb chops and I'm always in the mood for you, but the question is do you love me and are you always in the mood for me?" said Sandra in a very serious tone.

Archie was not quite sure where she was going with this line of inquiry. For the first time ever he began to think that maybe he had become too reckless with his illicit sexual affairs. He thought about last night and tried to picture everyone at the nightclub to see if there was anyone there who knew Sandra…because they could be the possible snitch.

She just suspects she don't know I did anything with another woman. Because if she did know she wouldn't have come out to dinner with me. But knowing Sandra if she was to ever find out its fire and brimstone...she can go a little crazy. I always cover my tracks, though. Plus she loves me too much to leave me. Still, though, why would she ask me these questions?

"Why would you ask me a question that you already know the answer to, Sandra? Of course, I love you and I'm always in the mood for you."

"Archie, are you two-timing me?" Sandra asked as she looked Archie dead in the eye.

"Am I what? Am I two-timing you? Who told you I was messing around behind your back?" Archie said trying his best to sound flabbergasted.

"Lil Archie, just please answer the question. Don't ask me one on top of it," Sandra said softly.

"Stop listening to them heifers from Hanover baby. They are jealous of you and they want what you and only you have. So no, I am not two-timing you, Sandra," Archie said.

"Do you love the sound of your own lies? Big Mama always told me to stay away from folks who love the sound of their own lies. Are you lying to me Archie or are you telling me the truth? I swear I'd rather you tell me now that I am asking you point blank than to find out on my own. At least if you tell me to my face it would show me that you have some respect for me instead of telling me a bald-face lie," Sandra said again without flinching.

Archie was getting nervously perturbed by the line of questioning. To him, it came out of nowhere. Truthfully he was starting to get scared because he did not know for sure if she was speculating or if she knew it to be a fact. For the past two years, Archie had been with several different women. His street wealth played a huge role in the surplus of sex he received. But Sandra was with him and found him attractive whether he had money or if he was penniless.

"I love you and only you. I'm here with you now and nobody else ends of the discussion. You making me lose my appetite," he said sternly.

"Ok, Lil Archie, I believe you that you love me. End of the discussion," Sandra said mysteriously.

Before Archie had the chance to respond the waiter came with the wine. For the rest of the dinner, they enjoyed polite and safe conversation. He dared not go to the earlier topic of cheating and love. After the meal, he raced back to their house to drop her off.

"Why are you rushing to get me back to the house, Archie? It's only 9:30."

"You know I like to keep you out of the business that I do for your own safety. There are a lot of crazy people out here that are desperate. Junkies and

Vietnam vets are always looking for the big score. So I have to keep you in the dark about some of my business 'cause if somebody hurts you in an attempt to find me…I will kill everybody, plain and simple. So please darling, let me do what I have to do and you enjoy the spoils. I'll be here tomorrow afternoon first thing. We will go to see *Beyond the Valley of the Dolls* at the Capitol, ok? I know you said you wanted to see that movie."

"Ok, Archie, I'll see you tomorrow."

Sandra waited for him to open up her door. *Something is telling me this joker is lying to me and he got no business doing what he's about to do.*

They walked to the front door and Archie kissed her hard as if his lips could convince her of his piety. He hugged her hard and told her, "I'll see you tomorrow, sweetheart. I'll be here around one." Black Archie hopped into his black and orange Torino and sped off.

■

Black Archie hated to be late. He knew he was on the verge of tardiness. Turning on Mt. Hope Avenue, he was on his way to Carol's restaurant to pick up who he hoped would be his next conquest. He met 'Red' a couple of weeks ago picking up burgers for Sandra. Red worked as a cashier at Carol's. She was a few years younger than him he figured. Red was a pretty and stacked light skinned woman with sandy brown hair. Archie loved the shape of her body.

The time he invested by talking and wooing Red was about to pay off in spades. Archie had convinced her to stay the night with him at his apartment. The only stipulations were that he had to be there to pick her up by ten when she got off and that she had to be home by eight in the morning. Red told her father that she was staying at one of her co-worker's houses.

Arriving five minutes to ten Black Archie smoothly walked into the fast food restaurant. He could see Red in the back counting her drawer with her manager. He took a seat, crossed his legs and patiently waited for Red to finish. After changing into her lime green button up shirt that suggestively showed her navel and abs and lime green bell bottoms Red came out from the back and gave Archie a very juicy kiss.

"I told you I'd be on time to get you from work," he said confidently.

"Yes, you did. I like a man who knows how to keep time. Now you also promised to have me back home by eight in the morning. And trust me you want to make sure I'm home before eight. My father loves his only daughter very much and he sleeps with his shotgun. I can't believe I'm even doing this because if he found out I lied to him he might use that shotgun on me," Red said as they walked outside to cool autumn night.

On his way to his apartment, Archie pushed his girlfriend Sandra and her pleas for him to come clean into the back crevices of his mind. He looked at the seductive eyes of Red and got lost inside of them. They were barely inside of his apartment when he went for her clothes. Red tried to resist but failed miserably and gave in to Archie's advances.

They woke up tangled in clothes, bed sheets and covers from hours of pleasure. "Come on, mama, wake up...its quarter after seven. I wanna make sure you make it home on time. Plus I got some business to take care of too," Archie said to Red who was still stretching underneath the blanket resembling a caterpillar running in place.

"I'm up, I'm up. Just let me go to the bathroom, wash up, and brush my teeth and then we'll go ok?" said Red as she yawned.

"Cool," said Archie as he threw on some clothes quick and went into the kitchen to eat some breakfast. After finishing his Corn Flakes and toast, Red emerged from the bathroom and was ready to go.

Kissing her one last time they made their way to the door. Archie lived in an upstairs apartment above a neighborhood store. Going down the stairs slowly one by one with Red close by, he hoped the breakfast he had just eaten would help to restore some of his depleted energy.

When he opened up the door he immediately closed it back as fast as he could. Sitting on the hood of his car with a seven-inch switchblade in her right hand was Sandra with an ugly look of disgust on her face.

I swear before God I'mma cut him. I'mma cut him and that bitch.

Archie's heart did not know whether to hide in his throat or deep down inside the bottom of his guts so it went from one to the other. Archie was frozen with fear.

"Black, what's the matter?" Red asked.

"You gotta get outta here! I fucked up. Go to the payphone up the block on Hamilton Street and call for a cab. Here's a fin take it and go now! I gotta deal with this...I fucked up," Archie said as he opened up the door and stepped out of his apartment slowly with Red closely behind him ignoring his instructions.

"I guess you do like the sound of your own lies huh, Lil Archie? If you didn't want me no more or if I wasn't enough for you why couldn't you be man enough to tell me," Sandra yelled as she crossed the street and was closing in quickly on the exposed pair. Tears fell slow and deliberate from her swollen eyes.

Archie was stuck. He wanted to say something but the words refused to leave his mouth. Trying his best to gather his senses Archie turned to Red and pushed her up South Avenue. Sandra who now was crying uncontrollably ran up and took a lunging swipe at Red with the switchblade. Grabbing her from behind Archie pleaded with her to stop. She responded by sticking the knife in his right leg. Red quickly made it north toward the phone booth leaving Archie to clean up his own mess.

Yelling from the intense pain and the sight of his own blood spurting from his leg, Archie was confused and dazed while still trying to calm Sandra down. He let her go and tried to plead his case.

"Sandra, I'm sorry I fucked up. I love you and only you. Please, you gotta believe me. Please just calm down so we can talk. You already stabbed me. Please let me explain."

Sandra went from heartbroken and sad to mad as hell in a matter of seconds. She was not hearing anything that Archie said because her eyes had seen all she needed to know.

"So this is the business that you take care of, Lil Archie? You black ass liar! I can't stand you! I thought I was your business. My heart wasn't your business? My pride wasn't your business? Basic respect for me wasn't your business, Lil Archie? You out here fuckin these tramps behind my back! I ought to fuckin kill you right now for doing this to me!" Sandra cried out as she went in for another piece of Archie's flesh just missing it by an inch.

Archie began to get upset at Sandra for staking him out and exposing him. He thought she could never find out about his affairs. Now his anger and resentment began to build because he knew their relationship was over forever. Desperation kicked in as the pain from his leg intensified.

"Sandra, forgive me! I swear I'm done messing around behind your back. Don't leave me please!"

"Fuck you!" Sandra said as she rushed Archie once more stabbing him in his bullet-scarred shoulder. Archie screamed out in pain and pushed her away, knocking the knife out of her hand. Seizing the moment he rushed her and slammed her to the ground back first. The hard jolt knocked the wind and consciousness out of her. Realizing the force he used was excessive, he rushed to her side.

Sandra, baby doll, please. I swear to God I'm done messing around behind your back. Wake up, Sandra. Wake up, please.

About a minute later Sandra came to and started to cough.

By now he was beside himself with grief and sobbing like a freshly slapped newborn. "Why didn't you just stay home, Sandra? I told you I was gonna be there today!" he said as he stood up above her.

Sandra sat up and began to cry herself. Archie had never heard anybody cry so hard. He begged and pleaded with her, again and again, to take him back while her reply was simply more tears. He needed to take a different approach.

"You know what, Sandra? You wanna leave me...then leave me. I don't care no more. You can't hurt me! That switchblade ain't shit! My mama shot me in the shoulder with a shotgun and I survived that, so I can damn show survive a couple of stabs from you. So if you gonna leave me then do it. Fuck it! It's over," Archie said as he fished for his keys in his pocket. As he began to walk gingerly to his car Sandra's voice stopped him in his tracks.

"You have hurt me more than anybody ever could, Lil Archie, and you don't deserve to see me anymore," Sandra said just before she slit her left wrist and throat and fell to the ground.

Archie was silently hoping his tactical shift would soften Sandra to him. Instead, it backfired disastrously. Time slowed as he made his way to his dying first love. He ran as hard as his injured leg would carry him. By the time he reached her all he could do was cover her throat and wrist with his hands. He looked up South Avenue and saw Red standing helplessly near a phone both with a look of absolute horror on her face. Archie begged the blood not to leave Sandra's body and her not to leave this world. Both were exercises in futility.

20 December 31, 1989

Camara Truth was a young woman with a plan. Camara and her accomplice one Rhonda Wheatley had set gears in motion to fool not only Brenda 'Mama' Truth but also Rhonda's unsuspecting parents. They planned to reserve a hotel suite in Rochester and bring the New Year in together. Camara and Chase would occupy one room, and Rhonda and her on again/off again boyfriend in the other. However Rhonda's on/off again boyfriend was currently off, putting their plans in jeopardy.

The two young ladies were in their respective bedrooms, burning up the telephone lines in hopes of getting everything right so that they could pull off the ruse without a hitch.

"Ok, girl, listen. It's 1 p.m. now and I need you to be here no later than four. Make sure you have your license so we can show it to my mother. I'm glad you two met a couple times and she's comfortable with you. As long as I'm back home by two tomorrow afternoon it doesn't matter if we stay here or if we go back to Buffalo," Camara said while twirling the white telephone cord in her right hand.

"Cool, I'm a give your mother my Auntie Diane's phone number so just in case she calls we're covered. My aunt said it's no problem because she knows I don't drink or wild out like that and I told her you don't either. I was going to drop my asshole ex off at the hotel in Rochester first and then come and pick you up but he fucked that up! I swear some of these dudes are so trifling. I should have left him alone like you left what's-his-name alone...Harold. So anyway you said Chase got a homeboy right? I'm feeling naughty tonight and if his homeboy is cute and plays his cards right...he might get to play with it," Rhonda said as her and Camara both let out huge laughs.

"You're a hoe! I'm telling your daddy!" Camara giggled back to her.

"Uh-uh, you're the hoe! Who's the mastermind behind this whole scheme, huh? You probably going to give Chase some too. I should tell your mama that you about to break her three-month rule. Put her on the phone," said Rhonda as she laughed even harder.

"Mama Truth is not about to kill me. Listen, I'm about to call Chase now and make sure his friend is still coming. Chase doesn't know about the Hyatt yet. He just thinks we're going out to eat and then to Club Pandemonium. If I have to, I could also use the hotel as a bargaining chip to make sure his homeboy comes. I'll get his friend's number, give it to you, and you two can start talking. His name is Will. He's a cutie too. But don't start making love on the phone and end up picking me up late."

They exchanged a few more jabs and laughs before they finally hung up. Camara was as excited about the night as she had ever been about any night in her life. She was completely and totally absorbed in the now. She did not worry about what would happen if her mother found out nor did she think that anything could disrupt the bold schedule of events she scheduled for their enjoyment. Tonight was indeed the night. She was in control and she loved it.

■

After getting off the phone with Camara, Chase left his grandparent's house and walked to Will's house across the street from the Genesee Gateway Projects. The best friends would often hang out in the dangerous Projects. Their connections and acquaintances resulted in a pass to enter and leave at their own discretion. By the time Chase arrived, Will was just getting off the phone with Rhonda.

"Perfect timing...I just got off the phone with your girl's homegirl. She better be straight too man, or I'm a walk off the job," Will threatened.

"Your horny ass won't walk off shit! I told you she straight. She a little on the husky side but she's not sloppy with it or nothing like that. She's cute. And even if she wasn't straight, as many times as I've blocked them defensive ends you done sent my way so you can score, I better not hear a peep out of you. Remember last summer? Yeah, the one that looked like she ate toddlers for breakfast?" Chase said to Will as he threw a fake punch at him.

"That didn't stop you from fucking her field goal blocking ass, did it?" Will fired back.

"Man, fuck you! She blew me, but that's beside the point. The point is, I took that one for the team," Chase said as he sat down on the living room couch.

"Yeah, you did jump on that hand grenade for me. Anyway, Rhonda seems cool you never know...she might be my type. Plus, I get to see that fine ass, Camara, up close and personal. I heard her sexy voice earlier," Will joked.

Chase balled up his fist and went at Will throwing more playful air punches. "Don't make you cut you to the white meat. That's cool you two already talked. We are going to Cathay Pagoda's around six or seven, then we'll hit a club. We're going to bring the New Year in with a bang, boy. 1990s here we come!"

Chase and Will had been friends since they were toddlers and had a brotherly bond that allowed them to freely and openly talk or joke about virtually anything. They had ducked bullets and dodged knives together. Over the years they fought each other and fought for each other, shared the same women and slept head to foot sharing the same bed. The pair also shared an intense passion for celebration and the opposite sex.

Cathay Pagoda's Chinese Restaurant and Bar, located in Downtown Rochester, had a reputation for great food and unpredictable behavior by its patrons after 9. Arriving around seven gave the freshmen foursome time to get properly acquainted and comfortable with each other.

The restaurant's walls were covered with bright and vibrantly colored oriental hand fans. The wicker-like ceilings were low and slanted which added a remote but exotic flavor to the atmosphere. Although the place was full, it still retained a degree of intimacy for its patrons. The restaurant was sectioned into four distinct dining rooms. The two couples, Chase and Camara and Will and Rhonda, were seated in the Dragon Room and engaged in spirited and colorful banter.

"Yo, I got the worst sneaker story ever. Neither one of you can top it. Check—" Will said defiantly as he sat next to Rhonda and across from Camara.

Rhonda jumped in before Will could continue, "Negro, please! I was a tomboy growing up, I was real rough and so I was always wearing out my sneakers. We got a Bell's supermarket in Buffalo...and I was young... probably around 7 or 8. But, anyway, I remember us going to the grocery store like we did every week ...you know nothing out of the ordinary. So we're going up and down the aisles getting food and shit, and I always ran to the cereal and cookie aisle like most kids. My mother told me to stay in that aisle because she had to pick up something. So I'm there with a box of Count Chocula in one hand and Apple Jacks in the other and I see my mother pushing the food cart back towards me. In the food cart on top, the meat I saw a pair of sneakers and I'll never forget the price tag on it read $4.99! I swear I could hear all my friends singing *Bobos they make ya feet feel fine, Bobos the cost a dollar ninety-nine.* I tried to burn those fucking sneakers but the toes on them were so hard, the fire wouldn't take to it!" Rhonda yelled as the whole table laughed.

Will chimed back in by saying, "Ok that's a good one but it doesn't top mine. My pops is one of those old school dudes who think he's so hip. So I'm in the ninth grade and I ask him if he could get me a new pair of Adidas because my Puma's was getting a little fuzzy. And you know shell-toe Adidas was hitting back in '85. So Pops was like, *Ok son, no problem.* The next afternoon when I got home from school I see these sneakers...if you can call them that...on my bed and I was pissed the fuck off. You know Adidas got three stripes, right? Well, these joints had four stripes. My pops comes in the room smiling like he did something great talking about *you got more stripes for a lesser price. I should have bought a pair too.* I wanted to kill him," Will said.

"Dude, cats wanted to kill you when came in for a rebound wearing those fire-stompers. My man Ray was like, *damn, what the hell kind of kicks he got on!* I told them I don't know but if he steps on my foot with them, I'm cutting him," Chase said as they all erupted in laughter.

Between the hard crunchy noodles dipped in duck sauce, shrimp fried rice, sweet and sour chicken, spare ribs, lo mien, fan-tailed shrimp, the couples shared embarrassingly funny stories and were having the time of their life. Camara cued Chase in on what he was in store for later so he was looking forward to having Camara for dessert.

■

"Ok, you two lovebirds, be safe and have fun...and oh, don't do anything that I wouldn't do," said Will as he left Camara and Chase and headed toward Rhonda's room with Rhonda hugging him tightly from behind.

"What you need to be worried about is what I'm a do to your sexy black ass, Will. Girl, I will see you in the morning. Goodnight, Chase. Will, assume the position!" Rhonda could be heard as she slammed the door behind her.

Alone at last inside of their hotel room, the couple sat down on the edge of the king sized bed. Without saying a word to each other they both started to slowly disrobe. Chase felt his rapidly beating heart more than ever as it threatened to take over his upper torso. He stood up to step out of his pants and turned to Camara who was already naked and simply smiled. They kissed each other beautifully for nearly five minutes nonstop.

Camara's trepidation about having intercourse again all but vanished. Wonderful thoughts played in her head as she pulled Chase on top of her while falling on top of the soft mattress.

"Wait, Camara. I hope you brought some rubbers. I didn't know we were going to end up here or I would have gone to Rite Aid or something," Chase said between kisses and fighting the urge to proceed unprotected.

"Oh God, Chase, you're right," Camara opened up the nightstand drawer and pulled out a remedy for the oversight. *If Chase didn't say anything I was going to have unprotected sex. I swear it didn't even cross my mind. That is scary.*

As the moment of truth arrived, the lovers locked eyes and never broke the gaze. Looking into Camara's eyes, Chase thought he stumbled upon a peephole into Heaven. Camara for her part had never felt such intense pleasure and wanted to remain one with Chase forever. She settled for the entire night. As the morning sun peeped through their hotel window, the lovers finally transitioned into a deep sleep.

21 March 7, 1990

Professor King loved everything about his job at McNair University except the faculty meetings. Most of his colleagues in the English department were well spoken, well read, and reasonably open-minded. There were a few professors who did not fit that description and unfortunately they were usually the most outspoken and the loudest. Not only did they love the sound of their own voice, but they also hated the sounds of others, especially those with opposing tones. Being that he had less than a year under his belt Professor King thought it would serve him best if he listened instead of talked.

The other aspect of McNair that bothered him was the dearth of black and Latino colleagues in his department and across the University. For this fact, Professor King did not know who to blame. He did know that knowledge yields power and therefore, he had to gather up enough of it before he made any kind of move.

Resembling a bored kid in class, Professor King chewed on his pen while looking out of the window. He was focusing on his lecture for tomorrow's class on Alice Walker's 'The Color Purple' and looking forward to the colorful exchange that was sure to follow. To Professor King, opening young people's minds early and engaging them in critical thought in and out of the lecture hall was paramount.

When he left the late morning meeting, Professor King was on his way to indulge in another one of his favorite activities on campus...eating. Harrison Dining Hall located on the far end of the campus featured an all-you-can-eat style buffet for breakfast, lunch, and dinner. An uncommon skipping of breakfast this morning quickened his pace to sit down and dine.

Upon nearly reaching the entrance, Professor King was slightly startled by a tap on his huge right shoulder. "How are you doing, Professor King?"

He turned to see a smiling Chase who had his hand out waiting for a handshake. "Well, well, Mr. Douglass, what a surprise. It's good to see you, sir. How is the semester going?"

"It's good to see you too, sir. This semester is going a whole lot better than my first one. No A's yet, but no F's either. I appreciate the time you spent tutoring me last semester and giving me a chance to take an incomplete versus an F. I plan on retaking your class next semester. Are you on your way to eat?" Chase asked as they approached the door.

"Yes I am, Mr. Douglass. I didn't get this belly by accident. I look forward to you not only surviving my course but thriving in it. And, because you are growing as a scholar, lunch is on me. I know how hard it is as an undergrad to find a good meal sometimes," said Professor King as he walked through the door smiling.

"The best meal is a free one. I gladly accept," Chase said as he followed Professor King up the stairs to the dining hall.

"Mr. Douglass, this meal is not free. Hard work has its rewards."

Professor King's not that bad...I guess, Chase thought as he and Professor King went through the buffet line and stockpiled food on their trays like bears prepping for hibernation. They took a table next to the huge bay windows and sat across from each other.

After watching Professor King engaged in a brief ten-second prayer Chase asked, "You from Rochester right, Professor?"

"Yes, sir! Born and raised in the Hanover Houses...the Projects," answered Professor King.

"Hanover? I've never heard of the Hanover Projects. What side of town?" Chase asked earnestly.

"Well, you probably haven't heard of Hanover because they demolished them in 1980. They were on Joseph and Upper Falls Boulevard. Back in the day, Joseph Ave was considered 'Negro Town'. You see you didn't have to go downtown for anything. Up and down both sides of the streets you'd find nothing but stores and businesses, economic commerce, all the way to Clifford. Joseph looked like Monroe Ave does now. Whatever you wanted or needed you could buy on Joseph Ave. As kids, we would leave the Projects and go there and just people watch all day long. It was a great time to grow up. Then came riots of 1964...started on Nassau and Joseph. The Seventh Ward—that's what our neighborhood was called then—would never be the same. Do you know the first northern city to have National Guards called in? It wasn't Detroit, Newark, Chicago, or Harlem. It was Rochester, NY. We were reacting with violence to brutality and racial inequity," Professor King said as he remembered both the ugly and gorgeous times his family had living in abject poverty. A tortured smile forced its way across his face.

"Wow. I never knew that. I never even heard of the riots of 64. I thought Joseph Ave always looked like it does now," Chase said as he tried his best to envision a sparkling and vibrant Joseph Avenue. All he could muster in his mind's eye was the patches of abandoned buildings, empty fields, and low-level flat project housing that replaced the high rises of the Hanover. "I'm from the South Wedge...real close to the Gateway Projects."

"I used to live on South Ave too. I'm very familiar with the South Wedge. It's a beautiful side of town to be raised on. Do you know any of the Browns or Walkers?" Professor King asked.

"Of course! Shawn, Antoine, Freddie, Huggy, Stacy...we all went to school together."

"Ok, I can't say that I know any of them...probably because they are too young. Let me see. What about J-Mike, Sammie, Markie, or Rodney?"

"Yeah I know them. They're older but...matter of fact, Markie is my best friend Will's uncle. Small world," Chase said.

"You are right about that. I haven't seen any of those cats in years. A lot of good times and bad times on South Avenue too," Professor King said as he lost himself to remembering his colorful past life.

"Can I ask you a question, Professor?" Chase asked as Professor King nodded his head yes. "Are you married?"

Immediately fond remembrances of some of the fellas that he used to hang around as a young adult turned to the horrible image of losing the only woman he ever loved due to his lifestyle. Professor King was losing his appetite. He honestly had not thought about Sandra for years. In order for him to maximize his potential after leaving jail, Archie had to mentally block the terror of watching her life leave her body. He almost wiped clean her guilt-filled memory—until this conversation with Chase. He felt shamefaced for temporarily exchanging her memory for advancement. Totally forgiving himself for her death was a slim possibility.

"No, son, I'm not married. As a matter of fact, I'm going to share something with you that only the man upstairs knows. I've been celibate for the better part of ten years."

"You mean you haven't had sex for almost ten years? Couldn't be me. I can't go more than a week without getting some trim," Chase said with a small laugh.

"Of course, you can't, at least not now. How old are you about 19... 20? Your testosterone won't let that happen. The best you can do is break even with it because you'll never beat it. My advice is to try your best to never mix your penis' business with your heart's business. At your level of maturity, they are for the most part diametrically opposed to each other's best interest.

Sometimes God puts extraordinary women in our path, regardless of if we are ready for them or not. The love of your life can come into your life too soon. Do you have a girlfriend?" Professor King asked as Sandra's face contorted in pain in his mind's eye.

Chase's initial instinct was to lie and say no. But he sensed no danger in being honest with the professor. "Yea, I got a girl. Matter of fact you know her. I go with Camara. We've been together for like three-four months now. I'll be honest with you I haven't cheated on her but it is hard not to. Not because she gets on my nerves or because she isn't satisfying me...because we are real good in that department. I don't know why...but I just want to have sex with other girls. If they got a nice ass or thick lips...it don't matter I want to have sex with them. I guess it's kinda like that testosterone thing you were just talking about. To be honest I'm surprised I've lasted this long."

Professor King was bothered a bit by the fact that Camara had chosen Chase as a romantic companion. It was not because he did not like him, it was because deep down he knew that Camara was ready but Chase was not. Chase had more growing to go in the professor's humble opinion. And, it was possible Chase was going nowhere fast and would need to truly crash and burn before he learned the lessons that would propel him to maturity.

"I did some things that forced me to reassess the nature of my relationships with women. The lack of respect that I used to show women was despicable. Chase understand me, son. There is no stronger, more beautiful, more spiritual, more awesome specimen on this planet than the black woman. So I understand when you say you want to have sex with them just because. They can be supremely attractive. But that's where your intellect and your heart need to intervene, especially if you're already involved with someone. Society has put the Black woman through so much and yet she is still there to love and support you. And when I say society, I'm not just talking about the white man...I mean you and I as well," Professor King said.

Chase began to think immediately of Camara. "I'm a do my best to not cheat on her, Professor King."

"Now a young, intelligent, handsome guy like yourself has no problems getting girls so I applaud your monogamy. But when you find that woman—and Camara may well be the woman—God made specifically for you, do...not...mess...it...up," Professor stared at Chase reciting the last five words very slowly.

Chase looked into the eyes of Professor King as he spewed his advice. He then began to think of his relationship and that, incredibly enough, he had not cheated yet. Of course, he had opportunities but they were few and far between because his spent much of his time with Camara. Chase had to admit that he enjoyed her company as much as she enjoyed his.

Leaving the dining hall Professor King had hoped his warnings would make Chase think before cheating on his girlfriend. He cared about Chase because he saw elements of himself in him. He, however, did not want Chase to make the same fatal mistake that he did. Once outside he looked up toward the area where they were seated and gave Chase a final wave good-bye. It looked as if Chase was actively flirting with a young female cafeteria worker although he could not be sure. *What's that old saying youth is wasted on the young…and bad memories continue to haunt the elderly.*

22 March 24, 1990

"Camara, can I ask you a question?" Chase asked lying face-to-face with Camara in her bed with Mr. Fizzy wedged in between them.

"Yes, baby. Ask away," Camara said lazily.

They both were still recuperating from the previous night's pleasure exploration. Under the warm cotton blanket, naked, and touching each other from their bent knees to their toes they revealed in the aftermath of their glorious debauchery on this late Saturday morning.

"Why did you name our son Mr. Fizzy? I feel funny calling my son mister. Shouldn't it be the other way around? My son should call me mister," Chase said as he put his hands theatrically to eyes and pretended to cry.

"Don't blame me, Mister Douglass. I met his dad, Papa Bear before I met you. You should've transferred to my high school and snatched me up before I got with him," said Camara.

"You right about that. I'm just glad Mr. Fizzy loves me like I'm his real daddy," said Chase

"Well for starters you definitely treat his mommy right. That's rule number one. So you're off to great start there. Secondly, you're a good daddy to Mr. Fizzy. Even if we broke up I couldn't keep him away from you. You're the only Daddy that he has known...you're the only Daddy that I have known too. So don't ever abandon your family. Bad things could happen if you do," said Camara as a serious smile slowly adorned her face.

"You need a crane and a blowtorch to get rid of me...because I ain't goin' nowhere," Chase said and then kissed Camara on her lips and left earlobe. He was too drained to do anything else.

They dawdled in the bed in a comfortable semi-silence for the next half hour. Rhonda would not interrupt as she was prone to do because she was in Buffalo for the weekend. The couple would have put Frosty the Snowman and his cold-hearted wife Crystal to shame as they were in serious chill mode.

Cracking jokes between yawns and mushy baby talk was a sure sign their guards were all the way down.

Bwwwpoomp

At first, Chase thought his ears were playing tricks on him. Then he played the familiar but seemingly out of place sound back in his head. *Hold on I know Camara didn't just fart!*

Chase did not know whether to act like he did not hear her flatulence or acknowledge it and let her know it was no big deal. He knew she passed gas but did not know how to react to it. Never had he been in the company of a woman when she broke wind. He refused to believe that someone that beautiful could do something so vulgar.

Camara who had her eyes closed at the time but clearly not sleeping laid on the bed as if she was oblivious to Chase's dilemma.

"Camara, did you just do what I thought I heard you do?" Chase asked presumably.

"Did I do what? What are you talking about Chase?" Camara asked not knowing where Chase was going.

"Camara, I know you didn't just fart and then act like you don't know what the hell I'm talking about."

"I did what?" Camara asked him as she busted out laughing. She was so relaxed she didn't realize the dilemma a little gas would create.

"That's not funny, Camara. You lucky it didn't smell that bad."

"Baby I swear I didn't even realize it," Camara said as she covered her face and then wiped away tears of laughter. When she gathered herself she continued and said "Girls poot they don't fart. That's the difference, Chase."

"Poot, fart, I don't give a damn! Don't do that around me. That's nasty. What you gonna go do next? Go take a mean shit?" Chase said as he too began to laugh.

"I guess it means that I'm comfortable enough around you to be me. I'm human too. I use the bathroom just like you. But you are right baby it isn't ladylike to pass gas. I swear it won't happen again," she lied.

"I'd tell you to check your panties if you had any on Garbage Can Annie!" Chase said as he exploded with laughter.

"Hold on you act like your shit smells like tulips! I caught your act when we were at your grandparent's house. I was surprised the paint didn't start chipping in the bathroom!" Camara said as they both laughed non-stop.

Chase loved to laugh and he loved the fact that as beautiful as Camara was she knew how to take a joke and was not above laughing at herself. Chase was use to 'playing the dozens' growing-up with friends and family members.

The thick skin and quick wit he developed in the process equipped him well for life.

"And speaking of the bathroom, that's exactly where I'm headed. And it's none of your beeswax what I'mma do while I'm in there so don't ask," Chase said.

"I don't care what you do when you go to the bathroom boy! Anyway if you take too long in there I know exactly what you're up too," Camara said while rolling over on her side, throwing the blanket over her shoulder, and turning her back to Chase.

"No, you won't big-head."

Chase put on his underwear, closed the door, and walked into the suite headed to the bathroom without a care in the world. After using the bathroom he opened the door and was startled to see Brandi standing in front of it wearing a bra and a pair of very tight green and yellow shorts. Next to Camara's figure, Brandi's was a close second and closing in fast as far as Chase was concerned.

He realized it was inappropriate for his girlfriend's suite-mate to be seeing him in nothing but his underwear. He covered his Fruit of the Loom covered genitals with his hands and tried to leave the suite as fast as possible.

"My bad. We thought nobody was here but us," Chase said quickly.

Brandi stepped in front of Chase and made sure their bodies touched. "I see Rochester is doing big things. I know how to keep a secret," Brandi whispered as she stretched out her hands making intimate contact with Chase's manhood.

Chase was instantly aroused. Chase was also stuck mentally. Brandi boldly reached inside his underwear while looking him straight in the face.

"Camara's a lucky girl. It's a nice length, nice girth...I'd give it nine out of 10," she whispered as she stroked him to a full erection.

As quickly as she started, Brandi stopped and then walked into the bathroom and closed the door quietly. Not knowing how to fully understand what he just experienced, he high-stepped it back towards Camara's room. His adrenalin was pumping like insulin to nearly every part of his body.

Chase opened the door to see Camara standing with her arms folded and a sour look on her face.

"Hey, baby. It was a number one," Chase said nervously.

"What the fuck are you doing going to the bathroom in just your draws! You forgot I got suitemates, dummy? Put on your t-shirt and pants! Don't go out there parading my goods, especially with that trifling hooker Brandi on duty. I will smack fire out of her ass," Camara said matter-of-factly.

"I hear you, baby. I'm sorry, my bad," Chase said as mistakenly hugged Camara and tried to take her to the bed. He paid for the error swiftly.

"Why are you hard?" Camara asked.

"Huh?" Chase asked trying his best to sound dumbfounded.

"Don't huh me, you heard me. Why are you hard? Between last night and this morning, you should be all worn out. Who's out there?" Camara asked as she wrangled herself out of Chase's embrace and headed towards the door.

Chase not knowing if Brandi was out the bathroom or not, hedged by grabbing Camara from behind and tried his best to calm her down before she could get out of her room.

"Baby you buggin' out...chill! All I did was go to the bathroom. And you know every time I push up on you I get hard. You're right, I shouldn't have gone out there in just my tighty-whiteys. You know what I'm—"

Camara stopped his speech with an unexpectedly powerful punch to Chase's lower abs. She had an innate feeling he ran into Brandi. Camara felt as if it would be in her best interest to send a strong and very clear message to Chase that she was simply not having it...just in case. Chase immediately doubled over and rolled on the bed pretending to be in excruciating pain. She then jumped on top of him and said, "You're lucky you are so sexy."

The lovers were interrupted by a very loud knock on the door. "Who is it please?" Camara said visibly irritated.

"Telephone for you," said Brandi.

"Can you tell whoever is on the phone to hold on a minute while I get dressed? Thank you," Camara said as she jumped off of Chase and told him to put some clothes on. Once they both were decent Camara opened up the door to a semi-dressed Brandi who held the telephone in her hand.

"Here you go. Good morning, Chase," Brandi said seductively as she handed Camara the telephone and quickly turned around so that Chase could get a good view of her assets.

Camara thought about snatching Brandi by the back by her weave and clunking her with the telephone until she passed out. Instead, she put the telephone down by her breast and mouthed the words, 'I'm going to kill you,' to Chase.

"What did I do? The girl just said good morning," Chase said haplessly.

"Hello, this is Camara."

"Hello, Ms. Truth. I hope I did not disturb you this morning. This is Professor King."

"No, not at all, Professor. How are you?" Camara said as she was still staring Chase down, giving him the evil eye.

"I'm fine. Ms. Truth, I attained your number through the student directory. I hope you don't mind me calling, but it is somewhat important," Professor King stated.

"I don't mind at all, Professor King," Camara said. *What in the world is he calling me for?*

"I'll go straight to the meat. I was so impressed by your performance in my class last semester and how well you tutored Mr. Douglass. I have a tutor position available for Black Literature 101. So naturally I thought of you. The good news is that it is a paid position and it looks great on your resume when you apply to graduate school. You'd sit in a room in Cooper Hall with other tutors and the students who need help will come to you. You will also be required to meet with me about an hour a week to go over class notes. You can do other work from your other classes while you wait to tutor students. This will start next semester and we will meet a few times before then to go more specific details. So, Ms. Truth, what do you think?"

"Umm…it's kind of sudden. But I can't find a reason to tell you no. Can you give me the rest of the weekend to make sure I want to take the job?" Camara asked softly.

"Absolutely and I tell you what. If you're interested come by my office at noon on Wednesday and we will discuss the particulars."

"Ok, sounds good."

"I will hopefully see you then. Enjoy the rest of your weekend, Ms. Truth."

Camara remembered how thoroughly she enjoyed Black Literature 101. She still had all of her notes. She also remembered how fond she was of Professor King and how he came to her aid when another student copied her work. She knew she would likely take the job.

Camara darted a look in Chase direction. The urge to choke some truth from him had subsided. She was falling deeper and deeper in love with Chase and was exhilarated and profoundly happy to be his girlfriend. Chase was kind, loving, and sweet. Popular, athletic, smart, and handsome Camara felt like she hit the bonanza. But deep down inside she felt uneasy about Chase's dedication to the relationship. Maybe it was the looks Chase furtively stole in the direction of other women. She looked into his beautifully perplexed brown eyes and could not imagine anyone else capable of loving him the way in which she did. She prayed that the feeling was mutual.

23 May 7, 1990

The contagion of spring fever threatened to shut down the motivation and thirst for higher knowledge at McNair University. The students were quarantined to fester under the sumptuous deep blue skies, ideal 72-degree weather, and blooming seven-foot lilac wedge wood blue shrubs. Green leaves pitted against the light winds swayed and gossiped about the deteriorating academic conditions. Skylarks circled above and chanted hopeful hymns of recovery.

Professor King leaving his office on his way to class bravely decided to walk among the lounging wounded and get a bird's eye view of fallout from spring fever and the devastation that it left behind. King spied smiling half-dressed students lying atop beach towels, impromptu volleyball games, and dancing as he walked. The infectious sights, sounds, and smells of spring were obviously intoxicating.

However, there was a group of students who had yet to submit to the frivolity of the changing season. In the middle of the campus square, two sets of six pledges stood at attention. The first set of six young men facing west were the pledges of the Omega Psi Phi Fraternity. These athletic looking men stood behind each other in perfect symmetrical distance from one another and stood perfectly still. The first pledge in line carried a torch that would have made Lady Liberty proud. All of the pledges wore black, tightly-tied, Timberland Boots, black cargo pants, black t-shirts, and winter camouflage coats. Bald heads and black shades completed their outfits.

There was another muscular student dressed in all purple and yellow who yelled periodically "Pass the torch!" to the pledges. The first in line took three steps forward, turned around, and took three steps towards the next pledge in line and passed the torch to him, then got back in line.

Professor King watched the young men and fondly reminisced about his days as an undergrad and being approached to become a member of a few black Greek organizations. Before submerging himself too deep in thought, he was interrupted by the call of his name by Camara who was also stricken with spring fever. She was sitting on a small grassy hill surrounded by seven other sick students, including her boyfriend Chase all of whom were laughing, debating, and listening to a humongous boom box.

"Professor King! Let me ask you a question. Do you believe it's a good idea for Black students or any students for that matter to join a fraternity or sorority?" she asked.

Blocking the sun with his massive hand he answered, "Well, Ms. Truth, the easy answer is it depends on the individual student. Do you work better with a team? How much of an individual are you? Can you blindly submit to the will of others for the duration of the pledging process? Can you sacrifice yourself for the good of the group? But of course, the answers and questions can go much deeper when you focus it solely on Black Greek fraternities and sororities."

"This is what I don't like about them, Professor King. Why do I have to jump through all these hoops just to be your brother? I mean I've seen a few of them get put through hell and look like clowns in the process. And all so that I can say I'm your brother now! Shiiiit! I'm sorry, Professor King, but they can kiss my ass!" Chase said while shaking his head no.

"Chase, you make a valid argument. Not about them kissing your ass but about the demeaning task that some fraternities—not all—make their pledges complete in order to be accepted into their order. But they would argue that going through hell with your line brothers or sisters actually bonds you. That is, it makes you true siblings because you have to have each other's back in so many instances during the pledging process," said Professor King.

Turning down his boom box which was playing "Hold On" by En Vogue Brad countered, "But Professor, college is hard enough already and there are going to be people that you just naturally bond with without doing all that extra stuff, dude. For example, if I'm in a real hard class with everyone here and all of us here decide to study together and work hard at passing the course doesn't that in a way bond us too?"

This is what turned Professor King's motor on, lively and thoughtful debate on real issues that mattered to his students. He hoped that they would gather enough facts and data leading them to make well-informed choices. He felt proud that Camara thought enough of him to ask his opinion on the matter. Professor King gladly continued to facilitate the conversation.

"That too is a very good point. But that doesn't necessarily mean that you wouldn't bond with your line brothers either. I know line brothers to this day that are the best of friends. They would literally die for each other in a heartbeat."

Rhonda, who would have pledged Delta Sigma Theta if it not for the freshmen ban on pledging quickly chimed in with her opinion, "I think it's cool to be part of a sorority. The main reason why because it promotes sisterhood. Too many of us black women are at each other throats for the silliest of reasons. I don't have the time or patience for it. Plus you automatically have great contacts in the professional world. For instance, if I become a Delta and it's on my resume and a Delta is doing the hiring then I know I got a great chance of getting the job."

Sean, Chase's slender homeboy from New York City, figured it was time for him to weigh in. He asked Rhonda, "But what if the person hiring is an AKA? If she's dressed in pink and green from head to toe do you think for a second that she is going to hire your ass once she finds out you're a Delta? I don't think so."

Then Cassie a mutual friend of both Camara and Chase jumped in, "In my opinion, I think it further divides us for that very reason. If you are five, ten years out of college and you still holding grudges against another sorority you're wack as hell, period."

"All fraternities and sororities are a big ass educated gangs, they're no different than the G-Boys, Crusaders, Gangster Disciples, Vice Lords, Bloods, or Crips. They got their own colors and hand signs...initiating and pledging...shit there is no difference at all," Chase said defiantly.

"To be honest with you, Chase, I never quite thought of it like that. It's an interesting perspective," Professor King said.

Another student named Hugh said, "Well, we all differentiate ourselves and pledge allegiance to one thing or another. Nupes and Ques are not killing each other over corners. I'm pledging! I don't give a damn. I can't wait for the 'sweethearts' to help me when I'm pledging next year. I heard they sho' know how to help a brother!"

"You're nasty ass would join just to get some, Hugh! And speaking of nasty, them Kappa Sweethearts are just that! Nasty!" Rhonda said with a turned up look on her face.

"Hey if they ain't nasty then they ain't worth it!" Hugh countered as he and the rest of the group laughed.

"Ladies and gentlemen, the conversation has been great, but I must press on. Don't enjoy the sun and fun too much now," Professor King said as he nodded his heavy head and walked away.

After watching Professor King walk away, Camara silently turned her attention to the other group of hopeful future fraternity members. Several young gentlemen were pledging Kappa Alpha Psi in black sweat suits and black boots. The hoods of their sweat suits were pulled over their heads. They stood side by side and would periodically turn from facing east to facing west. They were as quiet as church mice. Camara recognized the tallest pledge, Squeeze, and was hoping that Chase was not as perceptive.

Although she was still physically attracted to Mr. Squeeze she felt deep in her soul that she made the right decision in choosing Chase. This thought put her at ease. She was surrounded by newfound friends, the weather was gorgeous, and she had her man right by her side. Camara could not have been happier. There was a rhythm, rhyme, and flow to their relationship. They had the freedom to spend the night in each other's room, they could talk on the phone all hours of the night, and they literally lived across the street from one another. They had the freedom to spend as much time as they wanted with each other.

Yet, she shivered at the fact that summer break was a few weeks away. Camara feared the summer because she feared the unknown and uncertain future. Chase was a very handsome and attractive young college man, and she knew women could and would literally throw themselves at him. She hoped and prayed at that moment that he would be strong enough to resist. Camara did not want to envision Chase falling victim to the seductive powers of another woman.

24 June 16, 1990

Summer present numerous entertainment options. Beaches, amusement parks, basketball courts, street corners, and movie theaters were but a few of the choices that Chase and his friends weighed on a daily basis. For Chase, his summer job as a camp counselor at the YMCA and his college girlfriend Camara were the only anchors to his voyage through a carefree summer.

The night before, Chase and Will gallivanted from nightclub to bar to hole-in-the-wall courtesy of Will's Uncle Markie's infamous Chevy Nova and a couple of fake identification cards provided by their mutual childhood friend turned local drug dealer, West. Chase, a nondrinker, got behind the wheel once Will began glugging anything with alcohol he could get his hands on. Frightened of the possible repercussions of going home drunk Will decided to crash at Chase's house instead.

The morning after a night out on the town can be a revisionist historian's dream. Exaggerated tales of conquest and overall boasts of being *the man* were all too common. Facts, fiction, and a hazy hangover blurred to tell the tales.

"Man, that chick in them white pants. I swear she had the fattest ass I've ever seen! I got them digits too! I should call her ass up now and see if she wanna make a nigga some breakfast this morning—especially since your mother is mad at me for coming too quick. I gotta work on that," Will said as he laughed, rolled, and stretched on his makeshift palace on the floor.

"Let's get off of moms' cause I just got off of yours. But you right, she did have a fat ass, though...I can't even front on you homie. You get your stripes for pulling her, she was bad. Her homegirl with the dimples is real lucky I got a girl or I would've kicked the bass and snatched her up...word up," Chase said as he sat in his bed clinched hands behind his head.

"Stop lying, nigga! I saw you creep with her to the bathroom and get her number. You were grinding on her the whole time at Club 127!" Will said while laughing.

"Naw, man, she was grinding on me. There's a huge difference. And how you know I wasn't just helping her get to the bathroom? She was a little bit inebriated you know!" Chase asked.

"Come on, man! Who you think you talking too? Willy Lump Lump the neighborhood chump? I know you, Chase. And don't get me wrong Camara is fine as fuck. She is the flyest and sexiest girl you have ever had. And you had almost as many as me and that's a lot. I know you're trying to be faithful and I respect that. But, man, all this good pussy 'round here. We both look good, no jail records, and on top of that, we're in college too! We're like the cream of the crop. Good luck trying to keep them off you. Oh, and don't let one of them have a nice ass, flat stomach, chocolate complexion, thick thighs, hungry bedroom eyes or anything that turns you on. I hate to say it but whoever she is, is gonna get fucked faster than a speeding bullet."

"Thanks for having confidence in me, homie! Those words of encouragement are exactly what I needed to hear to stay on the straight and narrow," Chase replied sarcastically.

"Seriously, though, I'm very impressed that you haven't violated already. I'm proud of you and I don't want you to fuck it up. Camara must be pretty special. But if you do cheat, you better not let her find out," Will said.

Camara was indeed very special to Chase. Camara was unlike any woman Chase had ever met. Although he had yet to tell her the words he knew he loved her. He loved her from the moment she spoke to him behind her desk at the Student Union. When he saw her talking to Squeeze he was beyond furious. The jealousy he felt seeing them talking was intense and scary. Deep down inside he knew that Camara was the only woman capable of wielding the tools necessary to deconstruct the barriers that kept him from true intimacy.

However, Chase was also well versed in rhythm and cadence to the lures of his mortal enemy—sex addiction. Masturbating sometimes up to three times a day did very little to slow down his libido. An almost unquenchable thirst for sex was warring against his pledged fidelity to Camara.

A combination of Camara's and Chase's summer work schedule and Mama Truth's rigidity regarding their relationship meant that the couple had yet to see each other since their summer vacation started. They talked on the phone everyday but that was the extent of their contact. Chase felt as though they were losing their connection somewhat. He needed to be in close proximity to Camara. Chase's penchant for witnessing flesh was coming to a head.

Changing the subject Chase replied "Anyway so what we getting into today? What's up with West? He told me yesterday he was thinking about riding to Buffalo to go to the Juneteenth Festival. We should break out with him. I haven't been to B-lo in a minute."

"I don't give a damn. As long as they got some freaks in Buffalo I'm there," Will said as he got dressed.

The twosome hooked up an hour and a half later and made their way crosstown to the northeast side of Rochester via the city bus. On the corner of Portland Avenue and Lochner Place, West operated his new but flourishing drug spot. The building's facade resembled the color of perennially un-brushed teeth. Flattened Miller Beer cans, broken Genesee beer bottles, empty lighters, empty plastic crack bags, and used condoms were but a few of the accouterments that hid in between the towering uncut and thirsty blades of burnt grass. Lop-sided, run-down and ran over, the four apartment dwelling with a rickety covered diagonal staircase you could see from outside was on the city's shortlist of soon-to-be-demolished properties.

"Hey, what's happening y'all? Hey, can I put this bug in one of y'all's ear before y'all go upstairs? Who's trying to trick with me? I need a couple dollars. I wanna do something strange for some change," said a 40-something, nearly toothless, black woman with the shape of an eleven-year-old boy.

"I believe I'm speaking for the both of us when I say, we will both sadly have to pass on that offer. Now go and floss them five teeth in your mouth. Be easy," Will said as both he and Chase jogged up the staircase laughing and shaking their heads.

Chase rapped the four knock code on the chipped and battered white wood door. He did it twice because it took a while before someone responded. Chase and Will stood in mild surprise when the door opened.

"West told me to let you in. He's in the back bedroom," said a tall, very shapely, pretty, young female. They walked in behind her mouthing the word 'Damn' to each other. Her black spandex shorts hugged her apple shaped buttocks which bounced ever so slightly when she walked. As she entered the hallway which led to the two back rooms, West appeared from the same hallway wearing an oversized black Bart Simpson t-shirt, black leather African medallion, red shorts, and a tired smile.

"Fellas, what up? How you feeling on this beautiful day?" West asked breathing heavily as he sat down in lone black loveseat which faced the door. Although it was seventy plus degrees outside it felt like triple digits inside the grubby hovel that masqueraded as an apartment. Chase and Will grabbed a couple empty metal milk crates and turned them into makeshift chairs.

A very nappy navy-blue rug occupied every room in the house except the kitchen. The moldy living room smelled of stale cigarettes and funky fish. A non-working, RCA 35-inch floor model television humbled itself and agreed to let an older working 1970-something, Zenith television lay atop it. The television set, complete with vice grips where the knobs should have been and a twisted hanger for an antenna, was broadcasting the latest episode of Soul Train. The newest piece of electronic equipment was the gigantic 1988 boom box standing on the floor which was playing 'Only You' by Kwame'.

"We aren't doing as well as you. Damn, West, who was that freak who answered the door? She got ass!" Will said candidly.

"And I know she's not letting your fat funky ass dig her out!" Chase added as he and Will slapped hands and laughed.

"Nigga, you know I gets more ass than a toilet seat. I may be big but I'm charming like a motherfucker. I got dough and I'm far from ugly. That's an unbeatable combination," West said as he stood up and pounded his chest.

"I'm not talking about them raggedy hoes you usually mess with. I'm talking about the Amazon honey in the black biker shorts. I know you ain't fuckin her," Chase said.

"Man, listen. I was in a cab on my way back from re-ing up, and I saw her with a gym bag walking up North Clinton Ave. She looked lost and you know me. Come to find out she's from Elmira and she left cause she had a fight or something with her moms. She had some family here but couldn't find them. I told her she could crash at the gate till she got in touch with them. That was last week, and I been banging her out sometimes three times a day ever since. I hit the jackpot boy!" West said as leaned back in the loveseat.

Chase recalled the image of the young lady in his mind and was instantly aroused. Then almost immediately Camara's face popped in his head. The last time he had sex was with Camara before they adjourned for the summer. In his mind, he had hoped to make it the whole summer without cheating on her. He hoped he could resist. But trials, tribulations, and tests were in Chase's forecast.

"What's her name and how old is she?" Will asked.

"Well her name is Shontae and to tell you the truth man I never asked her how old she is. Shit, as magnificent as her pussy is I don't want to know how old the hoe is. I look at it like this man, her face looks like she fourteen, but her body look like it's twenty-one. So I just split the difference which is seventeen and a half and in New York State seventeen is legal. And if the law says its legal then I could give a fuck if it's morally wrong," West said as he headed to change the channel.

"Did Man-Lips or Bobby hit it yet?" Will asked.

"I think she let them both hit once, but that's it. She doesn't even ask for no bread or nothing. Basically, all I do is feed her. I bought a couple outfits and a pair of cheap-ass Nikes. If you wanna hit it be my guest. Don't be surprised if she just throws it at you. That's what she does. Besides I want some Buffalo flavor tonight anyway," said West.

Shontae emerged from the hallway on cue and sat on the loveseat next to West. Her eyes firmly attached to Chase's as the boys small talked. Shontae's gaze was becoming increasingly harder to ignore and Chase tried his best not to fall victim to the young temptress.

"You're cute," Shontae said bluntly.

"Who's cute? He's cute?" Chase asked pointing to and hoping she was referring to Will.

"He's cute too but you're cuter," she said.

"He's spoken for. I'm free, though," said Will looking at Shontae with hungry eyes.

It felt to Chase like the devil himself took a flamethrower and torched the room with a smile. Chase began to run multiple scenarios through his brain, all of them ended with Shontae on her back. "Yo, I gotta take a piss," he said as he stood up from the milk crate and walked to the bathroom hoping that the walk would re-focus his mind on the joys of being faithful.

"Oh shit! Let me find out Chase scared of some pussy," West said as he turned to Will and laughed.

Will came immediately to Chase's defense, "You know Chase is the boldest brotha we know when it comes to sex. He's trying to do his faithful thing. He got a girl he met at school. I've seen his girl and she is bad word life. There are not too many broads walking the planet that would make me give up my other chicks. But in all honesty, his girl might be one of them...I can't even lie. I think she is good for Chase and I like her as a person. So I respect what he doing, I just don't know how long he can hold out," Will said to West.

"Ok, I hear that. Love is a motherfucker. Let's go to the store and grab some forties. I bought some weed from Huggy so I need some blunts too," said West.

"That's cool is Shontae coming with us?" asked Will.

"Nah. She won't leave the house for shit. When the crew ain't here and I have to bounce somewhere, she catches all the licks for me. And my money and product be right," West answered as they headed toward the door.

Inside the bathroom, Chase successfully sidestepped two ten week old Pit Bull puppies and feces/urine drenched newspapers which covered some of the dingy white floor tiles. After urinating he splashed water on his face in hopes it would cool him down. Fully confident that he was capable of spurning any of Shontae's advances, he walked out of the bathroom. He found her sitting on the loveseat bare-footed with her legs crossed.

"Where's Will and West?" asked a perplexed Chase.

"They went to the store," Shontae' said.

"They went to the store? What they go to the store for?" Chase asked.

"Blunts and forty ounces. You're sexy as hell. What's your name?" Shontae said as she stood up and walked towards Chase.

"Chase. I'm going to the store too," Chase said as walked towards the front door.

"Really, you're going to leave all of this?" Shontae said as she twirled around so Chase could get a three hundred and sixty-degree view.

"Come on yo, you got to stop. I got a girl," Chase whined as he took in the view.

Shontae responded by beginning to slow strip down to a thong and bra. When she was finished she threw her shorts in Chase's face for good measure. Chase mind went blank and his body transformed for a singular purpose—to tear into Shontae like a grizzly bear in a room full of honey-dipped salmon.

25   June 17, 1990

The blacktop basketball gods were smiling on the many faithful ballers who came to the outdoor vestibule to give thanks and praise. The Gods weaved a day consisting of deep blue skies, seventy-two degrees of warmth, and no winds. Conditions were ideal for an outside basketball game. Both Chase and Will were longtime members of the 'Cathedral' on South Avenue, sometimes worshipping from early Sunday afternoons until well after dusk. Fire-breathing sermons warning of crossovers, fade-a-ways, no-look passes, and slam-dunks were being preached by the self-ordained chosen ones.

There was just as much glory on the sidelines as there was on the basketball court. Someone's uncle who was years past his prime could at any time be heard pleading his case for sainthood by saying, 'I was a bad joker back in my day' or 'Yall jitterbugs don't know how to play real basketball'. Barbeque grills, coolers, and 'oohs' and 'ahs' were hymns sung from both the lay and the holy. The basketball court and surrounding playground and park area were almost filled to capacity as 'church' began.

Chase and Will were the main attractions on the court. Over the past two summers, the boys built their reputation the hard way through wars with streetball legends, neighborhood ballers, and cross-town rivals. The duo embarrassed so many ballers on the court that some players stopped bringing their girlfriends. The young men were considered among the best point guard/swingman duo in the city. However, today Chase could not be considered the best at anything basketball related. As a matter of fact, Chase had never played worse.

"How come you didn't catch that pass?" Chase yelled at Will as their team walked off the court dejected after their loss.

"How come I couldn't catch that pass? Negro, Kareem Abdul-Jabbar couldn't catch that pass! I'm 6'3 not 7'3. The ball went way over my head," answered a growingly agitated Will.

"Jump, lazy fuck! Jump! You ever heard of that?" Chase asked angrily.

"What are you saying, Chase? Are you saying that cost us the game? One pass—way over my goddamn head? I scored damn near all our points! You were all over the place...a turnover machine. And what was that shit you threw to Levert? I couldn't tell whether it was a shot or a pass...I'll call it a shass!" Will said. The people standing on the sideline and the other three members of the team heard Will's last assessment of Chase's play and started to laugh immediately.

Frustrated and infuriated upon hearing the laughter at his expense Chase's first instinct was to run up on Will. He thought better of it as he looked down and took a deep breath. Today was not going to be his day on the court so he promptly interrupted the game that was going on by taking his basketball.

"Oh, that's funny? Fuck all y'all! Laugh at that! Find a new basketball, bitches!" Chase said as he took his time and walked the length of the court with his basketball in hand and left the court area altogether.

"That's some real bitch shit, Chase!" yelled a fellow Southside hoop artist.

"You can't be serious, man! Bring the ball back, homeboy!" yelled another player.

Chase was having absolutely none of it. He simply blocked them out and smiled while he walked away.

"Yo, Will, ya man is buggin' out. He lucky he is who he is or he'd get his ass kicked. He knows he can get away with that shit here because he home. But that shitty attitude kept him from playing high school ball! Go tell 'em to grow the fuck up, Will!" one man noted.

"You're right, I'm about to try and talk some sense into him," Will said before he galloped away to catch up with Chase.

Will caught up with Chase about halfway down South Avenue and yelled, "Chase, you acting like a true hoe!"

"Man, fuck you!" Chase said while still walking forward and bouncing the basketball between his legs.

Will was not sure if his best friend was serious or joking. What he was sure of was that Chase had been acting extremely strange since yesterday. Will continued, "Stop acting like a little bitch man. Come' on man! Come on back to the-"

"Eat me then if I'm actin like a bitch!" Chase yelled as he stopped and turned to Will in a semi-defensive stance.

Will sensed they were headed full speed and without a paddle into uncharted choppy waters. Over the years the two young men could count on one hand the real arguments they had. Will was also aware of Chase's penchant for holding grudges when the dispute, no matter how big or small, was over. Will did not want to go down any of those roads. He knew the value of their brotherly bond.

"Ok, time out fool! Mike Tyson got his ass whopped by Buster. You can be next. You've been acting real funny lately. Matter fact since we got back from Buffalo you been acting kinda crampy. Are you on your period? Seriously, what's the deal?" Will demanded.

"Ok. You wanna know what's wrong? Check it. You were supposed to have my back brother! It's your fault!" Chase screamed.

Clearly frustrated because he could not understand Chase's hostility over a single basketball game Will responded, "I told you the pass was too goddamned high!" Will roared.

Shaking his head in exasperation Chase said "I'm not talking about the game today. I'm talking about yesterday at West's gate. It's your fault I wound up doing Shontae. You saw how that she was all over me man! You know I was trying to be faithful! I come out the bathroom and you're gone! She practically raped me!"

"Wow! Is that what all this bullshit is about? First of all, a woman cannot rape a man, so stop frontin'. We were gone, what, maybe fifteen minutes tops? We come back and open up the door and see her riding you—very well I might add. So what was I was supposed to do? Run and tackle her off your dick? Get outta here. I did what any good homeboy would do…shut the door and let you get your nut off. You wanted to break her off, so you did. Don't put that shit on me. Your girl is not going to find out anyway so relax," Will said.

Chase turned to Will and moved closer. "It's not about my girl finding out man! You were supposed to be there and have my back. You know I was vulnerable. We had just talked about it early that morning. You saw how she was looking at me and what she was saying to me. Shit you might as well had put my dick inside of her yourself. You know I'm weak as fuck when it comes to woman. And now I feel real messed up inside. Man, if Camara finds out I'm screwed!" Chase said.

"No homeboy, you were screwed yesterday—by Shontae. Vulnerable? So are you going blame me for the skeezer you smashed up in Buffalo too? You need to stop shitting in the bushes and blaming it on the dogs," said Will nonchalantly.

"By that time I was already all-in. The day was already messed up so I had to finish it up strong or not at all. But that's beside the point. You were supposed to be there and the bottom line is you weren't. Thanks, friend," Chase said sarcastically.

"Man, eat a dick! That makes no goddamned sense. I be damned if I kiss your ass or be your scapegoat. I'm about to go back and hoop," Will said as he turned back around and walked towards the basketball court.

Wanting to save some face and not be considered a total jerk Chase figured it was all right if he let the rest of the guys use his basketball. "Don't forget my basketball either, sucka!" Chase yelled as he rolled the basketball up the street stopping directly in front of Will's Nike's.

"I won't, sweet cheeks. I'm snitching on you to your girl, though. Maybe me and Camara will have some revenge sex on that ass!" Will said as he laughed and dribbled his way back up South Avenue.

Chase could not help but chuckle to himself after Will's playful threat. But he had to admit after speaking his mind on how he felt was therapeutic. The guilt that he felt for cheating began to wane. Having pushed the blame on Will, he could begin the process of wiping Saturday out of his mind completely.

Now he was in the mood for one person only, Camara. Running over Camara's schedule in his mind he surmised that she should be home from church by now. They had actually planned to see each other after Chase had finished up from playing basketball around four or five. Extra hours of quality time with his girlfriend were just what the doctor ordered.

■

Chase was in a frustrated state of disbelief. Sitting in his kitchen staring at the phone he could not understand why he could not get in touch with Camara for the past three hours. Rotating between watching the white clock on the wall and the telephone, Chase was steaming. His anger triggered an unhealthy concoction of paranoia and reaction formation.

Why she hasn't called me yet? She knew good and damn well we had a date today at 5. Where is she? I know she's with Squeeze. They probably went to the movies or something. Why else hasn't she answered my calls? I know she got her mom looking out for her and playing it off. I'm not stupid. We haven't seen each other in three weeks and now she's standing me up. I know she's cheating on me. I wonder how long she's been with Squeeze behind my back? She is foul! That's some foul shit to do to a good man like me. Where in the hell is she-

Chase's stream of conscious thoughts was rudely interrupted by the ringing of the telephone. It barely finished the first ring before Chase picked it up and frantically spoke "Hello!"

"Hi, baby. Listen don't be mad at me. I got some good news and some bad—" Camara said before she was cut off by Chase.

"Where the fuck you been! I've been waiting inside this hot ass house all goddamn day for you!" Chase screamed.

Camara stopped, removed the phone from her ear and looked at it…examining it to make sure it was her phone and that she was talking to the right person. The voice on the other end sounded like Chase's but the fury and rage was unfamiliar to her. She squinted her eyes and pursed her lips and followed up, "Excuse me? Let me try this again because I know I must've dialed the wrong number. Hello, may I speak to Chase please?"

"Where have you been all goddamn day, Camara? Did it slip your pretty little mind that we had a date today at 4? Who were you with? Do you know what time it is now? It's 8 p.m.! The day is ruined!" Chase yelled totally ignoring Camara attempt to recalibrate the conversation.

Inhaling deeply before she spoke Camara countered with "Chase I told you before I am not your child. Stop cursing at me, please. Now I understand that you're upset and I apologize for calling you this late. But before you rudely started bombarding me with questions I told you I got some good news and some bad news."

"Just tell me where you were and who you were with that you couldn't pick up a phone and call me," Chase said.

"Ok, Chase, you're right. Rhonda gave me a surprise visit this afternoon. We went to the Marketplace and to Midtown Mall and shopped. After that we got our feet and fingernails done. We were having such a great time that I lost track of time. I already apologized for that. The bad news is that we wouldn't be able to spend time together today. The good news was that I'm off until Thursday morning and I had booked us a room for the next three days. Rhonda is going cover for us because my mother said it was cool if I went back to Buffalo with her. Of course, I wasn't because I was planning on spending—" Camara said.

"You were with Rhonda? Rhonda came all the way from Buffalo? You're lying to me, Camara. Were you with that clown Squeeze? Are you fucking that clown behind my back? Squeeze came up here and scooped you up didn't he? Not no damn Rhonda! The truth will set you free, Camara!" Chase said.

Camara thought she was inside of the dark side of Rod Serling's fertile imagination. The only thing that was missing was the creepy theme music. Chase's reaction to a missed date was over-the-top and unnecessary. Clearly, flabbergasted Camara had enough. "Are you on crack, Chase?"

"Am I on crack? Yea I'm on crack, Camara. And I'm bout beam up Scotty right now!" The receiver registered a loud click.

Chase had never hung the phone up on her. Camara did not know exactly how to react. She was going to call him back immediately but suddenly decided not to. *You look better gone,* Camara thought as she sat in her room in silence trying to collect her sanity.

After hanging up the phone Chase began talking loudly trying to convince himself that he did the right thing.

"I might have been born yesterday but I was up all night! She ain't slick. I should've known she was a snake. She was too good to be true. She really expected me to believe she was chilling with Rhonda all day long. Shit, Rhonda's all the way in Buffalo." It never dawned on him that Squeeze was all the way in New York City.

Chase kept repeating his charges and waited for Camara to call him back. The more he believed he was justified in hanging up the telephone on her, the more he believed that she was lying to him, and the more empowered he felt. Chase also felt that it was up to Camara to call him not the other way around and he expected her to submit to that reality before he went to bed. As the hours ticked away doubt began to slip into his mind ever-so-slightly. When 2 a.m. came around, Chase began to pray to God that he did not make the biggest mistake of his life.

26 June 28, 1990

Misery was extremely fond of Camara Truth. Misery would frolic and carry on inside of Camara's head. Misery was like that spoiled five-year-old who demanded in baby talk that he be pushed in his stroller while sucking on his binky. When Camara would wake up Misery would be there with hot morning breath that hummed like a 1950s doo-wop group.

Misery would mock her by asking condescending questions such as 'Rough night huh? How did you sleep? Not well I hope'. Misery believed in a multi-pronged approach which included jealousy, regret, and imagination. The terrible threesome would stake their claim inside of Camara's brain. They force fed her emotions a steady diet of insecurities, self-doubt, resentment, and pure uncooked anger.

Since the moment they met Camara and Chase never let a day go by without communicating with each other either in person or by telephone. The couple naturally felt the need to correspond and connect. However in the battle between the two young lovers, radio silence was the weapon of choice. Entering the eleventh day of the war Camara was beginning to suffer from battle fatigue and was wishing she had never been drafted in the first place.

Courtesy of her aunt, Camara had a nice paying and relatively easy summer job at Eastman Kodak. Her duties mainly consisted of keeping her designated three floors and clean of debris and non-toxic waste. The good thing about her job was that she could truly take her time to complete her aforementioned tasks. She had no boss or supervisor over her shoulder watching her every move or demanding that she pick up the pace. The laid back nature of the job suited Camara's sensibilities.

Today, however, the hours dragged on incessantly. Everything she did from the sweeping and mopping of the floors to the changing of the toilet paper in the bathrooms, to the dumping of the garbage, seemed like monumental feats which took everything she had inside of her to complete.

Her mind was in no mood to help because it was solely focused on Chase and trying to understand both how and why the couple ended up here.

Why he hasn't he called me? What possessed him to hang the phone up on me like that? Why was he even talking to me like that in the first place? I can understand him being a little upset. I can even deal with a little yelling but what he said was uncalled for and way overboard. I told him I was with Rhonda. Why in the hell would he think I'm with Squeeze? Squeeze? So his stupid ass would rather believe that Squeeze came all the way up here from New York City which is almost six hours away, but can't believe that Rhonda came up from Buffalo which is only an hour away? I wanna smack sense into him. He hasn't called to apologize yet! I am not calling him first. He has until the end of this week to call me or it's over for real. My head is killing me...

Having made it through the day, Camara was relieved to be finally on her way home. She was looking forward to a warm shower, Sade, and her bed. As soon as she put the key in the front door she heard her telephone ring. *I know its Chase and it's about damn time!*

Running top speed to the living room Camara picked up the telephone and greeted the caller while trying to catch her breath.

"Hi. Is this Camara?" a somewhat familiar but still unrecognizable voice.

"This is she. May I ask who's speaking please?" Camara asked in a puzzled tone.

"What's up, Camara, this is Will. How are you doing?"

"Will? Oh, Will. I'm fine. What's up with you?" Camara said confused.

"Ok, first of all, don't freak out. I know what you're thinking. Best friend goes behind best friend's back to try to steal his grieving and vulnerable girlfriend by using everything boyfriend ever told the best friend about her," Will said attempting to address Camara's suspicion about a phone call from him.

At this point, Camara did not know what to think or how to even take the fact that her boyfriend's best friend just called her out of the blue. But she aired on the side of caution and decided to not jump to any conclusions.

"I'm listening," Camara said politely.

Will cleared his throat and said, "Never would I do that. Chase isn't like my brother... he is my brother. And as gorgeous as you are, even if you threw it at me—which I know you'd never do—I still wouldn't take it. I have to say that early so that you know and understand there is no backstabbing stuff going on here."

"I always thought and felt that you and Chase's brotherhood was strong and genuine. But I'll have to admit I'm still wondering why you're calling me instead of your brother. But those backstabbing thoughts never crossed my mind," Camara admitted.

Happy there was zero chance of a misunderstanding, Will continued, "Camara, you need to understand this first and foremost. As much as you are missing Chase trust me he misses you double that."

Hearing those words Camara was immediately relieved on two levels. First, she was happy that she was not the only one miserable. Second, she now knew that Chase truly loved her. A long smile instantly opened up on her face.

"This dude is bugging out! I mean he's talking to himself. He barely comes out of his room. I know for a fact the only thing that dude has eaten for the past week or so is a pork chop sandwich and three slices of pizza. You got my boy fucked up. Excuse my French."

Camara laughed to herself as quietly as she could as Will recounted Chase's actions, "You're excused. But it's not my fault he's feeling that way. How does he think I feel?" she said very calmly as to not give away her true emotional state.

"The other thing you need to understand about Chase is that he is very stubborn. He will hold onto a grudge for dear life. Trust me I know. Camara, this relationship thing is all new to him. There are two Chases: Chase before Camara and Chase after Camara. And I know the difference. He was a wild boy. I not going to tell all his dirty little secrets but I will say this. The only reason why I called you is to let you know how he is really feeling so you don't break up with him. Give him a little time. Chase is my brother, I love him, and I can say this without a doubt that you are the best thing to have happened to him. I don't want to see him lose that. I should be so lucky," Will said.

Camara was blown away by Will's mature and honest assessment of her boyfriend. Her mood immediately turned better.

"Aww, Will, you're gonna make me cry. Thank you so much. But hold on what's up with you and Rhonda? Don't you two still talk?" Camara asked with a smile.

"See that's the thing, Camara. Don't get me wrong Rhonda is cool as hell. Thick, pretty, freaky, intelligent and she's nice. We got up and did our thing and it was fun. Camara, she did this thing with her—excuse me I'm getting carried away. My point is that if she walks through my door right now we would probably screw each other's brains out again and that's fine. But that is all it will ever be. And she knows that too. As cool as she is, she not my soul mate. Chase has found his. I'll find my Camara when it's my time to find her. But until then I'm going to shop around," Will said.

This was one of the most touching things that any man had ever said to Camara. The genuine nature of his deep compliment resonated soundly inside of her soul.

"Chase is a very blessed to have you as a brother. Thanks, Will, I can't tell you how deeply I appreciate you calling me. Oh, by the way, I'm curious how did you get my number?" Camara asked.

"Chase got your number pinned to that Teddy Bear in his room. It's like it's his name tag or something. He's like a zombie right now. He didn't even know I copied it down. Take down my number just in case you need to talk, 461-5555. And don't tell Chase I called. See ya Camara," Will said before hanging up the telephone.

He got my number pinned on Mr. Fizzy! That is so cute! Feeling exhausted from her recent lack of sleep she decided to follow through with her original plans and curl up in her bed with the music of Sade.

27 July 5, 1990

Will's phone call seemed to take place in another time and dimension. Camara's patience was beginning to wear thin. She was sure Chase would have called her by now and could not believe another whole week had passed. She was feeling progressively worse about Chase and their relationship. Every day when she got off of work she was expecting a call from Chase, in essence, apologizing and asking to spend time with her. Such a call never made it to the Truth's residence. Summer opportunities were being squandered and the season was wasting away.

Walking up to her front door from another slow and depressing day at work, Camara was at wits end. When she opened the door she was surprised to see her mother standing in the foyer.

"Mama? What you doing home? I didn't see the car in the driveway. Aren't you supposed to be at work?" Camara asked.

"Hello, Baby Doll. Yes, I'm supposed to be at work but I decided to take the day off," Mama Truth said as she walked into the living room.

"What! Mama Truth you playing hooky from work? I'm calling the cops on you. You missing work is like a kid missing the carnival," Camara said playfully following her mother and sitting next to her on the couch.

"Well, well, well, is that my daughter actually cracking a joke? I'm calling up In Living Color to get you an audition. I can't believe it! My daughter can actually smile," she said sarcastically.

"Very funny. Is something wrong with the car?" Camara asked.

"Brake pads, shoes, and a major tune-up, it'll be done first thing tomorrow morning. But my question is what's wrong with you? And don't say 'nothing'. I see you around here moping and carrying on. I know I haven't been the best mother when it comes to love and relationship advice. I have my own demons and disappointments but I see that something is wrong with you," Mama Truth said sincerely.

This was the first time ever that Mama Truth showed any sincere concern about Camara's relationship woes. She was always stern and apprehensive with respect to men. However, the rare show of womanly sensitivity was a mother and daughter moment that Camara had been waiting for.

"Well Chase and I had an argument and he hung the phone up on me and we haven't talked for over two weeks. And I'm not calling him first!" Camara said sternly.

"From what I have seen from Chase, I don't think that he is the devil. Maybe you should give him a call," Mama Truth said as she walked to the foyer and grabbed the mail. "This came for you today."

Camara's brown eyes became the size of chocolate chip cookies as she realized who the letter was from without looking. Chase had sprayed his signature Joop cologne all over the outside of the envelope and on the letter itself. The aroma brought back a flood of great memories. She wanted to rip it open immediately but instead, Camara chose to slow down and opened the letter slowly.

Dearest Camara,

Words cannot begin to describe how awful and how foolish I feel for talking to you in such a disrespectful way. I humbly ask you for your forgiveness. The only reason why I haven't called you is because I am truly embarrassed. What I did was extremely immature. I promise you it will never happen again. I had a very rough weekend and I not only took it out on you but I took it out on my friends as well. A rough weekend is no excuse. I don't know why I just didn't believe you at first. I know you would never lie to me. Again I apologize. Being in a relationship is new and very scary to me. So I know I'm going to make mistakes. But I never again want to make the mistake of letting you get away from me. You have changed my life forever. And I've always heard that change is good. I love you Camara....

Forever yours if you will have me,
Chase

Big juicy tears welled in Camara's eyes and fell onto Chase's letter like a monsoon. The warmness that her heartfelt refused to be contained so it visited each and every part of her body. Camara had never experienced such joy. When she looked at her mother she was surprised to see her mother wiping away a few tears as well. Feeling closer to her mother than she had in years all she could is embrace her and cry with her.

"I love him, Mama. I just do," Camara said through her tears.

"I know you do, baby…I know you do. I know I've been a little strict on you. I just want the absolute best for you. So if Chase is what's best for you at this point in time then he is who I want for you. Don't call him. Go see him. Just don't be back too late," Mama Truth said. She handed Camara cab money and proceeded to call for a pickup.

Between her mother letting her guard down and truly embracing her and Chase's heartfelt letter, Camara was soaked in emotional bliss. Instead of running upstairs to change her clothes or to put on some makeup Camara was so high she went straight outside to wait for the cab…smiling and crying the whole while.

Arriving in front of Chase's house she was surprised to see the man himself, sitting on his front porch with his head lowered and resting in between his hands. He did not even realize that there was a taxicab in front of his house, let alone who was inside of the vehicle. Camara could not help but to feel sorry for Chase, who appeared defeated, dejected, and thinner than when she last saw him in May. Feeling that it was time to let him out of the torture chamber Camara paid the taxi-driver and jumped out of the car.

She was amazed as she walked up the porch stairs that Chase did not even raise his head to look to see who was coming. *Will was right…he is worse than me.* "I hope you been taking care of Mr. Fizzy. If not I'm jumping right back in that cab and going back home," Camara said as she stood in front of him.

Slowly raising his head from his hands Chase squinted and shook his head a few times just to make sure what he was seeing was real and not a depression induced hallucination. He saw standing in front of him Camara wearing a sleeveless white button up shirt and tight blue jean shorts.

"Camara? Baby, I'm so, so sorry. Please forgive me. What are you doing here?" Chase asked her after he peppered her with hugs and kisses.

"I got your letter so I came to let you know in person two things. One, don't ever do what you did to me again. And two, I love you too. Chase, I love you," Camara said as the tears dropped down her brown cheeks.

The words Chase never thought he would ever say to a woman and truly mean came flowing out of his mouth like the Nile River.

"I love you, Camara. And I won't ever put you through that again," Chase said as he grabbed Camara again and kissed her gently.

For the rest of that afternoon and into the evening the young couple laughed, talked, smooched, and enjoyed comfortable silence together as they retied the string that held them together.

28 November 2, 1990

Playing point guard was easy to Chase. With the basketball in his hands, he controlled the flow of the game and everyone playing. If the man guarding him played him to close, Chase simply used his incredible speed to blow right past him. If he gave him too much room, then Chase would use his high arching rainbow jump shot to punish him. He was a developing sense of calm that allowed him to think before he reacted.

This newfound round ball serenity was put to the test as Squeeze jumped with Chase and landed a hard overhand right, just missing his face. Nevertheless, the solid blow landed across Chase's chest and arm area, knocking him to the floor. Squeeze got into his defensive stance ready for the certain retaliation. But to his surprise, Chase jumped up and walked the other way.

"I don't have to call ball on that one, right? That's pretty obvious. I guess the game plan is if you can't stop 'em then chop 'em. It's all good. Check ball," Chase said.

Chase's retaliation came in the form of a perfect alley-oop pass to one of his teammates. He winked at Squeeze and blew a kiss. Chase was as amazed by his non-violent reaction to Squeeze's rough play as much as anyone. Today he viewed retaliation as wasted energy. For one, he was obviously getting the better of Squeeze and everyone else with his play on the basketball court. The other reason he decided to let that rough foul slide was because he had won Camara. That victory outshined them all and gave Chase a sense of accomplishment that could not be attained on a basketball court.

After winning his fourth game in a row Chase decided to hit the library and study class lecture notes from the past week. Chase was well on his way to earning his first 3.0 GPA. Everything this semester seemed to come much more natural to him. Some of his rejuvenation more than likely emanated from his renewed fidelity to Camara.

Chase and his comrades had a fun-filled lineup scheduled for the weekend. On tap for Saturday night was the Bell, Biv, Devoe, Ice Cube, Salt-N-Pepa, and Big Daddy Kane concert at the Rochester War Memorial. The fact that it was Camara's first ever concert made Chase even that much more excited to attend.

Tonight, however, was the annual Kappa Ball and Dance. A year ago the concert and dance would be the only thing that Chase would plan for. School work was secondary at best and a non-factor last year. Now he was learning the art of how to prioritize. Some of his courses were also very intriguing to him. But more importantly, he was beginning to like the challenge of college.

He got back to his dorm room from the library around 5:00. Plunking down his now always full black leather book bag onto his bed, Chase went to use the bathroom. The dorm room telephone rang as Chase stood over the toilet. He hoped he could finish his business before the person on the other end decided that no one was home. When he finished and ran to the telephone.

"Hello."

"Hello. How are you doing today, Mr. Douglass?"

"I'm doing fine, Mr. Dance. Much better in fact since the last time we spoke," Chase said in a mildly gloating tone.

"It overjoys me to hear that dear sir. And from what I've been told by a few of your professors, you seem to be in a good place academically speaking," Mr. Dance said.

"That is very true. I don't know what it is, but things just seemed to slow down for me. I mean when I first got to school I wasn't really about school at all. I didn't apply myself. Plus half the time the coursework and the professors overwhelmed me. I didn't know what the hell I was doing. Well, I guess we both know what I was all about without going into all of the gory details," Chase said.

Chase was indeed in a great place in his life. He was starting to realize that fact. It started literally with a wake-up call from Mr. Dance and continued with heated but heart to heart conversations with Professor King. However, the biggest change to his life was meeting and falling in love with Camara. Lately, Chase had started to reassess his life and was actually beginning to think of the future and some of the glorious possibilities it could bring.

Chase continued, "I have to first thank you for getting me into McNair University in the first place and then giving a damn about me once I got in. I needed that and I thank you, Mr. Dance. I'm really starting to enjoy school. I even chose my major...English. I'm not sure yet exactly in what capacity I want to use my degree but at least I know I want a degree in English. I've always been fascinated by words."

"Mr. Douglass, you have acquired a most important trait that you will need to be successful. It is the ability to focus. You told me out of your own mouth that you want an English degree. This time last year I don't think those words were a part of your vocabulary. A lot of young urban men and women fail miserably their first year of college mainly because there is no thirteenth grade to prepare you for the sudden change in life and lifestyle from high school to college. It is quite a leap. But you Chase are starting to grow, and that my friend can be a gorgeous achievement," Mr. Dance said proudly.

"Yes, it can be. You know, Mr. Dance, I've changed too. You know I use to fuc—uh...I was very promiscuous. But I found a diamond in the rough. I sleep with her and only her. Now, I slipped up a few times, but I don't want anybody but her. She looks like an Empress, she smart as a whip has her own mind, she ain't no skeezer, and she loves Hip Hop! What more can a man ask for?" Chase asked enthusiastically.

He was indeed proud to call her his girl. Every now and then the guilt of cheating on her during the summer would creep into Chase's psyche. He felt horrible for making her feel like she was the culprit. What he appreciated most was the fact that Camara never brought up their summer separation. Even when he would piss her off a little she would never so much as even mention it. Chase quietly thanked God that Camara never found out about Shontae or Buffalo. Camara's ignorance of his indiscretions helped Chase place them in the rear view mirror.

"Congratulations are indeed in order. When a man finds his wife he finds a good thing. I know. I wouldn't trade my wife for all the tea in China," said Mr. Dance.

"Whoa, Whoa, Whoa! Hold your horses, Mr. Dance. I love her in all but it'll be a while before we do all that! Regardless, I got her on lock and she isn't going anywhere. And as for everything else in my life right now I'm pretty comfortable. I mean I'm content. My grades are good, my love life is good. I guess that means that I'm good," Chase said as he smiled.

"We have come so far and yet we have miles and miles to go. Son, contentment, and comfort are the hidden landmines buried on the road to success. Those particular states of being by their very definition stifle growth. You claim that you have your woman on lock. But then you turn and pivot in the same breath and crow about her intelligence. Mr. Douglass, if she is as intelligent as you say she   is then trust me her mind will never be on lock and her intellect will always take her somewhere. You just better be smart enough to either drive or ride on the passenger side with her. Or better yet make sure you have your own vehicle just in case she neither needs nor wants your company. Good day, Mr. Douglass."

The conversation seemed to end just as it was beginning leaving Chase thunderstruck. Remembering the last talk on the telephone he had with Mr. Dance ended just as abruptly, Chase decided to brush his former English teacher advice off as well.

■

Entering the Student Union with his friends Brad, Sean, and Hugh, Chase felt like an emperor. In his mind, everyone was waiting for him and his crew to arrive to make their grand entrance and to give their precious blessings for a great party. Chase prided himself on keeping up with the latest dances and fashions. He found himself reluctantly embracing House music, the newest sound invading college jams and parties across the country. House music forced both Hip Hop and Reggae music to move over a little so that it could take its place inside the imagination of young partying college students.

Going at 124 beats per minute, the song 'Everybody Everybody' by Black Box was pounding from the stage where the Disc Jockey was stationed to the back of the ballroom where the wallflowers and the unpopular populated. Chase and his crew stood front and center in the middle of the dance floor. Chase was sporting an African twist hairstyle with a ball fade on the sides and back of his head. He wore a tan, dark brown and black paisley button-up long sleeve shirt. To complete his outfit he had on over-sized blue jeans, black patent leather shoes, and his African beads.

Before Chase, Brad, and Sean started to take over the dance floor, Chase scoped out the crowd to see if he could spot Camara. The pseudo-darkness did not hinder his eyesight. After seeing Camara and Rhonda dancing by the exit Chase gave the nod to his friends and they broke into their well-rehearsed dance routine. They immediately drew a large circle around them as the onlookers clapped and smiled.

Chase loved the attention. He adored the stares from the young women who knew he had a girlfriend but would still give him that flirtatious stare. Every now and then he would give them a wink to see the reaction that it would elicit. Chase promised himself that it would go no further than that.

Right before Chase totally allowed himself to get lost in the music and the attention he spotted Squeeze and two of his frat brothers walking towards Camara and Rhonda. Suspecting that Squeeze was still very sweet on Camara he watched with a keen eye for any obvious signs of foul play. Squeeze got as close to Camara as he could and tried to steal a hug. Camara to her credit was simply not having any of it. Chase stopped dancing and smoothly walked over towards them.

"Excuse me…I think this is mine," Chase said as he grabbed Camara by the hand and guided her to the middle of the dance floor.

"Now, Chase, you know I'm no great dancer like you and you know I'm a little shy. Why are you pulling me out here like this?" Camara asked playfully

"Hold on, baby…hi, Squeeze!" Chase yelled and then waved dramatically. Wanting to drive the point home even harder, Chase started to French-kiss Camara lustily in the middle of the dance floor for all to see. At first, Camara was a willing participant. But half-way through the theatrical slobbering, something did not to feel right to her.

Pulling away from him she asked, "Chase, what are doing?"

"What do you mean what I'm doing? I'm kissing my girlfriend. Is that ok with you?" Chase asked.

"Of course, it's ok with me as long as you know I'm not your trophy or prize plaque that you show off to friends and enemies whenever you feel the urge to boast. I'm a living, breathing, and feeling person Chase," Camara yelled into Chase's ear trying her best to compete with the music.

"I know that. Listen, baby, I'll be right back," Chase said as he walked away from Camara leaving her in the middle of the dance floor to glad-hand a few of his classmates.

Camara looked at him as he seemed to be almost congratulated by people while Chase gloatingly accepted the praise. Camara's stomach felt queasy. Uneasiness and worry was knocking on Camara's heart as she questioned Chase's very public display of affection.

29   December 4, 1991

Chase was finding it increasingly difficult to pinpoint exactly what color the sky was. It morphed from gray to burnt orange in what seemed like milliseconds. Bulbous faces left as soon as they appeared. The phantasmagoric city skyline seemed familiar to Chase yet unknown to him at the same time. It was if he was looking through a time machine at Downtown Rochester as it was and then fused it with how he viewed it presently. At least that is what Chase was thinking before his alarm clock woke him up dazed and confused.

There was just enough time for Chase to jump in the shower, brush his teeth, and get dressed, before his 8:00 a.m. math course. To successfully fulfill McNair University's math requirement, Chase had to get a D or better in two classes: College Math 110 which he received a C last year and College Math 112 which he was barely passing. Chase loved words and conversely hated numbers.

He also hated the class and the fact that the only time it was offered was 8:00 a.m. Three times a week around 7:15 a.m. Chase was metal and his bed was a magnet. He literally had to talk himself into attending class on most mornings. Today was no exception. Sleepy-eyed and groggy he began the internal battle of wills. *I'll come up with a good excuse later.* Chase rolled over and rejoined his dream already in progress.

■

Shockow's Bookstore located on Main Street in the tiny village of Brockport was Professor King's favorite place to hangout. Although the establishment took up one-third of the block, it was able to retain a small and cozy bookstore feel. The limestone building had a huge mural of famous books and authors that covered it like a colorful newspaper headline. The picturesque bookstore looked like it was lifted out of a Hallmark Christmas special as the huge snowflakes rained on top of, and around, it. The late autumn snowfall had little chance of sticking but that did not slow it down from visiting Brockport.

Professor King had a wide and eclectic taste in books from fiction to non-fiction. On today's shopping list was three books: *The Firm* by John Grisham, *Homicide: A Year on the Killing Streets* by David Simon, and *Needful Things* by Stephen King. Professor King had been known to polish off up to three novels in a week when he was feeling ravenous. The smell of a brand new hardcover book was an instant gratification to the erudite professor.

Walking to the register to pay for his books, Professor King saw Camara emerging from the basement section of the store. She was slouched over and had her head towards the floor. He and Camara had grown close during the past two semesters since she decided to tutor other students taking his course. They talked about everything under the sun and had a great and growing rapport.

The keenly observant Professor King had begun to notice changes in Camara's demeanor, both subtle and at times flagrant. The smiles, the effervescence, and the shy but accessible persona were changing slowly in front of the professor's eyes. He had a good idea who was fueling the transformation.

"Hello, Ms. Truth. I see you have discovered my secret hide-a-way, my home away from home, Shockow's Bookstore the place that takes most of if not all of my discretionary income," Professor King said smiling as he walked up to Camara and extended his hand.

"Hi, Professor King," Camara said blankly as she shook his hand.

"Didn't find the book you were looking for?" Professor King asked.

"Ah, no they didn't have it so I had to order it. It'll be here in two to four weeks," Camara said flatly.

Seeing the sullen look in her eyes and hearing the almost imperceptible resign in her voice, Professor King felt compelled to prompt Camara to talk about what was truly bothering her. He did not want to cross any lines by unduly prying into her personal life. However, he genuinely felt that if she verbalized her feelings it would help.

"Are you going back to campus, Ms. Truth?" Professor King asked.

"Yes, I have to go to the library and study for my Econ final," Camara said as her voice trailed away.

"Well, what a coincidence. That's my destination as well. I'll accompany you on the way if you don't mind," Professor King said cautiously.

"I don't mind, Professor," Camara said as she walked head down and blurry-eyed to the door.

The first part of the walk was smothered in unpleasant silence. The juicy wet snowflakes from the smoke-silver sky refused to let up. Professor King obviously wanted to talk but did not know how to initiate the conversation. Despite numerous conversations with Camara, he knew this was different due to her dark and unresponsive mood. His first thought was to talk about the weather. He just as fast dismissed the thought because he felt the topic was trite and meaningless. Frustrated by his lack ingenuity, Professor King was happy to be helped out of his quandary by Camara.

"Professor King, can I ask you a question?" she asked.

Smiling from ear to ear he responded, "Of course, Ms. Truth, please ask away."

"How do you know...umm...I mean, how can you tell—I'm trying to figure out how to word this correctly I apologize," Camara said trying her best suppress her frustration.

Professor King stopped and turned to her and put his hands on her shoulder. "Relax. I'm here to listen and not judge."

Exhaling deeply Camara continued, "When you think someone is losing interest in you should you bring it to their attention? I mean should you point blank ask them if they are, and if so then why? Or should you wait to make sure it's the case and kind of ride it out? But if you wait too long you might be the last one to know that it's over and I guess that's no fun. Why do people have to change, Professor?"

"Ms. Truth, you said *a question*. If I'm correct you asked a multitude of them," Professor King said with a laugh hoping it would brighten Camara's spirits.

"You're right, Professor King. I apologize," Camara said sadly.

Sensing that she was not in her regular state of mind to appreciate the joke, Professor King stopped and turned to her. "No, no, Ms. Truth. You have no reason to apologize. It was my ham-handed attempt at humor that begs for your forgiveness. Your heart and mind are obviously heavy. I'm a professor I get paid to answer questions. It is my pleasure to help you in any way that I can."

Camara looked at him and gave a faint smile.

"But before we go any farther, let's get to the meat of the matter. I can safely assume that we are talking about Mr. Douglass?" he asked as they started to walk again.

When his name left Professor King's vocal cords and made its way from his mouth to Camara's ears she thought a poison dart hit her stomach. Never had she associated Chase's name with uncertainty. But she could not ignore the feelings of doubt that overcame her at times when she reflected on their two-year relationship.

Looking morose and withdrawn Camara reluctantly affirmed it was Chase.

"I do not know Mr. Douglass that well on a personal level. Therefore it would be wild speculation on my part to try and tell you why he did this or why he has not done that. However I do know a little bit about him and I have a good memory of how I was around his age. This is the funnel that I will pour my advice through. Ok?" Professor King asked again.

Nodding her head up and down vigorously, Camara was poised to take whatever advice was necessary to help remedy her situation. "I guess I'm just tired of asking women advice about men. I figure I can go to a man and maybe it would help. I get a little depressed at times."

A sudden swelling of pride filled Professor King. He felt privileged that she had enough trust in him that she would seek his advice on highly personal matters of the heart. In professor King's eyes, Camara was the model student and destined to be a success in whatever field she chose because she had the right mix of smarts, humility, and drive. Professor King believed in quality associations and this was the smelting of such a union.

"May I ask you a personal question, Ms. Truth? Trust me it will only help me to give you the best advice possible," Professor King said.

"Sure Professor."

"What is your relationship like with your father? Are you two very close? Are you two estranged? Please be very honest."

Camara rubbed her hands together to combat the expected cold weather. She then hugged herself before she answered.

"Well, Professor King, to be honest with you, I've never met my father. He was killed in the Vietnam War. His name was Barry Bell. My mother barely talked about him. But she did tell me about his death when I was young. I guess I just got used to not having a dad. I mean he was killed. It's not like he abandoned me on purpose. So I hold no grudge against him. It's just one of those things that a person has to accept about their life," Camara said.

"I see. And is this your first real, quote unquote, long-term relationship?" Professor King asked.

"Yes. Well, to tell you the truth it's my second relationship. But that one was nowhere close to this one as far as love and intensity," Camara said as the twosome hit the north end of campus.

"With that being the case, Ms. Truth, this bit of information may give you some sort of framework for you to address your situation. You see the fact that you have not had your father for any discernable time in your life may put undue stress on you and Mr. Douglass as well. You see sometimes a young woman's first relationship with a man takes on added importance especially if there was no father in place to set the benchmark. All children have an innate craving to be loved by their mother and father. So there are instances where she may go overboard, bend over backwards, or whatever cliché' you want to employ, to keep that relationship alive. That relationship sometimes will help her to cope with abandonment issues she may have had with her father."

Camara immediately began to think of her mother. Growing up as a child, her mother at times was a bit cold and aloof. Professor King's words brought back those memories.

"Relationships, in general, are of importance to the average women so, generally speaking, they will at times take the demise or perceived demise of a relationship much harder than the male. When a man gets older is typically when he begins to yearn for a more meaningful relationship beyond say sex. I'm not being a male chauvinist or echoing stereotypes, there always exceptions to every rule because there are no absolutes," said Professor King as they stood in front of the library.

"I didn't think about it on that deep a level. I guess I just seriously miss the way things used to be. Chase would make time for me now he's short with me. Don't get me wrong, Professor, it's not like he's abusing or using me or anything outrageous like that. But I can tell that he has changed his behavior towards me. It's not the big things it's the little things that he would do for me or the little things we would do together. It hurts," Camara said.

Professor King was all too aware of the pain a man was capable of inflicting upon a woman. Memories of his past womanizing flashed through his mind. Scared that some of those past memories would become more vivid, Professor King returned his focus to Camara.

"Listen, the bottom line is I think Chase is a decent young man. His potential is limitless. But you have to keep in mind that he is a young man. I emphasize the word young. I know that this is probably his first real relationship also. You should be very proud of yourself because you brought this young man from one phase in his life to another. From my understanding, you are each other's first love. That is very powerful. The problem is that he has much more growing to do. He is not at this point, the man that he will eventually become. But he will become that man. Patience can be your ally. Women seem to always mature faster than men. But always remember this, Ms. Truth. Never complain about the things that you have the power to change. There is no guarantee he will live up to his true potential. Ok, I'll see you next week," Professor King said as he disappeared in the bowels of the library.

Camara watched him for a few seconds as she allowed his words to reverberate in her head. She was very grateful to him for taking the time to talk to her. Readjusting her book bag Camara walked up the library stairs and went in. She decided to go to one of the individual study rooms located on the second floor so that she could concentrate on her work. When she reached the top of the stairs she saw Squeeze heading toward one of the individual study rooms as well.

Without thinking, Camara sped up her pace and caught up with him. Not saying a word to him she simply looked at him and smiled. Before Squeeze could properly react to Camara's welcoming smile, she turned right, went inside the tiny cubicle and closed the door.

30 December 11, 1991

What a difference a few semesters makes, Chase thought as he galloped up the administration building stairs for an informal meeting with Professor King, his former enemy. Knowing Professor King better than when he was embarrassed for not keeping up with the readings, Chase felt foolish for not seeing that the ordeal was a subtle way of encouraging better performance.

Chase was very curious, however, about what Professor King wanted to discuss with him. Whether it was the association, the quality of the discussion or the sincerity of the message, Chase felt and welcomed the sprouting kinship. Although Professor King was pleasant enough, there was something about him that intimidated Chase. Still, a conversation with Professor King always left Chase feeling smarter.

"Professor, how are you doing today sir?" Chase asked warmly as the two men shook hands. Professor King walked back around his oak desk and sat back down.

"I am doing fine, Mr. Douglass, how about you?"

"I'm good, I'm good. I am curious though as to what you wanted to talk to me about. You always have something very interesting to say," Chase said as laughed.

"You are starting to know me very well, Mr. Douglass," Professor King answered back with a laugh himself.

Before diving into what he wanted to discuss, Professor King remembered how perplexed with uncertainty Camara appeared at the bookstore. He wanted nothing more than to plant seeds in the fertile, still maturing mind of young Mr. Douglass without coming across as if Camara asked him to. Neutrality or the appearance of such was supreme.

"Do you know what the key to a happy life is, Mr. Douglass?" Professor King asked with a stoic face and tone.

Chase began to wonder where the question would lead. He thought he was in for a mental sparring session with the champ himself. With a smile, he answered, "I'd say being able to do what you want to do when you want to do it. That boils down to money. That's why I'm in school...to get a good job...to get those ends....get that dough! So, I'll say money."

Professor King shook his head from side to side and picked at his small but growing goatee. After readjusting and cleaning his black horn-rimmed glasses he stood up. "Interesting answer...I won't psychoanalyze it because I don't want to get side-tracked. Mr. Douglass, the key to a happy life is fruitful, mutually beneficial, happy and healthy relationships—as many as you can secure and maintain. For example, you and I have grown over the years to have a very productive relationship, would you not agree?"

"I agree," Chase quickly answered.

"Good people and strong relationships are important, Mr. Douglass. Good folks are rare, priceless, and always in demand," Professor King said.

"Again I agree. I also think it's important to be a good person yourself. Good attracts good right?" Chase asked.

"Very well put, Mr. Douglass."

A strong sense of fatherly pride overcame Professor King. He knew he played a significant role in helping show Chase how important it was to be a responsible student and man overall. It felt good to recognize the growth.

"So how is your music coming along, Mr. Douglass?"

"Good...real good. I just put the finishing touches on a demo tape. God-willing this is the one," Chase said as he knocked on Professor King's oak desk.

Professor King loved the fact that Chase was putting his dreams to land a recording contract in motion while still attending college. He thought of all of the many talented but troubled people he came across in and around the Hanover Housing Projects growing up. Most of them were either dead, in prison or worse. It takes a special soul to escape the traps and offerings of the ghetto. Chase was one of those souls. More than a few times coming up Professor King dodged bullets...both real and metaphorical. Professor King wanted none of that for Chase. *So far so good*, he thought before proceeding.

"You are a very talented young man, Mr. Douglass. I heard you perform more than once. The way you put your words together...the way you intricately twist them to do your bidding is quite remarkable. I am a music fan but honestly, I respect the art form of Hip Hop more than I actually like it. But you are gifted. I know enough about music to know that. You should not let that gift go to waste. I am very impressed with your hustle," Professor King said.

Chase believing the compliment to be genuine said, "Wow. Thanks, Professor. I appreciate that. Who is your favorite group?"

"I'm an O'Jays man myself," Professor King said proudly. The slick moves, the tight harmonies and the powerful voices of Eddie Levert, and Walter Williams reverberated in his memories. Next to reading, music was another passion of his.

"My grandmother would always play the O'Jays cleaning up the house on Saturday mornings. 'I Love Music' was my shi—my bad...I mean that's my favorite song by them," Chase said as he sat back in his chair.

"You have a good ear for good music. I see why you're good at making it. You know what my favorite O'Jays song is? 'Use to be My Girl'."

Professor King broke into an impromptu rendition of his very own version of the song. "*I used to neglect her. She wanted more than I could give but as long as I live, she'll be my girl.*" Realizing he'd gotten a little carried away he regained his composure and said very seriously, "It's funny that we stumbled upon that song because it is a perfect segue into what I wanted to discuss with you."

Fidgeting in his chair Chase thought, *What in the world do the O'Jays have to do with me? Professor King is bugging.*

Professor King continued "Do you know what separates a boy from a growing man? Do you know what separates a growing man from a grown man? I'm going to share this concept with you...like I wish someone had shared it with me at your age. It is incumbent upon you to implement what I'm going to tell you as soon as humanly possible. Your learning curve will be reduced significantly, thus saving you a megaton in pain. The last thing that you want to be is haunted as a grown man by the foolish mistakes you made as a growing young man. Those types of ghost will turn you into a bitter old man. Understand?"

Trying to follow the conundrums and logic laid out by Professor King made Chase dizzy. He answered honestly by saying, "Absolutely not sir."

"Of course, you don't at least not yet, but trust me in time you will," said Professor King.

"I hope I will. So tell me, Professor King, what separates a boy from a man?" Chase asked impatiently.

Knowing how volatile Chase was but also aware that the two were on much more solid footing, proposed two distinct ways Professor King could disperse the information to him: polite and subtle or raw and uncut. Professor King chose both.

"Perspective and the ability to reason are the pillars of maturity. The sooner this sinks into your subconscious the better you will be. I can all but guarantee you a fantastic and full life. I tell you this son because you are traveling down an icy, curvy road at top speed with four bald tires. Slow down, make the changes necessary and realize what you have, before you crash and kill everything in your sight."

"What do I have?" Chase asked.

"It's not what. It's who. Mr. Douglass, you are well aware that we are defined by the choices we make. In my estimation, you made a fantastic choice by making Miss Truth your girlfriend. Mr. Douglass, you are a fine young growing man. You remind me of myself at your age. Of course, I was much better looking than you but that's beside the point. Every day you have to make the conscious decision to not let your cock destroy the relationship with your girlfriend. Back in the days, I would have told you that your slip is showing. And if I can see it I know she can," Professor King said as he interlocked his hands pointing both of his index fingers skyward.

Over the past couple years, Chase slowly but surely warmed up to Professor King. He respected Professor King because he believed it was mutual. However, Chase questioned his expertise when it came to sexual relationships. *How can a man who hasn't had sex in ten years tell me about what I'm doing with my girlfriend?* He thought it better not to say it aloud.

"With all due respect, Professor, you sound like my roommate Brad," Chase said.

"You say that as if it is a bad thing? Does Brad have your well-being at heart?"

"Of course, he does. That's my boy. But I'm good and Camara ain't going nowhere. I got that on lock. I messed around behind her back a couple times like I told you before. I couldn't help that, though. The girl attacked me and then Mother Nature took over. This freak's ass was so big, I had to wax and tax it. I felt bad about it. I know I was wrong and I haven't cheated since," said Chase.

"Mother Nature made you tax it, huh? Mr. Douglass, it is truly amazing how little you know about women, relationships, and why you like what you like for that manner. For example, you have referred to the young lady's buttocks and the effect it had on you…a hypnotizing effect correct sir?" Professor King asked as wheels turned inside of his brain.

"Yea she got a real fat ass—I mean butt…excuse me," Chase said while tracing an imaginary butt in the air so that Professor King knew the exact size he was referring to.

"Well my butt is fat but I bet you aren't attracted to it. Mr. Douglass, there is a reason why a woman's body is shaped the way that it is. For instance, do you even know why you love a woman that has wide hips or big round butt for that manner?" Professor King asked. He listened for Chase's answer while he pulled out a white handkerchief from his white short-sleeve button-up shirt pocket and began to polish his black horn-rimmed glasses.

Chase paused and tried to figure out why voluptuous and curvy women turned him on so much. He and his friends would ask that question amongst themselves from time to time, but no one could properly answer it. Pulling from his past limited discussions on the topic, Chase said, "Yeah I know why I love a woman who got a big butt! It's soft, it wiggles when I'm hittin' it from behind, it's squeezable, and it feels good when I'm going up in it. Plus it just looks so nice in a tight pair of jeans, especially if she got a small waist and nice, big, and supple breast. I know you haven't had any for ten years Professor, but I know you got a good memory of how it feels, it's indescribable."

"Classy. Mr. Douglass, you have an awful lot to learn about the nature of women, their role in the universe, how you are supposed to operate within the dynamics of a relationship, and quite frankly you have a lot to learn about yourself," Professor King said.

"What you mean, Professor? Are you calling me stupid?" Chase asked.

I remember being his age, being defensive and believing everybody was always against me, or trying to make me feel beneath them. I do remember.

"Son, I just praised you and acknowledged your genius a couple minutes ago not to mention complimenting you on your taste and choice in women. Now you think I'm calling you stupid? No, I am merely highlighting your ignorance when it comes to a woman. For example are you aware that the rotations of the Sun, Earth, and Moon are based upon a woman's menstrual cycle? Do you know that a woman's orgasm on average can be up to four times more powerful than yours? Personally speaking, I have had some great orgasms in my day but if it was four times more powerful, it could possibly blow my mind," Professor King said.

Chase started to imagine an orgasm four times as powerful and it actually began to frighten him.

"Really? Four times more powerful. Get outta here!" Chase said as he laughed in disbelief.

Ignoring Chase's skeptical response, Professor King continued with his barrage of knowledge, "You like a woman with wide hips because it is engrained in your subconscious that she will be able to push your baby through her birth canal. The wider the hips, the higher the likelihood she will be able to produce. Historically many women have died in labor. We as men think that a woman with wide hips and generally more weight on her frame—thick as you all call it—gives her and your baby that much more of a chance at survival. We all want to live forever. The birth of a child or many children almost ensures that. Beauty demands replication. So when you see a beautiful woman you instinctively want to reproduce her form of beauty. That's part of the reason why it is called reproduction."

Chase was fascinated by what the professor was saying. He never equated his love for a 'thick' woman with childbirth. "That's interesting, Professor. I never thought of it like that. You may have a point there," Chase said.

Professor King continued without taking his eyes of Chase, "You like a woman who has a big round butt because it reminds you of the Earth and how round it is in the context of the universe. When you are at a social gathering and music is playing and a woman starts to dance, what does the lower part of her body automatically do? It winds in a circle or rotates around and around. When you're making love to her, you watch her body as it goes around and around. What goes around comes around 360 degrees. What you sow is what you reap. The round butt of a woman reminds you subconsciously of pregnant woman's round stomach. You are reborn through the roundness or circle of life. If you could magically put one hand on her stomach and one hand on her butt and move them so they could connect, then you would have the shape of the earth. Your woman is your Earth. She is your world. God designed a woman's body to be a magnificent vessel that carries the most precious of cargo. A woman is the doorway to infinity. We as men have the key. That's partly why women mesmerize us so much."

"That's deep…I definitely never thought of it that way," Chase said.

Chase's face crinkled with confusion and curiosity. Never had he looked at a woman's body beyond its useful pleasure to him. Camara was the first woman that he loved beyond her sexual capabilities. In the past, Chase was accustomed to leveraging a woman's body against her natural affinity for him. Professor King was telling him to see and think on a deeper level.

"Why do you think women show cleavage, Mr. Douglass?"

Chase wanted to show Professor King that he was indeed paying attention and was intelligent enough to contribute to the discussion.

"Ok. Hold on lemme think. They are showing off part of their breasts," Chase said.

"What is the primary function of a woman's breast, Mr. Douglass? And here is a hint…it is not for your pleasure," Professor King said with a smile.

"I know that, Professor. It's to feed her babies," Chase said.

"Exactly, Mr. Douglass. When she shows you cleavage she is showing you that if you procreate with her, the baby produced will be well fed. Now your responsibility is to go and provide for her. Since she has given everything of herself even risked death to bring your child—your rebirth—into this world, this means your responsibility to her is epic. A woman feels emotions that we could not possibly fathom. Stay on the straight and narrow and do not test their emotions by doing stupid stuff like taking them for granted or cheating on them," said Professor King sternly.

Guilt began to wash over Chase like a squeezed wet sponge. He remembered the day he betrayed Camara and immediately felt horrible again. Professor King had the hot water faucet turned all the way on.

"Do you know the greatest gift that you could possibly ever give your woman? No, it's not diamonds, pearls, furs, flowers, cards, candy, sweet nothings, sex or even love. The greatest gift that you could possibly ever bestow upon your woman, Mr. Douglass, is respect—pure, unbiased, unequivocal, unadulterated, uncompromising, and unconditional respect. Give that to your woman, Mr. Douglass, and you can sit back and truly experience just how bright and beautiful the sunshine really is," said Professor King as smiled harder than ever.

"I thought it was all about love. I thought love is all a relationship needed," Chase said as held his head low.

"Respect stops you from doing what love won't. Don't, believe me, I'll give you a concrete example. Who is your very best friend?" Professor King asked.

"My man Will. Well, he's in school too—Cornell. But we have been through so much together. I can say that he would take a bullet for me just like I'd take a bullet for him," Chase said almost defiantly.

"That is most honorable, Mr. Douglass. Now let me ask you this. Would you sleep with his girlfriend?" Professor King asked provocatively.

"Hell no!" Chase said sounding as if he was on the cusp anger.

"Would he sleep with yours?"

Chase went from a perplexed look on his face to a murderous grimace when he imagined Will sleeping with Camara. This thought never crossed his mind, so when the image appeared in his mind it was jarring.

"Hell goddamn no! Neither one of us would do that to each other at gunpoint!" Chase yelled even louder.

"Exactly! That's not out of love for your best friend—your brother. Love doesn't have a damned thing to do with that. You wouldn't do it out of respect for him. Understand me, son? You have to transfer that same level of respect you have for your best friend to your girlfriend as well. All respect means is that no matter what, I will not cross this line and do this because I hold our relationship in that high a regard. No matter what, I'm not going to call you a bitch. No matter what, I'm not going to hit you. No matter what I'm not going to cheat on you. Why? Respect! Respect is the highest form of love," Professor King said with a quiet scream.

Chase's head was twirling like a baton in the Labor Day Parade. Information overloaded his brain. He was not sure if he still liked Professor King. He needed time for everything to sink in.

Professor King finished, "You know why a woman is, and will always be, more powerful than us? When the seed necessary to make a baby comes out of you, it just feels good. However, when a baby comes out of a woman it hurts like hell before it feels like heaven. You will never know the depths of pain and pleasure the way a woman knows it. You should respect her like you respect God. The difference between the two may be smaller than we think. See you around, Mr. Douglass."

31 January 26, 1992

"This game sucks ass! Why in the hell would they play the damn Super Bowl in Minnesota? I thought they were supposed to play it outside in the warm sun, not in a wack ass dome," Chase yelled from his booth inside the Pub to the group of onlookers and friends in his immediate vicinity. Most of the spectators were bored out of their minds watching Gloria Estefan, Dorothy Hamill, and Brian Boitano perform at halftime of Super Bowl XXVI.

Sensing the urge to be seen and heard, the Chase whispered a few words in Brad's ear. Chase was prone to 'showing his behind' as his grandmother would say and today he was prepared to get buck naked. As soon as the network went to commercial, the Chase show began.

"Brad hit that beat box for me, and turn down that bullshit television. Everybody gather around. I'm about to rhyme and my man Brad is on the beat box. We are the real halftime show!" Chase said as he commandeered a center spot directly in front of the projection screen, facing the crowd.

The Pub which was located in the middle of campus was hosting a free Super Bowl party for faculty and students. It resembled a sports bar minus the alcohol. Spacious but cozy, it had a capacity of 500 people. The walls were painted touchdown green and adorned with all kinds of collegiate and professional sports memorabilia.

Chase and Brad were very comfortable performing in front crowds, having pulled off victories in the last two McNair University talent contests. Although Will was his rap partner and they had plans on submitting their just completed demo to several Hip Hop labels, Chase was open to the idea of adding Brad to the 'Monster Crew' if Will approved. Chase grabbed the microphone and proceeded to move the crowd for a 10-minute set.

The sizable crowd applauded and gave its approval. As Chase made his way through the crowd a female voice asked, "Why don't you do a rap for the ladies up in here. Come on, Rochester."

Chase, surprised to see Brandi, took her in visually from head to toe. Her short hairstyle which was tapered on the sides was sophisticatedly spiked to give it a chaotic but orderly look. She wore a red long-sleeved shirt that was cut clean out in the middle from the top of her bosom to the back of her neck to accentuate her impressive cleavage. Her tight white leggings and red high heels made Brandi a must see at the Super Bowl gathering. Chase needed to oblige.

As soon as Brad restarted to beat box Brandi got up from her table and started to dance her way seductively towards Chase. Brandi turned her mammoth backside to him, making sure it rubbed against Chase in the friendliest of manners. Chase did not back down or push her away. Instead, he went with the flow and moved rhythmically with her as she was grinding up against him. He continued to rap as if it was par for the course.

Chase self-censored himself for the virgin ears in the crowd but cared not for the virgin eyes as he performed a hybrid of Hip Hop and Burlesque with Brandi. When Brad, who was lost in the moment, realized who Chase was dirty dancing with he was visibly appalled.

Brad slowly wound down beat-boxing, waited for the crowd to finish clapping and then pulled Chase over in front of the men's bathroom and asked sarcastically, "Yo Chase, what you doing homeboy? Isn't that your girl's roommate?"

"No...they used to be suitemates but Brandi moved out at the beginning of last year," Chase answered missing the point.

"That's beside the point. I know at the very least they're not exactly fond of each other," Brad said becoming more and more concerned.

"Man, all I did was dance with her for a minute. It's not like we had sex. I wouldn't do that Camara," said Chase as he waved Brad off with his left hand.

"You have no idea who might be in here. You don't know who is watching you and waiting to go back and blab to Camara. It's no skin off my nose I'm just telling you, you're being a little reckless, dude," Brad said while pointing his finger at him.

"Come on, Brad, we at a Super bowl party. It's just a few broads here but mostly its people who don't know me or Camara. I told you, man, Camara ain't going nowhere. I got that on lock!" Chase said.

The two headed back to their table but before Chase could sit back down and watch the second half of the Super Bowl, his new improvisational dance partner Brandi wanted a couple words with him. She watched Brad head to the counter for pizza and swooped in opportunistically, taking his seat.

"You kinda nice with your little raps, Chase," Brandi said while batting her eyelashes.

"Thanks, Brandi. You're a pretty good dancer. You most def know how to move that thick body of yours," Chase said as he sat down and looked Brandi up and down imagining what she looked like naked.

"Thank you, but I think I'm getting fat, especially my ass. See?" Brandi asked as she stood back up and turned slowly putting her hands on the top of her waist before sliding them down each rounded butt-cheek.

"Very impressive," Chase said as he thought about Professor King's hypothesis on women and the shape of their bodies.

"Even though you from Rochester, I can't front on you. I always thought you were sexy as hell. Are you still with your girlfriend… whatever her name is? I was just curious."

"Camara," Chase answered playing along but purposely ignoring the first part of her question.

"I'm getting ready to go soon and I was hoping you could walk me home," Brandi said then licked and bit her lips.

Chase was stuck. He knew Brandi was detrimental to his relationship. Although it was well over a year ago, her bold and brief hand-job was still fresh in his mind. With Camara a few feet away, it was clear she would do anything to get under Camara's skin. Yet, her brazenness exhilarated Chase.

"Umm…we—"

"Yo, Chase! Can you excuse us for a second please, Brandi?" Brad said as he walked towards the jukebox by the wall.

"I'll be right back," Chase said to Brandi as he smiled and walked over to Brad.

"Dude, what the hell are you doing? You're screwing up. And when you're all fucked up beyond all recognition you're going to remember I tried to stop you," Brad said with growing concern.

"Brad homeboy, I get what you're saying but please man, relax. All we're doing is talking. I promise you I am not gonna do anything I'm not supposed to. Listen, man, I'm a little tired plus, look—it's 24 to zip now. I'm breakin' out. The Buffalo Bills are done," Chase said.

Brad looked at Chase and shook his head smiling. He knew there was little he could say to dissuade his roommate and friend from possibly making the biggest mistake of his young life.

"If you're breaking out with Miss Brooklyn all I'm going to say is watch out for Camara. Cause if she happens to see you two walking somewhere together, it's on," Brad said.

"You think I'm stupid, Brad? Camara is gone for the weekend. She's not getting back here till Monday afternoon. But that immaterial, like I told you, I am not going to violate Camara and do some bullshit. Alright, man?"

Brad looked at Chase hard. "Ok, dude, just don't say I didn't warn you."

The two friends shook hands and walked in separate directions. Chase quickly spotted Brandi's seductive smile waiting for him at the table. Chase meant every word he said to Brad about not letting things get out of hand with Brandi. But once he took another good look at her, he wasn't so sure. He began to eye-hump her on the way back to the table.

"Yo, Brandi, I'm getting ready to break too. I'm not sure if your friends are staying for the second half or not. If they are staying then at the very least, I could walk you to your dorm and make sure you get there safe," Chase said as he licked and bit his bottom lip.

Brandi stood up as slowly and as provocatively as she could, pushing her backside out. "Ah…how sweet. Yeah, I better walk home with you. It's a whole lot of crazy people out here. I don't want to have to give an eye jammie to some creep. Plus I don't really understand football anyway. My girls dragged me here. If you promise to keep me safe we can leave now."

A smiling Chase grabbed his black on black Shearling coat and said, "Cool, let's make it like cake."

Unfortunately, Chase did not notice Rhonda, who entered the Pub in the middle of the first quarter. Being a native of Buffalo Rhonda arrived to quietly root for her beloved Bills. She promised to keep her emotions in check because of an all-out brawl she nearly started at a downtown watering hole last month rooting for her team. She remained mostly reserved while her team showed little signs of life deep into the third quarter. However seeing her best friend's boyfriend dancing suggestively with a heated rival, Brandi, and then leaving with her was worse than the shellacking the Buffalo Bills were taking.

■

Chase and Brandi stuck close to each other as they navigated their way through the cold and clear starlit winter night. The soft crunch of the snow underneath their boots echoed through the biting breeze. The noise was slowly beginning to worry Chase. For some odd reason, he thought the sounds their boots were invisible alarms transmitted to the friends and associates of Camara. He looked to Brandi's firm but switching hind quarters for reassurance that he was doing the right thing. Going back and forth in his mind on whether Brandi was a tease or full-on-freak kept Chase walking forward with the young beauty. He pretended his only motive was purely ensuring she made it to her off-campus apartment safe. His furtive looks behind him and at each person, they passed suggested otherwise.

"You ever been to New York City? Or you just stayed in Rochester your whole life?" Brandi asked sarcastically while putting her arm in the middle of Chase's back.

Chase had done his research. Brandi had tons of family in the City but she was actually from Rockland County. That was close enough to give her pass—he figured she flew out of JFK and LaGuardia like everybody else. "Yes ma'am, a couple times. I stayed at Brad's house in Spring Valley and went with Sean went once. He's from Brownsville. I can't front, I had a blast both times. We went to the Bank and one club called Demerara. I've never had so much fun," Chase said as he remembered putting in a full six-hour shift and leaving the club with a pocketful of numbers from the female patrons.

Brandi stopped and looked at Chase. "What you know about the Bank and Demerara? You from country ass Rawchesta!" she said with a laugh.

"For once and for all Brandi there is nothing corny or country about the Roc. Ain't nothing sweet either...we got the highest murder rate in the state. We got plenty of money coming out of there with Kodak, Xerox, and Bausch & Lomb. Hell, Rochester practically invented photography and movies. Not to mention that Cab Calloway, Susan B. Anthony, and Frederick Douglass are all from the Rochester," Chase said.

"Actually honey, Frederick Douglass was born in Maryland. He is buried in Rochester," Brandi said smartly.

"I know where he's buried...Mt. Hope Cemetery. But I can't front I didn't know where he was born. How you know?" Chase asked.

"I'm a Black History major. I'm supposed to know these things. Don't think I'm just another pretty redbone with a fat ass. For real, though, I can't lie, for the longest time, I thought you were from the City too. The way you carry yourself...real fly and sexy," Brandi said to him as they walked up the porch stairs of her apartment.

Chase's ego blew up to the size of the Goodyear blimp. He tried his best to hide his smile to no avail. His sexual attraction to her began to swell. All Chase could think about was ripping her clothes off and exploring every inch of her naked body in meticulous fashion.

"You coming in? I'm a little cold still. I was hoping you had something to warm me up with. Just make sure your girlfriend don't find out. I don't want you getting in no trouble," Brandi said as she stepped into the doorway and placed her hands and her hips.

Camara's face entered his mind the moment Brandi referenced her. Chase thought her hologram transported to Brandi's porch and dared him to walk past her. Instantaneous memories of both their courtship and relationship barraged Chase. Even his conversation with Professor King reverberated in his head. For the first time ever the thought, *Do I really want to risk losing Camara? Even if she never finds out, I'll know.*

As he reached the top of the stairs Chase looked at Brandi and said, "You know what, Brandi, you're right. I don't wanna get in trouble either. My girl has been known to throw a few eye jammies in her day too. I'm glad I got you here safe, I'd better get ghost. See you later."

Brandi was so shocked that Chase did not succumb to her invitation that she stood in her doorway slack-jawed for more than a minute. By the time she recovered, Chase was halfway down campus road headed back to his room thinking of ways to make up to Camara for his near indiscretion.

32 February 1, 1992

Rhonda Wheatley was fuming worse than the tailpipe attached to her 1985 Yugo GV. Her tightly gripped face refused to relax as she listened to the vile goings on between her best friend Camara and Chase. The muffled giggles and the constant but playful pleas, "Stop playing, you know my roommate is outside", were too much for her to ignore. In fact, the fun they were obviously having was making Rhonda furious. She sat in their dorm suite and stewed.

The slow burn of anger directed towards Chase was a growing fire that she could not extinguish. On one hand, she could only speculate as to what Chase and Brandi actually did once they left the Pub. *Chase could have walked her home like a perfect gentleman. Or he could have fucked her dry. I don't know which is true but the way they were dancing...* Rather than speculate, Rhonda steamed about what she knew was true. Chase violated about ten unwritten relationship rules according to Rhonda that night. She was questioning whether or not she should turn him into the proper authority.

Rhonda found herself being very short with Chase or almost immediately excusing herself from their company in situations where she was always a welcomed third wheel. All week she would make veil references to his behavior with Brandi to Camara without actually spilling the beans. Her affinity for both Chase and Camara stopped her from telling everything she knew about the infamous Super Bowl Sunday. But Rhonda's conscious persistently threatened to her. *If you don't tell her, then I will.*

With her white t-shirt, oversized pajama bottoms housecoat, and rollers in her hair Rhonda got up from the love seat in the suite and knocked on the door.

Camara opened the door only halfway signifying someone was not dressed appropriately. "Hold on, Rhonda," Camara said as she then playfully yelled to Chase to put on his shirt before she opened the door fully. Chase happily complied and sat up fully clothed on her bed.

"I need to talk to Camara—girl talk and it's kind of important," Rhonda said while walking into the room methodically and looking away in the distance, never meeting Chase's eyes.

"No prob, Rhonda. I gotta finish up this paper anyway. Baby Cakes, what are you doing tonight? This paper is going to probably take me all day to finish. Maybe I can come through and chill with you later on?" Chase asked.

"I'm not doing anything tonight, I don't think. More than likely I'll be here. I got some reading to do to. Just call me when you get back to your room," Camara said before she kissed Chase good-bye.

Chase was hoping that Camara did not mention going to the Kappa House Party. He was not even sure if she knew about it but he was relieved that she had no plans of attending. They both enjoyed parties produced by the Kappa Alpha Psi fraternity but this one was different because of the time and location. Instead of it being held at the campus Student Ballroom, it was going to take place off campus at the Kappa House. Instead of the party having no alcohol and ending at midnight, this party was going to be filled with adult beverages and was more than likely going to end the next morning.

Chase remembered how many times he got 'lucky' at frat house parties. Drunken girls whose inhibitions were relaxed, coupled with a quick jaunt up the stairs to a free bedroom equaled sex, sex, and more sex. He hated when she thought about going to one of these parties and would argue fervently about her going alone. No one's girlfriend or boyfriend was safe if they slid unprepared down the slippery slope to a bacchanalian orgy. He certainly did not want his queen in that environment.

However since his ill-fated walk with Brandi, Chase made a conscious effort to be more respectful of Camara overall. Breathing easy, Chase walked back to his dorm room to focus on finishing his short story for Creative English due Tuesday.

Once she was sure Chase was long gone, Rhonda carefully and quietly began to spill the beans. At first, she was hesitant as she watched Camara clean out her closet while singing along to the Boys II Men song, 'Uhh Ahh'.

"That's my song girl! I love the way they harmonize," Camara said.

Rhonda walked towards the small but very effective boom box and turned it off.

"Why'd you turn the music off? I just told you that was my shit," said Camara.

"I know and I'm sorry but I want to talk to you about something if you don't mind," Rhonda said in a quiet voice and serious tone.

"What's up, girl? Talk to me," said Camara who picked up instantly on the urgency in Rhonda's voice. She closed the closet door and turned her attention to Rhonda, who was pacing back and forth, before finally deciding to sit on the bed.

"You know I like Chase, right?" asked Rhonda.

"Of course, I know that. I'm glad that my boyfriend and my best friend are cool with each other. I truly appreciate that neither one of you have ever asked me to choose. To be honest, I don't know what I'd do without either of you," Camara said.

Rhonda was lost. She was afraid of giving Camara information that could break her heart. She loved how Camara and Chase the individuals came to be Camara and Chase the couple. But Rhonda loved Camara as a sister and knew firsthand how embarrassing it felt to be the last to know. Her own cousin knew that Rhonda's first boyfriend and first love was cheating on her. Rhonda found out the hard way when she unexpectedly visited him. When she found out that her cousin knew about the infidelity, she vowed never to speak to her cousin again and followed through on the threat. She felt her cousin owed her the facts she uncovered about her relationship. By extension, she felt she owed the same to Camara.

"The best way to do this is just to come right out and say it. Ok…I'm not saying that Chase is cheating on you because honestly, I don't know that to be a fact. I mean I see that you guys have been going strong as of late. But I saw Chase do something at the Super Bowl party that I feel you must be aware of," Rhonda said.

"The Super Bowl? What did he do?" Camara asked quizzically.

"Well, he was rapping at first like he does…putting on a halftime show for everybody at the Pub. That was fine. But then Brandi decided she wanted to become part of the show. So when Chase was rapping, Brandi ran right up under Chase ass-first and started rub-a-dubbing with him. And he was definitely enjoying himself…I mean he never pushed her away or told her to chill or nothing. He started grinding on her ass and shit…it was fucking disgusting."

Camara was dazed by the quick right verbal jab Rhonda threw her way. It stopped her briefly. The threat of another strike gave her reason to pause. But Camara remembered all of the roadwork she put in with Chase by her side. The blood, the sweat, and the tears in the gym were not going to flow in vein. After the standing eight count, Camara countered, "What's a dance? A dance is nothing. Worse crimes have been committed."

Rhonda blocked Camara's counter punch and fired a mental overhand right and then floored her with devastating word-filled upper-cut, "I probably would have kept it to myself if it was just that. But unfortunately, it didn't stop there. Chase and Brandi left the Pub together. And I know he walked her home because I watched them walk towards her apartment."

Camara's eyes rolled into the back of her head as her brain told her legs that this weight was too much to carry. Knowing soon that her legs were going to betray her Camara sat slowly on the bed beside Rhonda.

"I'm sorry, Camara. I love you like a sister and I couldn't live with myself if I just stood by and watched you get played. Again, I don't know if he boned her but I felt I had to tell you what I witnessed. I'm sorry," Rhonda said as she began to tear up. She sat on the bed beside Camara and rubbed her back.

Camara answered with silent screaming tears.

■

For the rest of that day, Rhonda walked around campus feeling like leftover manure. She hated to see anyone she loved and cared for in any kind of pain. After doing her best to console her somber roommate for at least an hour, Rhonda could not take it anymore and darted to the newly constructed computer lab on the west side of the campus.

When the lab was closing up for the day Rhonda decided to kill time at Off the Tracks. Packing up her book bag all she could think about was the Super Bowl party, Chase, Brandi, and a grieving Camara. She felt sick to her stomach. Knowing she had not eaten all day and not in a rush to go back to the room, a burger sounded great to her. The only problem with her plan was the fact that her meal card sat on the desk in her room. Hunger offset the feelings of dread in returning to the dorm and Rhonda trudged back there reluctantly.

Upon opening the door to the suite, Rhonda was surprised to hear music coming from the room. She immediately recognized Naughty By Nature's song 'Yoke the Joker' with Camara's melodious, feminine voice on top of it rapping along to every word with flawless passion.

"It looks like someone is in a much better mood," Rhonda said.

"What I look like worrying about something or somebody I can't control? So anyway what's going on tonight? I feel like getting loose and having some fun. Who's throwing parties tonight? U of R, RIT, UB?" Camara asked in an excited tone.

"You really feel like going out tonight, Camara? Are you sure?" asked a surprised Rhonda.

"Yup," Camara said calmly.

"You're joking right?" Rhonda said with a guilty giggle.

"Nope, so where are we going tonight? I need to shake my ass a little bit," said Camara.

"Well it's funny you asked. Guess who's throwing a party off-campus tonight? The Kappas! I wasn't going to bring it up but since you asked, the party won't get jumping until midnight and it could go up until the morning. I'm just warning you," Rhonda said.

"I'll be ready by quarter to twelve," Camara said and then left their room altogether.

Stunned by the sudden transformation of her best friend, Rhonda was wondering if she should have kept her big mouth closed.

33 February 2, 1992

Chase had driven down this road before. He hoped the winds and turns would not be as treacherous as they were previously. The last time he was on this curvy stretch of pavement he nearly totaled his vehicle along with himself. He was drunk with rage, speeding, and had a depraved indifference for anybody else's feelings besides his own. Chase blew his head gasket and crashed headfirst into his own vulnerability, nearly getting his license revoked. But that was then. That summer when love was garden-fresh, unpolluted and virtually new, Chase reacted recklessly when he tried to reach his girlfriend Camara via the telephone and she refused to answer.

That was then. He was a better man now. However, his unanswered calls on Sunday morning just after midnight were testing his newfound maturity. He had been trying to reach Camara for the last two hours and was beginning to feel more than a bit uneasy. His patience was being pushed to the limit and beginning to overheat.

Chase decided to call it a night after his last unsuccessful attempt and ruling out a quick visit to her dorm room. *Camara is sleeping...don't trip. Don't over-react.*

■

Sweltering and oppressive heat surrounded and invaded Camara like she was an occupied country. Sweat slid down the side of her face diving into her half exposed bosom. The sauna-like heat inside of the packed-to-capacity Kappa house party was forcing her to reconsider her decision to attend. She stood as far as she could, back against the living room wall, hoping not to get noticed. The wall seemed to stick to her white blouse with bell-bottom sleeves.

Camara squinted and tried her best to locate Rhonda but the red light bulbs, one on the ceiling and two in each lamp, proved to be very little help.

Rhonda promised her that she would run interference and block anyone's attempt to dance with her or to get her alone.

Camara was still livid at Chase for his alleged escapades with Brandi...so much so that it brought her to a house party to unwind. As Camara's anger towards Chase began to wane, her discomfort level was rising fast. She finally spotted Rhonda dancing suggestively close with a fellow uninhibited student to the song 'Come and Talk to Me' by Jodeci. Not wanting to interrupt, Camara simply stood up against the wall and stewed.

"Please tell me you're finished dancing, Rhonda! I'm ready to go back to my room. It's too damn hot in here," Camara said hoping to convince Rhonda along with herself that it was time to leave.

"That's my point girl. Here, this should cool you off," a very relaxed and Rhonda said as she handed Camara a plastic cup filled with a dark purple colored drink.

"What's this, Rhonda?" Camara asked pointedly.

"Purple Rain—with a twist. I told you, it'll cool you off. Just take a big sip. It's not gonna kill you. Drink at least half of it," Rhonda said as she giggled and then was suddenly whisked away by a fellow male party-goer.

I see we aren't going nowhere anytime time soon...What the hell I'm here now. Why not relax and enjoy the party. Camara looked at the pretty purple drink. She was going to smell it to see if it had any alcohol but at the last second she changed her mind and sipped through the tiny straw as hard as she could.

Her tongue and taste buds were confused. She liked the sweetness of the Southern Comfort but disliked the strong nature of the Vodka. The cranberries and blue Curacao combined for a sour but tasty concoction. *I better drink the rest of it to see if I really like it or not.*

By the time she finished the drink she could not definitively decide on whether or not she liked it, so she made her way to the bar and asked for another and 15 minutes later another one for good measure. She decided she liked the drink only after she drained half of the third one. 'Remember the Time' by Michael Jackson was playing and for the life of her Camara could not remember the words to the catchy chorus. The number of the people in the huge carpeted living room appeared to have doubled. The stress that she had been feeling was being replaced by a light tickly feeling emanating from the middle of her stomach. The alcohol made Camara want to have fun and nothing else. It was perfect timing because fun came looking for Camara.

"Hello, Camara. How are you this evening?"

She looked and focused hard on the face coming towards her in the red light. "Hi, Squeeze. I'm doing just fine, and you?" Camara asked with a slight slur to her words.

"I'm doing better now. I'm in your beautiful presence," Squeeze said as he moved closer to Camara.

"Oh…is that a fact?" Camara asked.

"Just like Morris Day said in Purple Rain…Yay-ess!" Squeeze said as he rubbed his hands together like an evil scientist while looking Camara up and down. He was still floored by her devastating dimensions. Squeeze knew Camara was drinking. Although she was not drunk yet she was well past tipsy. Squeeze figured this might be a good opportunity to finally make some headway in his over three-year attempt to get Camara.

Camara laughed, "I just had a Purple Rain…with a twist."

"Huh? Oh yeah…we call it a Funky Cold Medina. Vodka *and* Comfort instead of Gin and soda water. How many did you have?" asked Squeeze with an ounce of concern and two ounces of opportunity in his voice.

"Three," Camara said holding up two and then finally three fingers.

"Who you here with?"

Camara had to think for a second as she recalled who she journeyed with to the party. "Oh…Rhonda brought me here. Yeah, that's who I'm with…Rhonda," she said with a laugh that came out of nowhere.

"Well Rhonda done messed up," Squeeze said as he put his right hand on the side of her waist while slowly moving down to her hip.

"What you mean she messed up?" asked Camara.

"Because she let you get into my evil clutches," Squeeze said dramatically.

Camara laughed hard. While she laughed Squeeze slyly pivoted and repositioned himself so that his body was directly behind hers. Before she could protest or move away Squeeze whispered into her ear, "Where is your man?"

Camara's thoughts quickly went to Chase and Brandi and their impromptu performance. She quietly raged. "He's probably here dancing with that skeezer Brandi."

"Probably is, knowing Brandi. Well, let them do what they do. We can focus on the here and now," Squeeze said seductively, excited by the opportunity Chase's actions had provided.

The Deejay mixed in 'Pretty Brown Eyes' by Mint Condition and almost on cue Squeeze whispered, "Come on. Let's dance." He gently forced a willing Camara to the middle of the crowded dance floor. She still had her back to him and her drink in her hand.

Oh my God. Am I really slow dancing with Squeeze? I must be drunk as a skunk. I don't even like Squeeze…at least I know I'm not supposed to. He does feel good up against me. Chase would kill me if he found out I was dancing with Squeeze. But that would be just deserts for him, wouldn't it?

She slowly began to feel how happy he was to finally dance with her. Squeeze made it his business to push up and grind on Camara's backside as hard as he could. Surprisingly she offered little resistance and even moved her body to match his rhythm. Squeeze wanted to look into her fascinating eyes for some reassurance and Camara playfully complied.

"Camara, when are you gonna leave that clown Chase and get with a real nigga? I've wanted you since I first saw you. Give a brother a chance. Please, I swear I'll treat you like no other," Squeeze pleaded into her ear, making intimate contact with her earlobe.

Squeeze's peppermint hot breath and wet tongue sent more than a shiver or two up and down Camara's spine. She was so happy with Chase sexually she never even considered sex with anyone else until now. She looked into his pretty green eyes and initiated a kiss. Squeeze welcomed it and returned the passion. For the next fifteen seconds, they were French kissing for all who were paying attention to see.

Camara's misbehavior finally ended when an aghast Rhonda found her an hour and two drinks later grinding with Squeeze to Beres Hammond, 'Tempted to Touch". Rhonda did not know Camara had it in her to move her body like that. She decided to intervene before Camara took things too far.

34

When Chase woke up early Sunday morning the first thing on his mind was eating. He was so hungry that he began to plan his brunch after a short middle of the night visit to the bathroom. The second thing on his mind was completing his short story assignment for his Fiction Writers Workshop. He found himself truly enjoying the whole writing process. From coming up with the character list to writing the one-page treatment, to using his fruitful imagination to come up with wild and inventive scenarios for his characters, Chase was fully engrossed.

But what he loved most was writing the story itself. Chase found writing a short story similar to writing rhymes, although it was a much more involved undertaking. The assignment was a short story about anything the student wanted to write about. It had to be seven to ten pages, the characters had to have an arc, and it had to have a clear beginning, middle and end.

Chase went straight to Brad's Acorn Archimedes A5000 computer which sat on the oak desk. He sat down and began to two-finger-plunk his way toward completion. Just as Chase began to lose himself in the arch of the story, he was interrupted by an early morning call.

"Speak what's on your mind, Chase is on the line," he said arrogantly as he picked up the phone in the living room suite and sat down on the love seat propping one leg on the armrest.

"What's up, Chase, this is Sean."

"What's up, homeboy?" Chase asked enthusiastically.

"Nothing much man. Hey, are you going to brunch over at Harrison? Hugh and I are going be there around 11. I need to drop some knowledge on you, brother."

"I'll be there. Peace."

An hour later Brad awoke surprised to see Chase up early on a Sunday and working on school related matters. "Chase, I remember when you and schoolwork were not too familiar with each other. Now I wake up and you're working on shit? I have to say it, brother, I'm proud of you," Brad said as he stretched.

"Well to tell you the truth Brad, I think I just found something that I enjoy doing. I hate math so I know I'm never going to be a mathematician. Languages and psychology bore the hell out of me. And I guess the rest of the courses I've taken over the past three years are just tolerable. But the bottom line is, I want my degree now. I never thought I'd make it this far, let alone be a year away from getting a Bachelor's degree. I guess you can say I've matured a little bit. I remember when I didn't give a damn about school work. I got a long way to go—don't get me wrong—but I believe I'm on my way," said Chase.

"Keep doing your thing man," Brad said as he headed toward the bathroom.

"Hey, are you coming to brunch with me? Sean and Hugh will be there at 11," Chase asked.

"Brunch with you? Well, I'll come but only if there is tea and crumpets and Antoine and Bartholomew are serving them with complimentary blowjobs afterward," Brad said in a mocking faux English accent laughing hard before he could finish.

"Whatever man. I'm leaving five till!" Chase yelled as he refocused on writing his story.

■

In one hand Chase had a plate with a huge Belgian waffle, two pieces of toast, three strips of bacon, and four link sausages. In the other hand, he had a plate of fresh fruits, specifically grapes, melons, and cantaloupes. Chase's face carried an enormous hungry smile as walked to the table nearest to the huge bay windows to join his friends Brad, Sean, and Hugh who were already knee deep into their food.

"Damn dude! You pregnant? I see your head is already swollen. Where are the pickles and ice cream?" Hugh said as he and Brad laughed loudly.

Chase put both plates down at the same time and sat next to Sean and replied "The only things swollen up on me is my pockets and my dick. Get it right. And I'm a growing boy. I'm hungry, so max out before I go visit your chick and swell up something on her. You know I'm working with that super sperm," said Chase. He laughed and pulled out the cutlery.

With his focus firmly on the hot golden brown Belgium waffle, he poured butter and syrup on it, cut it, stabbed it with his fork and shoveled it into his mouth. He followed it up by wrapping a link sausage in bacon and shoving it whole into his mouth. As he reached for the toast when Hugh looked at Sean and nodded his head. Sean cleared his throat, took a sip of cranberry juice and started off the planned information session.

"It looked like Camara had herself quite the ball last night."

Immediately Chase knew why he could not reach Camara with his repeated calls. *Kappa Party*. Sean's discomfiting statement felt like a switchblade cutting into Chase's guts. Camara had not crossed his mind since last night. He coached himself into not worrying about her whereabouts after he failed to reach her by telephone. Simply assuming she was in her dorm room sleep was enough to send Chase on his own sandman journey. Chase wondered why he went to bed without a worry. Was it because he truly trusted her? Or because he felt he had Camara wrapped around his finger so much that she would not dare go to a party that he frowned upon.

The ravenous hunger he felt just moments ago was replaced by an uprising coming from the pit of his stomach. He was afraid to entertain Sean's assumption in the form of a statement. But still wanting to save face and not be looked upon as weak Chase lied, "Well, I told her if she was going to go to the party just make sure she had fun and don't get back to her room at some crazy hour. You know what I'm saying?"

"To me, it looked like Squeeze was having all the fun. I know that's your girl and yall business is y'all business but that shit was foul," Hugh said shaking his head.

Chase's stomach sucked itself into inward upon hearing the name Squeeze coupled with the words *fun* and *foul* in relation to Camara. His imagination began to assault his fragile psyche.

"I know she knew me and Hugh were there. She thought we were just gonna ignore them or look the other way? Shit, I can't hold water. You know I was going to tell Chase if he hadn't heard about it yet," Sean said strongly.

Now Chase's face turned beet red and he felt the strong urges to both vomit and defecate at the same time. *Oh God! Please don't let them say what I think they're about to say. I feel sick.*

Brad noticed the signs of torture in Chase's movements. Chase hadn't taken another bite of his food since the nibble of toast and looked like he was about to regurgitate what he had eaten. Brad sought to end the slow torment of the Chinese-water-torture-like release of information drip by drip. "Yo, what are you talking about? Don't pussyfoot around the issue. Come out with it. Exactly what are you saying," Brad asked.

Chase wanted to leave but his body would not allow it. Even though the dining hall was perfectly heated at 72 degrees, beads of sweat began to trot down the side of his face. His condition only worsened once Sean began to rattle off a raw, blow-by-blow description of what went on between Camara and Squeeze.

"Chase, I hate to have to drop this bomb on you like this but you my boy and I'd want you to tell me if the situation were reversed. It was kinda dark because of the red light, but man this is my eyewitness testimony. I saw Squeeze all up on Camara's ass. He was palming her ass like he was dribbling. Then they started dancing. She turned her ass so that he could get it doggy style. She was bending over, grinding back with him, and all that dumb shit. But that wasn't the worst of it. Word to my mother, Chase, they started kissing in the middle of the floor man—tongue action and everything. I swear to fuckin God! I always liked Camara. She's fine and sexy and all that, but I never would have thought she would get down like that with Squeeze of all people. Maybe she was drunk or something because I did see a cup in her hand. They were basically fuckin' on the dance floor with their clothes on. And like I said, it looked like she was enjoying it…"

Poor Chase listened, mouth agape, trying to find ways to reconcile the story with what he knew about Camara. Brad believed Chase needed a standing eight count and began to signal the *cut it* sign to Sean by moving his hand quickly back and forth across his neck. Hugh seized the opportunity in the brief silence.

"That ain't the worse. When the reggae came on, they got some more drinks and moved in the back toward the wall. Camara was working dude. I mean dancehall-queen style. They were all tangled up in a twisted position like they wanted to get inside of each other. When I went on the study group to Canada, the white boys up there used to call that sexual position the Kinky Jesus. Imagine that Chase!"

Hugh, undaunted by spewing sacrilege on a Sunday, bit into a moist blueberry muffin and continued, "If I were you I'd go check her ass! I'd punch her damn lips off for starters—"

"Whoa! Kinky Jes—Hugh, you are going straight to hell for that. Hold on! First of all, there is never a reason to hit a woman. Don't go punch nobody's lips off all right? Listen, Sean said it was dark, maybe it wasn't Camara. Don't overreact! Find out the info first from the horse's mouth," Brad said cutting of Hugh.

Chase was pure Novocain. He felt like he was being buried alive with the dark words coming out of his friend's mouths when the words formed sentences they resembled a shovel full of dirt landing on his casket. Chase sat motionless as they buried him and listened.

"I'm just trying to give homeboy the visual. And, yeah my girl's mouth would be as big as Mr. Ed's if I caught her up against another dude winding, twisted up on a nigga like Jesus on the cross. But that's me. That's how I get down. I wouldn't even be mad at dude because he is only gonna go as far as a chick lets him. Plus, you weren't there Brad, we were. I know what Camara looks like. It was her," Hugh said.

After wiping his mouth and taking a big gulp of his orange juice Sean said, "I agree with Brad to a certain extent. I wouldn't hit her or no dumb shit like that, but I'd verbally blast her ass. That was some foul shit. You can't let that go unpunished. Put her ass in the panic room until she begs to come out. Give her the silent treatment after you unload on her ass."

Chase's spirit could not take anymore and exited his body along with hope, pride and honor. They hovered over the table and looked down at the lifeless shell formerly known as Chase. The three unhelpful doctors in the room sitting around the table continued to try and operate on his heart.

"Hold on man. We all know Camara. And the Camara we know would never dance with Squeeze, let alone kiss him. She had to have been drunk or something. Or maybe he put something in her drink…I don't know. But we do know that he didn't bone her," Brad said.

"Well, you mean he didn't bone her with clothes off. They were definitely boning on the dance floor," Sean said with a mouth full of French toast as if he was being constructive.

"You know what? Come to think of it, she was probably trying to get you back, Chase. Somebody told her about you and Brandi last week. I told you to chill but you didn't want to listen. Now look what happened! Somebody saw and probably told her what you did. Maybe she wanted revenge. Chalk it up as a lesson learned. I wouldn't even bring it up to her. Let it go and move on. Like I said she probably was drunk anyway. It's not worth losing her," Brad pleaded with Chase.

"Yo, you fucked Brandi, Chase?" Sean asked, pointing at him with two fingers.

All Chase could do was shake his head involuntarily no.

"That's it! The best revenge is the one they don't know about. You know what I'd do, Chase? I'd break Brandi sexy ass off. She's been dying to give you the ass anyway. Fuck her first then talk to your girl. Act like nothing ever happened. At that point yall even," Hugh said offering what he believed the perfect remedy. He leaned back satisfied as if he had just articulated the solution to the problems in the Middle East.

"Now I'm not saying go that far. I'm saying go and give her a chance to come clean. If she doesn't, then as a last resort you may have to do that. But in any event, she did disrespect you, homeboy. And you need to check her ass for that regardless of if she was drunk or not," Sean said.

Chase was demolished. The nightmare-like conversation seemed surreal and ridiculous. It was too much for his brain and heart to take in at one time. His soul finally returned to his body and his legs finally relented, allowing him to leave the table.

"Yo, Chase, where you going? You didn't even finish your food! Don't let her get to you man," Hugh said in a vain attempt to stop Chase from leaving.

Chase left the dining hall with no clear destination. His head was pounding, his breath was short, and his stomach was in his chest. *I'm having a heart attack. I can't believe she was kissing Squeeze. I'm about to explode. I never knew such pain existed.*

By the time Chase realized where he was, a half hour had passed. He was by the town river. Standing on the bridge and leaning on the wooden rail for a split second Chase thought about jumping into the cold river. Thinking better of that he got down on one knee and cried uncontrollably.

35

Camara went from one side of her bed to the other in a vain attempt to find comfort. Her head would not stop pounding. Going in and out of nightmares Camara thought a gremlin burrowed its way inside of her skull and went to work on her frontal lobe with a hammer, chisel, and irritating giggle. Her blood vessels expanded because of the cups of 'Funky Cold Medina' she consumed at the party. Her dry mouth begged for water but her queasy stomach wanted nothing to do with any movement. All Camara knew was that the sun was up. The exact time of the day was a working mystery.

"Rhonda. Rhonda. Please, if you don't mind can you bring me some water? It's a jug full in the fridge. I'd get it myself but my stomach won't let me. Rhonda? Are you sleep?"

Camara could not see if Rhonda was sleeping partly because she was facing the wall and found it very difficult to turn over to see for herself. Somehow she mustered the strength to twist her upper torso around far enough to see that Rhonda's bed was still made up and empty.

Disregarding her thirst because of pure exhaustion Camara prayed for rest. Through some divine miracle granted by Hypnos, Camara was actually able to doze off. Right, when the sleep was getting good the jingle-jangle of Rhonda's keys disturbed her slumber and gave the go ahead to the gremlins to continue their demo job inside of her head.

"Girl, you still sleep? That had to be your first time getting drunk. I should've given you something light...like some Bartle's and James. My bad girl, I see it put you on your ass," Rhonda said while kicking off her pumps and plopping on her bed back first.

Camara was able to contort enough of her blanketed body to face Rhonda. "Yeah, it put me on my ass all right. But who put you on yours? Somebody had to because you're just getting back."

"You right about that. I had to give Tim some. He's been patient enough. Plus that Seagram's I was drinking last night made sure Tim was getting some.

He put something on me, you hear me, girl? And there's nothing like a hard dick for breakfast. Wakey, Wakey, Eggs, and Bakey," said Rhonda laughing hard.

"I agree…but right now sex is the furthest thing from my mind. What time is it? I'm sick to my stomach. Rhonda, I don't even remember when or how I got back into the room," Camara said lying on her back shaking her head.

"It's almost 1 p.m. girl, you know my number one priority was to make sure you made it back to the room safe and sound. I had to stop you from dry humping Squeeze in a dark corner. I didn't know you could move like that girl. You almost turned me into a lesbian! When pulled you away Squeeze was all pissed off. We walked back to the room and I made sure you were safe and sound. I locked the door and then I went back to the party. You don't remember?" Rhonda asked.

Camara racked her brain to trying to remember as much as she could from last night. The only things could recover were her memories of arriving at the party, getting her first drink then two more and Michael Jackson.

"That's a damn shame, girl. I swear I don't remember shit. If you see me with a drink in my hands again slap it out, please! I need some water. Better yet can you run to Off the Tracks and bring me some ginger ale? The money is in my purse…even though you're partly responsible for my condition so you should pay for it. You should also nurse me back to health. I swear girl I'm never drinking again."

She was praying that she did not vomit. The last time she did, Camara thought her face was coming undone from her skull.

"Ok how about I get you some water now, then once I get finish showering, I'll run and get some ginger ale and some Alka-Seltzer to help with your stomach. Cool? It's on me ok?" Rhonda answered.

"I'll try and go back to sleep…half of the day is wasted anyway. Wake me up when you get back, please. Thanks for the water," Camara said. After gulping as much as her belly would allow, Camara snuggled back up under the cover with Mr. Fizzy for moral support.

■

Chase could not fathom shedding tears over any woman besides his mother and grandmother. Yet there he was sobbing wildly because of Camara's reported sexy salsa and lip-lock with Squeeze. Gaining his composure Chase took some deep breaths and wiped the tear residue from his face. Pain and embarrassment began to egg him on. Re-focused by his surging anger towards Camara, Chase quickly decided that it was time to pay his girlfriend a visit.

Heavyhearted and despondent Chase trudged his way from the bridge, through town, through campus, to the front of Camara's dorm room. In usual circumstances, Chase would use the courtesy telephone inside the first door to call Camara to either alert her that he was on his way up or that she needed her to come downstairs and open up the door.

Chase was not interested in either of those options today. He waited for a resident of the dorm to enter and he simply piggy-backed behind her inside. Once Chase reached the stairs he was inundated by déjà vu. He recollected all the times he joyfully climbed these very stairs to reach his princess, his goddess, his first and only love Camara. Chase would have paid a pretty penny to the highest bidder for this to be one of those times. The closer he got to her dorm room the more anxious he felt. Chase wanted to know why she would violate him especially with someone she knew he hated above all others.

When Chase stood in front of Camara's door about to knock, his heart started to retreat by pounding up against the inside of his spinal column. His heart wanted no part in the knowledge of Camara's vile transgressions and why she committed them. Chase's brain, on the other hand, needed to know. Chase's fist obliged and knocked on the door.

"I'll get the door. I'm getting ready to go and get the ginger ale now," Chase heard the Rhonda's muffled voice say.

Rhonda opened up the door and jumped back when she realized it was Chase. He had a foreign look in his eyes and a cold demeanor that gave her some pause. Something inside of Rhonda told her to lie when Chase asked if Camara was there. Instead, she told the truth and slowly stepped aside.

"Ok, I'll be right back," Rhonda said trying to convince herself that everything was just fine.

Chase waited a good three minutes before he went inside of Camara's room to make sure Rhonda was truly gone. He entered her room without knocking to see Camara cuddled up with Mr. Fizzy and snoring louder than an inebriated sailor.

I used to love to watch her sleep. It was peaceful to me. But what hell is she doing sleeping after one in the afternoon? Probably tired from doing Squeeze all night. I know it didn't just end with a kiss and a dance!

"Camara, wake up!" Chase yelled as he stood over Camara screw-faced and angry. She did not reply and instead began to snore louder. Chase took a deep breath, and with his right hand, shook her shoulder hard enough to dislodge Mr. Fizzy from her clasp and yelled again, "Camara, wake up!"

Not knowing exactly where she was at first, Camara turned around to see Chase with a twisted face and arms folded. "Chase? Hi, baby. Did Rhonda let you in?" she said while trying to adjust her eyes.

"Yeah. What are you doing sleeping until this late in the afternoon Camara? You had a long late night last night?" Chase asked as calmly as his resentment would allow.

Camara unwrapped herself from under her blankets and realized she was completely nude. She was never the one to sleep nude.

"Oh…you sleep naked now? Wow, you must have had a real good night last night," Chase stated sarcastically.

Looking on the floor directly underneath her bed, Camara saw all of the clothes she wore the night before including her bra and panties. She sat up and as fast as she could, and put on a red oversized button-up blouse, and sat back down.

"Actually, I didn't," Camara said grabbing her turning stomach.

"It ain't hard to tell. So what did you do last night, Camara?" asked Chase. He grabbed her chair from the desk and turned it around and sat never once breaking eye contact with Camara.

Her first instinct was to lie but she sensed Chase both knew something and was mad about it. The fog that covered her mind was slow to clear even though she desperately wanted to speed up the process. The previous night's escapades were coming to her in bits and pieces.

"I asked you a question, Camara. What did you do last night?" Chase asked in a slighter loud and more aggressive tone.

Now she knew for a fact he knew something. She scrambled to buy time while her mind went into autofocus. "Rhonda and I were chilling."

"So you and Rhonda, huh? Ok, let me ask a more specific question. Where did you and Rhonda go?"

"Huh?"

"Did I stutter? I'm assuming that you left the room. As a matter of fact, I know you left the room because I called last night and no one answered the phone. But I didn't trip. I just figured that everybody was sleep. I gave you the benefit of the doubt. So I'll ask you once again 'cause you seem slow this afternoon. Where…did…you…go?" Chase asked in a slow and very deliberate tone.

Her recall and what Chase knew hit her like a ton of bricks. *He knows I went to the house party last night. The Frat house where for the first time ever I got drunk.*

The frat that Squeeze, who Chase absolutely hates, belongs to. Oh my God...I danced with Squeeze. I kissed him too! What in the world was I thinking! I kissed Squeeze!

Camara started to shake from both nerves and embarrassment. She did not want to meet Chase's piercing eyes. "We went to the Kappa house party last night," she said quietly.

"Oh you did, did you? Have fun?" he asked.

"I don't know," Camara said even quieter.

"What you mean you don't know! How in the hell you go someplace, spend half the night there, and then not know if you had fun or not? Well, tell me what did you do at the party Camara?" Chase asked smartly.

"I'm afraid to tell you. I got drunk for the first time last night. I'm ashamed," Camara said trying to hold back tears.

Chase was seething with anger. It took all he had to stay seated. For the first time ever her beautiful face began to look different to him. Her once warm slanted eyes looked sneaky and unfeeling. Her mouth appeared to hide secrets deep down. The power she had over him was now readily apparent to Chase and he resented every watt of it.

"What else did you do at the party Camara?" Chase asked.

"Huh? What else did I do? I told you I got drunk. I'm ashamed and I apologized."

"Oh, you think I'm stupid! You going to blame alcohol for what you did with Squeeze? Dancing with him like you some harlot stripper! And that's not even the worst of it! You kissed that bitch-made clown! How could you play me like that and think you would get away with it!" Chase screamed. He stood up from the chair pushed it violently away from him and bent over towards Camara stopping just short of her face.

She thought she would never see Chase this upset with her. The effects of her hangover, and the stress of trying to explain why she was cavorting with the one person on campus she should have never been seen with had Camara hyperventilating and afraid.

"Chase, baby, I'm so sorry, I was drunk and I swear we only danced for a minute. He kissed me and I was too drunk to stop him. It was nothing. You know I love you and have zero feelings for him. You have every right to be upset with me. I promise you it won't ever happen again. Please, baby, accept my apology," Camara pleaded as she leaned back as far on the bed as she could as she held up her left hand for protection.

Chase had never considered physically attacking Camara. Seeing his own mother fall victim to the horrors of spousal abuse, he vowed to never raise his hands in anger to his romantic partner. Still, he was mad as hell. Recognizing Camara's fear, Chase turned the other way, walked towards Rhonda's bed, and picked up her chair and threw it against the wall. "I'm not accepting your bullshit apology! You don't care about me. If you did you wouldn't have did that to me. What the hell were you—?"

Chase's question was interrupted by a hard knock on the door followed by Rhonda's voice, "Camara, are you all right in there?" Rhonda slowly opened up the door.

"Oh, here's your cut buddy! Yeah, she's all right. Her and that ball-licker Squeeze both gonna be all right. I bet it was your idea to take her to the party to knowing I didn't want her anywhere near there. Damn cockblocker! You probably mad because you don't have a man of your own...so you wanna mess up your so-called best friend's happy home. Well, you succeeded. Gold star for Rhonda!" Chase yelled as he turned his anger towards Rhonda.

"Hold on, nigga! First of all don't worry about who, or what I'm doing because trust me I get and keep mine! Second, Camara is like a sister to me. We haven't had one argument. If she's happy then I'm happy. Third, I have never had no problem with you—until recently. I thought you were cool. That is up until I seen you and Brandi at the Super Bowl party dancing all nasty and shit! Oh yeah, and I saw you leave with her. So I told my best friend about it...so what! That's what friends are for," Rhonda said tearing into Chase while standing toe to toe with him.

Lucidity finally conquered Camara's mind. "That's right! You got me here feeling all bad for dancing with Squeeze when you had your nasty ass all up against that rotten bitch Brandi! Did you take her to her house and screw her? You talk about me. You hypocrite! The only reason I was at the party was because I felt so bad behind what you did. How you think I felt when I found out that you took her home, Chase. You walked her home and did God knows what. You know I hate her ass! How could you do that?" Camara asked as she began to burst into tears.

This wasn't how it was supposed to go. How did she turn this shit around and now trying to blame me for what she did?

"How you feel about that, nigga? You built the yellow brick road—out of Brandi—that led us to the Kappa House," Rhonda sassily stated.

"First of all Rhonda, you need to leave. This is none of your fucking business. If your fat ass would've kept your pie hole shut we wouldn't be arguing right now! And yes Camara I'll admit that I did dance with her. But she came on stage by herself. I didn't ask her to come up. I'll also be a man and admit that I did walk her home, but I swear on everything that I love I did not fuck her. She invited me in but I did not go inside her apartment.

Professor King opened my eyes to a few things. I know I shouldn't have walked her home. That was clearly disrespectful. I apologize. But I repeat I did not have sex with her. I was happy with you. Aren't you happy with me?" Chase pleaded

Wiping her tears away as fast as they came rolling down her cheeks Camara answered, "Of course I'm happy with you Chase. I love you so much. But that shit killed me when I found out you walked her home. Just like you don't like Squeeze you know I can't stand Brandi. Why would you do that to me? And stop disrespecting my friend!"

Feeling cornered, mad and sad all at the same time Chase was clueless. He looked at Rhonda who was standing next to him ready to pounce on him if she had to and thought, *I never had issues with Rhonda before. She is one of the coolest girls I know. But why did she have to snitch!*

"Ok…ok…you're right. I apologize, Rhonda. But I wish you wouldn't have said anything. I do understand that Camara is your best friend so I can't blame you for telling her what you thought you saw. I just wish you would have just come and confronted me about it first. Maybe we could've straightened it out. But let me be clear…I did not fuck her," Chase said with all the honesty he could muster.

Relaxing her stance a bit, Rhonda relented. "Maybe I should've come and talked to you first. We have always had a good relationship. But I love Camara just like you love Will and I'm quite sure you would've snitched too if you saw Will's girlfriend bumping and grinding and then leave with some dude."

The tension in Chase's heart began to ease and miraculously he began to feel a bit more relaxed. He looked at Camara who was sitting on the bed clutching Mr. Fizzy tighter than best friends on a rollercoaster ride. Chase's heart could not help but soften.

"You got a point, Rhonda. I'm sorry for real. Listen, can I please talk to Camara alone so we can straighten this out?" Chase asked in his almost regular voice.

"Camara…are you all right?" Rhonda asked.

Exhaling Camara shook her head yes.

"Well then by all means. I got some work to do anyway. Apology accepted Chase. Camara, I apologize to you if I did or said anything to hurt you. You know I love you girl. I'll be back later," Rhonda said as she made her way out of the room.

Camara remained motionless on the bed. The totality and shock of the whole weekend were hard for her to absorb fully. All Chase could do was look at her as she looked to the floor not ready to look back at him. He sat down on Rhonda's bed and began to look towards the ceiling. Neither one of them knew how to reboot the fragile conversation. They sat in silence for twenty minutes. The only communication between them was the sniffles and silent tears.

When he felt that he had an ample grip on his ever-changing emotions Chase stood up and asked, "Camara, is it all right if I talk to Mr. Fizzy?"

Camara looked up and finally met Chase's eyes. She could see in them that he was scared but would risk everything for her love and adoration. Camara knew that she would lay it all on the line for him too as she truly believed Chase was the only man she would ever love this deeply.

"Sure, I think he'd like that. He loves his daddy almost as much as mommy does," Camara said as she reached over and picked up Mr. Fizzy.

Chase stood up and walked slowly over to Camara who was trying her best not to crack a smile. She handed Chase Mr. Fizzy with love as if she was extending an olive branch. She struggled to understand her complicated feelings. A moment ago she was screaming at the top of her lungs in anger but now she wanted to show Chase how much she loved him. Camara felt unstable and crazy.

Chase also recognized the sensual turn the mood in the room took. Neither one of them wanted to fight anymore. They both wanted and needed to believe that they would be safe if they let go of all inhibitions and simply trusted that they would never betray one another again.

He slowly took Mr. Fizzy from Camara and began to tell him, "Could you do me a favor son? Mr. Fizzy I need you to tell mommy how sorry I am that I danced with that jezebel. I exercised very poor judgment when I walked her home. It won't ever happen again."

Putting him up to his ear he listened to what Mr. Fizzy had to say. Nodding his head accordingly, Chase appeared to agree with Mr. Fizzy's recommendations by saying "Camara, Mr. Fizzy would like to whisper something to you."

Quickly standing up to oblige, all the traces of her sadness vanished. Despite the slight hangover, Camara was feeling just fine. Chase now put Mr. Fizzy to Camara's ear and patiently waited for him to finish his message of forgiveness and renewed love. Once Mr. Fizzy finished, Camara responded alluringly, "Chase, I wholeheartedly apologize to you for that public display of disrespect. I should have never danced with him and I most definitely should not have kissed him. I'd really like to show you how sorry I am."

Chase walked over and carefully placed Mr. Fizzy on Rhonda's bed. Chase wanted to make love to Camara in every way imaginable.

"Rhonda won't be back for a while right?" he asked.

"When she studies, she studies. She's a regular eager beaver," she answered smiling hard.

Before they could repair the relationship permanently with a kiss the phone rang.

"Let it ring baby. I need to taste you," Chase said as playfully tried to stop Camara from picking up the phone in the suite.

"Hold on, Chase, it could be Rhonda. See, she left her keys. I'll take them downstairs and tell her to stay gone for about three hours, ok? Then it's just you and me," Camara said as she grabbed the keys and ran to the phone.

"That's cool. I gotta drain the main vein anyway," said Chase.

Camara answered the telephone, "Hello."

"Why did you leave so fast Cinderella? You didn't even let me walk you to your carriage."

Immediately Camara's heart dropped as she recognized whose voice it was on the other end of the phone. Instinctively she looked at Chase in horror. Unfortunately, the telephone and bathroom were in an earshot of one another and Chase left the door wide open.

"What's wrong, Camara?" Chase asked walking towards her.

Camara did not know whether to respond or to hang up the phone. She was in complete shock that Squeeze actually called her phone.

"Who is that on the phone, Camara?" Chase asked suspecting something foul.

"Nobody...I gotta go," She said and attempted to hang up the phone quickly.

But Chase was too quick. Before she could successfully do so, he snatched the phone out of her hand. "Hello!"

"Hello, what? Is this bitch-ass Chase? Put Camara back on the phone dude. We didn't finish our conversation yet," Squeeze said arrogantly.

"What the fuck you doing calling my girl's room? How'd you get this number?" Chase screamed.

"How did I get this number? How in the hell you think I got this number dummy? Camara gave it to me after I waxed that ass last night, that's how. You know the rules of the game, your bitch chose me," Squeeze said as he laughed.

"Clown, when I see you I'm tapping your jaw!" Chase said and slammed down the phone so hard the receiver cracked.

"I knew it! I knew it! All this time you've been lying to me! You broke him off last night and now you want to butter me up so you can fuck your way back into my good graces! You getting down like that now? No problem so can I!" Chase said as he headed towards Camara's room.

"Chase, hold up! That boy is lying through his teeth! You are the only man that I have ever been with—minus Harold and that was only one time and before I knew you existed. I can't believe that you would actually believe that bullshit. Why did you break my phone?" Camara said.

"Speaking of phones, how did he get your number? Please tell me that! And please don't say he had it, 'cause you've changed numbers twice since freshman year. You know what? I'm done! We are finished. You won't make me look like a damn fool no more. You and Squeeze can fuck till the cows come home for all I care. I don't want to see you again. I'll take the goddamn teddy bear and look at him before I look at you. I'm outta here," Chase said as he grabbed Mr. Fizzy and stormed out of the room.

"Oh my God, Chase, you can't be serious! Baby, I would never do that to you. Don't leave me on account of some lie!" Camara said as she followed Chase down the hallway and to the stairwell.

As the tears flowed down her face once again, Camara realized that there was nothing she could say that would have stopped Chase from leaving. With that realization, anger dominated her emotions. She stopped calling his name and instead offered some choice words, "Wrong choice asshole. You run when things get hard because you're a big pussy! Eventually, you'll run out of places to run. Then you'll be nowhere—just you and the memories of all your dumb choices. Go fuck yourself!

Brandi, Squeeze, Funk Cold Medina, Kappa Party. This is without a doubt the worst weekend of my life.

36 February 13, 1992

Brilliant sunshine beamed throughout the picturesque deep blue smeared skies to cover the length of the entire McNair University campus and the greater Rochester, New York area. The beautiful weather stood in stark contrast to the actual frigid air that occupied the region. The air was so cold outside that when Brad, walking home from his final class, breathed it in it actually burned the inside of his nose. The Arctic air did little to take Brad's thought off Chase's fragile mental state.

When he got to their dorm room he was disappointed to see Chase still in his bed wide awake and looking terrible. Very little these days mattered to Chase. School was merely background music and the weather was of absolutely no consequence. For all, he cared the skies could have been colored purple with people running everywhere like Prince forecasted in his apocalyptic hit '1999'. Not seeing the inside of a lecture hall or shower stall since his argument with Camara, Chase was in a physical funk.

His once crispy faded haircut with his trademark tight African twists was now frazzled and unkempt. Small patches of skin peeked out from his wool covered face. Deep dark circles and bags big enough to carry groceries settled underneath Chase's disenchanted eyes. One athletic tube sock and one black dress sock covered up his size 13 feet. Camouflaged pajama bottoms and a dirty white t-shirt adorned the rest of his body.

With his appetite all but gone, Chase survived on Christmas cookies, water, and an occasional hot dog. Nothing on television would help Chase to escape from the constant re-run of the 'Camara and Squeeze Porno Show' in his mind. Imagination and jealousy were the wicked step-sisters that refused to abandon their campaign of fear and resentment. They were in complete and total control of Chase's brain.

Was he better than me? Bigger than me? But why would she let him? I can't believe she would do that! I wish it wasn't true. I wish to God it wasn't true. I could just see him sweating all over my girl. But if she fucked him then she was never my girl in the first place.

She just never was. Maybe Squeeze was lying? But why would he lie on his dick? I want to believe her. But I can't be nobody's sucker for love ass clown. I don't know. I know he can't lay it down better than me. Maybe-

"Chase! Dude, I'm starting to get worried about you. First of all, if you don't get out of this bed and take a freaking shower right now, I'm go to the RA. You fucking reek. Come on man! Snap out of it. Nobody had sex with your girl. You should know her better than that," Brad pleaded with Chase. Brad's frustrations were beginning to boil over upon seeing Chase and witnessing his zoned out response to his tirade. "You're starting to look like a crackhead man. Why don't you just go and talk to her?"

Brad still could not tell whether Chase fully heard and understood what he was saying or not. Faint grunts and murmurs were the only reply he got.

"Listen, dude, I'm 99.9 percent sure Camara wouldn't sleep with Squeeze. As long as I've been around her she has never come across to me as that type. But Chase I'm telling you now if you don't snap out of whatever it is you're going through and get your girl back you are going to push her right into someone else's arms, maybe even Squeeze," Brad said.

"Whatever man. I don't have a girl. You got one right? Why don't you go there and be with her? Mind your business, man," Chase said as he rolled over on his bed turning his back to Brad.

The coldblooded retort wounded Brad. This was not his good friend and roommate of almost three years. Whoever was lying in Chase's bed was unrecognizable to him. He wanted to help but after Chase's response, Brad knew it was useless. Chase's heart and mental state seemed inoperable.

"You know what dude I'm going to do just that. Best of fucking luck," Brad said while slamming the door behind him.

This did little to jar Chase into a more reasoned line of thought. He simply dug in deeper. Jumping from Camara to Squeeze to their activities afterward, Chase's mind was on trampoline mode for the next four hours.

■

BOOM BOOM BOOM. The hard knocks barely registered to Chase. Between the blaring television, boom box blasting EPMD's 'Rap is Out of Control', and his own twisting thoughts Chase simply thought it was a part of the sonic wallpaper. Ignoring everything, Chase delved back into his downhearted stupor.

One by one the sounds inside of the room began to get noticeably quieter. The newswoman reporting about another murder in the Rochester area suddenly went mum. Erick Sermon's flow was cut short. Then the twirling thoughts inside the mind of Chase Douglass amazingly stopped. His dulled focus started to sharpen as he realized he was not in his room alone anymore.

"Mr. Douglass, how are you this evening sir?"

Immediately Chase recognized the familiar deep baritone voice of Professor King. Turning around and sitting up on his bed Chase answered, "I've been better."

"That is absolutely correct sir," Professor King said as he took an old gray McNair University sweatshirt and a pair of jeans off of the chair closest to the door and sat down.

"Why are you here?" asked Chase in an annoyed manner.

"I received a phone call from Mr. Dance. Apparently, for almost two weeks you have been missing from your classes. Mr. Dance asked me to find you and remind you that you have a fiduciary responsibility to him and everyone who gave their life for you to have the privilege to be here. But even more important than that, you owe yourself. A missed class here and there is expected but two straight weeks? You know Mr. Dance has ways of finding out this information. So if you are sick I'd be glad to point you in the direction of the campus clinic. If it is something else then I'd be delighted to listen and help. That's my primary function…to help you graduate. I promised you, Mr. Dance, and myself that I would do just that so help me God," Professor King said.

Chase stared blankly into the distance then turned right back around to face the wall. Professor King felt insulted by the apathetic response. Probing the way to best combat a potentially one-sided and uncomfortable conversation Professor King remained silent.

Then surprisingly Chase responded, "What kind of answer you want from me? Not that you or anyone else deserves one. I'm going through something personal right now. When I'm all the way through it I'll either be in class or back home in the Roc. It isn't yours or Mr. Dance's business whatever I chose to do."

"So you're contemplating absconding from this educational institute?" Professor King asked.

"Talk English man, damn! What the hell does 'absconding from this educational institute' even mean? How you gonna say you from the Hanover Projects and talk the way you do. You always try to sound smarter than what you are. Or you try to make me feel dumb by using all of these big words that I don't know and my major is English. Who are you trying to convince that you're smart? These crackers, or yourself? Don't front on me homeboy nobody's here but me and you," Chase said as he got up from his bed and stood near the door.

The piercing critique hit Professor King hard. His first thought was, *Does he have a point?* He had hoped that this was not the impression that he left on his students. Not knowing if this was a well thought out opinion Chase harbored all this time or if it was an off the cuff remark designed to push him away, Professor King folded his fingers together and closed his eyes to simmer his reaction.

"Mr. Douglass, I will not be confined to your or anyone else's narrow parameters on how I should look, talk, be or achieve simply based on where I was born and raised. I have the right to grow…and so do you."

Ignoring Professor King's response Chase instead piggybacked off of his own last statement. "You feel like an Uncle Tom inside sometimes don't you, Professor? All confused and shit. I bet when those Big Wigs at the office talk that shit to you, you take it like a good house nigga! *'I don't want no problems I just wanna keep my job.'* Big, black, ugly ass dude like you talking whiter than a picket fence…shit, I'm confused now. I bet you didn't talk like that when your fat ass was eating Twinkies in the Projects, huh?"

Professor King smiled faintly. Knowing Chase was venting, he simply took it in stride in hopes that once all of his venom was ejected, he would be able to charm him into being reasonable.

After he realized Professor King was not going to answer such a question Chase kept going. "You know who you remind me of Professor? You remind me of a faggot in the men's restroom. I mean he is supposed to be there…but on the other hand, he ain't supposed to be there. Know what I mean, homeboy? You don't know where the fuck you supposed to be."

Now it was Chase who was smiling. He knew the acid-laced quip hurt Professor King. Sensing victory he went in for the kill shot, "You need to go get some pussy. How a grown ass man gonna go years without getting some ass? I'm not with that gay shit man. You better pay for some pussy or something. Either that or you might end up eating dick like Dr. Fellner."

The escalation of tension was something that Professor King wanted no part of. Chase was swinging for the fences in order to provoke him to leave him alone. Instead, Professor King remained seated and said, "Adrenalin junkie overdoses on a college campus film at eleven. Mr. Douglass, you are wise beyond your years. You must be psychic to know that you could say what you just said to Professor King…and not to Black Archie. You see because had you been loud talking Black Archie in the disrespectful manner you just did, he would have picked your light ass up and shook you, literally. Had you said what you just said to Black when Black was in jail—and especially since you want to dabble in that comparing him to a homosexual stuff—you'd be washing your mouth out right now and I am not talking about with soap. But since you are talking to a grown fully realized man that went from Lil Archie to Big Archie, to Black Archie, to Black, to Archibald, to Dr. Archibald Moses King II, to Professor King you are indeed wise, sir. I'm going to let those insults ease on down the road. But make no mistake I am not the Cowardly Lion nor am I, Dorothy. I am the tornado that blew her ass to Oz in the first place."

"Are you threatening me?!" Chase yelled as he stood up over Professor King.

"No son. I am helping you. That's all I want to do. Now if I had to make an educated guess as to the root of your hostile yet indifferent stance, I would dare venture to say that it would involve a woman, to be more specific, your woman Ms. Truth. Am I correct, sir?" Professor King asked plainly.

"Ms. Truth is a goddamn whore! She is not my woman no more. She's Squeeze's problem now, not mine," Chase said as he looked in the direction of the door.

Professor King was happy to be able to take the focus off of him and get to the spotlight on the real issue which was his deteriorating relationship with Camara. Not coincidentally he remembered that Camara was absent from their weekly meetings as well. He asked almost sarcastically, "You allowed another man to take your woman away from you?"

Chase quickly looked at Professor King while involuntarily moving towards him and yelled "I didn't allow shit! She was never mine, to begin with. Come on man, how you gonna fuck the nigga you know I can't stand and then lie about it straight to my face? She had my dumb ass believing that she didn't do it. But I heard it straight from the horse's mouth that he fucked her," Chase said despondently.

Sensing that he might have a small chance to appeal to Chase's intellect Professor King asked, "And you believed him just like that? You would summarily dismiss a woman who you have known intimately, a woman who has never shown you anything but love, devotion, and respect, a woman who has always for as long as you have known her had your best interest at heart? This gentleman must have presented to you some pretty damning evidence linking her to her guilt."

Chase wanted so bad to cry. The cutting pain of Camara's alleged indiscretion seemed to bleed all over his grubby white t-shirt and seep into his heart. Not wanting to appear unmanly Chase turned his head to gather himself and then said, "He told me they boned! Plus she told me herself that she kissed him at the Kappa party. She couldn't lie about that because my boys saw her do it. I don't have to be Columbo or Matlock to solve that case. So don't talk to me about respect."

"I'd be lying to you if I was to say that I'm familiar with the particulars of you and Ms. Truth's dispute. But knowing how deeply she feels about you, I seriously doubt that she did what you are accusing her of doing. Perhaps you are feeling this strongly about her supposed infidelity because you know that you yourself have been with other women during your relationship. You know as an absolute statement of fact that you had extra-relationship sex with other women. You are projecting your own feelings of anger, betrayal, and guilt onto her. You are simultaneously selfish while screaming for help," said Professor King.

Feeling attacked Chase's heart began to physically hurt. The temperature in the room felt hotter. His breath was shortened and his stomach began to feel as if made out of dust bubbles.

"First of all, that was a while ago when we weren't as close as I thought we were. Second, I don't need your help. I listened to your great advice before and look where it got me. I should've boned Brandi when I had the chance. At least we'd be even now," Chase said.

Professor King recalled how he mistreated the love of his life and how she paid for it with her life. Wanting to honor her memory he chose celibacy as a way to never forget her. The development of Chase Douglass was also a way to never forget her. Professor King wanted so badly to impart his knowledge to Chase so he would not make the same machismo-minded errors he did. He considered Camara to be of the highest of quality which made his mission all the more important.

"So she gets no benefit of the doubt? Does she not deserve the chance to at least explain her side? What in her past would lead you to believe that she is capable of doing what you have nailed her to the cross for doing? Did you consider the source, Mr. Douglass? Did you think that the gentleman in question could...I don't know...could be telling an untruth to get you to break up with her so he can come in and play shoulder to cry on? He does not have your best interest at heart. At the very least you should listen to what your lady has to say. Give your lady a chance to explain herself and her actions," said Professor King standing up.

"What Lady? She ain't my lady. A hoe is as a hoe does!" Chase yelled as he stepped out of the room into the suite bumping Professor King.

"Mr. Douglass, please do not disrespect Ms. Truth in my presence. That's the second time you called her out of her name. She's entitled to—"

"Why, you fucking her too? Oh! That's why she got those good ass grades. Figures!" Chase said dismissively.

"Mr. Douglass, I'm telling you!" Professor King said loudly.

"You telling me what?" asked Chase daringly. Chase had a plan if things got out of control. He would use his speed to maneuver behind the large professor and use his own weight to bring him down and place him in a choke hold. Then, if necessary, he would choke him out. He felt his plan was foolproof.

Professor King calmed himself as best he could. This was unfamiliar territory for him as a college professor. "I think it is best that I leave before things get out-"

"Man, fuck you and that bitch!" Chase screamed as he stepped aggressively to Professor King.

Instincts took over Professor King's left leg and right fist as he stepped forward and connected with brutal accuracy on the bottom of Chase's chin, knocking him from the suite back into his room. Chase was sleep before he hit the floor. Professor King methodically walked into the room and stood over a snoring Chase. "If you ever question my morals or call another black queen a bitch in front of me I will dismantle you. Now sleep tight. When you wake up I'm quite sure you will thank me for knocking some sense into you."

Chase was vacationing in dreamland with Camara flying across the enchanted city holding hands during the flight. *Blissful peace with the woman I love...it can't get any better than this.* As for Chase's idea for getting the physical one-up on Professor King, the great boxing philosopher Mike Tyson was spot on when he said, 'Everyone has a plan...until they get punched in the face'.

37 February 14, 1992

Waking up abruptly out of an unremembered nightmarish dream, Camara thought her heart was literally on fire. The usually reassuring pink comforter with silver and brown teddy bears on it was clammy and bristling. The warm cozy temperature in her dorm room did nothing but mock her cold sweating body. All around her in the bed were a litany of items including folders, pencils, her purse, her blue backpack, three teddy bears, notebooks, and textbooks ranging from Statistics and Intermediate Microeconomics to Principles of Marketing.

Even though she could not make up her mind as to whether or not she was cold or hot Camara was certain she was thirsty. Sitting up to stretch Camara was surprised to see what she had slept in, a black bra and jeans from yesterday. Not believing that she could sleep but thankful for the few hours that she did get, Camara tossed the items on her bed to the floor and went to the bathroom. She retrieved a bottle of water from her tiny refrigerator as the clock flipped to 7:15 a.m. She had just enough time to shower and make it to her 8:00 a.m. macroeconomics course.

Camara walked back into her room to disrobe and to grab some toiletries for her shower. Upon entering her room she could not help but hear and see an idyllically sleeping Rhonda who snored like she did not have a care in the world. She loved Rhonda dearly and would not have traded her friendship with her for the world. In Camara's eyes people like Rhonda were rare and very hard to come by. Rhonda was always warm, open, and honest with Camara. Their friendship was built on genuine love and respect for each other instead of heavy platitudes.

However, looking at her friend peacefully snoozing, Camara got somewhat angry. She knew Rhonda's intentions were of the purest order when she informed her about Chase and Brandy. Nevertheless part of her secretly wished that she had decided back then to not be such a great friend. If she had not said anything to her about their naughty but ultimately fruitless walk she thought *maybe I would not be feeling all twisted up inside*. She fought through bouts of slight and silent resentment towards Rhonda the last couple of weeks. Guilt was always the end result.

Camara left her dorm and walked to class in a semi-fog. Sitting in her normal seat in the front of the classroom she mechanically took out her various scholarly accoutrements. Camara's focus oscillated from economic indicators and the causes of short-term fluctuations in the economy to why Chase would not answer her calls and what level of violence should she unleash upon Squeeze when and if she came in contact with him. Every time she thought about her love life the bottom of her stomach felt like chewed bubble gum. This was a feeling that she was dead set against getting used to, subsequently vowing to concentrate more intensely on her course load.

After attending all of her class lectures Camara raced to Harrison Dining Hall for an all-you-can-eat lunch buffet. Her appetite remained healthy despite her turbulent emotions. She chose baked tilapia with bacon, tomato and tumbleweed and three glasses of fruit punch to wash it down. Walking out into the dining room she immediately noticed how everyone eating was not only with someone but also having a great time. The circle of true friends that Camara kept outside of Rhonda was small and most of them were connected to Chase in someway. Rhonda had no classes on Friday and was planning on going home to Buffalo by mid-afternoon. Camara wished she could have dined with her best friend today to fend off that lonely feeling that was creeping her way.

Walking through the curled table isles while witnessing the laughter, frivolity, and merriment associated with a college cafeteria, Camara began to feel awkwardly old for some reason. She wanted and needed to be a part of a click or motley crew to help wash her mind of her heart's troubles. Hoping she would recognize someone that she could dine with Camara walked around the dining hall almost two times. By the time she settled for eating alone at a two-seat table in the middle of the dining hall, Camara's baked tilapia was lukewarm.

Each time she cut into her food she felt as if she was being ridiculed for eating alone. The overwhelming sense of being watched by everyone raised her panic level. Self-consciousness invaded her psyche and pushed reason to the curb. Camara felt sorry for herself and stupid for eating alone. She could also feel the sympathies from other students pouring her way. *How could it come to this?* She thought. Too embarrassed to finish, she left her half eaten cichlid fish on the table.

Needing to getaway and escape mentally Camara thought the perfect place to go was the library to stay on top of her studies. The refreshing calm and steadying solitude that most libraries offer made it a preferred destination growing up. The Drake Library at McNair University was no different. Friendly students and staff greeted her kindly, seated behind a long dark blue desk to her left. Ahead of Camara stood a large green carpeted staircase, leading to literally thousands of books that dealt with hundreds of thousands of topics. Large files of meticulously kept records were buried in black file cabinets that measured from one end of the library to the other.

Camara chose the stairs and galloped to the second floor. She sat down at a desk and took out her books she intended to read. Before delving into her work Camara always took a brisk walk around the inside of the library. Walking ignited her thinking. Under any other normal circumstances, her walk would have gladly propelled her into any academic world of her choosing. Camara had the rare ability to focus for hours on end on almost any task. Her mental acuity landed her nearly straight A's through not only high school but through her first three years of college.

This time walking only helped to muddle her mind. Seeing couples snugly studying together made her heart yearn for the time when her and her beloved Chase did the same thing. She took pride in helping Chase raise his grade point average from a 1.25 to a 3.0. Suggesting and giving him books to read for pleasure by authors like Dean Koontz and Thomas Harris helped Chase's writing dramatically.

However now, Chase was nowhere to be found. Stopping herself from sliding any further into the memory abyss that is Chase, Camara shook it off and walked back to her desk. While she was able to get into her book *Economics: Principles, Problems, and Policies* by Stanley L. Brue somewhat, Camara could not fully leave her very real world. The combination of a lack of sleep and a brutal reading regiment began to physically hurt Camara's eyes. They felt dried out and strained thus giving her a headache. *I'm not getting anything done today. Let me take my ass home.* Putting on her coat and making sure she had everything that she brought with her, Camara went back to her dorm room.

While walking home Camara wished Rhonda decided to stay at school for the weekend. Knowing the chances of that were slim to none did not stop her from planning things that they could do together to make it a fun weekend. For a while, her imagination took over and an anticipatory smile made its way onto her frosty face. By the time she got to the door of her suite she could not wait to inform Rhonda of the fun that lay in front of them.

When she opened up the door Camara was greeted by no one. Rhonda had neatly cleaned up her side of the room and her luggage was gone. Camara was quietly crestfallen. Then today's date all of a sudden popped into her head. *It's Valentine's Day. Oh my God. I have never felt so totally alone in my life. Chase I miss you so much.* Camara took off her coat, sat on the floor in front of the door, and cried silently alone.

38

For the first time in almost two weeks, Chase was forced to look into the bathroom mirror. Blood soaked and strange looking eyeballs stared back at him daring him to make a move. Emaciation shanghaied his face leaving a gaunt impression. Chase's slightly swollen jawbone was covered with ingrown hair bumps and a furry checkerboard beard. The abysmal look he wore on his countenance was matched by his deplorable feelings toward McNair University, Camara, and Professor King.

While shaving himself with a butter knife and Magic Shaving Powder, Chase keen on revenge, began talking loudly, "That fat nigga lucky he caught me off guard. I'm weak 'cause I haven't been eating right. He's lucky I'm not a snitch or he'd be in the unemployment line right now. It's all right, though. I'm going to have a couple of my boys come pay him a visit real soon."

After carefully shaving his face Chase jumped into the shower. The hot water cascaded onto every inch of his body. He wanted the water to wash away the incident with Professor King. Chase hoped the scolding water would wipe clean the stench of soiled pledges and purify him from his own indiscretions. Chase scrubbed hard. It was hard for him to differentiate which was hotter when it hit his face, the hot water or the hot tears. *God, I miss you, Camara,* he quietly admitted.

Once he dried himself off, Chase walked into the suite butt-naked and sat on the loveseat. In front of him lay two distinctly different roads. One road led to Camara Truth. If he chose to drive down that road, he would be forced to work things out with her. Truthfully speaking Chase did not know whether or not Camara was lying or telling the truth when it came to her alleged infidelity with Squeeze. There was something in his heart that made him fear an all-out open discussion to clear things up. To follow the road that led to Camara also meant that he had to clear things up with not only the professors of the classes that he had missed but Professor King as well.

The other road stretched back to the mean and uncertain streets of Rochester, New York. There was obvious comfort afforded to Chase in letting go of all of his collegiate responsibilities. Remembering to study, to read this book and that book, the writing of ten-page papers, trying not to fall asleep in class, sometimes going hungry due to the mismanaging of meal points, and stress due to exams were all aspects of life at McNair University that Chase was not fond of. The question in Chase's mind still remained *what is waiting for me if I decide to leave and go home?*

■

"Yo, did somebody just page me from this number?"

"Yeah I did about an hour ago. What up West, this is Chase."

"Chase! Oh shit what up man."

"Chillin."

"I thought you were at school?"

"I am…but I'm headed back to the Roc for the weekend. What's going on tonight?"

"Club Superior is what's going on tonight my nigga. Tomorrow night Savoy's is jumpin'!"

"I'm down. I'll be leaving here tonight. Can I crash at the spot?"

"That's cool but we ain't on Portland no more."

"Where y'all at now?"

"The Motor Lodge on South Ave. Around these parts we hit it and split…quick."

"Cool. I'll page you around 9 when I get home."

"Alight. You straight for the weekend. You might make a few bucks too. Peace."

Chase hung up the phone temporarily invigorated. The last bus leaving the school going into the city was scheduled to leave campus at 8:15 p.m. This gave a Chase a few hours to decide whether or not he was packing for the weekend or if he was packing for good. *I'll take as much stuff home as I can and decide Sunday if I'm coming back or not. That way if I chose to stay home for good I won't need to come back to this bitch ever.*

Going back and forth from his room to the suite packing up things, Chase thought he heard a faint knock at the door. Chalking it up to hallucination from improper nourishment, Chase continued packing. The knocking was louder and much more pronounced. Putting his two suitcases and his book bag in the suite closet Chase went to open up the door. Wondering who would be visiting without calling Chase was hesitant at first about opening the door. He certainly did not want round two with Black Archie. Slowly looking through the peephole he could see a female but could not quite make out exactly who it was. The one thing that he was sure of was that it was not Camara.

Feeling somewhat apathetic about who it actually was, Chase thought there was very little damage to opening the door. A twisting of the doorknob revealed Brandi wearing a waist high short black leather Shearling coat. Seductively smiling she said to Chase, "Happy lover's day, can I come in?"

Chase's pulse rate immediately rose as Brandi walked into the suite meticulously slow. Brandi walked over to the loveseat turned and smiled at Chase. Taking off her coat she revealed a tight Valentine Day red mini-skirt that came to the high middle of her thick yellow thighs. The top of the mini-skirt ended and went straight across from the top of her left bicep to the top of her right one…leaving everything above the center of her cleavage bare. Her breast needed no bra for stand up support. Brandi's rock solid nipples tried to poke a hole through the sheer outfit.

Flabbergasted, shocked, and impressed all Chase could mutter was "Brandi, what are you doing here?" as he walked up to her shaking his head.

Brandi sat down and crossed her left leg exposing even more of her thick as a tree stump thigh over her right thigh and said "I heard through the grapevine that you would be spending Valentine's Day all alone because somebody was busy being a little tramp. I came by to make sure you got your just desserts. I've been told I taste like cherries jubilee. I'll need you to verify that for me." Beneath her vixen persona, she had genuine feelings for Chase.

It was hard for Chase to get over how gorgeous Brandi looked to him. His instinct first told him to resist because he and Camara were officially still a couple. Then one by one his human wants and needs began to come back to him. Hunger resounded in his belly as well as in his loins. Chase began to feel more like Chase and then his effortless charm took over. Camara left his mind as soon as she entered it.

"Is that a fact? A taste test huh? I haven't eaten in days," Chase said as he smacked his lips.

"Well I think it's time for you to pull up a seat at the big boy table, grab you a knife and fork and dig in," Brandi said as she grabbed Chase's buttocks with both hands and pulled him close to her. She began kissing him, making him harder than Japanese science with a stuttering teacher.

Savagely returning her kiss he was lost to the moment. Chase grabbed the back of her thighs and kept going north until he reached Brandi's panty-less backside lifting up her mini-skirt. Chase squeezed Brandi's soft backside like he was kneading dough. He picked her up causing Brandi's legs to latch on to his waist.

Walking while still kissing her, Chase carried Brandi into his room by memory. He kicked the door closed behind him. Brandi's eyes were sensuously closed ready for the incoming penetration. Ever since she put eyes on Chase, Brandi dreamed about having sex with him. At first, it was purely out of spite for Camara who for some unexplainable reason she despised. As time went on she wanted to sleep with him because Chase turned her on pure and simple.

The loneliness, the hunger, the stress, the moment, the attraction, the pain, and the curiosity all wove together to make Brandi simply irresistible. Stopping only to go get a condom out of his desk drawer, Chase was fired up and went for broke. For the thirty minutes that he was inside of Brandi, Chase's problems ceased to exist.

Once the lovers reached the finish line, Chase pulled out of Brandi exhausted and overwhelmed. *What did I just do?* Chase stood up and looked at Brandi who was still recovering. Brandi's legs were shaking involuntarily as she put her thumb in her mouth and rolled over on her side to sleep. Reaching down to pull up his pants that were still down by his ankles, Chase was overcome with a sudden feeling of nausea. Making his way to the bathroom commode, he dropped to his knees and violently vomited.

Feelings of regret and guilt flooded Chase's heart as all he could think of was *I just cheated on Camara.* Chase had enough of McNair University and the whole being in a relationship thing. Flight was the only option that he felt was available to him. Thanking God that he had his entire luggage already packed and in the suite closet, Chase decided to make a run for it. Tears welled up in his eyes because he knew this was the last time he was going to see the inside of a dorm for a long time. His friends Hugh, Sean, Cassie, and most of all Brad surged in his mind.

Once he put on his coat and gloves Chase was about to leave the dorm room when the image of Mr. Fizzy flashed before his third eye. Chase looked towards the door and very quietly crept back into his room so he would not alert a relaxing Brandi. Lying flat down on top of his desk was Mr. Fizzy. Chase grabbed him by the neck and left the room, quietly closing the door behind him.

When Chase took a good look at Mr. Fizzy all he could ask was, *How did we get here? We were so in love and happy. I am completely lost and ashamed of myself.*

Reaching the exit to the dorm Chase turned to his left and saw the courtesy phone. *I have to call her one last time.* Chase nervously plucked Camara's number.

With each unanswered ring, Chase's guilt level vaulted. By the twelfth ring, Chase was beside himself. *I need to hear her voice one last time!* He fidgeted with the faux metal cord attached to the telephone receiver in the hopes that it would help the telephone in Camara's room to ring loud enough for her to hear it.

"Hello," said Camara groggy from a desperately needed nap. Whoever was on the other end was silent in their response. After a few more seconds Camara said hello again, this time in a clearer throated voice. "Whoever this is I'm about to hang up. I hope you got your jollies off for the nigh—"

"Camara."

Camara's heart nearly stopped when she heard her favorite familiar baritone voice. She knew of no one else who could speak her name and instantaneously stimulating her. For the last two weeks, he dominated her thoughts. It scared her how much she adored him. When the plug on their relationship was pulled disconnecting their blended circuitry a good portion of Camara's spark for life ended with it. Hearing Chase's voice electrified her.

"Chase! Baby oh my God! Listen, baby, I swear I never had sex with Squeeze. The only thing we did was kiss and that's because I was mad at you, got drunk and didn't realize what I was doing. I am so sorry for doing that to you! He got my phone number from Ginger the Jamaican chick I tutor. I found that out because she told me he needed a good tutor and he asked for me by name. She didn't know about all the drama. I called you so many times but you wouldn't pick up the phone or come to the phone when Brad answered. I just knew you were going to call me or just come by but you didn't. I got scared. I thought you were done with me so I was scared to call you back again. Baby, I just want to move on. I have never been so miserable in my life. We can put this behind us. I miss you so fucking much. I can't wait to see you," Camara said without so much of taking a breath. The weight of what Camara had been holding seemed to lighten with each word she spoke into the telephone.

Chase began to cry. The full gravity of his conquest with Brandi yanked him down exponentially. Until he met Camara women were the solely viewed by him as a carnival. They were designed for all kinds of fun. Pleasurable experiences from one ride to the next ride. To Chase each ride was different and that is what made it so fun. When the ride was over it was just that, over and on to the next one. Having a favorite attraction or ride was dangerous. That ride could be closed for repairs. It could stall halfway and breakdown, killing certain passengers. Or worst of all to Chase that ride could have more fun entertaining other patrons while refusing to let him on.

Camara was altogether different. Camara was the ride that God engineered specifically for Chase's mind, flesh, heart, and soul. He also realized that it was not about just his fulfillment. Chase had an obligation to Camara's feelings as well as being all he could be for her as well. The path to Chase's manhood goes through Camara Truth.

"Why are you crying, Chase?"

"Camara, I know now you didn't sleep with Squeeze. I feel stupid that I thought you actually did. But sweetie, I'm not right. This whole experience is simply too much for me right now. I'm not right. I know I need help," Chase said fighting through tears.

"Chase, baby, what do you mean you need help? I'm all you need! I love you! You're scaring me. What do you think you need help with?" Camara asked.

"Me. I'm not right. I have to leave school. I will come back to school and I will come back to you I promise you that. But I have to go. I am so sorry. Camara, I love you more than I love me. You are the light at the end of my tunnel." Chase hung up the phone, picked up his two suitcases and left for the bus stop.

Camara was beyond devastated. *Chase just left me. He just ups and leaves school? How? Why?* For the rest of that Valentine's night, such questions would not stop harassing her.

39   February 23, 1992

Sometimes before he went to bed, Professor King would read to help him unwind. Lately, more often than not a good read was becoming essential to a good night's sleep. The Sandman on this night came in the form of Chancellor William's book *The Destruction of Black Civilization* which was sprawled flat across Professor King's fully clothed chest. Sleep had been very hard to come by in the wake of his physical confrontation with Chase. He awoke with the book that brought him to sleep and paged through it before fully emerging from the bed. He ate his usual big breakfast of grits, scrambled eggs, three link sausages, four strips of bacon, and a stack of buttermilk pancakes alone at his kitchen table built for two

For obvious reasons Professor King was nervous. If Chase had decided to go to any of his higher-ups or even worse file a police report against him, Professor King would cease being Professor King. In fact, his well-deserved moniker could be replaced by some hand stitched numbers in a prison uniform. He simply lost control and felt horrible about the whole situation.

The life he was living as a respected up-and-coming professor at a mid-level college was one of the best things to happen to him. His innate intelligence served him well whether he was debating a theory with the president of the college or if he was relating a point to a freshman student. Challenging himself to critically thinking about the underlying themes and messages delivered by the great African-American authors of our times was a luxurious rapture to Professor King. It took his mind to places where it was prohibited to think about other things. Things that if he pondered on too long could drive him insane.

The tiny but efficient two-bedroom apartment Professor King had been residing in for almost three years was beginning to feel confining and lonely to him. The sparsely decorated bedroom consisted of a queen size bed, a black dresser drawer, brown throw rug, and a lone nightstand complete with a lamp. The other bedroom was a carbon copy of the other. It came in handy as a guest bedroom whenever one of his sisters decided to visit. Professor

King's living room boasted a maroon sofa, black leather Lazy Boy recliner set, and rust colored twisted cage floor lamp. There were no televisions in his apartment.

Always good with money, he could have easily bought a house if he chose to. However, he was not one to waste space or invest under uncertainty. The only justification for upgrading to a house was a family. Professor King knew he had to have a special lady in his life for that to happen and the last thing he was interested in was muddying up his life with the fickle and unpredictable nature of finding, keeping, and maintaining love.

On the last Sunday of every month for the last several years, Professor King had a Sunday dinner date with Alvin Dance and his family which consisted of Alvin's wife Nicole and their five daughters. Professor King and Alvin had become fast friends ever since their days at Morehouse College where they were roommates. Alvin was a native of Harlem, New York and never thought that he become lifelong best friends with someone from Upstate.

The stark physical differences between the two friends were easy to document. At 5'11, Alvin was slim with a caramel complexion, curly hair, and hazel green eyes. Archibald was tall, husky, and dark skinned, with rugged facial features. However, both men shared an almost endless supply of charisma underwritten by their formidable intelligence. This fact meant that the women of nearby Spellman College did not stand a chance against their charm. The two bold underclassmen would routinely one up each other with wild and unabridged stories of their sexual conquests. This was indeed the fact until senior Alvin Dance met freshman Nicole Miles. Alvin found something that day greater than all of his lewd encounters combined. Nicole stopped his dalliances cold turkey.

Archibald's liaisons would also stop right before he finished graduate school. After a wild campus party, Archibald took to his room a very willing young lady. The next morning his name was sullied. The drama infatuated young woman gave Archibald a proposal. Either be her man or she would go to campus police and file a complaint of sexual battery against him. Choosing the later almost put Archibald in the nuthouse not to mention the 'big house'.

Between sleepless nights and worried days Archibald was petrified that he would lose everything that he had worked so hard to finally become. This was when he began to re-question his rash and impetuous use of his sexuality. After his beloved Sandra's suicide Archibald mourned for a few months and then began to bury his pain inside of as many agreeable women as possible.

Building functional relationships or investing his emotional currency within any of his sex partners was a complete impossibility.

With both Alvin and Nicole's tireless intervention and help, they were able to convince the young woman to recant her allegations and not go through with filing a complaint against Archibald two days before he had to orally defend his dissertation. This cemented his bond with the couple for life. Once he was given the title of Dr. Archibald Moses King II, he gave up sex as a sacrifice to God thanking him for providing a new perspective on respecting women and himself.

■

Archibald thought he was driving inside of a freshly shaken snow globe. Although the Christmas season was over, Wellington Street in the Nineteenth Ward section of Rochester was picturesque and postcard as they come, especially with huge wet fresh snowflakes as the backdrop. The neighborhood was home to many solidly middle-class African-Americans including the Dances.

The light tan and white trimmed colonial styled house was almost camouflaged by the snow. Making his way carefully from his Honda Accord through the semi-crunchy snow Archibald finally reached the top of the front porch. Instead of ringing the doorbell like he would normally do, Archibald instead decided to look through the window.

Archibald saw Alvin and Nicole playing what appeared to be some sort of board game with their five daughters. The girls ranged in age from 3 to nine. Upon further inspection, they were playing twister and having a laugh fest. Alvin tried to contort his body so that his hands and feet were touching the red and yellow circles. Alvin failed miserably falling flat on his bottom touching off a chorus of giggles and belly-deep laughs that would have made any comedian proud.

Watching this beautiful family in action made Archibald proud to be a part of it in the manner in which he was. He was a treasured honorary brother to both Alvin and Nicole and a beloved uncle to their children. Archibald adored The Dance Family with all of his soul. However, there was deep inside of him a twinge of envy. Because of the path that Archibald took in life he sincerely felt that he would never know the exquisite comfort of being able to come home to a woman who loved and respected him to the highest order. *To know the distinguished pride of going half on a brand new innocent soul and then to wholeheartedly accept the awesome responsibility of molding and guiding that new person into the best person that they could possibly be was a dream that was going to have to be realized in another life,* Archibald quietly lamented. *I would love to be somebody's husband* was the refrain that played inside of his head more often than he would have liked to admit. Making his way from the window to the door Archibald rang the doorbell.

"Ooh, Daddy, can I answer the door? I know what to say and everything. Who is it please...before I open the door," said Alvin's snaggle-toothed, six-year-old daughter as she stuck her tongue out at her older sister.

"Ok, little lady, we are going to try you out as our official door answerer for a trial period only. If you can handle that then we may have something bigger and better in store for you. Go ahead sweetheart and get the door," Alvin said as he readjusted his baby blue button up shirt and gray slacks.

The new doorman ran to the door and screamed at the top of her lungs "Who is it please may I help you!"

"Yes, you can, sugar. It's Uncle Archibald."

Archibald's booming voice was loud enough for the rest of the younger Dance Clan to hear as they rushed the door. Before Archibald could take off his galoshes and tan trench-coat he was swarmed by Alvin's and Nicole's offspring's with kisses and hugs.

"Hi, Uncle Archie! Where you been?" asked the youngest girl.

The question warmed Archibald's heart like few others did. His love for his nieces was pure and unrestricted. To keep from tearing up Archibald laughed hard and then answered "I've been at school, my love. How have you been? How's work? How is your husband and kids?"

The youngest daughter frowned as she turned to one of her sisters and asked "What Uncle say? I'm a kid I don't have any kids!"

"You funny, Uncle Archibald. She's too young to have a job or a husband," said another of the little ladies with a huge smile on her face.

"Better have your shotguns ready, Al," Archibald said as he was finally able to put his coat on the rack.

"I don't have my gun license for nothing. How are you, my brother?" Alvin asked as he and Archibald hugged.

"Not bad. You're looking good."

"You say that as if you expected something different, big boy. My wife wouldn't have it any other way," Alvin said.

"Don't pay him any mind. How are you, Hun?" asked Nicole as she came up and gave Archibald a big warm hug. Archibald returned the favor and kissed her on her cheek.

Nicole had a complexion similar to a cozy cup of hot chocolate. Her sincere smile illuminated an ever so slight gap between her white teeth. Senegalese-twisted locks that fell just below her shoulders appeared perfectly kept. She stood five-foot-six, petite but had a backside that sprung forth like an Irish rainbow.

"I'm fine, Nick. You know I don't pay Al no mind. How have you been?" asked Archibald.

"Good! My clients are driving me crazy at work, though. I'm going to need my own psychologist when I retire. If I could tell you what these rich white folks consider problems…anyway dinner is almost done, honey. Sit down and relax," Nicole said as she went back into the kitchen to check on the food.

"So what's on the menu, Nick? Whatever it is its smelling awful good," said Archibald as he rubbed his hands together like an evil scientist explaining his master plan.

"Black eyed peas, greens, macaroni and cheese, potato salad, beef ribs, cornbread, and banana pudding for dessert. How does that sound?" Nicole asked.

"It sounds like to me my future wife is in a world of trouble if she can't cook like my mama or you. My only question is how did you wind up with this knucklehead?" Archibald asked as he pointed to Alvin with a grin.

"I ask myself that all the time. One of these days I'll get an answer. Y'all relax we got about a half hour before everything is done."

Archibald loved the snug and welcoming feel of the Dance's home. With the brown carpeted staircase in the middle of the home the dining room and living room stood on the left and right side of it respectively. The cinnamon wooden archway greeted you into the living room. Scores of beautifully framed family portraits stood up on the coffee table begging to be admired. The biggest one was placed above the red-brick fireplace with all seven members of the Dance family.

In the middle of the living room was a three piece burnt pecan sectional sofa. The left arm sofa, armless loveseat and right arm chaise, all upholstered in a premium soft microfiber were conjoined to form a shape similar to the letter 'U'. Before the two men could sit on the sofa various toys, missing board game pieces, Ebony magazines, and a basketball had to be removed first.

Of course as soon as they sat down all of the children came pouring in and around their father and uncle. "Ladies, ladies please give Uncle Archibald a break ok. I promise you all will have time to play with him before he leaves. I have to talk to Uncle Archibald about icky man stuff. I know mommy needs some help with the food all right? Thank you, ladies," said Alvin in his soft but firm fatherly voice.

"Okay, Daddy. Bye, Uncle Archie. See you later!" was said in various ways by the young ladies as they exited the living room.

"I love your girls like they were my own Al. You and Nick are doing a fabulous job raising them to be young ladies. I congratulate you early on a job well done," Archibald said respectfully.

"I'm only doing what I am supposed to be doing as a man, father, and husband. And those girls are yours too Uncle Archie. I firmly believe in the mantra it takes a village to raise a child. If they can't get it from me for whatever reason but they get it from you because of whatever reason then I'm a happy dad. I just want them to get it from a person who loves them and will always have their best interest at heart…and that is you, my brother," Alvin said reassuringly.

"I gladly accept the responsibility."

"Cool. Now, what's this with you hitting Chase?"

Archibald took a deep breath and shook his head. Shame overtook his emotions. If he could go back in time he never would have gone over to Chase's room in the first place. However what was done is done and the only thing that he was doing now was regretting his actions ever since.

"If I could take it back I would Al. I simply lost control and knocked his dick in the dirt. I mean it's not like I hate him or anything remotely close to that. In all honesty, I actually grew to genuinely love Chase like a son. I see so much of myself in him it's scary. He is so smart and gifted. But he also is troubled and has plenty of demons…I just sense it. I'm scared for him," Archibald said as he looked out the window.

Archibald was on a first name basis with his demons. Even though he felt he had gotten over most of his troubles the most dangerous demons were the ones that hide deep inside your closet, the ones that you are afraid to admit exist at all.

"We all have our Demons, Archie. Luckily God gave us something made specifically for eradicating demons, angels. My angel is in the kitchen. From what I know about Chase he has trouble sticking his dick in as many halos as he can find. Maybe one day he will find the one angel God sent to him," Al said.

"That's just it, Al. He has a girlfriend. She is highly intelligent, sweet, gorgeous, and she is head over heels in love with him. I know that she is the best thing to ever happen to him. But because she came to him so early in his life he is too ignorant to realize it," Archibald said passionately.

"Oh yeah, that girl named Camara, right? We all had lunch at G&G's Steakout this past summer. I didn't realize they were still together. I concur totally with your assessment of the young lady. She was quite impressive, so I can definitely understand where you are coming from in wanting the absolute best for your students in and out of class. However and I must be honest with you Arch, it appears as if you are internalizing Chase's problems and making them your own."

Archibald and Alvin decided a long time ago to always be as honest and as forthcoming with each other as possible. They both knew that a true brotherly bond would wither and die without it.

"Maybe you're right, man. I love them both. I just don't want him to make the same fatal mistake that I did, not only for his sake but for Camara's as well. She is a beautiful person and I don't want him to hurt her in any way. They can do all sorts of great things together. I know how it feels to mess up royally and live your life with the consequences," Archibald said as he buried his head in his massive hands.

Alvin waited for Archibald to compose himself. Once he finished Archibald stood up and took control of his emotions. Alvin embraced him hard.

"Forgive yourself. Clear your path, my beloved brother. Your angel is closer than you think," Alvin said as the two men smiled and made their way into the dining room.

40 April 19, 1992

"I thought it was supposed to get easier as time goes on, Rhonda? I feel worse and worse almost every day. I don't have an appetite, my schoolwork focus is blurry, and I cry when the wind blows," Camara confessed to her best friend via telephone as she sat on her bed in her room in Greece, New York.

Camara's spring break week consisted of helping her mother with varying degrees of house and garage spring cleaning, catching up on missed assignments, and reminiscing tears. Her now defunct relationship dominated her thoughts no matter what she did to push it out of her mind. Mama Truth sensed something was different about Camara but was hesitant to drill down to get the true and living facts. For the most part, Camara stayed glued to her telephone and the friendly voice of Rhonda.

Camara continued, "Rhonda, it feels like someone close to me has died but on purpose just so he wouldn't have to be around me. It's just not right."

"I know how you feel, girl. I can't believe how things between yall got so messed up so quickly. Again I can't apologize to you enough if I was in any way the cause of the breakup. I only told you what I would've wanted you to tell me if you saw my man walking with the next bitch," Rhonda said.

Brandi's face popped into Camara's head and rage immediately filled her heart. From the moment she first saw Brandi and her cohorts in the dorm room she knew they would never like one another.

"Speaking of bitches that bitch Brandi has been looking at me real funny lately. I don't know if she knows we broke up and now she's gloating about it or something else. But Rhonda I'm telling you if that heifer looks at me sideways one more time I'm getting thrown out of school," Camara said half-jokingly.

"That skeezer is a small thing to a giant. An elephant never wastes its time swatting at flies. But for real, girl, listen to me. I need you to know that the night of the party I made sure that you made it home safe. I locked all the doors behind me before I got up with Tim. So no, Squeeze did not come in the room and drunk fuck you or anything like that unless he got a key and broke in," Rhonda said defiantly.

"I know he didn't come in the room or anything like that. Girl, I know what it feels like after you've been fucked. I know nobody touched me that night. And Rhonda for the last time I do not blame you for anything. I know you feel bad about the breakup just like I do. I know you have my best interest at heart. But the bottom line is I feel so empty and angry inside. Why did Chase do this to us? Girl, I swear I wanna pick up that phone so bad and call him but why should I! I didn't leave him he left me. But I am so horny Rhonda. I can't lie!" Camara said they both laughed.

"I know that's right! But my gut is telling me that you two are meant to be. I don't know when but I guarantee that he will find his way back to you. But for now, we need to worry about tonight, Carpe Diem! Are you ready for your first nightclub?" Rhonda asked.

Although she had been to a number of college-related parties Camara had never been to a nightclub in the city. Mama Truth reluctantly gave her blessings even though Camara was a few short months away from becoming a full-fledged legal adult. Camara herself reluctantly agreed to go after Rhonda practically begged her.

Rhonda knew that Camara was in no way ready to meet a new man, however, she felt it was therapeutic to have men show a heartbroken woman the attention she so richly deserved. With the all black slinky miniskirt and pumps that Rhonda had picked out for Camara to wear she knew precisely that she would be receiving just that.

"I suppose so. Since you won't let me ball up in a corner and grow old and die, I'll be ready. What time are you coming to pick me up?" Camara asked.

"I'll be there around 11," Rhonda said.

"All right girl let me go and deal with my mom and her sisters for Easter Dinner. I'll be ready," Camara said before hanging up the phone.

As hard as she tried to drum up the requisite excitement about attending a nightclub for the first time Camara's anticipation was tepid at best. *I miss my baby* she thought over and over again as she stared at her bedroom telephone. *I just need to hear his voice. Whatever it is we can get through it. This is the longest time since we've known each other that we haven't heard each other voices. Why is he doing this to me?*

Camara picked up the phone and dialed six digits of Chase's phone number angrily ready to give him a piece of her mind for destroying their precious relationship. *But what if he really doesn't want me anymore? What if he has another girlfriend already?* The last question she posed to herself was enough for her to not pluck the seventh digit. Blistering tears singed her chocolate face almost melting it. It took her almost an hour to put out the cold fire.

■

The line from the main entrance of Carpe Diem stretched onto Court Street. The muffled thumps and melodies taunted the anxious groups of party seekers. Well-dressed twenty-something Hip Hop culture loving patrons were excited about getting a chance to party with the legendary DJ B-Swift at the hottest club in Rochester.

Knowing that after midnight getting into Carpe Diem was a virtual impossibility, Camara and Rhonda were in line by 11:20 p.m. and fifteen minutes later they were about to enter the club.

An Italian man dressed in a brown suit with a black button-up dress shirt stood at the entrance and yelled for all standing in line to hear, "Ladies and gentlemen please have your IDs out so that the line can move faster. Benefit cards or McCrory's picture booth IDs will not be accepted. Only a New York State license or college ID will be accepted. No sneakers. Gentlemen, no hats or hoodies. Ladies to the right and gentlemen to the left."

Camara was surprised at how militaristic the process of having a good time was. What also raised her eyebrow was people's nonchalant acceptance to being frisked, told what they can and cannot wear or where to go.

After Camara raised her arms to the side and spun herself around to be inspected and wanded by security for weapons she heard *ID please* by a stocky built white man who could have easily been an off-duty policeman.

"Sure," Camara said as she nervously fished through her tiny black purse and took out her New York State identification card.

After suspicious back and forth looks between the ID and Camara the bouncer with a reluctant nod granted her entrance into the club. She walked in slowly and was immediately greeted by a throng of fluctuating bodies matching the rhythms of Joe Public's song 'Live and Learn'. The festive feeling of profligacy permeated Carpe Diem. Neon green, yellow, and purple lights pooled with stage and marijuana smoke to color the atmosphere carnal. Camara was overwhelmed but loved the feeling.

"This is not the student ballroom that's for damn sure," Camara said as she grabbed Rhonda's arm and surveyed the huge square shaped room that held five hundred plus easily. Karl Kani and Cross Colour cladded young men could not take their eyes off of Camara as she walked through the thick crowd. Some dared to attempt to touch her backside but to no avail. Rhonda yelled "Don't even try it! My daddy, brother, and uncle are all security guards! Touch her ass or mine you will get dealt with!"

Camara went from being mildly embarrassed to actually reveling in the attention that she was getting from the males. A Tribe Called Quest's classic collaboration with Leaders of the New School 'Scenario' overtook the club as the crowd went crazy rapping along in semi-unison.

"Here girl, try this," Rhonda said as she handed Camara an electric neon blue colored drink.

Immediately Camara remembered the last time she consumed alcohol and the results were nothing short of disastrous. Then she realized that she was in a relationship then but now she was free to do whatever she wanted with whomever she chose. "At least tell me what it is you're trying to poison me with this time, Rhonda, before you do it," Camara asked loudly.

"It's called a Motherfucka!" Rhonda yelled over the music.

"It's called a what?" Camara screamed back.

"A Motherfucka!"

"That's the name of the drink? And you're actually giving me, your best friend, this to drink?"

"Yup! Drink and enjoy. You can only have one, though. It's got like seven or eight different liquors in it. I got your back. Enjoy your spotlight!" Rhonda said as she backed it up on a willing male dancer.

"What the hell?" Camara said as she sipped the bright blue drink through two tiny red straws. The combination of bitter, sweet, sour, and salty danced politely on her tongue. Camara was feeling the music so it did not take long for the drink to have its desired effect. *Motherfucka!*

For the first time, ever Camara's beauty felt different to her. Whenever she would look at a man provocatively, his whole façade would change from hardcore to smiling and shy little boy in mere seconds. Once she started dancing slowly and giving in to the rhythm of the music she could feel the hungry eyes feasting on her. Although she was famished herself Camara realized the power in feeding and loved it.

After dancing with the fourth different guy Camara was ready to sit down to stop the club from spinning. She stopped at the bar, put her empty drink on the counter-top and requested some bottle water. She sat at the far-east end of the club next to a window overlooking the Genesee River and the multitude of boulders that filled it. The cold water helped to balance her.

Right before Camara had most of her bearings and was ready to attack the dance floor once again she thought she recognized a very familiar male face. Focusing to overcome the influence of the foul-mouthed drink, Camara stood up and walked closer to the man to get a better look at who she thought it could be.

Camara stopped halfway when indeed she realized who it was talking to a young woman. It was none other than her first boyfriend Harold who dropped about 30 pounds along with the thick glasses. Wow. Harold didn't look half bad Camara thought as she confidently strutted her way over to him.

41 April 30, 1992

Boredom and quiet resignation glazed the face of Chase Douglass. Sitting alone on the worn out off-brown sofa in the dank tiny den of his grandparent's house, Chase pressed the buttons on the remote control passively. He flipped through the six available channels going between the coverage of the Los Angeles riots and The Video Jukebox Network. Anquette's 'I Will Always Be There for You' did its melodious best to keep Chase's mood non-committal.

With nothing but time on his hands since Leaving McNair University, this was where Chase spent the bulk of his time. He wanted to record more music but two factors stood in his way of that goal. The first was the fact that his rapping partner and best friend Will was still attending school. The other reason was a severe lack of funds.

Although he tried to never admit it because he wanted to be strong, secretly he missed Camara more than he missed anyone in his life. He was seriously considering giving her a call if only to say hello. Every morning as soon as he awoke his mind would flashback to one beautiful memory of Camara after another. To say that he was second-guessing his decision to leave school was a gross understatement. Besides Brad, Sean, and Hugh, Chase even missed the knockout master, Professor King.

Day in and day out Chase followed pretty much the same routine: waking up around 11 a.m., watching television until 3 or 4, eating what his grandparents cooked, and then hanging with a few neighborhood friends until he got tired. His grandparents for some odd reason did not force Chase to seek employment or make him go back to school. On the other hand, he knew neither of them would ever put money in his hand. All they would provide Chase was a roof over his head, a bed to rest his head, and at least one meal per day. Once a week he would go job hunting with no profitable results.

Feeling the pinch of hunger, Chase fished his pockets and caught $6.50, just enough to provide his favorite meal, a steak and cheese submarine sandwich, cheddar and sour cream potato chips, and a Canada Dry ginger ale. Pat's Store on the corner store on South Ave and Alexander Street was the best place in the South Wedge to get a cheap but tasty meal. Chase also thought a walk up the street could help to break up the monotony of his day.

He walked into the cozy corner store he knew like the back of his hand and was greeted warmly by the store's middle-aged Hippie owner Pat Breedlove. Wearing his tie-dye shirt with a white apron over it Pat extended his hand warmly from behind the counter and said, "Chase is in the place. How goes it, brother?"

"I'm ok, Mr. Breedlove. How are you?" Chase asked politely.

"Hey, man, everything is peace. So let me guess, you'll be having the usual today? A medium steak and cheese sub with extra mayo, tomatoes, Swiss cheese, fried onions, and Boss Sauce? Is that correct?" Mr. Breedlove asked kindly.

"You know me well, Mr. Breedlove," Chase said.

"Chase, I've watched you come into this store since you were five. Your grandparents were among my very first customers. Good people. Hey, a little blue birdie flew into the store and informed me you're not in school anymore. Is that true?" asked Mr. Breedlove.

"It's just a blip on the screen, for now, Mr. Breedlove. I'll be back in the fall," Chase said trying his best to convince both Mr. Breedlove and himself.

"Whatever you do, Chase, please go back to school. When some folks leave school they get use to life without it and they never go back. But until then, I can always use some help around here. You got a job with me until the last weekend in August. I can only give you minimum wage and no more than about thirty hours a week. I'd have to pay you under the table as well. If you're interested you can start Monday."

Chase wanted and needed money especially for the upcoming summer. Mr. Breedlove was a trusted family friend and respected neighborhood fixture. He thought *what the hell? Why not? I need some money for the studio anyway.* "What time do I start?"

"I open by 8:00 a.m. Come in at 7:00 a.m. to help me open up the store and you will be outta here by noon. Stock shelves, sweep up and help me run the cash register and lotto machine. That's pretty much it. It won't take long for me to teach you and get the hang of it. So we have a deal?" Mr. Breedlove asked.

"Yes we do," Chase said enthusiastically. "As a sort of signing bonus, how about my sub, chips, and drink on the house?"

"You drive a hard bargain, Chase. Agreed! Rodney, please take care of this gentleman's order," Mr. Breedlove said as he handed the slip to another employee working alongside him.

Chase thanked Mr. Breedlove and walked outside to wait for his food. To his left, he heard a deep bass filled boom emanating from a maroon and tan custom painted Mitsubishi Montero driving down South Avenue about three blocks away. The low-end bass from 'The Bridge is Over' by Boogie Down Productions was played so loudly in the sports utility vehicle that the words were completely drowned out.

As the truck came closer to the store the slower it went stopping directly in front of Chase. The darkly tinted windows dropped down to reveal the driver. "Whatup, pimpin'?" West asked smiling hard showcasing his gold and diamond encrusted teeth.

"West? Damn playboy, I haven't seen you in a couple of months. You don't even answer a nigga pages no more. I was gonna ask what's up with you but I see what's up with you. You got the Cuban Link, dookie rope, and the gold wonder woman bracelet on. Business must be good!" Chase said as he hopped into the passenger side of the truck.

"Business is great, my nigga! I'm actually looking to expand and maybe you can help me," West said as he turned down the music.

Chase had been paid by West to be the lookout on occasions but he never sold drugs for him or anybody else for that matter. For some reason, he was always against it and could not see himself as a drug dealer. But now he wanted money for the studio. Chase figured to do three songs which included a $100 per beat fee and studio time at $40 per hour could cost him around $1000. He also had to add about $300 for some quality black and white glossy pictures and a nicely typed biography for a fully completed press kit.

Although he had a legal job offer in hand Chase thought it would take him nearly all summer long to come up with that amount of money working for $4.25 an hour minus his minimal living expenses. Knowing that Will's upcoming summer job money was used to help his family, Chase had to foot the entire bill if their Hip Hop dream was going to come true. If it did not come true by the end of the summer, he promised himself that he would re-enroll back at McNair University.

"I don't know if I could sell drugs man. I mean don't get me wrong I'm not holier than thou or no shit like that. I'm not judging the way no man makes his money especially you. I mean we grew up together we're family. I done been around it and I know how it works. It's just that I'm not sure if it will work for me. Selling that poison to our own people, I don't know if I can do it dog. It takes a certain mentality to be able to do that shit day in and day out and be all right with it. You know what I'm sayin'?" Chase said trying his best to not sound melodramatic.

West put his vehicle in park, turned off the ignition, and looked Chase dead in the eye and said, "You know the difference between you and me? You would stay in your grandmother's attic for the rest of your life and be happy with that. I, on the other hand, would front my Nana some dope sacks until the third when she gets her SSI check. We both would be waiting on the mailman. But if she was to front and not pay me my money, I'd knock her clean the fuck out! I'm talking dentures, wig, and bifocals—all over the floor. I'm about money and pussy, in that order, plain and simple. Fuck everything else."

Chase was floored by the transformation of his once jovial friend. West always loved money but he also loved to have fun. Since returning home Chase had heard from mutual friends about how West was slowly becoming monstrous in the dope game. Chase was seeing for himself that there was more than just a little truth to the whispers on the street.

"If all you care about is money and pussy, I know you don't give a damn about me 'cause I don't have neither one," Chase said half-jokingly hoping to illicit a positive response.

"Nah man. You got to understand this. I'm about you because you can help get me money. Money gets me things like this truck and these jewels. This truck and these jewels gets me pussy. So as long as you getting me along with yourself, of course, that money…You ain't gotta worry about nothing or nobody fucking with you," West said as he opened up the glove compartment showing a second generation all black Glock 17 pistol.

"That's cool. So tell me the details man. Where will I be, who will be with me, and how much money I'm gonna make?" Chase asked.

"I keep the math simple. I give you 100 sacks at $10 dollars apiece. 100 times ten is a thousand dollars. You get two dollars off of every sack sold I get the other eight. So at the end of your shift, I gotta have $800. Not $798, not $799, I need $800 or for the sacks to add up to $800 with the money you got in hand. Take no shorts. Are we peace on that point?"

"I got it. Straight money no shorts no credit. But a hundred sacks seems like it will take all week to get rid of. I'm not gonna risk jail or my life for $200 a week. Mr. Breedlove just offered me a job for that kind of money. Shit, I might as well take that job," Chase said rhetorically.

West looked at Chase and smiled. He rubbed his face and said, "Nigga, do you think I'm driving around in this truck making $800 a week? I got two spots, one on Parcels and Chamberlin and one right down the street at the Downtown Motor Lodge. I move anywhere from 200 to 400 sacks apiece from both spots on a slow day. Now take a day like tomorrow. It's the first and the first happens to fall on a Friday too. I can make up to 20 g's cash on that day alone! Oh, and I almost forgot to mention another fringe benefit to this job—all the pussy your dick can handle."

Frantically Chase tried to do the math in his head on how much of that could actually land in his pockets. Then he thought about all the sex he could have. Surprisingly enough his episode with Brandi riddled him with enough guilt that he had not engaged in any sexual activity since he returned. He did not want to appear as if he was shocked by the dollar amounts or the promises of bottomless cups of coffee-colored women so Chase quickly asked another couple of questions.

"How many days a week do your spots stay open? How long each day?"

"Nigga, 24-7! Crackheads don't sleep. But, I never count the next nigga's pockets so you figure out how long you want to work. I got three dudes working at my Parcels and Chamberlin gate. They all do eight-hour shifts. I had three at the Motor Lodge but I had to fire two clowns for fucking my money up. Needless to say I damn near broke 'em in half but that's beside the point. I got two shifts open. You can have one or both of them, the early morning shift from 6:00 a.m. to 2 p.m. or the late night shift from 10:00 p.m. to 6:00 a.m. The choice is yours," West answered.

Throughout Chase's life money was never the focal point. Sex was the driving force behind his passions until he met Camara. Always having just enough to function and live, Chase never thought or fantasized about the things that he could do with lots of money at his disposal. Now these thoughts rushed through his mind at Mach speed. *The possibilities…*

Before Chase could say anything else Mr. Breedlove came outside with his steak submarine in hand. "Oh, there you go, Chase. Here's your sub. So we'll be seeing you first thing Monday morning right?"

"Let me think about it, Mr. Breedlove," Chase said compassionately. West knew Chase well enough to know that he was not going to work at the corner store anytime soon. So before Mr. Breedlove could try one more pitch, West turned on the truck and pulled off. It was time to show Chase some more spoils of his drug dealing success.

42 May 1, 1992

The Downtown Motor Lodge once stood as the proud gateway into the historic South Wedge neighborhood in Rochester New York. The neighborhood was even once home to famous African-American abolitionist Frederick Douglass. Firmly anchoring the corners of South Avenue and Byron Street, the two story 105 unit motel wormed its way around a two and a half acre plot. The predominantly concrete tan structure with splashes of arctic orange and black welcomed drivers heading into the South Wedge from either Downtown or from the Inner Loop expressway. The rooms were small and cozy but clean and inexpensive. This fact, coupled with its central location, made it a popular stay for both city residents and out of town travelers alike in the 1970's and early 80's. When the crack cocaine epidemic hit Rochester, New York around 1986, the Downtown Motor Lodge and its clientele changed right along with it.

A young enterprising man from the nearby Gateway Projects named Antoine 'West' Cotton sat in a movie theater in early March of 1991 and was mesmerized and inspired by the movie *New Jack City*. West envisioned the Downtown Motor Lodge as a mini-version of the fictional 'Carter' apartments immortalized by its infamous takeover by Nino Brown and his CMB crew. Although it was on a much smaller scale, West was indeed building a drug empire by moving almost a kilogram of cocaine a week from the Downtown Motor Lodge alone.

West bagged up a quarter kilo of crack in dime bags and further separated those into thousand dollar portions. He was locked, loaded and ready for the first of the month. Looking at his cream-colored Motorola pager the time read 11:42 p.m. which meant he had eighteen minutes to make the first call for crackheads.

Feeling invincible as he drove from the east side to the south side of town blasting 'Deep Cover' his new favorite song by Dr. Dre and Snoop Doggy Dog, West cruised into the motel's parking lot and double-parked arrogantly.

To his right pushing, a dingy yellow maid's cart was Mary Carter the head maid. She was a white woman with feathered blonde hair in her early to mid-forties but looked somewhere north of sixty due to stints that ranged from a street walker and waitress to a mindless alcoholic. Now hopelessly and happily addicted to the highs and lows of crack cocaine she found the motel to be a perfect place of employment. Upon seeing the familiar Montero, Mary stopped mid push and galloped to the truck.

Rolling down his tinted windows West asked "Yo, Mary, what's up? How many new lodgers did we book for an overnight stay?"

"Hey. We got plenty. You got something on ya? All I need is a blast and off I go. You know me," Mary said smiling hard doing a little two-step dance.

"I got you. Listen, go and book room 201, 202, 203, 208, and 211. We're moving everything through 202. I'll be parked out back. Bring me the room keys and any info I need. You got five minutes," West said as he turned his vehicle on and went around to the back of the motel.

Besides being the head maid at the Downtown Motor Lodge she was also chief informer to West. She would alert him to the residents who smoked crack and those who did not. Mary was personable and relatively loyal. The fact that she was a functional crack cocaine addict made her pure gold to West. She would also find out through the manager—who himself sniffed cocaine ninety going north—how the patrons paid for their rooms. In return for her information, Mary was allotted up to three free dime bags a day.

West had been doing his research and due diligence on the hotel. Instinctively he knew the customers of the Downtown Motor Lodge were the most important aspect of the whole operation. They could get a cheap room for $19.95 a night and do their dirty deeds all night long. This was tailor made for prostitutes who could trick with their johns and then turn around and literally buy crack next door. West would often target the prostitutes and pay for their rooms and in turn, they would bring him business all night long.

When he began moving product out of the motel it was important to West to know how they paid for the room. If the Department of Social Services paid for a person's room then they were pretty much safe to serve to. Credit card customers were generally low risk as well. In West's best estimation it was a bit too much for the police to go through credit card companies and establish legally fake identities to then bust local small time motel drug dealers. When they would go to that extent it would usually involve the kingpins who moved real weight not grams and ounces. Customers who paid with a credit card, for the most part, had well-paying or steady jobs and just wanted to get away for the weekend. Those customers, as a rule, would spend a thousand dollars before they realized it, but would never be a minute late for work Monday morning.

The riskiest customer to sell to was the customer who paid cash. Police liked to use cash when they engaged in undercover sting operations. West made Mary peddle the crack to customers who paid cash. She would then arrange for them to go to the smoking room where they were observed unknowingly by West through cleverly drilled peepholes. Then West would have them smoke the crack in front of him. Once they were initiated they were gladly welcomed inside the club and prescreened to use cash going forward.

West quickly spotted two very familiar cars in the parking lot with their headlights on, a white 1992 Chevy Corsica and a 1990 fire engine red Ford Mustang GT 5.0. Out of the Corsica stepped Man-lips and Pharell. Bo Mack and Chase exited the Mustang shortly thereafter. All were reporting to work for West in some capacity. Running from around the corner, Mary had all five keys in hand.

"Here you go, hun! How soon before I can come up and get a taste?" Mary asked almost out of breath.

"Be easy yo. You see me and the crew just getting here. Call 203 in twenty minutes. We'll be set up by then. I'll pay the bill tomorrow morning. Come on fellas," West said as he grabbed a huge Nike gym bag and began walking up the concrete stairwell to the second floor. Once inside room 203 West unzipped the gym bag and took out a bottle of Wesson cooking oil, baby oil, a jar of Vaseline, a silver six quart covered stock pot, a chrome metal electric hot plate and $20,000 in crack wrapped in plastic bags and towels.

Bo who was dark-skinned and built like a weightlifter stood by the balcony sliding door next to a slightly uncomfortable Chase. Man-lips, tall and lean sat on one of the room's two beds. Pharell who was short and pudgy stood close to West who positioned himself between the exit door and the bathroom. Once everybody settled in, West began his speech.

"Fellas listen up. Man-lips, you got the back. Pharell, you park in the front of the motel and make sure you got a wide view of the whole joint. If you see some stick-up kids headed up to the room, page Bo. Same shit for you, Man-lips. Follow anybody that don't look like a geeker. Keep your Glock loaded and on cock. The code for a potential 211 is 840. Bo, you and Chase grab the street sweeper as soon as you see 840 in your pager. Man-lips and Pharell, if it's Five-O then page Bo the code number 666. Bo if you see 666, burn up all the dope in the sauce. Put the guns in the drop ceiling and haul ass to 201. That's a clean room."

Chase who was never good with numbers began to worry if he could remember everything when the time came. Math 112 was probably easier than this. Chase knew there were certain inherent dangers involved in selling drugs but now it was clear to him that he was taking penitentiary chances or worse.

West continued, "Pharell start mixing the sauce now and put it on the hot plate so that shit will be good and hot. I want Chase to be the one serving the fiends. I need my smartest nigga on point. Chase they will call the room next door, 202. That's where you will be. If somebody just knocks on the door, don't answer that shit. The customers have to call the room first. Don't ask them what they want over the phone. Don't let them tell you what they want over the phone either. That's conspiracy, twenty-five years."

Chase thought *You get more time for talking about selling drugs than the actual selling! That's really weird.*

"So, West, how do you know who is good to sell too? Or what can they say over the phone so that I know they're cool?"

"All they have to say is one of three things to you for you to know they're cool. One, can I bum a cigarette from you? Two, I'm drinking, you want a shot? And three, can I come watch the game with you. Saying yes to any of those questions means were on and we got it. Saying no means we are empty—temporarily out. Once they get to the room they will tell you exactly what they want. You close the door and go get it from room 203. They wait outside until you get them what they need. Once you got the product open up the door, let them in and close the door. Sell them the shit and send them on their merry fucking way."

I'm actually going to be a certified drug dealer. Am I up and ready for all this shit? What if I get popped? What if I go to jail? These thoughts bombarded Chase but were not enough to make him walk away for the thousands that waited for him. He shifted his focus back to West.

"Use the balconies because they're connected. Bo will be back and forth between 202 and 203. It's a hole we drilled between the balconies that's big enough for Bo to pass you this tennis ball. Inside the tennis ball will be how many bags they want. Just tell Bo. The dope in 203 will be stashed inside the bathroom mirror. Remember don't take no shorts. I don't give a fuck if a motherfucker bought a hundred bags. No discounts, nothing free."

Chase was surprised that no one had any questions or objections to anything West was saying. The militaristic way in which he now spoke stood in stark contrast to his once laid back persona. Chase was also amazed at the brainpower, ingenuity, and guts it took to build this all night and all day, money generating monster from scratch. West's business acumen was off the charts.

"Any shorts are coming out of your pay. If you're hungry call me. I'll make sure somebody bring some grub to you. But whatever the food cost comes out of your pay too. Don't leave the room at the same time. Somebody needs to be here at all times. No missed money. 211 is the chill room—get your freak on if you want. 208 and 201 are the sleep rooms. It's Friday the first so I'm giving you four g-packages, two apiece. If you run out, text me using the code 911 and I'll be on my way with reinforcements." Like a good general, West stayed around long enough to handle any questions and check the morale of his troops. He then traded fist pumps with the crew before slamming the door behind him on his way out.

Not two minutes had gone by when the phone rang for the first order. Looking at Bo for approval, Chase tautly picked up the phone and mouthed hello in his best impression of an adolescent boy trying to convince himself he's hit puberty.

"Yeah hello this is Jim in 118. Can I bum a cigarette off one of you?"

Chase again looked at Bo for an answer that he would not give.

"Yea sure." Chase walked to door gingerly not really knowing what to expect. After what seemed like an eternity a knock came from behind the door. Quickly Chase looked through the peephole to see who it was. The fish-eyed view showed an older white man in a blue baseball cap of some unrecognizable team. To Chase's best guess this had to be Jim. Once he opened up the door, the gray stubble-bearded man waddled in. The checkered lumberjack shirt he wore did it's very best to hide his pot-sized belly. He smiled a missing-tooth-smile and took off his beat up hat which hid a folded up $50 dollar bill.

"Hey, how's it going there? You the new guy huh? I'm Jim," he said while reaching out his paw.

"C. What you need?" Chase said as he remembered to never use a real name.

"Can I get six for 50?" Jim asked in a low voice.

His voice was not low enough to escape the ears of Bo who came from the balcony sliding door to towering in front of Jim's face in mere seconds. "Ain't nobody new to this shit Jim! Slick bastard. You know ain't shit like that going down here! Give the money up and wait your hillbilly inbred ass outside before I punch a hole through your fuckin kidney!"

"Geez-us Christ, brother, calm down. It was just a question. I'll take the five for fifty no problem," Jim said as he scurried outside as fast as his waddle would allow.

Chase stood back and waited for Bo to get the five bags of crack from next door. The only other things that Chase really knew about Bo, besides the fact that he and West went to school together, was that he was from the Olean Projects and he was a hell of a power forward on the basketball court. Taking note of his size and quick temper Chase thought it would be most prudent at this juncture to follow Bo's lead.

For the next four hours straight the phone did not stop ringing. Crackhead after crackhead patronized room 202. Chase had never seen this much money in his life. He couldn't understand how the same crackhead who looked poor as dirt could keep coming back with loads of money. When they stopped for a money count break they had made close to $4,000 in four hours. Chase sat back slack-jawed in amazement.

43 May 14, 1992

"I don't give a damn what none of y'all say! White chicks are the best," Pharell said defiantly.

"A nickel-and-dime ass nigga like you would say some shit like that. I wouldn't fuck one with your dick. They smell like baloney. I bet your simple ass love them offensive line-sized hoes!" Bo said laughing and slapping hands with Chase.

Pharell, Bo, Chase, and Man-lips stood outside in the Downtown Motor Lodge's parking lot. Bo sat inside his car sipping on a full cup of E&J and coke while Chase leaned against the driver's side door. Both Pharell and Man-lips sat on the pavement smoking marijuana. The AOP Posse, as they affectionately nicknamed themselves, threw jabs at each other while they waited for West to return with a brand new batch of product. The sun and clouds played peek-a-boo with each other as the spring time warmth filled the air.

"It's all pink inside nigga. Look at that snow bunny checking in. I know she loves black dick! Look at the way she walks," Pharell said while shaking his head.

"You're attracted to that? If I ever get down with a white broad you can bet she gonna be finer than a motherfucka! But not that hoe. Man, I can smell the Chlamydia from here," Bo said laughing hard.

It would not have been a normal day at the Downtown Motor Lodge if the four young men did not insult one another or make incredible claims about their abilities in a variety of arenas. They all felt the overwhelming need to compete against each other in everything from games of Spades and basketball to money and especially woman. It was amazing how they vacillated from severe name calling and put-downs to teaming up and making thousands of dollars.

"You know why the teen pregnancy rate for white chicks is so low? 'Cause they stay sucking. Black hoes don't like to suck. So, that's the number one reason I prefer white hoes," Pharell said.

"I guess you conducted your own scientific research in a double-blind study, huh Professor Keen-Bean? No, wait you couldn't possibly do that because it would require you to be in the presence of some pussy, let alone actually getting some," Chase said sarcastically.

Chase knew Pharell for the better part of ten years but never quite liked him. To Chase, Pharell was a bit on the plastic side not to mention phony. However, he did not completely dislike him. Pharell has thick skin so Chase knew he could chide him a bit. What really surprised Chase was how quickly he bonded with Bo.

"Fuck you Chase! You just mad cause I was your new stepdaddy last night. You need to get some of the E&J or at least hit the chronic nigga! You might get some hair on ya nutsack! Frontin' like you don't drink or smoke, you was in college. That's all they do! Anyway, number two you could tell a white broad to do anything and she'll do it. You remember Sammy? Man, listen…I know for a fact he got busted in their house messing with Sara from Gateway. His white broad—umm what's her name?" asked Pharell.

"Oh you are talking about Maureen with the big ass titties," Man-Lips said.

"Yeah, Maureen. Yo, she caught the nigga Sammy with Sara in their bed! She wilded out on him and kicked him out the house. But, the next day Sam got popped on Jefferson and Bronson selling to an undercover. State my word, Maureen went downtown and bailed that nigga out! Ten grand cash! You think a black chick would do that for you?" Pharell asked.

"Hell no! And why should she? I don't want no broad that will let me just run all over her and do what the hell I want when I want. That shit will get boring after a while. I don't want a broad that don't respect herself either because she damn sure ain't gonna respect you. Your woman is a reflection of you. She represents you and what you stand for. If you get a woman with no respect for herself no matter what color she is, then that says more about you than it does her," Chase said somewhat sadly.

Damn! Where did that come from? Chase asked himself after his mini rant.

"Ok, Farrakhan X. Yo, when is West coming? I've been paging him. All we got is five dimes left," Bo exclaimed.

"You know that he with some broad. He trick off more than David Copperfield. That young chick Tammy got his nose wide open. She is sexy as fuck though I can't even front," Man-Lips said.

"Damn, I wanted to hit that," Pharell said.

"You don't like black women, remember? Yo, I'm about to pack up," Chase said as he jogged upstairs to room 203.

In the two weeks that Chase had been working for West, he was averaging about $500 dollars a day in pay for himself. He gave himself an allowance of $50 a day to blow on whatever way he deemed fit. For the most part, it was spent on food, particularly Chinese. The rest of the money he put in a brown paper bag and tucked it underneath his mattress. He had his studio time more than covered.

Quickly developing armor against his own revulsion to selling drugs, Chase adapted to the lifestyle with relative ease. At times he found it difficult to ignore the obvious havoc that prolonged drug use could visit upon the human body. Nevertheless, he pressed on in impressive fashion for a rookie, earning the respect of his crew.

Entering the room Chase was greeted at first by empty condom rappers, empty dime bags of weed, Styrofoam boxes filled with leftover soul food and empty bottles of Canada Dry and Smirnoff. Chase picked up the phone that began ringing almost as soon as he opened the door, "Hello?"

"Hello. Hey I'm drinking do you want a shot?" the sexy and distantly familiar voice asked from the other end of the phone.

"Hold on one second," Chase said as he searched for the tennis ball to see if they had any product left. He found it behind the mirror and squeezed it so that the cut that was along the seam would open and show its insides. There were four dime-bags left inside.

"Yeah, I wanna shot. Come on through," Chase said.

There was something about the voice that resonated in his subconscious. Chase was anxious to put a face to the voice to satisfy his curiosity. About two minutes later Chase heard a very soft knock on the door. When he opened it, Chase's belly immediately went into hyper-drive. Although he knew that he had come across this woman in her mid-thirties before, he could not put his fingers on where exactly.

She was tall with saggy breasts. From her stomach down she was nearly pencil thin. Chase could not decide whether she lost her thickness due to smoking crack or if she was skinny, to begin with. Smelling of stale cigarettes and musk, the woman tried her best to bat her once beautiful sleepy eyes. Her hair had seen better days. It was straightened but was all over the place like bad-ass kids in church. She wore a slightly over-sized dingy Buffalo Bill's football jersey.

"Where do I know you from? I know I know you from somewhere. Do I look familiar to you?" Chase asked.

The woman folded her hands in front of her stomach and looked at Chase hard, "I don't think so. I need five here you go." Strictly business she handed Chase two twenty dollar bills and a ten dollar bill. Continuous sniffing accompanied the constant rubbing of her nose. Her mouth would involuntarily twitch with the help of her ever moving tongue.

"I know I know you from somewhere. What side of town you from?" Chase said as he reached into his pocket and grabbed the tennis ball.

"Nigga ain't nobody got time for twenty questions. I said I don't know you, damn," the woman replied in an aggravated tone.

"What did you say to me?" Chase asked angrily. He had to stop himself from almost grabbing her by the throat.

The woman jumped defensively and quickly copped a plea. "Damn, I'm sorry! Look I get like this when I'm either horny or ready to get high. And right now I'm both!"

"Well answer my simple ass question without all that disrespect or I'm not selling your geeking ass anything. Crackheads have no goddamned patience! You turn into some ignorant, impatient bastards once you start smoking," Chase lectured and blackmailed.

The woman ran her fingers smoothly through her hair while she attempted to assess Chase's angle. Clearly nervous she slowed herself down enough to focus on Chase and his request. "Ok baby, what you wanna know? Whatever you ask me I'll tell you."

Exasperated Chase said, "All I said to you was that you look familiar to me. What side of town you from?"

"I'm from all sides of town. You name it I've lived there. Westside, Northeast, Southside...shit just all over," she said as she wiped her mouth in anticipation of satisfying her withdrawal symptoms.

The woman's hygienic practices were thoroughly out of shape so her natural body scent hit Chase he began to get sick to his stomach. Her voice was eerily familiar. "Here, I only got four."

"Ok baby. Shit momma happy now. When I feel like getting high then I feel like getting some dick. As fine as you is, I'll do you for free," the woman said as she walked up to Chase.

Chase pushed the woman away as his taste buds went sour. He darted towards the bathroom, making it just in time to vomit into the commode. *Was it her smell that made me throw-up? Was it that steak and cheese sub?* Something was fundamentally wrong with the scenario to Chase. Flight was his only way out. Once stopped vomiting he looked in the mirror and told himself loudly, "I'm Done!"

"You all right in there, baby?" The woman asked.

"You got your dope from me but you will never get anything else. Now get the fuck outta here!" Chase yelled.

"You ain't gotta tell me twice," the woman said as she exited the hotel room rather quickly.

Chase sat on the edge of the bed and looked around. He began to think about how he wound up becoming a drug dealer. Just a few short months ago he was a college student with decent grades, good friends, and a great girlfriend. Now he was selling drugs to some of the most pathetic people imaginable. Something deep down inside of Chase knew this was not the life for him. Not only did he want to go back to school but for the first time since the breakup, he admitted that he needed Camara back in his life. Chase knew he had to make a clean break from the A.O.P. Posse as soon as humanly possible.

44 May 15, 1992

"Check please," Harold asked as he sat across from Camara in a snug booth at Red Lobster. The more he looked at Camara the more he hated himself for letting her slip through his hands. Being young, overwhelmed, and immature was not an excuse that Harold was going to let himself accept. Graduating from college with a business degree a year earlier than planned, gave Harold a keen sense of achievement. This helped to bolster his confidence overall.

"Camara, relationships are easy to get into but hard to get out of, especially emotionally. My ex at school was cool but she just wouldn't let me go. I mean I could have stuck around because we both got used to things—the sex, going out, doing things together. I think I just outgrew her and the relationship. Kind of like how you outgrew ours. I understand that now but I had a hard time accepting it then," Harold admitted.

"We were kids, Harold. I did what I thought I was supposed to do instead of what was in my heart. But when I followed my heart, it wound up getting smashed. Life and love is crazy. I do truly thank you for at least being there for me," Camara said while half-smiling.

"No need to thank me, that's what friends are for. Besides, I see bigger and better things in our—I mean my future. And please don't think it's just the new job at Xerox that I'm referring to," Harold stated assertively with a frisky wink of his left eye to punctuate it.

It was hard for Camara to ignore the obvious expansion of Harold's aura. He still retained the sweet gentlemanly aspect to his character but it was now more relaxed and refined. Camara found that very appealing. Harold's gangly approach to her in the past was replaced by a smooth and understated swagger. His attire suggested he was business cool. He looked powerful in his white buttoned up shirt with French cuffs and gray slacks.

At no point during the time they were a couple had Camara been so impressed and attracted to Harold. All things being equal he was perfectly suited for her. However, the gorilla in the room was beating its proverbial chest while howling ferociously. Camara was still hurting and she was still in love with Chase. She maintained a tenacious grip on the precious moments they shared together

Simply letting go of their love was the hardest thing Camara had ever tried to do. Her brain would not allow it. The thought that truly shook her up was the possibility of having to stomach the rollercoaster ride of another relationship. Although she liked Harold and appreciated him, she was not sure as to how far she would go with him.

It was painfully clear to Camara that he wanted her back as his girlfriend. However instead of asking her constantly or putting pressure on her, Harold simply chilled and he let things happen in their own good time. Time was the great healer of all kinds and levels of pain.

Harold knew that Camara was still hurting from her breakup. So instead of putting pressure on her to be his girlfriend and claim how much different it would be this time, he chose a different path. Since their reconnection, he played the background while insisting upon being her friend. He called only on occasion and anytime they met in person he made sure it was her suggestion. The most important thing he did was to create a safe space for her to talk and then listened to her.

Harold quietly schemed on winning Camara over as he opened the car door for her. Harold drove a black 1992 BMW Three Series car which was a graduation gift from his parents. "Damn you make my car look sexy! I may not let you leave," Harold exclaimed.

"I may not want to leave," Camara said provocatively. Flirting felt good to her. Anything beyond that felt sketchy at best.

Harold wanted to savor every moment he could with Camara. Taking the scenic inner city route from the Henrietta suburb south of Rochester to the Greece suburb northwest of the city would ensure maximum opportunity. Opening up the sunroof and turning up Arrested Development's tunes added to the ambiance of the ride. 'Everyday People' the group's rendition of a Sly and the Family Stone classic track, perfectly meshed with the rhythms of Rochester, New York's residents out and about enjoying a taste of early summer.

Instead of yammering on and on, Harold was smart enough to be quiet and let the scenery do all of the talking. He sincerely enjoyed being in Camara's presence. By the time they reached Camara's house, Harold felt it was time to express his intent and feelings.

"Camara, please wait. Before you leave I'd like to say something to you if that's all right with you," Harold asked.

"Sure."

"I am honored that you have allowed me to be your friend. Whenever you need someone to talk to, I'm here. But I can't lie. I want you more than I ever did in High School and I was head over heels then. I know you're going through the aftermath of a failed relationship so it would be in nobody's interest to rush you. With that being said when you are ready to try another relationship, I want to be the one you try it with. If you would only give me the chance, I swear I would make you as happy as you have ever been," Harold said as reached over from the driver's side and kissed Camara softly on her left cheek.

"When you allow me to kiss you on your lips, then I know you're ready to give me that chance. Enjoy the rest of your day love," Harold said as he kissed her once again on the cheek. After a brief embrace, he watched her walk into the house. All that Harold could do was smile.

Harold's statement unexpectedly brightened Camara's mood. *Harold is a really nice guy. No, he's not Chase but he is more mature and has a bright future. I may just give him another chance.*

Grabbing her keys from inside of her little black purse, Camara opened up the door to a small letter sized white envelope. In big red letters, it read 'CAMARA'. "Who in the hell would slip a letter underneath my door?" she asked out loud to herself in a clearly puzzled tone of voice.

When she bent down to pick up the envelope, the sweet smell of Joop Cologne told her exactly who placed it underneath her front door. Her hands literally shook and her heart palpitated to the point of dizziness. Making sure that her mother was at work before she opened the letter, Camara called out "Mama Truth! Mother Dear, are you home?"

She ran up the stairs skipping three steps at a time. An assortment of emotions boiled inside the heart and mind of Camara Truth. Nervousness, euphoria, anger, excitement, adrenaline, and fear united to form a ragbag of feelings never felt before. Sitting on the edge of her bed she slowly opened up the envelope exposing the letter. An even stronger burst of the French cologne hit Camara's olfactory nerves, causing an explosion of fantastic memories. Immediately she started to cry. She reached for the Kleenex box and wiped her eyes with some tissue. Once she had a sufficient hold on her composure, Camara opened up the letter.

Dearest Camara,

I hope all is well in your world. To be very honest with you, all is not well in mine. I would first like to apologize to you for any and all pain that I have caused you. This was never and will never be my intent. An old-timer told me once that adversity introduces a man to himself. Hello, pain…my name is Chase.

What you need to understand is that God made you for me. I am convinced of that and nobody can convince me otherwise. What I clearly need to understand is that God also made me for you. I have not held up my end of the bargain. God would never give a woman of such genuine sophistication and regal qualities some garbage to haul around for the rest of her life. Right now Camara my life is trash and I refuse to put my rubbish in you.

My chocolate empress I humbly request some time to get myself in order. I will spare you the gruesome details of my mistakes and ask that you accept my most gracious and heartfelt apologies for crimes I committed against you. No longer will I bargain with my dysfunction. I will not negotiate with my unhappiness. I will not lose you. My goal is to be back at school by the fall. If I work hard enough I can walk the stage with you and graduate on time. Please give me until the fall to kill my demons once and for all. This must be done by me and me alone. Another wise man once told me to respect your woman even more than you love her. I hereby pledge to you that I will do just that once I am back safely in your warm and loving embrace. I need you, Camara. I want you, Camara. I love you, Camara. I respect you, Camara.

For now and forever…Chase

Chase's hand-written words flooded every part of Camara's very soul. The sincerity in the words was never in question. She took the letter and put it underneath her pillow. Each and every word was seared into her memory. So she closed her eyes and read the letter over and over again.

45 August 31, 1992

Waking up early this morning felt good to Chase. Once the shock of the 7:00 a.m. alarm clock blare wore off, he laid quiet in a state of supreme happiness. Today was the first day of the brand new semester at McNair University. After going through and completing an exhaustive amount of paperwork with the help of Alvin Dance, Chase Douglass was reinstated as a student.

With the money he earned working for West, Chase was able to put together a full press kit for his rap group, Absolute Monarchy. After sending off material to more than ten major record labels, Chase made up his mind that he was going to graduate before he signed any offers that may or may not come his way.

The rest of his money was spent on a tan 1987 Cutlass Ciera Oldsmobile which he was happily packing up for the school year. The low-level clouds, foggy mist, and light drizzle made it look like a classic black and white horror movie outside. Chase loved it when the weather was like this. The raindrops did little to dampen his enthusiastic mindset.

Once his car was packed and ready to go, Chase reached in his cassette tape holder and pulled out Mary J. Blige's 'What's the 411?' Since purchasing the tape that previous Tuesday, Chase was hooked. The driving Hip Hop beats over harmonious arrangements consistently mesmerized his musical senses. It was difficult for him to understand how a person could sing about certain aspects of pain so beautifully. The melodies from Blige vocal cords literally gave Chase goose bumps as he listened to the tape over and over again.

Since his car was missing a tape deck, Chase played the songs on his Walkman as he drove to school. 'Reminisce' by the songstress was his absolute favorite. It was apropos that every time he listened to the song it reminded him of McNair University and all of the wonderful memories he had experienced there. One person with whom he shared his most precious times with was dancing a solo on the stage inside of his mind. Camara Truth was the prima ballerina assoluta as the song consumed him.

Camara was the chief motivating force driving him back to school. All he could do was smile as he thought about her lustrous eyes. Chase was resolute about practicing monogamy within his relationship with Camara although he quietly admitted to himself that it would be a struggle.

Honesty forced him to face the fact that he was indeed obsessed with having sex with different women regardless of his relationship status. Honesty also forced him to acknowledge that sex with Camara was unlike anything he ever experienced with any woman. The main reason for that was there was so much more to their relationship beyond sex. This brought on an intensified fulfillment that was life altering. Chase was going to give fidelity his very best effort.

Camara respected the fact that Chase requested some time to get his head together and only communicated with him through a couple of handwritten letters. The anticipation of actually seeing her face-to-face after six months was hard to quell.

Should I kiss her first? Should I just hug her? Or should I hug and kiss her? Damn it's gonna be hard to not just breakdown and give her some head on the spot, Chase thought as he drove his way back to college.

Before long Chase entered the Village of Brockport, New York. Making a left onto Monroe Street, Chase cut through the southern end of campus. Some of the same images he remembered greeted his eyes once again. Because of the damp conditions, students hustled from one building to another doing their best to dodge the raindrops.

Chase drove to the back of Thompson Hall and began to unload his car which included three suitcases, a backpack, a box full of footwear, other miscellaneous items and of course Mr. Fizzy. The teddy bear had become a favorite and constant reminder of his relationship with Camara. It provided some comfort to Chase whenever those lonely feelings started to creep up.

"Mr. Douglass. May I or my colleague be of some assistance to you?"

Chase who was fidgeting with a broken box inside of his trunk quickly identified the deep and smooth voice. The last time he and Professor King were around each other it did not end well. Time did help Chase to see that he played a huge part in getting concussed. Wanting to begin anew, Chase turned around and replied "Sure, why not?"

To his surprise standing next to Professor King, under his own umbrella was a sharply dressed Mr. Dance. Although he helped Chase gain re-admittance to the school, most of his help was administered via telephone.

"What you doing here, Mr. Dance?" Chase asked while going over and shaking hands with him.

"I'm here for you, young man. My brother Professor King asked me to make sure that the next time you leave this campus, it will be with a smile and a degree in your hand. Let me grab this box for you," Mr. Dance said.

"Chase, can I have a word with you?" Professor King asked as both he and Chase walked into the foyer of Thompson Hall. They sat across from each other in a pair of standard issued lounge-area chairs as Professor King continued, "From one man to another man I'd like to apologize to you for my role in our incident. Although you did deserve a punch, it is still no excuse for my overzealous reaction."

To see Professor King exercising humility and not bombastically scolding him was a welcomed and much appreciated departure from the norm. All Chase could was respect Professor King that much more.

"Apology accepted. I was out of control too. It's nothing, water under the bridge," Chase said as he put out his hand. Somewhat surprised by Chase's response, he shook his hand and smiled heartily.

"Son, you are indeed growing. Let's get you moved back in," Professor King said as he shadowed Chase from behind to get the rest of his belongings from the car.

■

Things seemed to fall right back into place quickly. Chase was at the McNair University Student Union cafeteria sitting and cracking jokes with his three best friends from school. The only difference was now he could call them all his roommates as well. Hugh and Sean were now suitemates to Chase and Brad. Chase loved this fact because it solidified his support system, thus lessening the chances of another withdrawal from the college.

Sitting at the table long after they finished eating was a Me-Phi-Me tradition. The brotherhood of Chase, Sean, Hugh, and Brad began calling themselves the mock Greek name a year ago when they decided the Black Greek fraternities simply was not for them. They had met and became brothers organically.

"Speaking of aquariums, I'll never forget when I was six I wanted to fry our goldfish because I wanted to know what gold tasted like. So I grabbed the chair and pushed it up to the aquarium, and then I tried to dip my hands inside the bowl to get the goldfish. The fish must've known what was up because he started to dart across the aquarium swimming super-fast. I got dizzy as hell watching and trying to catch him and then I went head first into the aquarium. Then the aquarium came tumbling down," Brad said while laughing.

"Word? What else came tumbling down Sir-yap-a lot, oh great one," Sean said to Brad in an exaggerated sarcastic but very playful tone.

Hugh chimed in with "You are one yapping motherfucka, Brad. No matter what we talking about, it could be some baking soda, you got a story about it."

Picking over a few stray French fries on his tray Chase revealed in the environment. The relaxed atmosphere brought about a renewed sense of calm and belonging. Thinking back to the thousands of dollars a week he could have earned by working for West made Chase enjoy this moment with his brothers that much more. It was indeed priceless.

"Seriously, have you seen ya girl yet? I mean you two are still a couple, right?" Brad asked.

For a few moments, Chase actually forgot about Camara. He forgot about some of the bad things he did while he and Camara were officially a couple. At the mention of her name, some of those things came rushing back into his head. Chase's stomach felt it first as it dipped and dived. Although everything pointed to a full reunion for the young couple, Chase was more than a little nervous.

"I'm picking her up around six. She and Rhonda are staying in Dobson. We going out to eat and talk and get things settled. So by the end of doing all that it should be safe to call us a couple once again. I thank all you sassy hoes for your help in making that happen," Chase said jokingly.

"Fuck, you man!" Hugh said as lovingly as possible.

"Yeah I love you too. Anyway, I gotta go to the bookstore and buy these expensive ass books for class and then I'm going to the room take me a power nap and get ready for my hot date. Peace, you sassy hoes," Chase said as he went around the table and slapped five with his friends.

The McNair University Bookstore was directly underneath the Student Union cafeteria. It was predictably bustling and busy as students made their way to buy various college related supplies. When Chase got in front of the bookstore, he reached into his back pocket and pulled out his folded up schedule for the semester. Leaving his book bag by the security counter, Chase went to the English section and started to match up the numbers on his schedule with the numbers on the bookshelves.

From the corner of his eye, he recognized Brandi walking slowly his way. She was the last person he wanted to see. Hoping she did not see him Chase turned and focused even more intently on finding his books.

"That's how you doing it now, Rochester?"

Chase's heart skipped three beats or more. The fact that Brandi was still enrolled at the college honestly never crossed his mind. He pushed their episode so far back in his subconscious that seeing her again actually scared him.

"Hey, what's up, Brandi? How are you?" Chase said trying his best to remain casual and calm.

"How I'm doing? What you mean how I'm doing? Played the fuck out is how I'm doing," Brandi quipped somewhat loudly.

The damp weather did little to stop Brandi's provocative choice of clothing. A black jean jacket barely covered up the black bra she sported. A pair of tight black shorts, black fishnet stockings, and black high ankle boots completed her sexy ensemble.

Upon further review of Brandi's revealing wardrobe, which showcased her impressive six-pack abs, and calculating the months since their sexual encounter, Chase breathed a sigh of relief. *Thank God she's not pregnant.* He remembered that he left her ass-naked and leg-shivering in his room, without as much as a goodnight kiss. This was the probable source of her anger.

"Ok, first of all, please lower your voice, Brandi. I'm not into putting on free shows for people," Chase said.

"Oh, I see. You don't want word to get back to your little ex-girlfriend huh? Well, I could give two fucks about her! What about me? How you just going to leave me like that? And I haven't seen you again until just now!" Brandi asked with one hand on her hip and the other pointing directly at Chase across the narrow aisle.

"You know what, Brandi? You're right. You have every right in the world to be mad at me. I was dead ass wrong for that. I apologize. I had a lot going on personally and I had to leave. You are a beautiful woman and I should have never done you like that. Do you accept my apology?" Chase said sincerely without trying to be sexy.

Brandi was genuinely upset with Chase for months. When she woke up from the multi-orgasmic induced sleep she had no idea where he was. Thinking she would catch him early that morning back at his room she was surprised when no one answered the door. By the end of that following week, she found out that Chase left school.

Around her friends, she would put on the façade of indifference when it came to Chase. Fear of embarrassment prevented her from telling them that they had sex and he ditched her five minutes post-orgasm. So she kept the full details a secret. Plus, she liked the fact that she had something over Camara, a secret she harbored that if unleashed would blow Camara's world apart. That fact brought her a twisted sense of pride. Besides that she wanted Chase for her own so she could rub it in Camara's face that she took what she held near and dear to her heart. When she would see Camara going about her business on campus, she so badly wanted to spill the proverbial beans but she decided to wait for the right moment.

"Aight. Apology accepted. You're pardoned for now. So what you gonna do to make it up to me?" Brandi asked seductively. Before he could answer she kissed him and grabbed his crotch area.

For two seconds Chase enjoyed Brandi's touch and sweet lips. Physically the only woman he was attracted to more was Camara. "Naw," Chase said pushing her backward.

"What you mean no? No man tells me no! And anyone who I let have a taste of me always came back for seconds and thirds. You better stop trippin'. Your dick is rock hard! How you gonna tell me no?" Brandi said sounding frustrated and no longer concerned with discretion.

"Like I told you, Brandi, you're a beautiful woman and if I wasn't in love with someone else I'd never tell you no. But I can't have sex with you ever again. It was the biggest mistake in my life. I swear I don't mean to come across rude or disrespectful. What I mean is I can't hurt the woman I love anymore. If I was with you I swear I'd give you that same respect," Chase said in hopes of getting through to Brandi's reasonable side.

"So it's like that? You think you can just fuck me and leave me alone?" Brandi asked.

"I don't think it. I've done it. I swear I mean no disrespect. I just want to be faithful to my girlfriend from here on out. Is that wrong? I don't want any issues between you and me, and I damn sure don't want any issues between you and Camara. I want harmony," Chase pleaded.

"Ok Rochester, it's cool. I don't have to sweat you or any man. From here on out don't say anything to me and I won't say anything to you. But when she winds up blowing Squeeze again don't think I'll be there for you to sweat on. Bye!" Brandi said as she walked away slow and deliberate. Chase hoped that he successfully dodged a bullet on his way to bliss. *But with Brandi, you never know.*

46

"Camara! Girl if you don't hurry up! I swear you're going to be late for your own funeral. You know I have to make my doctor's appointment and be to work by three thirty. Let's get a move on girl!" Mama Truth yelled from downstairs to her beloved yet much more laid-back daughter.

"I'm just about ready, Mama Truth. Patience is a virtue," Camara said in a bouncy tone.

"And making you walk to school would be a vice. If you don't want me to wind up in Hell, then I'd suggest you get a move on. I'll be in the car," Mama Truth said.

All Camara could do was smile and shake her head as she picked up the pace. Most of her things were packed in the car already. She went one last time to the bathroom mirror to make sure she looked as gorgeous as ever. Camara was not a heavy makeup user. Instead, she used only eyeliner and lip gloss. Satisfied with her look, Camara smiled and posed seductively in the mirror. This was the happiest she had been in a longtime.

Camara celebrated the fact that she was finally a senior. She adored her mother and always appreciated her for being a little strict and overprotective. Making sure she stayed close to home for her Bachelor's Degree was the absolute best thing for her. She was close enough to home to go there whenever the need arose yet far enough away where she could develop her own sense of independence and self-assuredness.

Mama Truth always had Camara's best interest at heart and she knew this. However, Camara was ready to take that next step. Adulthood was calling her. She was ready to go to school on her own time and no one else's. Being accepted to the NYU Stern School of Business doctoral program next year was a near certainty. Her outstanding 4.0 GPA all but ensured that fact. Dr. Camara Truth had a nice ring to it she often thought.

New York City always fascinated her as well. The hustle, the lights, the smells, the food, the different assortment of races, and the electric feel to the city made her want to experience it on a daily basis. Rhonda also loved New

York City and if she too was accepted at NYU for their social work program they would tackle the big city as roommates once again.

The other reason why Camara was so happy this morning was that she was going to reunite with Chase. Trying to get him out of her system was useless. The mere thought of his rugged smile was enough to make her cake-like moist. Waves of unrelenting sexual escapades they shared together would not leave her mind. To say she was horny for Chase was an absurd understatement.

Although the sex between them was fabulous, the intimacy they shared was orgasmic. Whether she was hugged up on Chase in a roomful of people or if they shared a pure kiss alone in a room, Camara felt the securing warmth emanating from him. Her very presence healed Chase on a profound level that neither of them could articulate but both silently recognized as tangible and vital.

Chase sent a copy of his demo tape to Camara and she was blown away by it. She had high hopes that he would land a record deal from a record company based in New York City. This would mean they could continue their love affair without the barrier of unseen miles between them. Missing him terribly over the past few months only added to her growing blaze of passion for Chase.

Camara sat shotgun in her mother's brand new deep-sea blue Cadillac El Dorado sports coupe thinking pleasant thoughts. Making it to McNair University a little before 1:00 p.m. gave Camara some time to go see Professor King.

Surprisingly enough Rhonda had not made it to school yet. The last time they talked she informed Camara that she would be leaving for school after church Sunday. Without a doubt, in Camara's mind, she knew she had a dear friend for life. The good mood she was in was quickly elevating itself to greatness. Savoring the rush of endorphins, Camara sat on the bed to gather hold of the moments. Then she ran down her schedule for the day aloud.

"Go and talk to Professor King about the syllabus and my availability for tutoring this semester. Go to the library and checkout the recommended books on my reading list. Meet with my senior advisor and check out how high I rank in the class of 93. Grab something to eat, see if Rhonda made it back on campus, and last but certainly not least, call my baby. Definitely make sure we are set for our dinner date and our fantastic make-up sex session!" Camara said as she laughed hysterically.

The occasional splashed mini-puddle and side-stepping of homeless earthworms, was what Camara had to navigate her way to Professor King's office. Decked out in a white ruffled shirt, a black Santoon hippie long skirt, nearly knee-high leather boots and a thin waist high leather coat, Camara oozed class and elegance.

Professor King, who was busy writing an editorial on the Central Park Jogger trial, heard the tapping of Camara's heels and looked up. "Ms. Truth, you have graced this learning institution with your presence once again. I hope all is well," Professor King said as he stood up from his desk to reached out and shake Camara's hand.

"All is very well, Professor King, how are you."

"I am doing fine, Ms. Truth. Please sit down. So are you ready for your senior year?" Professor King asked eagerly.

"Am I! Professor King ,I swear it feels like I just walked on campus yesterday. But I have learned so much in these last three years, especially from you," Camara said warmly.

"To teach is to learn. Ms. Truth, I have learned so much from you, let alone from all of my other students over the past three years. I feel blessed. You have a remarkable future ahead of you. You know I kind of feel like a senior too. After all, I am going into my fourth year as a professor," Professor King said matter-of-factly.

"That's right. You know I never really thought of it like that. You, Chase and I are officially seniors today!" Camara said happily.

He wondered what would Camara think of him if she knew he cold-cocked Chase. That episode was still fresh in his mind. Regretful and embarrassed, he hoped that Chase did not tell Camara about the incident. From the loving and appreciative tone of her conversation, Professor King surmised their secret was safe.

Professor King was curious about the state of their relationship. The natural affinity he had for them as a couple was indisputable. He wanted them to succeed where he and Sandra had failed. Doing whatever he could to ensure their continuing relationship was something he felt obligated to do. Along with Alvin Dance, he pulled some strings to make sure Chase was re-admitted. Professor King figured there was only a slim chance that Chase would graduate with the class of 1993, but believed he would graduate eventually.

"Yes, we are! I actually saw Mr. Douglass earlier today and he looked refreshed and focused. Somebody must have given him some really good news," He said with a beatific grin.

Camara's face lit up even brighter than it previously was. Anyone with eyes could see the naturally intense love that swelled in her heart at the mere mention of his name.

"Well, Professor King, I am happy to report that starting today, we are giving it another chance. As of today, we will be officially a couple again. We both needed time to think, to reflect, and to see if we liked life without one another. To be honest with you, Professor King, I want to spend the rest of my life with Chase. I don't want anybody else. During our time apart I have had the opportunity to be with whoever I wanted to be with. But I don't want anybody but Chase. It is that pure and simple."

Once again pride and humility combined to almost bring Professor King to tears. He felt so grateful to Camara for sharing this joyful information. Before any tear could fall Professor King countered, "Ms. Truth, as your mentor it would be reckless of me to shower you and your decision with empty platitudes. I have way too much respect for you as a woman and as a scholar. I feel obliged to give you my honest assessment of what you intend to embark upon with Mr. Douglass."

Camara began to feel nervous. The respect that she had for Professor King was immense. She clearly wanted his endorsement of their relationship. This would have given her that extra jolt of confidence that she was making the right choice. However if he disapproved, Camara was still bent on finding out for herself.

Professor King continued, "My first impressions of Mr. Douglass were that he was troubled, immature, flawed, angry, and dangerously promiscuous. When I think of Mr. Douglass today, I think gifted, intelligent, caring, and he possesses a rare human quality—he is actually learning from his mistakes. Ms. Truth, you are the reason that he is growing from a boy to a man. I could not be happier for the both of you and I hope you remain together for a thousand years."

All Camara could do was hug Professor King. Taking off his glasses to wipe the few tears that fell from his strong-featured face, Professor King hugged her back and kissed her on the forehead. "Ok, Ms. Truth, you have discovered my secret, I'm a big teddy bear inside. Please keep it to yourself," he said as he smiled to hide his awkwardness.

"No can do! The world needs to know that men like you actually exist. See you next week," Camara said as she left his office soaring higher than any bald eagle dared.

47

"Hello," Chase said after running to pick the telephone.

"Don't hello me with your sexy ass! You better not have been giving my stuff away either," Camara warned in a tough yet loving and playful tone.

Chase grinned and replied "I would never do that. I like having all my teeth. Being able to chew my own food is pretty cool."

"You goddamn right! Yeah I'm from the suburbs but please, believe me, I will clean knock you out!" Camara said sounding remarkably serious.

"It's just so sexy when a woman not only takes ownership of me but threatens me with violence. Such a turn on!" Chase said in a clearly fake dramatic accent.

Both he and Camara laughed. Camara, however, was no one's dummy. Chase was sexy, handsome, intelligent, charming and women were naturally drawn to him. Realistically she knew opportunities would present themselves to him on a constant basis. So during their 'hiatus' from each other, she assumed that Chase cashed in on an offer or two.

To swallow this unthinkable pill, Camara thought of these women as nameless and faceless. On the other hand, if there was a face or an indelible image to attach Chase's infidelity to, it could prove to be calamitous. Technically they were not a couple so she also did her best to convince herself that anger was a waste of energy. *What I don't know or never find out about will never hurt me. We were not together so I can't get mad.*

Instead of speculating about Chase's possible trysts during their hiatus, Camara focused instead on her present pure lust for him.

"You are my turn on," Camara said sweetly.

"I love you, Camara. I can't see life without you. For me, it is that simple. I am now ready to be your man, not your boyfriend…your man," Chase said smoothly.

"I gotta go and take care of something, Chase," Camara said and hung up the phone without waiting for a reply.

With the dial tone suddenly ringing loud in his ear, Chase hung up the phone perplexed. He began to disrobe for a quick shower. He began as always making sure the water was as cold as possible. He then slowly turned the temperature up until it was a few degrees short of scalding. Somewhere in the middle of this process, he heard someone knocking extremely hard on the door.

He turned off the water and draped a towel around himself and went to open the door. Pulling open the door slightly, Chase tilted his head to the right to see the owner of the heavy-handed knock.

"Sorry, it took me so long to get here. I see you're ready for me," Camara said as she boldly pushed the door open.

Chase had never seen a more a beautiful woman in his life. He dropped the towel and began to kiss Camara like God himself ordained it. Exhilaration ran amuck through Camara's body. She could not take her clothes off fast enough. The narrow and confined space between the bathroom door and the closet was as far as the couple would travel. It would meet all the required dimensions necessary to execute their carnal sentence.

After extensive foreplay, Camara stared into Chase's eyes and begged to be set free. Chase administered deep punishing strokes without breaking his gaze. A trance-like euphoria slowly consumed him. It was hard for him to distinguish between what was real and what was in his mind. The one constant that he knew was real was Camara. He clung onto her for survival as primordial moans bolted from his throat. The faster he pumped the quicker she equaled it.

Camara hollered between deep breaths in a vain attempt to reason with Chase to slow down before he made her reach another orgasm. Chase forged ahead unmercifully stroking Camara with no regard for pity. The lovers soon reached providence together and melted into each other. Tears dripped from Camara's very pretty brown eyes.

■

The crisp autumn air could not cool the fire of the most memorable sexual experience of her twenty-one years of life. Her legs were both wobbly and a touch sore but they may as well been flotation devices as she moonwalked across campus. Camara could still smell Chase's sweet mix of Joop cologne, baby powder deodorant, Ivory Soap and his body sweat on her personage. The more she smelled it on her, the more she wanted to turn around for round four with Chase. *I'm not taking a shower or bath. I want to smell my baby on me all day.*

Looking at her watch and feeling the pangs coming from her stomach Camara thought better of it. She had an hour and a half to go before their 6 p.m. dinner. The first thing she had to do was to take a picture for a new college identification card. She lost the previous one during a wild night partying with Rhonda in Buffalo last month. *I have never been happier in my life! This is the perfect time to take this picture. My after-sex glow will be frozen in time forever. God, I love that man!*

After receiving her new identification card Camara headed over to Off the Tracks to grab her favorite beverage, a bottle of Orangina. This was her favorite places on campus because it was where she and Chase decided to become a couple. The bells and whistles of the various video games and pinball machines filled the decent sized but very cozy eatery. Camara resisted the smells of the Buffalo chicken wings, hot submarine sandwiches, and pizza and stuck to her original plan.

There were a number of students there both sitting down dining and in line waiting for their orders to be taken. With about four people ahead of her Camara leisurely walked up and pulled out a five dollar bill from her purse. Without actually turning around to look behind her, Camara could feel someone staring at her. Being a very attractive young woman she was use to this. However, this felt different. Her space was being invaded as she sensed someone was standing very close behind her.

"Umm, excuse me? I think we need to have a talk."

Camara did not have to turn around to know who was talking to her. The distinctive pseudo-Brooklyn, New York accent and throaty voice told her it was none other than Brandi Tubman. Having only seen her in passing since she found out about the dirty dance and subsequent walk home with Chase, Camara had to first calm down before she responded. She could hear Mama Truth's voice saying to her, 'Always remain a lady, especially when dealing with those who are not'.

Still feeling relatively calm Camara smiled and said "Sure. But I have no idea why we would need to talk about anything."

"Oh trust me. We need to talk. I'm not one to put my business in the streets like that so if you don't mind can we go to the ladies room?" Brandi said smartly.

"After you," Camara said as she followed Brandi into the ladies restroom.

The closer they got to the bathroom the more Camara began to feel uneasy. *What does this tramp want to talk to me about? We barely spoke when we were suitemates. She lucky I don't go upside her head! This can't be good.*

Once both young ladies were inside the bathroom in front of the middle stall Brandi said dismissively, "Look, I'mma need you to tell your man to stop bothering me. I don't want him. That's your man. I don't want to mess with him like that anymore."

She could not comprehend how Brandi wound up interrupting her day, a day that was supposed to be exclusively hers and Chase's. The day that started out so beautifully for Camara was starting to feel tainted and oddly surreal. The seriousness of what Brandi was actually saying hit Camara hard.

"Hold on…what did you just say?" Camara asked as her stomach muscles began to clench.

"I said to tell ya man to please stop bothering me. I saw him this morning at the bookstore and he was all on my bra strap begging me to let him taste it again. I asked if he was still with you and he said y'all was getting back together soon but in the meantime, he still wanted to fuck me at least one more time. I told him that's foul and he is a foul ass nigga for trying to play me like that," Brandi said again in a louder more aggressive voice.

For Camara, everything after 'begging me to let him taste it again' was a sonic blur. Involuntarily her head began to shake no back and forth. Her temples pounded. The muscles in her face stretched to register disbelief.

Clearly dumbfounded, Camara asked, "What are you saying, Brandi? Are you saying that you had sex with Chase?"

"Yeah, we fucked majorly," Brandi said quickly.

"What!" Camara screamed.

"What? Bitch, are you hard of hearing? I said I fucked your man! As a matter of fact, we been fuckin' on and off since y'all been together. Why you think I moved out and stopped being your suitemate? I didn't want to have to whoop nobody ass over no man no matter how good the dick is. And it is good," Brandi said with a snicker.

Camara whole body felt like it was caught up in a tornado. The eye of the storm was staring at her and dared her to blink first. Panic stricken she incredulously pointed out, "You're lying! I know your lying. Chase would never play me like that. I don't know why you doing this but I'm getting ready to go before this gets ugly."

"I never lied on my pussy and I ain't about to start now. You don't believe your man tasted this? Ok, check it! In his room, he got a poster of EPMD over his bed. He had some sort of teddy bear on his dresser, and the nigga is packing heat!" Brandi testified.

Brandi knew by grossly exaggerating the number of times that she had sex with Chase it would be that much more humiliating to Camara. To embarrass her pleasured Brandi to no end. That the lies that she was telling were based in truth made it extremely difficult for Chase to refute.

This was fast becoming a horrific nightmare for Camara. Dazed and traumatized, she found it nearly impossible to speak. Nevertheless with tears falling she summoned the strength to ask, "How could he do this to me?"

Ready to unleash the coup de grace Brandi asked "Do you want to know the real reason he left school? He got me pregnant. I told him I was keeping the baby and he left like a coward. The only reason he is back because I had an abortion. Still, don't believe me? Here."

Brandi reached into her purse and pulled out a yellow medical form. Camara was too shaken to read it. Anger and resentment began to seep its way into Camara. *How could I have been so stupid? I swear before God I will never let anyone hurt me like this again. I'll be damned if him and this skank don't pay for this!*

"So lemme get this straight. You have the gall to call me outa my name, embarrass me, curse at me, talk down to me, tell me that not only did you fuck my man but you were fucking him on and off the whole time we were together? And on top of all that you tell me, he actually got you pregnant? Thank your lucky stars I'm a lady. I swear I'm mad as hell, but I'm not even gonna fight you," Camara lied as she took three steps towards the door.

With a huge smile on her face, Brandi began to do just the same until Camara's overhand right hook knocked her into the bathroom stall. Luckily for Brandi, her head hit the toilet paper spool. Camara jumped on her and punched her repeatedly knocking out Brandi's front tooth. This felt therapeutic to Camara. Brandi tried her best to get Camara off of her by counterpunching but to no avail. Camara stood up and grabbed a screaming Brandi by the back of the neck and pushed her head face first into the commode.

"Bitch, I've wanted to whoop your fake, New York City ass ever since I laid eyes on you! Thank you for giving me the reason. You obviously had too many teeth in your mouth. I had to remove some for you, slut!" Camara said as she pulled Brandi up from the toilet water and slammed her head against the wall as hard as she could.

Camara straightened herself up as best she could and walked out of the bathroom. Exhausted from the lack of oxygen, Brandi crawled out of the stall and nearly passed out underneath the bathroom sink.

Camara left Off the Tracks with one thing on her mind…finding her soon to be ex-boyfriend. *Wait until I find that cheating motherfucker Chase! He is going to wish I never existed!*

48

"Damn dude! You're sleeping in the middle of the day? Wake your lazy ass up!" Brad said as he walked into the suite to see Chase half naked sprawled out on the sofa snoring.

"Oh shit! Damn, what time is it?" Chase said yawning.

"Almost 5:30. Don't you and Camara have a date or something like that tonight?"

"Yup sure do. She just left here…I'm not sure how long ago, but why you think I was sleeping like a baby? Man, that girl got the best punany God ever made! She is the only one that can knock me out," Chase proclaimed as he stood up and walked into the bedroom.

"Dude I hear you. The wonderful powers of a good woman will never cease to amaze me. I'm glad you came to your senses, dude. Camara is a good girl," Brad said sitting down on the couch.

"You're right, she's a great girl. I mean I always knew she was great from the first time I saw her, I just had to go through my own bullshit to see just how great. I don't know man, it's like a light switch came on and I can see. You, the rest of the fellas, and Professor King really told me some things that made me look at women in a totally different way. I never knew what having a real girlfriend meant. I mean the responsibilities you have to a woman's heart I simply never knew existed. Camara changed me forever."

Reflecting back on his mentality towards women growing up, Chase was starting to feel embarrassed by some of his past tasteless antics. The careless attitude toward a woman feelings, the bold displays of reckless sexual power, and the overall lack of respect that he had for females or himself felt so foreign to him since falling in love with Camara.

"I hear that lover boy. No seriously dude, I have seen the change in you, and I—"

Brad was interrupted by the loudest knock ever heard at McNair University.

Chase yelled from the bedroom to Brad, "Damn is that the police!"

"I'm about to find out," Brad said as went to open up the door. As soon as he opened it Camara rushed through it by pushing the door open, hitting Brad in the forehead.

Chase heard the yelp from Brad. With only a pair of jeans on he went into the suite only to be met by a fierce open-handed pimp slap from Camara across the left side of his face leaving a handprint. Bright electric blue stars cascaded from Chase's brain and pranced in front of his orbital socket. Before he could blink them away another vicious swing this time from Camara's left hand landed on the right ear. A dull buzzing sound tried to replace the shrieking words coming from Camara. "Why did you fuck that bitch? You dirty dick bastard! I fucking hate you!"

Instinctively Chase folded up and put both hands over his head to block the incoming barrage. Thankfully for him Brad came in from behind and grabbed Camara taking her out of the bedroom. "Get the fuck off me Brad! This cocksucker motherfucker has hurt me for the last time!" Camara said trying her best to wiggle out of his grasp.

"Camara Please calm down! What in the hell are you talking about?" Chase said shaking his head.

"You know what I'm talking about!" Camara screamed even louder. Brad, who still had a decent hold of her, was finding it increasingly hard to maintain it.

"Let her go, Brad, please. Thank you, I got this," Chase said as calmly as he could. Brad quickly complied and exited the suite area into his room. This was Chase's problem to handle solo.

Remarkably Camara calmed down enough to not attack Chase again once Brad let her go.

"Baby, why are you beating on me? You blacked my eye and my ear is ringing...what did I do?" Chase asked once he got his bearing. Taking a good look at Camara he barely recognized her. Her hair was disheveled, her face was scratched up a touch and bleeding, along with a slightly ripped shirt that also had a few blood stains on it. Camara was fuming.

Taking a huge breath to try and gather her composure as best she could, Camara exhaled and said to Chase, "I'm going to ask you one time and one time only and you better tell me the truth or we are done!"

"Camara, baby doll, whatever it is I'm going to tell you the truth. I mean look at us we was just fucking and in la-la land, I mean pure bliss what a couple hours ago? And now this? This is crazy! So yes whatever you wanna ask me, Camara, I swear I'll tell you the truth," Chase pleaded.

For a split second, Camara thought everything was going to be fine. She hoped with every fiber of her being that this was all some huge misunderstanding. Wavering on whether or not to trust her instincts that said Brandi was a liar, Camara exhaled as much tension and angst out as she could to help clear her mind. She then asked Chase, "Were you sleeping with Brandi the whole time we were together? Did you get her pregnant? Is that why you really left school? Did you tell her that we weren't back together and that you wanted to screw her one more time at the bookstore today?"

Chase's intestines felt like they were being force fed into a sausage grinder by Brandi who was smiling while churning the handle. Compunction and regret filled his very soul. *I made the biggest mistake that I will ever make in my life by sleeping with that girl. How can I make this right and still keep Camara? Will told me to deny, deny, deny. Lie to get to a greater truth.*

"All right…I can tell you how much I love you and then lie to you or I can show you how much I love and respect you now by telling you the truth," Chase said.

"Just tell me the truth!" Camara screamed as she stood arms folded while her right foot tapped uncontrollably.

How badly Chase wanted to lie and deny everything. However knowing how intelligent Camara was, he knew for her to react in such an extreme manner Brandi had to have some pretty damning evidence. Professor King's words came to his mind, 'Respect will stop you from doing what love won't', as he looked into the now angry and distant eyes of his girlfriend.

"First and foremost she is making a whole bunch of bullshit up because she knows I'm yours and she don't like you. Yes, I did see her at the bookstore this morning, but she came up to me. She came up to me flirting like she always does and asked me to have sex with her. I told her no because I was with you," Chase said as he did his best to surmise if Camara had softened her stance a bit.

"Ok, so why did you leave school really? And if I remember correctly you called me that night crying. This shit doesn't add up Chase!" Camara yelled.

"Camara, I was fucked up in the head behind what you did! Don't forget you kissed Squeeze!" Chase said defensively.

"Nigga you're gonna try and flip this bullshit around and blame me! What the hell is a kiss compared to a fuck! No, not just a fuck, because according to your other girlfriend, yall been fucking the whole time we been a couple! That's what…three years?" Camara said.

"I'm not trying to turn anything around on you! And I don't have another girlfriend. You asked me why I left school and I told you why. My head was fucked up behind what you and Squeeze did at the party and that's the God's honest truth. Did I overreact? Yes, I did. I should have never believed all the extra bullshit he was telling me about you. I was dead ass wrong for that," Chase said genuinely.

"Yeah ok Chase...but you still haven't answered my goddamned question! Have you been sleeping with Brandi the whole time that we have been a couple? She said she's been in your room and proved it by describing all the little funky shit on your walls and on your dresser and shit! That stank slut also said that your dumb ass got her pregnant...and then showed me the papers to prove it! So don't lie to me, Chase! Answer the question!" Camara barked.

"We used a rubber," Chase admitted sadly.

"What?" Camara asked as her anger was replaced by a severe sense of loss.

"I didn't get her pregnant because we used a condom. We only had sex one time. So no, I was not boning her the whole time we were together. The night I left school she happened to pop up at my door. If she would have come by 20 minutes later I would have already been gone and we wouldn't be having this conversation. But she came by and you and I were not really together officially. I was convinced that you had sex with Squeeze. I was mad at everybody so I was going to leave school because the thought of you and him together messed my brain up! I never gave a flying fuck about any female until I met you, Camara. I had no idea how to process my love for you or my jealousy over what you did and what I thought you did. So I reverted back to the old Chase and did something that I will regret until I die. I was so sick about it afterward I threw up because I knew I was wrong. That's why I called you up that night and told you that I wasn't right and that I needed help. When I wrote the last letter to you I told you that there were some things that I did that I was ashamed of—this is chief among them. I have never been sorrier about anything ever in my life," Chase said despondently.

Camara felt like she was having a heart attack. Pain besieged every part of her body. Words wanted to come out of her mouth but were headed off at the pass by her cries. What began as quiet crying escalated quickly to wailing. Feeling completely drained Camara buckled onto the ground and curled into the fetal position. Each time she cried out Chase felt like someone's voodoo doll getting stuck by dirty 9-inch needles.

Chase had no idea how to proceed. So he sat on the bed and stared at her helplessly for the next twenty minutes as she cried. Needing to say something Chase said, "Camara, that happened so long ago. If I wanted Brandi I would have took her up on her offer this morning. But I didn't. I don't want or need any other woman but you! I've changed. Can't you see that? You changed me forever!" Chase said.

"And now Chase, you have changed me forever," Camara said as she summoned up the strength to stand up and walk out the door.

49

A cold dark numbness settled inside the body of Camara Truth. The pit of her stomach felt like a rotting diseased tooth just waiting to get yanked. The water running through the shower head—no matter how hot and powerful—could not wash clean the stains of disgust that she felt covered her very being. Her tear ducts refused to help any more tears pass through. They hoped the waters from the shower hitting her face would suffice. The hot water began to run cold but Camara could not detect the difference.

Stepping out of the shower, she grabbed her towel, closed the lid on the commode and sat down on it and zoned out. "Camara? Are you all right?" Rhonda yelled as she knocked gently on the door.

Almost robotically Camara draped the towel around her body and walked out and said, "I'm fine. I just had the worst day in my life ever. That's all."

"What happened? I heard that you and Brandi got into a fight. Tisha told me the bitch came out of the bathroom all wobbly and shit. Said she was falling all over Off the Tracks like she was Trevor Berbick after a Tyson hook—tooth missing and the whole nine," Rhonda said trying not to laugh.

"That's all you heard? Well, that's just the tip of the iceberg. Wait until you find out why I whooped that her ass, that's really going to bug you out," Camara said as she went into her room to put on some clothes.

Immediately Rhonda knew it had something to do with Chase. By the looks and sounds of Camara's voice along with the resignation that it suggested, Rhonda feared the worst. Although they had a blowup or two, Rhonda liked Chase an awful lot, especially for Camara. For now, she was reserving judgment.

Walking into their room slowly while her heart was beating at breakneck speed, Rhonda said, "Please don't tell me what I think happened actually happened."

"Of all the skeezers on campus that Chase could have slept with, he had to choose the one person he knows I cannot stand!" Camara explained to Rhonda.

"Are you serious?! Get the fuck outta here! I know good and damn well Chase did not have sex with Brandi!" Rhonda exclaimed.

"Hmmph…yes the hell he did. 'They used a condom'! You know what I'm about to go and whoop both their asses again!" Camara said as she found her shoes and started to head out the door.

"Wait, Camara—both their asses? Chase put his hands on you?" Rhonda asked now getting angrier by the second.

"No, he's not that stupid. But I damn sure put my hands on him. Rhonda, I swear to God I will never ever let another man hurt me like how Chase has hurt me. I feel so stupid for believing him when he said he loved and respected me. Obviously, he didn't love or respect me because if he did he would not have slept—" Camara said as she abruptly stopped and started to cry once again.

Rhonda knew that there were no words that she could string together that would help to put an end to Camara's pain. Starting to cry herself she walked up to Camara and simply hugged her silently.

Mary J. Blige's song "Changes I've Been Going Through" did its best in the background to match Camara's ever-changing moods. Her eyes were swollen and puffed from her continuous crying. Camara's knuckles were still slightly swollen.

After their embrace, Rhonda got up and went to the bathroom to get Camara some more tissue. After wiping away tears and blowing her nose Rhonda picked up the waste paper basket as Camara dropped the tissues into it. Then the two best friends sat next to each other on Camara's bed.

"I am so sorry that you have to go through this Camara. You are too good a woman. I'm not making any excuses for Chase, but I bet you dollars to donuts that it was Brandi who initiated it and pushed up on him. Some bitches only want a man if they got a woman. I'm so glad you whooped her ass, though," Rhonda said.

After gaining some composure Camara said, "It's still an empty victory. I can't help it, Rhonda, I still love him. I am trying my best to take him at his word that it only happened once. But once is one time too many. I can't stomach the thought of them screwing. Even with that being said part of me still, wants him back. Part of me wants to say fuck, Brandi! I be damned if I let that slut win! I don't know what to do or how to feel."

The sundry of emotions and feelings left Camara shattered. She quietly thanked God for Rhonda's friendship during the turbulent and topsy-turvy day. Camara then stood up herself and said "Rhonda, can I ask you a question?"

"Sure, what is it?" Rhonda said.

"What if I give Squeeze some? I might just do it to kinda even up the score. I wouldn't tell Chase about it but I'd know and maybe it might make me feel better about forgiving him," Camara said probingly.

Rhonda looked at Camara sideways and with a boatload of skepticism and said "Don't play yourself, Camara. First of all, Squeeze would know. And you know he would rub that shit all in Chase's face. 'I fucked your girl homeboy and this time I ain't lying about it'. It would cause more problems than it would solve. Plus Chase would kill him and you."

"Yeah Rhonda, maybe you're right. But remember, Brandi just rubbed it all in my face! I did nothing to Chase to deserve this! If I was to give Squeeze some then he would know exactly how I feel right now," Camara said as she sat back down on the bed screw-faced and arms tightly folded.

In Rhonda's mind, Camara was thinking recklessly out of anger and frustration. She was not about to let her friend make a foolish error without first speaking out about it.

"Now I know you're mad and you would rather get back at Chase than to get back with him right now, and I totally understand that. But to go sleep with Squeeze purely out of spite or revenge…umm, I hate to say this and please don't take this the wrong way but I think it would be kinda whore-ish."

Camara immediately offended stood up and said, "Oh now I'm a whore?!

The two women never had so much as a cross word to each other since they met and became close friends. Rhonda was not about to let Chase's indiscretion and the fallout associated with it ruin their friendship as well.

"Whoa, Camara, first please calm down. I don't hang with nor associate myself with whores of any kind and you know this. I'm your best friend, Hell we're like sisters now! I feel that it is my duty at all times to be as honest with you as I can possibly be, especially if it is in your best interest. So if you were to sleep with Squeeze that would be a whore-ish act. I never called you a whore because I know you could never be one," Rhonda said firmly as she could for clarification purposes.

Camara was unsure as to how to take Rhonda's words at first. The events of the day had her questioning everyone's loyalty to her. So instead of saying something that Camara knew that she would later regret, she simply sat back down and listened.

"I know you had a rough day today so I am pointing this fact out to you before you do something really dumb, that you can't just wish away because your mood or your circumstances suddenly changed. I know you don't want Squeeze. And under normal circumstances, it wouldn't even be a thought or option. I'm simply reminding you of this, understand me?" Rhonda said gaining confidence.

Camara understood and smiled. Rhonda could have easily gone along or even encouraged her to do something careless. However, she possessed the courage to tell her friend exactly how she felt about her possible choice no matter the consequence. At that point, Camara knew she had a friend for life.

"I'm so sorry, Rhonda. I am just so hurt right now, please forgive me," Camara asked as the two best friends hugged warmly. "I'll tell you what I do need is a drink! I guess I just need to get away from campus at least for a night. Maybe I'll go home. Maybe I can get my mind together and figure this out," Camara said exasperatedly.

"Now that is a good idea. Yes, girl, get-away! Even if you miss a day of classes or two, you're smart enough to make it up. So please, I insist that you do just that and come back refreshed. Just remember…don't do anything stupid," Rhonda warned.

"I won't, Rhonda. I'm just going to chill maybe get a drink or two, get my mind right. I'll be back in a day or two," Camara said.

"Ok but how are you getting home and who are you going to chill with? I know it's not anyone here on campus," Rhonda said smartly.

"Nope, it's no one on campus. I'm going to kill two birds with one stone," Camara said as she walked over to the telephone to call Harold.

50 April 16, 1976

Gloria Davis was no stranger to running late. It seemed no matter how early she started to get ready for work, for one reason or the other, she always found herself running frantically to the bus stop. By some miracle, she never missed the bus or was late to work. Today was the day that she made it her mission to be there early.

Ever since Xerox hired her last month part-time, Gloria worked hard to ensure that her probation status would be soon turned into full-time status. Since yesterday marked her 30th day at the plant without being late or having any disciplinary issues, Gloria was now a full-time employee of the Xerox Corporation. Her reward was working her first double-shift from 3 p.m. to 7 a.m.

Gloria a pretty and very shapely woman was also a young mother of a boy and a girl ages five and three respectively. Self-reliant and hard-working, she hated to depend on anyone for anything, especially her mother. Nevertheless, her mother was the designated babysitter while Gloria worked odd hours. Her mother's only rule was to pick them up after work so that the children could sleep in their own bed. Being that she was working a double overnight shift that was not going to be possible.

Luckily for Gloria and her kids she had another option. Penny Williams a good friend since high school with a four-year-old son of her own gladly volunteered to help Gloria out. "Y'all hurry up and eat them pot pies. Momma is running late as usual," Gloria said as she went into the bathroom to fix her hair and make-up.

The two children sat at the small kitchen table built for two and stuffed their faces as fast as they could. "Mommy, could we have some Kool-Aid please?" Unique asked her mother.

"Yup. I'll be in there in two minutes to pour both of you some. Make sure all your food is done. Y'all know you gets nothing to drink unless that food is done first," Gloria yelled from the tight bathroom.

The family lived downstairs in a two bedroom apartment on Wilkins Street in northeast Rochester. Wanting desperately to move from the cramped apartment that had five other families living in it, Gloria knew that a steady and decent paying job was the ticket. She had enough of the Department of Social Services and the hoops that they would make someone jump through in order to get basic human needs met.

After putting on her blue short sleeved uniform along with her work boots Gloria told her children "Ok, time to go to Penny's house so mommy can catch the bus to work. It's warm outside but please put on jackets anyway."

The two vibrant youths ran into their room and grabbed some prized toys along with their spring jackets. Gloria looked at the white and black clock above the refrigerator and grabbed her maroon purse. She had twenty-eight minutes to drop her kids off on Alphonse Street which was three blocks over and make it to the bus stop.

Once everyone was all buttoned up they headed out the door. Unique's red wagon, which was being pulled by Gloria, carried in it a box of Cinnamon Captain Crunch, an Evil Knievel miniature stunt bike, a stuffed Charlie Brown doll, and two baby blue folded blankets.

By the time they made it to Penny's house, her son named Timothy who was already playing in the front yard ran to greet his friends.

"Hi, Timmy! Is your mother in the house? Tell her Gloria is here ok?" she said as she looked into her purse again to make sure she had her house keys and bus fare.

"Hey, girl! Getting ready to go to that j-o-b huh?" Penny said as she walked out on the porch with a cigarette dangling from the edge of her pouty lips. Penny was a thick and tall, dark-skinned, twenty-one-year-old woman with a smoky voice and fiery disposition. The blue and white striped halter top she wore had a hard time containing her rather large breasts.

"Yes, Penny! I am so glad that I don't have to worry about keeping them welfare appointments no more! Girl, I can't thank you enough for watching my babies for me. Whenever I can return the favor or if you need a break from Timmy just let me now," Gloria said as she picked up the wagon and walked up the front porch stairs.

"You know I will, girl. As a matter of fact next weekend I'm going to The Caribbean Club, so I will need you then," Penny said.

"No problem. Listen I gotta run so I don't miss this bus. I get off at seven tomorrow morning and I probably won't be here to get the kids until around 8:30. Thank you so much!" Gloria said.

"Girl, don't worry about it! Now get on outta here before you're late," Penny said.

Gloria walked to both of her children and gave them both big hugs. "Chase, you watch out for your little sister ok? You are the man of the house."

"I will mommy…bye!" Chase said as he ran into the house with Unique, Timmy, and Penny.

As Gloria walked down Hudson Avenue she thanked God for having a safe place for her kids to be, while she worked to move them to a much better lot in life.

"Ok go in and take your coats off. Timmy, help them hang their coats up in the closet. Get that chair from the kitchen," Penny said as she walked into the living room to use the telephone. The dark blue shag carpet clung to her toes as she sat down on the off-gold colored couch.

"Larry…hi this is Penny on Alphonse. I need to see you, baby. I'm watching all these kids and as soon as they take they ass to sleep, momma needs to get as high as a kite. Bring me some of that good ass reefer. And you know if I feel like getting high then I feel like getting some dick! What time you coming by?" Penny asked suggestively.

Penny quietly listen through the speaker as Larry responded.

"Ok baby, see you then," Penny said as she got up and walked happily to her bedroom. Penny knew he was not coming until after nine. That was fine with her because all of the kids would more than likely be sleep in Timmy's room. So Penny kicked backed in her bed as the children watched Sesame Street in the living room.

"Nine can't come fast enough. Chase come here handsome, come give Auntie Penny a big hug."

51 August 31, 1992

"To be honest with you, Camara, I was pleasantly surprised when you called me. I was even happier when you said you wanted to hang out," Harold said as he stared into the puzzling but still beautiful eyes of Camara. Dressed in a sleek all black mini-skirt along with five-inch black heels, Camara was simply stunning.

The twosome sat at a table near the back of Jack's Restaurant, a quiet but well patronized out of the way eatery on Park Avenue which served traditional American cuisine. Camara really wanted something to drink, specifically Bombay Gin. Eating something solid was out of the question because her appetite went on strike.

Picking up a glass of water without it spilling all over the table was a monumental feat for Camara. Her whole body was still shaking uncontrollably with rage and fear. An undefined future along with an unutterable tête-à-tête involving her boyfriend and the person she disliked the most on campus, drove her to drink—literally.

Although she tried her best to remain as calm as possible, Camara could not help feeling nervous and somewhat paranoid sitting next to Harold in a cozy and romantic restaurant. Nearly every face that came into their circumference, Camara thought was either Chase or his evil doppelganger ready to visit upon Camara unspeakable horrors because of her imminent departure from their relationship. Camara was convinced Chase's minions like Brad, Hugh, or Sean were waiting just around the dark corner of the dining area ready to pounce on her. Once they completed their dastardly deed all Camara would hear is Chase's evil filled laugh while rubbing his hands atop of one another.

"To be honest with you, Harold, you're not more surprised than I am, trust me," Camara said as she finally sipped the water.

"Is it something that you would like to talk about or would you rather like to just forget about it and focus on having some fun tonight," Harold asked cautiously.

Harold was smart enough to know that something went horribly wrong between her and Chase in order for her to call him out of the blue for drinks on a weekday evening. He knew Chase had a third-degree black belt in fucking up fast but this was a new world record. However, Harold could care less about the reason that it happened because he was overjoyed at the fact that it did happen. His love for Camara never stopped, in fact, it grew exponentially.

"I don't want to think about anything, Harold," Camara said sadly as she tried her best to not tear up.

"I'm so sorry about whatever happened to you today. But I promise you I will do whatever it takes to a smile back on that pretty face, ok?" Harold said as he inched his chair closer to Camara's while putting his arm around her.

A faint smile was all Camara could muster as the weight of the day's events anchored her in misery. The resentment that stemmed from the Chase and Brandi fallout was palpable. The fact she had little to no control over how horrible she felt because of someone else's actions made her furious.

"You are so sweet, Harold. I'll be back. I have to go to the little girl's room…ok?" Camara said as she gracefully exited the table.

Walking through the dimly lit restaurant Camara noticed that nearly every man she walked by was breaking their neck to see her and some of these men had dates already. Some smiled others winked their eyes. Camara did not know whether to be appalled or flattered.

What she did take from it was a sense of power that her impeccable femininity wielded. As it went straight to her ego, it actually began to make her feel somewhat better. She was accustomed to the power as it pertained to Chase over the course of their relationship. However, she figured it was limited to Chase, maybe Harold and possible Squeeze. Now she recognized that she had the ability to employ it more broadly and wherever she deemed necessary. It was liberating. *I'm a pretty girl. If Chase can't see that, then there is a roomful of men that can see it. Screw Chase…it's all about Camara now.*

By the time she got back from the bathroom she had formulated a bold plan of her own to exact some revenge. All she needed was some help from Harold. If the newfound power she possessed was as potent as she believed it to be, then getting Harold on board would be a piece of cake.

"Hello guys, are you ready to order?" A pretty blonde waitress with long flowing hair asked the pair.

"For starters, we will have three shots of Bombay Gin. After we knock those back we will order dinner. Thank you," Camara said boldly.

"I just need to see both of you guy's ID please," The waitress asked kindly.

"No problem," Camara said as both of them showed that they were the legal drinking age as required by the state of New York.

When the waitress left Harold looked at Camara somewhat astonished and said, "Where did that come from? Plus you know I don't drink."

"Well guess what, Harold? You're drinking tonight," Camara said looking at him seductively. When the waitress arrived with their drinks Camara sat up and grabbed her drink aggressively waiting on Harold to follow suit. "What you gonna do, Harold? Remember I was a virgin once too. If you don't want to have a drink with me I'm quite sure I'll have no problem finding a man in here who will."

Harold was now in semi-shock. Never had Camara talked to him so assertively before. He could also tell that her uncompromising stance was not a façade and that she meant every word that came out of her mouth.

"First time for everything," Harold said as he poured the gin down his throat. "Oh shit! That tastes horrible!" He yelled as he coughed for the next half minute.

Camara was already finished with her second drink when Harold stopped coughing. The triple distilled alcoholic beverage although bitter also tasted sweet and tangy. Immediately Camara began to feel even more relaxed as the gin began to work its white magic. "That hit the spot! One more and I'll be feeling nice."

Three shots was her limit. It would make her tipsy but not get her drunk. Control and controlling her surroundings was the key. Upon making eye contact the waitress she put up two fingers and then pointed towards the table to indicate that they needed two more shots.

"Two shots weren't enough for you, Camara?!" Harold said in a vain attempt to gain some sway back.

"Nope but two shots is just enough for you for what I have in mind. Now throw it back and stop acting like a little bitch. I don't want to have to replace you," Camara said as she dared him not to follow her instructions to the letter.

Harold was as captive to her beauty as every other man in place. He had no choice but to do exactly as she told him. Strangely enough, Harold found obeying Camara when she was in this mode quite stimulating. Tossing back the drink fast so that the weird taste would make the least possible contact with his tongue, Harold held his head to stop it to ensure it went down with speed.

Feeling sexy and invincible, Camara was ready to put her plan into action. *It ain't no fun when the rabbit has the gun...huh, Chase?* Camara reached underneath the table and unzipped Harold's pants, and grabbed him firmly. Harold was beyond astonished, never witnessing this type of behavior from Camara.

"What are you doing, Camara? You trying to get us kicked out of here or something?" Harold said in a slurred whisper.

Camara slid over close to Harold and matter-of-factly yelled into his ear, "Shut the fuck up, Harold! You got two choices. Either follow me into the men's bathroom around the corner or I'm going to get on my knees and suck your dick underneath this table. One way or the other I'm going to get what I want. This gin got me horny and you are the only one I'm comfortable with. Now make a choice!" Camara said as she got up and walked around the bend to the restrooms.

I gotta be dreaming or drunk. Either way, I'm not stupid! I'm going into this bathroom with her, Harold thought as he staggered behind her.

Luckily for the naughty couple, the men's restroom was nestled behind the coatroom with no one in sight. Quickly Camara ran into the first of three stalls as Harold followed.

"Pull down your pants and sit on the toilet," Camara said as she slowly took off her panties and draped them over Harold's head. The gin had worked as Camara thought it would because Harold's penis was standing at attention and ready for duty.

Harold grabbed Camara's thick hips and pulled her close to him. "Slow down you aren't that drunk and neither am I," Camara said pulling away from him. "First of all, I'm in control. This is my show. Second I know you don't think I'm about to let in me raw. You know the rules. I know you got a condom in your pocket."

Harold quickly obliged. Once Camara felt it was securely on, she sat on it slowly. She had to cover Harold's mouth as he screamed with joy. He called for his mother at least three times, and Jesus twice more. Camara took full control, going up and down, deeper and harder to meet her specific needs.

Although she was still supremely angry with Chase, she imagined him thrusting hard as he begged her for her forgiveness. Closing her eyes all she could see were his eyes crying as he told her, "I want you to be my wife, Camara. I will never fuck up again. I promise."

"You promise! Oh god, that's it!" Camara screamed as she held on to Harold harder than a grudge.

Once her trance was broken Camara looked at Harold who looked wiped out. It was 10 times better than what she expected. As she stood up to ease him out of her she understood why. Harold was bareback.

"Harold! Did you come? Please tell me you didn't?"

"Of course, I came. Oh my, God Camara, I swear you are the best!" Harold said this time with a more sluggish voice.

"Harold! You asshole! Couldn't you tell that the damn condom broke?" Camara asked sounding livid.

"My bad, Camara. I was in another world. Damn, I'm the luckiest dude in Rochester!"

Camara snatched her panties off of Harold's head and put them on in a hurry. Pissed off and suddenly sober, Camara walked out of the bathroom. She could not help but smile a little as she imagined Chase curled up in a fetal position watching her episode with Harold on playback.

52   October 15, 1992

After the huge discovery, fight, and subsequent break-up, Chase was determined to not overreact. The last time he did that it cost him more trouble than it was worth. All he wanted to do was to have the opportunity to sit down and plead his case to Judge Camara Truth. These days Judge Truth was known as the hanging judge who handed out stiff penalties for the slightest of infractions. Life without the possibility of Camara was something the young man refused to accept. Chase hoped to appeal to her sense of justice. If that failed he was going to throw himself to her tender mercies.

The gloomy weather outside of Chase's dorm room mirrored his own dark feelings. He was poised to miss his 10 a.m. British literature class for the second time this semester. Staring at him with the same blank look since Camara first introduced him to Chase was Mr. Fizzy who was chilling on his desk. Mr. Fizzy always provided Chase with a certain sense of calm.

Clad in only his navy blue pajama bottoms, Chase sat on his bed in the dimly lit room and talked to his best friend Will Garvey who was acting as his chief 'consigliere'.

"Will this shit is crazy! I mean she won't take my calls, when I go by her dorm room Rhonda always says she isn't there. I wrote her two letters that she hasn't answered back. I don't know what to do man. I thought it hurt before when we had the big blowup. That ain't shit compared to now! I really fucked this one up man," Chase said

"Well, my friend, I'd love to disagree with you but I can't. You did fuck this one up big time. However, you are not alone in this. Camara did play a role in getting you both to this place too. But that don't mean shit now," Will said with a nervous laugh.

"Man, who are you laughing at?" Chase asked defensively.

"I'm laughing at your dumbass! You didn't learn from my mistakes, you didn't learn from your own mistakes, and you didn't listen to your boy Brad when he told you to be easy and leave Brandi alone! You should have at least denied it. Now look at you. Walking around looking like Rusty Jones on his period, I hear. I laugh because I love you and I know for sure you two will get back together eventually. Now I can't say that it will occur anytime soon so until you do, best believe she's going to run your ass through the gauntlet," said Will again with a sarcastic chuckle.

"You know what, Will, she has every right to. I'm just stupid as fuck that's all. I don't blame you for laughing at me," Chase said sadly.

"You gets no sympathy from me, brother. All you will get from me is some solid advice. Camara is running everything through her emotions and using that as her guide. All of her other senses are compromised due to the fact that she is in mourning over the death of you two as a couple. Therefore she has no use for logic right now because she is hurting worse than you are. Camara is using her emotions to help her cope and function. Alas, this is why she is ignoring you now. In her eyes you are dead," Will said.

Will had the benefit of growing up seeing his parents in a loving, happy, and respectful relationship. His father would often times sit down and talk to him at an early age about the do's and don'ts when it came to women. Chase was never privy to such luxuries because his relationship with his own father was non-existent. Will was making it his business to share the wealth.

"We as men are generally not as emotional as women are, so we tend to rely more on logic in these situations. And that's what's kicking your ass. Don't expect logic," Will said.

Chase remembered back to when he first looked into Camara's eyes following an altercation with Squeeze. He knew he was in love with her right then and right there without ever actually being in love before or even having a clear concept of love.

"You see, Chase, in your mind logically she should understand that you made a mistake. You proved that you don't want anything to do with Brandi anymore, and she should know how much perfect sense it makes for you two to remain a couple. So logically she should accept your heartfelt apology and forgive you."

"That's exactly what I'm saying, Will! I don't want nothing to do with Brandi. If that was the case I could be banging her right now. I just want Camara, man," Chase said despondently.

"Camara is lost in the land of emotions. And guess who drove her there and dropped her off with no map?" Will said roughly.

"Ok, man, I get it. I did. But you know how we grew up! Yeah, you had your moms and your dad but that still didn't stop you from doing some reckless shit as far as sex and females are concerned. And I know because I was right there with you. Hell, I just would take it up a notch or two that's all. I had no clue how to be someone's boyfriend. I'm surprised as anyone that I could slow down enough to be someone's boyfriend! So please cut me a little slack. So the question is what do I do to get her back?" Chase asked desperately with a crack in his voice.

Will hated to hear his best friend and brother in this heartbroken and desperate state. But he knew this was a lesson that Chase had to learn for himself in order to fully appreciate real love. Finding love himself fairly recently, Will was determined to drive this point home to his beloved brother.

"You can't do anything. You've been fucking around on her since day one! Remember Shontae and those hoes in Buffalo?" Will asked pointedly.

"You right, I fucked up back then. But I was blaming everybody else for me fucking up except me. At least now I am taking full responsibility," Chase said.

"You're right, bro, and that does show some growth on your part. However, I hate to say it but you have no power or control over her anymore. You gave all the power to Camara once you gave the dick to Brandi. When a woman opens up and, for all intents and purposes, 'submits' to you and you betray her by sexing another woman especially a woman as beautiful as Brandi is…brother it don't look good. The only chance you have, and the only ally on your side, is time," Will said.

"Time? I don't understand," Chase said as he searched his mind to see why Will would say that.

"Time because the more it goes by the more pain it takes away. The memory of you smashing Brandi will never go away but the pain associated with it will…over time. How long that'll take only God knows. The other aspect of time that may save you is the amount of real quality time that you two spent together. She will reflect on that and she will yearn for the closeness that you shared with her. To tell you the truth she wants it now. But her emotions won't let her forgive you just yet," Will said smartly.

"So you want me to just sit back and wait? I can't do that, man. This is a small ass school. I couldn't take it if she stopped seeing me and started seeing somebody else. I barely make my classes now. I'm stressed the fuck out," Chase said.

"Welcome to Camara's world my friend. The only thing that you can do is—when you see her—be sincere and put all of your cards on the table. See where her head is and then go from there. And Chase, I should warn you. There is a saying by that fat Chinese motherfucker. He says relationship are like glass. Therefore, sometimes it is better to leave a thing broken than to cut yourself putting it back together. You and Camara might be at that place," said Will as he ended their conversation to make his way to class.

■

Camouflaged in between a few students sitting in the main student courtyard, Chase was determined to have his day in court with Camara. Black hooded up he looked more like a thug than a lovesick college student. If Camara kept to her schedule then she should be walking by him in a mere matter of minutes. Chase nervously cracked his knuckles and said a quick silent prayer.

To his left, Chase spotted Camara leaving from Edwards Lecture Hall. Although she was still gorgeous to Chase, he could not help but notice a few subtle differences in her face as she walked closer to him. The first was that she was slightly thinner. The second and most disturbing to Chase was the twisted scowl that seemed to be plastered on it.

"Hello, Camara. How are you doing?" Chase said smiling as much as his face would allow him to.

Initially, Camara was shocked to see Chase. Instantaneously her surprise was replaced by disgust as the images of Chase and Brandi cavorting and frolicking popped up in her head. Camara went to great lengths to avoid running into Chase. She wanted nothing to do with him or his reasons for destroying their relationship.

"Chase, please leave me alone. Do you think it's by accident that I haven't seen you in over a month? Go fuck Brandi again and please just let me be," Camara said coldly as she walked away from him.

Exhaling and jogging behind her Chase gently grabbed her right arm and stood in front of her path and said, "Please, Camara, could you please just listen to me? I can't tell you how stupid I feel for violating you like that. I have never been sorrier about anything else in my life. I was not in my right mind. It's no excuse for what I did, I'm just trying to explain where my head was. I don't want Brandi. I want you, Camara. Please find it in your heart to forgive me. You know I love you!"

Pausing before she responded Camara did her best to gauge his truthfulness. She then asked passionately, "Chase, do you have any idea what it feels like to find out that the person that you are hopelessly in love with had sex with the person that you absolutely without a doubt hate? Can you put yourself in my heels and try to imagine the horrific pain associated with that discovery?"

"I know I messed up. And I know how bad you feel, hell I feel even worse! But, baby, please understand when I did what I did with her, technically we were not a couple," Chase said.

"So freaking what! So by that rationale, if I would have had sex with Squeeze the same night that you screwed Brandi then would you be as understanding and as forgiving as you are begging me to be now because 'technically we were not a couple'?" Camara said mockingly.

The thought of Squeeze or any man having sex with Camara hurt Chase to the back of his gut. Slowly the realization that Camara was going to leave him for good and eventually would make love to another man-made Chase furious.

"So what are you saying, Camara? Are you finally gonna admit that fucked Squeeze? I mean you did admit to kissing him," Chase said angrily.

Camara looked at Chase as a tear fell down her face. "You still think that I had sex with Squeeze? After me finding out what you did, don't you think that by now I would have rubbed it all in your face if I did actually screw him! But you know what, Chase, you believing that I did actually stoop so low is the reason why we're here having this conversation in the first place. So I'm going to tell you exactly what you want to hear so you can leave me alone forever! Yup, I fucked Squeeze and it was good! His dick is bigger and better than yours and he made me come ten times in one night! Whoop-tee-do! You happy? I haven't been feeling good lately and honestly you are making me sick to my fucking—," Camara yelled as she rushed a nearby garbage can and vomited.

Chase's head literally wanted to explode. He regretted making another accusation about Camara and Squeeze while defending his known transgression with Brandi. Hearing Camara say the things she said about her and Squeeze although he did not believe it to be true still hurt nonetheless. However the thing that puzzled him the most was the fact that Camara vomited for no apparent reason.

"Camara, are you all right? You've been sick lately? Was it something you ate this morning? Baby, why didn't you call me? You know I would have brought you over whatever you needed," Chase said.

Reaching inside her coat to grab some napkins, Camara wiped her mouth. She then inserted a few mint Tic-Tacs in her mouth. After she gained her composure she said to Chase, "I'll be all right."

"Listen, Camara, I told you I know you didn't have sex with that clown. I'm sorry. I just get upset sometimes at the thought of him even touching you. I was wrong and I apologize. I just want us to be us again," Chase said.

"Chase, you need to get this through your thick skull. I don't want or need you for anything. I hate you. You never loved or respected me. I have moved on and suggest you quit wasting your time on me and do the same," Camara said fighting through nausea.

"I never loved or respected you? You have moved on? What are you talking about, Camara?" Chase asked frantically.

"Just what the hell I said I have moved on. I am talking to somebody else now," Camara said dispassionately.

Cold shivers went through every part of Chase's body. For a split second, he actually felt his heart stop beating. The words that Camara uttered were words that he believed he would never hear from her. Chase stood there slack jawed. Immediately crying Chase said, "You can't be serious, Camara. You're talking to someone else? A month after a damn near three-year relationship you are talking to somebody else?"

Camara thought she overplayed her hand. She did not want to tell Chase that she slept with her ex-boyfriend. Knowing that she did it purely out of spite and Harold meant little to her would have been of zero solace to Chase. When he started to cry she knew truly how sorry and how sincere he was. Deep down she still loved Chase and wanted to remain his girlfriend but she knew she could not handle the embarrassment of being cheated on. Brandi and her friends would take every opportunity they could to humiliate Camara. That was something she was ill-equipped to deal with without resorting to violence again and risking getting kicked out of college her senior year was not an option.

Yet, the hurt that she felt upon finding out about the indiscretion still remained the same. The pain in a strange way to Camara was comforting. She knew exactly what it was and where she stood with the pain versus being blindsided by the devastating news of love betrayed. Doubling down on her statement she said "I have never had a stuttering problem and I know your ears work fine. For the last time, Chase, I am talking to somebody else and I am done with you. Have a good life."

Chase watched her in stunned disbelief walk down campus. He simply buried his head in his hands and cried for the next several minutes.

53 October 19, 1992

"I bet you it's just stress. The breakup with Chase, my fight with Brandi, the increase in my course work so I can graduate with honors, pressure to get into NYU…I bet you that stress explains why my period is late," Camara said to Rhonda as the two sat side by side inside the waiting area of the campus health clinic for her appointment.

The unfathomable thought of pregnancy was too overwhelming for serious contemplation. Growing up she rarely fantasized about being a mother. For the most part, her indifference towards motherhood prevented her mind from grasping the enormous responsibility it would bring. She wanted to be someone's wife for sure, but being someone's mother was a thought that she never fully explored.

For the duration of her sexual relationship with Chase, the couple mainly relied on condoms and the rhythm method to prevent pregnancy. Camara insisted that Chase get a clean bill of sexual health before she let him have unprotected sex with her for the first time. Although they had a couple of minor pregnancy scares, Camara never truly thought about becoming pregnant. Now, however, she was more than a little worried about it, she was not ready to admit her uncertainties to Rhonda yet. So instead she chose to play it cool.

"Camara, I'm not trying to jinx you or nothing like that, but girl when you come out of that doctor's office I bet you dollars to donuts you are going to tell you that you're pregnant," Rhonda said.

"Oh don't tell me…wait…you dreamed about fish! So I know for a fact I'm knocked up now!" Camara said sarcastically.

The idealistic Rhonda was used to her more practical friend doubting her womanly intuition from time to time. For some reason, Rhonda was convinced that Camara was with child. This was part of the reason she came with her to the appointment.

"Keep playing, Camara! When that doctor gives your ass the news you won't be joking then. I know you like clockwork girl. Your period comes when mine does without fail. And by my calculations you are around four weeks late," Rhonda said matter-of-factly.

"Well damn, Dr. Wheatley, can you tell me when I'm due and what I'm having too?" Camara said smartly.

"You threw up twice already last week when you started smelling the food from the dining hall and you complained about your boobs and how different they've been feeling lately. Girl, you pregnant," Rhonda said.

"Why are you trying to throw a baby on me, Rhonda? You wanna be an aunty or a god-mommy that bad?" Camara asked suspiciously.

"Yup! I'll be the prettiest aunty god-mommy ever!" Rhonda said.

"Well I agree, but you're just gonna have to wait about five or so more years that's all!"

What Rhonda did not know was that behind the calm doubt was extreme and palpable fear. Camara never told Rhonda about her bathroom adventure with Harold that resulted in a broken condom. Rhonda presumably thought that if Camara was indeed pregnant then naturally Chase was the father. Shame forced Camara to hide the fact that she had sexual intercourse with two different men in the same day. All she could do was to confide in her denials and hope for a failed pregnancy test.

"Camara Truth," a student nurse said from the back.

The moment of truth was about to arrive and Camara had never been more nervous in her life. She walked behind the nurse and into a small cubicle and sat down on the elevated bed that was covered with a paper bed sheet. "Dr. Tompkins will be with you in a minute or two. In the meantime can I please take your blood pressure?" the friendly student-nurse asked.

"Sure," Camara said as she took off her coat and extended her right arm. The nurse smiled and wrapped the sphygmomanometer around Camara's arm. "120/80—your blood pressure is quite normal."

Camara's tension level dropped a notch or two. *Maybe I'm really not pregnant. If I was pregnant my blood pressure would be through the roof…right?*

"Ok, Camara, relax, Dr. Tompkins is on her way. Have a great day," the nurse said as she exited the room and closed the large taupe colored hospital drapes behind her.

Camara looked around the small room and saw medical posters warning of the dangers of smoking, the importance of brushing and flossing three times a day, understanding depression, and early care for the unborn. The next ten minutes seemed like forever as endless scenarios danced in Camara's head. *If I'm pregnant and it's Chase's baby, do I forgive him and get back with him? If it's Harold's baby do I start a relationship with him even though I don't have those types of feelings for him that I have for Chase. Should I get an abort—*

"Hello, Camara. So what brings you in to see me today?" Dr. Tompkins said. The mid-thirty something African-American woman dressed in white doctor's jacket and a bright smile extended her hand to Camara.

"Well I'm hoping…I'm not and I don't think that I am…but I'd like to take a pregnancy test just to know either way," Camara said as her stomach did somersaults.

"I can relate to your nervousness, Camara. I was a young mother too. I am here to help you in any way that I can. Ok, so when was the last day you completed your menstrual cycle?"

"August 18th," an unsure Camara said.

"So today is the 19th of October. When does your period usually begin and how long does it usually last for?"

Although Dr. Tompkins seemed like a nice enough and very professional doctor, Camara still did not feel comfortable telling anyone besides Rhonda and her gynecologist back home this type of personal information. It was extremely embarrassing to her.

"Around the middle of each month, I'd say. Sometimes it's a day or two early or late but mostly around that time. It lasts no more than four days. On average it's about three days most of the time," Camara said quietly.

"Ok and you are sure you have had no PMS symptoms or any sign of your period since August?" Dr. Tompkins said as she wrote down everything Camara told her on her clipboard.

Camara began to feel more and more like she was being cross-examined by the lead prosecutor about her involvement in the sex crime of the century. Camara was pretty tall for a woman standing 5'9. However, she felt dwarfed and mildly intimidated by the six foot tall Dr. Tompkins who towered over her as she sat down on the bed. There was nothing threatening about what the doctor said or even how she said it but Camara somehow just felt very small.

"Positive," she said sounding even quieter than before.

"Ok, so when was the last time you had sexual intercourse?" Dr. Tompkins asked as she took a seat across from Camara still writing.

Anger and resentment began to build up deep down inside of Camara. She began to hate Chase and herself for winding up inside a doctor's office being asked intimate details about her private life by a complete stranger. She bit her lip and answered, "August 31st."

After doing the quick math in her head Dr. Tompkins said, "It is possible that you are pregnant. Have you vomited, or noticed certain sensitivities to certain foods all of a sudden, or have your breasts been more sensitive than usual?"

All of Rhonda's words came rushing back to Camara. She exhaled and admitted to Dr. Tompkins. "Yes, all of the above, unfortunately."

"Well, Camara, if indeed you are pregnant—and it sounds like so far that you just may be—I will walk you through each of the choices you have," Dr. Tompkins said.

"If I am pregnant I am not getting an abortion. I just couldn't do that to something so innocent. It didn't ask to come here so it should not be killed as a result of my recklessness. I guess I'm telling you that now so that you don't waste your time. I really only have one choice," Camara said somewhat defiantly.

Almost immediately Camara began to feel strongly about keeping the baby if she was pregnant. She did not know if she was fighting with herself internally and then abruptly came to that decision once Dr. Tompkins began to allude to her choices. It surprised her how protective she was of her possible unborn child already.

"Well that is a very brave decision but first, we need to find out if that decision needs to be made at all. Are you familiar with how a pregnancy test works?" Dr. Tompkins asked politely.

"I've never taken one before if that answers your question," Camara said smartly.

"Well, you take a simple urine test. If we find in your urine a hormone called Human Chorionic Gonadotropin or HCG, then you're pregnant. It is as quick and as simple as that. I just wish I could say the same thing about motherhood," Dr. Tompkins said.

"I'm ready Doc. I need to know," Camara said as she stood up from off the bed.

"There is a lavatory around the corner to your left. Take this container, urinate in it, and seal it up with this lid. After that just give it to the student nurse. It won't take very long at all to find out. Good luck Camara," Dr. Tompkins said as she smiled and handed Camara a plastic container.

It felt like the bathroom was miles away as she turned the corner. As she got to the bathroom door she went inside and locked the door. She quietly prayed to God. *God, I have never been so scared in my life. I know I'm too young and I don't want to bring a baby into this world under these circumstances. Please God let it turn out to be negative. Please...*

After her quick entreaty to God, Camara unbuttoned her snug jeans and grabbed the plastic medical container. She positioned herself as such between the container and the toilet bowl and did her part to comply with the doctor's request. Afterwards, she washed her hands and left the bathroom. The student nurse was waiting just up the hall and walked towards Camara to grab the container.

"Thank you. You can have a seat back in the examining room and Dr. Tompkins will be back with you," the student nurse said with a clinical smile.

Still hanging on to the hope that she may not be pregnant, Camara made her way back to the examining room. She closed the curtain behind her. Thumbing through a few magazines, Camara did her best to remain calm. As each minute ticked away so did the confidence she had in a negative result. She felt like a criminal awaiting the verdict from the jury, with a life sentence hanging in the balance.

The curtains pulled back and from behind them emerged Dr. Tompkins. Camara immediately tried to read her face but to no avail. Instead, Dr. Tompkins decided to cut straight to the chase and announce the verdict.

"I know how nervous you are Camara. Like I informed you earlier I have been in your shoes. With that being said I won't leave you in suspense any longer. It looks like you're going to be a pretty young mother."

Numbness overtook Camara's body. She had no idea what to say or how to feel. She sat on the bed in stunned disbelief. The last thing Camara remembered hearing was Dr. Tompkins talking about the importance of prenatal care to help ensure a happy and healthy pregnancy. She instinctively thanked the doctor and walked back out into the waiting room with a look of fear on her face.

Rhonda saw the look of intense sadness on Camara's face and immediately knew her prediction was deadly accurate. She ran to embrace her best friend. The full gravity of what Camara was about to embark upon hit Rhonda and she felt horrible for being right about her being pregnant.

"It's ok Camara. You have me here to help you with whatever needs to be done. I know you're still upset with Chase but I know you all can work it out and get back together for the sake of your baby. You guys genuinely love each other. That love can overcome anything," Rhonda said.

Camara fell into a chair and then slipped slowly to the floor completely devastated. She informed Rhonda, "The baby might not be his. I slept with Harold that same night. I feel like a complete slut."

Rhonda was confounded by this new piece of news. The two women sat on the floor, against the chairs clutching onto each for strength and understanding.

54 October 26, 1992

For Camara Truth, her bout with morning sickness was a walk in the park compared to the deep depression that all but consumed her every waking moment. Insomnia often laid its smothering hand across Camara's shoulders. When she was able to get a wink or a nod in here or there, continuous nightmarish visions plagued her. The soon to be young, pretty mother was denied access every time she fancied herself attempting to visit with the Sandman. Twisted images of Chase, Harold, and her unborn child challenged her emotional stability and triple-dog-dared her to do something about it.

Her first class of the day was Managerial Economics which begin at 9 a.m. The digital alarm clock which was set for 8 a.m. read 7:13. Having no real interest in going to class, Camara reached underneath her bed and unplugged the clock. Cold sweat poured from her temples and forehead as her stomach did its best gymnastic routine.

To deny her true feelings any longer was futile and ineffective. Camara wanted to speak to Chase it was as simple as that. She regretted her extreme hard-line stance against forgiveness. She now understood why men and women get married and raise a family together. *No woman should go through her pregnancy alone* Camara often thought to herself when she yearned for Chase's presence.

With a 50/50 chance that the child was Chase's, Camara was willing to conceal her night of carnal retaliation with Harold for the sake of her future family's happiness. For the past week, she had been seriously flirting with the idea of forgiving Chase fully and getting back together. This morning she made up her mind to see where his head was. Whether it was out of want or necessity made no difference to Camara's lonely heart.

*This is his final test. I know this is his baby. God wouldn't do that to us. I'm sure I could get over what he did with Brandi. I just need to check Chase's temperature...*Camara thought. Looking into the mirror at her ever-so-slightly bulging belly, Camara was amazed that a human being was actually growing inside of it. She wondered whether it was a boy or a girl and all kinds of names shot through her brain.

Miraculously, Camara was beginning to become excited about bringing a new spirit into this world. However, she knew she based a lot of her newfound joy on the premise that she might be raising the baby with Chase. Still finding it hard to wrap her head around the fact that she was with child, Camara smiled bravely.

Unaware of Chase's schedule for this semester, Camara suspected that his first class was not at least until 10 a.m. Chase was not a morning person in the least so more than likely he was still sleeping. Her first impulse was to call his dorm room. But she quickly decided against that because she felt an actual in-person visit would send a much more powerful message. With her confidence and mood soaring, Camara sprang into action.

9 a.m. was her target time to knock on Chase's door. This gave her a little time to doll herself up. After getting out of the shower Camara thought it would be a good idea to wear the outfit that she wore on their very first date. Being a couple of months pregnant would do little to mute the effectiveness of the sexy form fitting miniskirt.

She pulled her white Lycra mini-skirt and three-inch white pumps out of the closet. This time, she decided to forgo the white leggings for flesh colored stockings. She sat on the edge of her bed after squeezing into the mini-skirt and put on her pumps. Camara walked in front of the mirror a few times to gauge how alluring she looked.

"Damn, girl! You're wearing that to class? You must be trying to get an A the easy way or something," Rhonda said in her morning voice as she rolled over to see Camara all decked out.

"Never that. I'm just going to see Chase, that's all. I'll see you in a few," Camara said as she made her way into the mild, Indian summer morning without giving Rhonda a chance to talk her out of it. Rhonda had a special place in her heart for Chase but as of late, he seemed to be on a one-way trip to Loser-ville. She felt Camara deserved a lot better.

The sun seemed to smile as Camara took in the unusual warmth. Along the way to Chase's dorm room, Camara was trying to figure out the best way to let Chase know that she had forgiven him, she wanted to become a couple again and that he was going to be a father. Unsure of how much he could handle at once, Camara decided to play it by ear.

A severe craving for glazed honey wheat donuts was the only thing that stood between her and reconciliation with Chase. Walking by the Student Union which had plenty of donuts on deck, Camara remained steadfast and continued undaunted. A steak garbage plate from Nick Tahoe's this evening would more than makeup for her sacrifice.

Walking in behind another student who was entering the dormitory, Camara calmed herself as much as she could and went straight to Chase's room and knocked on the door.

"Hold on one sec," Brad said as Camara immediately recognized his voice. "Oh hey, what's up, Camara?"

"Hi, Brad, how are you?" Camara asked politely.

"I'm fine. Umm…is everything ok?" Brad asked somewhat suspiciously as he stood in the doorway looking at a very provocatively dressed Camara.

"Is everything ok? Of course, it is why would you ask that? Camara asked.

Brad stepped to the side and invited Camara inside of the dorm room suit. "I don't know I just thought that something happened because I'm not quite sure why you would be visiting me this early in the morning dressed the way you are that's all," Brad said.

"Visiting you? Are you trying to funny, Brad? I'm here to see Chase. I'm here to talk to him about us and how we can get things back on track. I know he's not in class this early…so I'm going go to wake him up," Camara said as she walked into the bedroom.

"Well that's just the thing, Chase isn't here as you can now plainly see," Brad said as he walked in behind her.

"What he have an early class or something?" Camara asked?

"Camara, Chase is gone. He left school again…I don't know about a week or so ago. Look in the closet. All of his clothes, sneakers, posters, books, cassette tapes, everything is gone. He went back home to Rochester for good he said," Brad said.

"He's gone?" Camara said stunned.

She looked frantically in the closet and on top and underneath the naked bed. It was as if Chase never existed. He left nothing behind and Camara was disgusted and shattered.

"Not to be all in you guy's business but I know a little something about what happened with Brandi and what happened with Squeeze. Don't get me wrong I don't know every intimate detail but I know enough to say this. Chase knew he messed up. He wanted to put all that dirt behind him. You couldn't get past his extra-curricular activities with Brandi—which by the way I totally understand and I don't blame you for. I guess he had enough of trying to convince you to believe him so he left school. It hurt me to my heart because dude didn't even have the guts to tell me he was leaving. I came up to the room after class last week and he was like dust in the wind," Brad said sadly.

Emotionally devastated, Camara was blindsided by Chase's sudden departure from school once again. The fact that he would leave school never crossed her mind. She began to blame herself again for not listening to Chase and at least trying to forgive him. *What have I gotten myself into? How am I supposed to bring a baby into all of this? Chase might not even be the father…Coward!*

"Thank you, Brad. I gotta go call Chase," Camara said as she took off her white pumps and practically ran back to her room.

■

Camara was committed to keeping it together emotionally. She was tired of crying. Deep down she knew that the fact that Chase actually packed up and left school for a second time was not a good harbinger as far as the future of their relationship was concerned. Nevertheless, she was determined to talk to Chase. His penchant for fleeing was not one of his admirable qualities.

Sitting on the couch in the suite, Camara nervously dialed Chase's house phone number. He had a separate line from his grandparents that went straight to his bedroom. At first, she hung up before the first ring. Not knowing if she could handle a rejection of this magnitude at this point gave her a reason to pause and think about if she really wanted to make this phone call.

What if he has a new girlfriend? What if she picks up the phone? I couldn't even get mad. Even if we do get back together what if the baby isn't his? I couldn't do that to Chase. He wouldn't go for that. I couldn't handle that. But I know it's his baby. I know God meant us to be together. Ok! I'm calling him.

"Hello," A very groggy sounding Chase said as he answered the phone.

"Good morning, Chase," Camara said nervously.

"Good morning…who is this please?" Chase asked as he yawned.

Camara was instantly annoyed that Chase failed to recognize her voice. She quietly began to second-guess her decision to call him at all. The thought of hanging up immediately crossed her mind but instead she simply inhaled and answered his question. "It's Camara."

This was the last person Chase was expecting to hear from at this time in the morning. He sincerely had no idea why she would be calling him. The last time they spoke she made it abundantly clear that their relationship was over. So he finally believed her and reacted accordingly.

"Did something happen to Brad, Sean, or Hugh?" Chase said.

"No, not that I know of. Why would you ask me that?" Camara asked.

"Because, I'm trying to figure out what reason you would call me. Unless of course, it was a life-or-death emergency," Chase said.

Camara wanted to tell Chase, *Yes it is a life-and-death emergency… my life, your life, and the life of this unborn baby growing inside of me.* But as soon as she thought it Harold's face popped into her head. Shame washed all over her.

"No, it's not an emergency. I called you because I want to talk to you. I want to know where we truly stand Chase. I want to know if you still want to give it another try," Camara said.

Chase exhaled smartly and said, "So let me get this straight. For damn near two months, I was practically begging you. Begging you to forgive me, begging you to look at the bigger picture and give us a second chance. Remember that? And now that you are finally ready to give us another chance I'm just supposed to jump up and say sure Camara anything you say! You're the boss! Yeah right."

"Chase, I am just trying to see where your head is. You gotta a lot of nerve! If you hadn't stuck your dick in Brandi then we would be together right now and we wouldn't be having this awkward conversation," Camara said.

"You see that's my point. The last time I checked I'm far from perfect. I messed up, Camara! But I apologized both humbly and sincerely to you. You know Brandi don't mean shit to me now and she didn't then," Chase said.

"Chase, did you seriously expect me to just get over that—just like that? To tell you the truth thinking about it now makes me sick to my stomach," Camara asked

Camara instinctively started to rub her belly. She figured her baby knew that it was audibly witnessing her parent's first argument. Walking over towards the bathroom she grabbed the wastepaper garbage can just in case and sat back down on the couch.

Chase scolded, "I'm not dumb or insensitive, Camara. I never expected you to get over it like that! I only wanted you to understand the part that you played in it. And that don't mean I'm blaming you for what I did because at the end of the day I am responsible for doing what I did."

At the very least, Camara had to admit to herself that it was mature of him to own up to his indiscretions. It did not, however, make her feel any better about the fact that it actually happened. She bit her tongue and continued to listen to Chase.

"But all I wanted you to do was to acknowledge the part that you played in the whole fiasco. Brandi had me in her sights since you all were suitemates…but I didn't bone her then. It took me to find out that you and Squeeze kissed and him telling me that you two sleep together in order for that to happen. It was dead ass wrong what I did but you are not innocent in all this. You simply exercised more restraint than me but nobody is an angel here!"

Camara wanted to debate him. She wanted to tell him no matter what she did he had no right to have sex with Brandi. Instead, she put herself in his shoes and for the first time although it still hurt, she could somewhat understand his mind-set back then.

"I could refer back to your initial walk with Brandi as the catalyst but you know what, Chase, you're right…and I can see that now. I see that the two or three messed up things that we did could never equal the thousand great things and days we spent together. You think we can make this work? You should at least come back to school so you can get your degree. You are so close to graduating. I don't want to be the reason why you left school forever. I love you," Camara said.

"I love you too, Camara. But I think your new man would have an issue with that. You said I couldn't expect you to just get over Brandi just like that and I agree. But damn I didn't expect you to be talking to somebody else just like that either," Chase said.

Suddenly her last words to Chase prior to this conversation exploded in her mind. Camara actually forgot that she told him about a new friend. Sensing that she was losing him forever, Camara felt it was time to go for broke and tell Chase everything.

"Chase, baby…we got to talk. I wasn't exactly talking to somebody. You see there is something that I—"

Interrupting her Chase countered, "I'm done, Camara. I can't take the ups the downs anymore. I'm too young to settle down. I don't know if I can be monogamous to anyone. Maybe when I mature more or get older. Maybe then I'll be ready to settle down. But for now, I just can't do it. Plus it hurts me so much when I think about you being with somebody else. I hate that you have such control over my emotions. I need that control back."

"Don't say that, Chase! We have control over how we treat each other. God meant us to be together. I swear you will never have to worry about me being with anybody else. Plus I have something to tell you."

"Camara, I love you with all my heart and soul. But if you love me the same way, please let's go our separate ways. I don't want us to keep bringing the worst out of each other. I just can't do it now. My mind and my heart needs a break from all this drama. I love you but you gotta let me go. I'm done," Chase said as he hung up the phone.

Her first instinct was to call Chase back. After dialing his number she hung up. What surprised her most was that no tears fell from her eyes. Anger replaced the sadness.

55 October 31, 1992

Saturday mornings were the only day of the week that Professor King allowed himself the luxury of sleeping past 5 a.m. Pushing his normal wake up time back two whole hours was all the extra rest time that the Type A personality and his industrious brain required to replenish the necessary juices. After relieving his bladder and brushing his teeth, Professor King, never one to break traditional or routine, kneeled in front of his bed and silently thanked God for waking him.

Dressed in his baby blue pajama's he quickly turned his attention to the favorite room in his two-bedroom apartment, the kitchen. Breakfast was his favorite meal of the day because it represented the initial fuel he needed to be as productive as humanly possible for the day. Before he went to sleep Professor King had waffles and beef sausages on his mind. Now was the time to put those culinary thoughts into action.

Turning on the faucet he filled up a small pot with water and placed it on the stove. Opening the large off-yellow refrigerator, Professor King grabbed a pack of hot beef link sausages. After poking holes into four of them, he placed them in the hot bubbling water. Singing Cameo's 'Why Have I Lost You' in his best falsetto while trying to dance, Professor King plugged in the waffle iron. He mixed the waffle batter with the adroitness of a master pastry chef and poured it into the machine.

The kitchen smelled like a potpourri of tasty ingredients once Professor King sautéed the peppers and onions to accompany the beef sausages. *Four waffles to go with four beef sausages, a great meal for a growing man to begin the day. My future wife is going to love me and the way that I cook for us* he happily thought. The finishing touches consisted of a bowl of fresh strawberries on the side and his favorite Alaga Syrup. Professor King was ready to dig in like he was in deep negotiations.

Being a big man and a single man to boot, Professor King felt it was a necessity to be able to cook and cook well. As a little boy, he would watch his mother and aunt as they prepared meals mentally taking notes on cook times, seasonings, and food prep. Cooking was his peace of mind but eating what he had cooked was sheer Heaven.

Professor King had to finish everything on his entire plate before he allowed himself to wash it down with a beverage. This was another rule that his beloved mother never allowed him to break. His drink of choice this morning was ice cold apple cider. The thick naturally sweet liquid became his absolute favorite since trying it on a junior high school field trip to a local farm. He gulped one cup after breakfast and poured another cup and took it onto the front porch with him.

The fall foliage in the Village of Brockport was nothing short of spectacular. The chlorophylls degrade forced the falling leaves to reveal to everyone in sight its true colors. Shades of yellow and orange exploded visually in stark contrast to the nearly colorless gray morning sky. Professor King smelled the oncoming rain in the air.

Right before he was about to head into his apartment, Professor King looked to his left and thought he saw a young female walking towards him. As the young lady got closer to his front porch he realized it was Camara.

"Camara?" Professor King asked incredulously.

Picking her head up suddenly Camara said "Good morning, Professor King."

Immediately he knew something was wrong. The sunken shoulders, blank expression, and poor slumped over posture was a dead giveaway. "Good morning, Camara. You are up kind of early for a Saturday morning. I pray and hope that everything is all right."

"To be completely honest with you Professor, things have never been worse. I was hoping that you had a moment to talk. I really need a male perspective on things. Unless you're busy I can always come back at—" Camara said before Professor King interrupted her.

"If I was busy I'd still make the time for you. Please, Ms. Truth, come on in."

He opened up his door, smiled at her warmly and ushered her inside. She did her best to smile back but the usual radiance that made up Camara's smile was all but gone. She took off her coat and plopped onto his sofa as if the weight she was carrying was just too much for her.

"Hey let me take your coat. Please, Camara, make yourself at home. Can I get you something to drink? Let's see I have water, apple cider, milk, Canada Dry, and orange juice. Or if you're hungry I can whip you up something for breakfast. I'm pretty handy with a spatula, a pan, and some heat. Please don't be shy," Professor King said

Camara sat on his sofa with her legs and arms folded and said, "You know what, Professor? I walked all the way over here on a whim. I have no reason to be shy. I've been craving some buttermilk pancakes and fried porgy for the longest. I've been afraid to eat it though because I didn't want to throw it back up. But you know what? Why not? If you have that I'll definitely do my best to eat it."

"If I got it? Ms. Truth, I was raised on fish and grits for breakfast. My family was born and bred in the south. I always keep some porgy handy! Here try some apple cider while I whip it up. It is delicious!" Professor King said as he handed a tall glass filled to the rim to Camara.

Delighted to be showing off his skills in the kitchen, he went to work on Camara's order. He rolled both sides of the fish in lightly seasoned cornmeal and placed into the frying pan. For the pancakes, he added a pinch of cinnamon and a touch of vanilla extract to the pancake batter.

He continued "I'm sorry I don't have a television for you to watch. I don't believe in it. However if you look to your right there is a nice little boom box that I invested in a few years back. I do love music."

To Camara's surprise, there was a nice sized black boom box almost hiding in the corner. She turned it on and 'Love Serenade' by Barry White came blasting out. WDKX's 'Memory Lane' showcased Funk, Soul, and R&B hits from yesteryear and it was Professor King's favorite radio program. Camara allowed herself to let the melodious groove transport her back to when things were so much simpler in her love life.

"Breakfast is served Madame," Professor King said in his best English butler voice. Camara smiled and walked into the kitchen to see three fluffy pancakes dripping with butter garnished with fresh strawberries and another plate with two golden brown porgies fried to absolute perfection.

"Wow, Professor! This looks good!" Camara exclaimed.

"Well, we all eat food with our eyes first. But please sit down and give it the ultimate test. I love Alaga but I know you up north folk enjoy maple syrup a bit better," Professor King said as he pulled out Camara's chair for her and grabbed a bottle of Mrs. Butterworth's Syrup from the cabinet.

Taking her knife and fork Camara cut into the pancakes and placed a good size piece of all three into her mouth. They were without a doubt the best that she had ever tasted in her life. Wanting to immediately see how good the fried fish would taste Camara put down her eating utensils and tore into the porgy. The food was so good it eased the burden of everything else she was dealing with. Professor King sat back and watched in glorious silence the effect of the meal on Camara's soul. The best part about the whole dining experience for Camara was her ability to keep it down.

"Professor King, I have had some good food in my day. But that is without a doubt the best breakfast I have ever had! Thank you so much!" Camara said as she gently rubbed her belly in a circular motion.

"It was truly my pleasure. Now that you have eaten and you are nice and full, let's step into the living room so we can talk about you being pregnant and all the joys and pains this brings to your life," Professor King said with a wry look to his face.

Camara's face registered bewilderment as she asked, "How did you know?"

"How could I not know, Ms. Truth? Your body language along with your subconscious mind screamed it to me. But let's talk turkey. How has Mr. Douglass taken this glorious news?" Professor King asked.

Shame and embarrassment once again took Camara in a corner and started to choke the life out of her. Everything inside of her tightened up as she began to recount every event that led her to this moment. Second guessing and what if situations sent ripples to her stream of consciousness. Nevertheless, she summoned enough courage and told Professor King the facts as she knew them.

"He doesn't know?"

"Well, I hope you plan on telling him at some point in time. I hope it is sooner rather than later. I know he left school again and it doesn't take a genius to figure out that you two are no longer a twosome. I do not know the reason for your breakup. However as painful as it may be, it is a must that you inform him on his impending fatherhood so that he can make the necessary adjustments," Professor King said.

"Why tell him when there is a 50% chance that he might not be the father?" Camara said sadly.

The color from Professor King's face seemed to all but vanish. He never once considered a Camara pregnancy scenario where Chase was not the father. His heart ached for the both of them. Professor King realized just how much he had personally invested in them as a couple. It appeared to him now that this stock was going belly-up, literally.

It took him a minute to actually come to terms with what he just heard. He knew Camara was not loose or easy. Therefore something pretty dramatic had to take place for her to be in such a drastic situation. Professor King walked into the living room and sat down in his recliner and Camara followed sitting on the sofa. The question that popped into Professor King's mind was *who is the other candidate?*

"Ms. Truth, to say that I am saddened and shocked is an understatement. To say that I am disappointed in you that you have placed yourself in this position is also a vast understatement. In fact, I am angry with you right now. I hope to God that the third person in this equation is not the gentleman named Squeeze. I'm not sure that Mr. Douglass would be able to handle that fact in a mature or sensible way," Professor King said calmly.

"No, it's not Squeeze. He and I never had sex. My ex-boyfriend Harold is the other possible father. I only had sex with him twice in my whole life. The first time was the night of my prom and the second time was the night I found out about Brandy and Chase having sex. I was so angry I truly didn't care, Professor King, and that's the God's honest truth. I just wanted to get even."

Flashbacks of his beloved Sandra *getting even* with him came rushing back to nearly all of his senses. Professor King's hands started to shake with abject fear as his mind's eye showed him the crimson fluid squirting from Sandra's wrists. Not wanting to have a nervous breakdown in front of Camara, he quickly went into the kitchen and poured himself a cup of water to help keep him calm. After gulping a half of cup and filling it back to full capacity he walked back into the living room and asked, "I hate to be graphic. But was some form of contraception used?"

Not as much as flinching when he asked the very personal question Camara answered flatly, "Chase and I did not always use protection. Harold and I did use protection, but the condom broke. At the time, becoming pregnant was the farthest thing from my mind. But the fact that I had sex with two different men in the same day…I still can't forgive myself for it…regardless if I became pregnant."

Camara's face read like a dull tombstone. Her eyes were void of hope and luster and glazed with indifference. Professor King wanted to hug her and tell her everything was going to be all right but he was positive with Camara's current mindset that it would fall on death's ears.

"Ms. Truth, to err is human. I hope I didn't come across as too heavy-handed or judgmental by expressing my sincere disappointment. You came here to me for advice and not to be scolded. I will give you my best advice for the sake of you and your unborn baby. I only want and wish the absolute best for all parties involved, including Mr. Douglass," Professor King said.

"I know you're not judging me, Professor King. And there is no way in Hell that you are more disappointed in me than I am with myself. I haven't even told my mother yet. So I don't blame you one bit. I should have handled the situation better," Camara said.

"Again, Ms. Truth, the saying may be trite but it is apropos. We all fall down. What makes us men and women is if we decide to stand back up. And I know you will rise to the occasion and stand," Professor King said optimistically.

Almost on cue Camara stood up. Soon, however, he knew it had little to do with his cheerful outlook.

"Professor King, I do have one question that I believe that you are the only man I know on Earth that is qualified to answer," Camara said.

"That's what I'm here for, Ms. Truth. I love answering questions, especially intelligent ones. My motto is if you don't put any thought into the question then why should I put any thought into the answer. But knowing you the way I do, I'm quite sure you have put much thought and intellect into your question. Please, fire away," Professor King said.

Camara looked Professor King and asked coldly, "Why do men cheat?"

At first, all he could do was chuckle. For some reason, he did not quite expect that question to be asked in such a point-blank manner. All Professor King could do after he finished laughing was to answer her question as best he could.

"If I knew the answer to that question I would have a bevy of women lined up around the block to thank me personally for answering the question that has haunted them for years. However I can make a valiant attempt," Professor King said smiling.

Camara kindly maneuvered herself back onto the sofa to get in a preferred good earshot position to hear the answer to her question. This perked her up and the expression on her face stated 'I'm all ears'.

He stood up and paced slowly taking on his normal lecturing style and said, "First of all there is no one reason why men cheat. I will also not give you excuses used by some men as to why they cheat, although it may be some form of the truth buried in some of their reasoning."

Taking a quick glance at Camara who had her arms folded and her right leg twitching unconsciously Professor King knew she was deeply invested in his answer.

"In my humble opinion the answer is unsettled because of the deep, multi-pronged and thickly layered conditions associated with infidelity. Each individual man has very specific biological and environmental factors either singular or combined that play a role in his misogyny," Professor King said.

"That sounds like a bunch of bullshit, Professor," Camara said while looking Professor King straight in his eyes.

"All right, let me first ask you a question. Can you be pregnant by four different men at the same time?"

"Are you trying to be funny, Professor King?" Camara asked in a slightly more agitated tone.

"Am I trying to be funny? Why would you...oh! I get it. No, Ms. Truth, not in the least. I apologize for not being more sensitive to the fact that your dilemma with the two gentlemen may slightly mimic my question. But please trust me I am attempting to make a larger point unrelated to your particular situation," Professor King said nervously.

Camara had been on edge and ready to explode as of late. The last thing she wanted to do was to alienate any of her true friends, namely Rhonda and Professor King. Doing her best to calm herself down, Camara took a deep breath and said, "It's ok, Professor. I am a bit sensitive these days. I'm quite sure you can understand why. So to answer your question, no a woman cannot be pregnant by four different men at the same time."

"Of course not, but a man can impregnate four different women at the same time. Do you think that is by accident?" Professor King asked picking up his favorite erasable black pen.

"So what are you saying, Professor King? Are you condoning a man having four different women pregnant because he can?"

"In this country, because relationships are built on monogamy and trust, I absolutely do not condone such behavior. It is irresponsible, selfish, and reckless to be with two or more women at the same time. Lying and misleading women who truly love you is reprehensible."

Wanting to scream as she thought about Chase and his lewd involvement with Brandi, Camara abruptly walked to the bathroom and slammed the door. Before any tear could adorn her face, she raised her shirt and looked at her belly. Taking her index finger and rubbing it in a circular motion she found the strength needed to fortify and fence in any oncoming tears.

Camara walked back out of the bathroom, sat down back on the sofa and said, "I thought breakfast was coming back up false alarm. I agree with you, Professor, it is reprehensible for a so-called man to do that to any woman."

"Now the important flip-side to that argument, Ms. Truth, is as follows. Monogamy is a relatively new phenomenon. Polygamy, however, has been practiced for thousands of years. There are many cultures, tribes, and civilizations in the motherland both past and present that have functioned— some would argue even thrived—with polygamy as a relationship method. Again, it is a fairly common practice. Since women have historically outnumbered men, the elders of some of these nations did not think that it was fair for any woman to be without a husband and therefore without children. You also have to keep in mind that the more children a family would have, the wealthier they were considered in some African civilizations. This was because you had more hands to till the fields and raise your crops," Professor King said sounding quite professorial.

Camara shook her head slowly and said, "Again, Professor King, I am having a hard time understanding the correlation."

"We as African-Americans are 440 years removed from Africa. However, the polygamous mentality is still in plenty of us, both men and to some degree women. Keep in mind in America black women outnumber black men eight to one. Then you factor in how many of our men are in prison and how many of our young men have been killed young due to life in the ghetto and now you're up to twelve to one. Sometimes the math is exactly what it adds up to be," said Professor King.

"So are you saying that some men are genetically predisposed to cheat and some women are born to idly stand by?" Camara said in raised voice.

"There are some men who believe it is their God-given duty to impregnate or to bed as many women as humanly possible. There are some women who know for a fact that their man is cheating on them but turn a blind eye to his extracurricular activities. Why would a woman ignore such a thing? Because some women would rather share a man than have no man at all," he said.

Professor King instinctively knew that if he did not word his theory correctly, he could taint his pristine image in the eyes of Camara. Yet, he was willing to risk alienation in order, to tell the truth to Camara as he viewed it. His hope was that she would be able to discern what she needed from their conversation and apply it accordingly.

"Ok, Professor, removing myself and my situation, I can honestly say that I can at least to some degree understand what you are saying. But to my understanding, the difference between polygamy in Africa and straight up cheating here is honesty and respect associated with it. I would guess that if a man had four wives, for example, they all knew about one another so there were no surprises when wife number three turned up pregnant. I guess they were one big family. I also understand that women do outnumber men. But you know what? Some women are so low down and dirty that they don't deserve a man. And some men are so sneaky and underhanded that they don't deserve to be with a real woman like me. I still don't condone polygamy. You can't tell me that some of those women on some level aren't jealous at least a little bit. I personally don't want any parts of it over there or here," Camara said.

"Ms. Truth, I was a habitual liar and world renowned cheater. When that aspect of my personality manifested itself it resulted in a beautiful young woman taking her own life. There is not a day that goes by that I don't think about how cold and unfeeling I was. I think about how self-serving and self-based my thinking was and it astounds me. But a lot of that was based on my immaturity, my unawareness of how deeply a woman feels, and just plain old youth. To be honest with you, Ms. Truth, it is so hard to be a young handsome black man with a normal sexual appetite and not gorge yourself on women. Between the ages of 16-25 testosterone is a beast. It drives some of us men to make sexual decisions that any sane person would refuse. In other words, if you are a female with compatible body parts we are having sex. It is that pure and simple. That's why it is so remarkable what true love can do to a young man. It can tame that beast. Your true love for Mr. Douglass tamed his wild beast. But sometimes the true love of your life comes to you too early in your life."

The love of Camara's life went back home to Rochester and did not want anything to do with her for the foreseeable future. With a baby growing inside of her stomach, Camara had no time to mourn for the love lost. She had no time to wish she could go back in time and not go to that frat party. There was only time to plan for the future. She figured that this future, unfortunately, would not involve Chase raising a newborn baby with her. This fact was excruciating.

"Well, Professor, the love of my life is gone. And now my chief concern is going to be to the new love of my life, my baby. I know beyond a shadow of a doubt that I am fully capable of raising my baby alone. I know this. The moment that I decided to keep this baby is the moment that it stopped being about just Camara Truth. Although I was raised without my father and I turned out ok, that does not mean that if I raise my child without his or her father that he or she will turn out ok," Camara said solemnly.

"I could not agree with you more, Ms. Truth. Every child born deserves the love and protection of both their mother and father," Professor King said.

Undaunted Camara continued, "In a perfect world, Chase and I would raise this baby together and be as happy as anyone could ever imagine. But Chase is cowardly and isn't mature. He made that painfully clear when I tried to get back with him—after I found out that he slept with someone else mind you. I had every intention of telling him that I was pregnant on that last phone call. But he hung up. If a man doesn't want me then that is fine. I will not beg him or make him be with me by telling him that I'm pregnant with his child. I will not ride nobody's jock-strap. Besides, this baby may not be his at all, which would make everything a mute point," Camara said.

Professor King knew the direction Camara had chosen. That road was slippery and wrought with deception. It hurt him badly that Camara had somehow wound up here so close to graduation.

"It sounds like that you are telling me this in advance of the decision you have already rationalized, justified, and basically made prior to your coming here this morning," Professor King said astutely.

"I guess to a degree you're right, Professor. For the sake of my child, I am going to give him or her something I never had, two parents. My ex-Harold is in love with me and when or if I tell him that I am pregnant by him, I know for a fact he won't shut me down or turn me away like Chase did. I know that he will love me and my baby and he will provide and do his part. That's what I need now. That's what my baby needs to be the very best person he or she can be. My baby needs a mother and a father who loves and wants them, period. My personal feelings can go on the back burner for now. Me and love aren't too fond of each other right now anyway. It would be real easy for me to be by myself, send both Chase and Harold notices to be at the doctors on such and such a date so that they could be tested to see who the father of my baby is. I thought about doing that," Camara said.

"But you won't because you want a family environment for your child. You want a two-parent household for your child instead of two one parent households for your child. I understand, and somewhat admire and respect you for that," Professor King said.

"Somewhat admire and respect me?" Camara asked pointedly.

"Ms. Truth, all you are planning to do is well and good. I know you are coming from a good place with it. But understand this. That child that is growing inside of your stomach has the unalienable right to know exactly, without dispute, who his or her father is. So if you decide to say the hell with Mr. Douglass and you and the other gentleman go on and tiptoe through the tulips happily together, just know and understand that you could be contributing to a hoax of the highest order. If it turns out indeed that the baby that you are carrying is not Harold's and is, in fact, Mr. Douglass's child, then no one wins. For the sake of everyone involved and not involved, I hope you are putting your chips down on the right man, because if you crap out you will only have yourself to blame. You have been properly advised. Please excuse me while I get ready for my day. Please stay as long as you deem necessary. Do the right thing, Ms. Truth," Professor King said as he exited stage right to the bathroom.

Camara sat on the sofa for the next fifteen minutes trying her best to collect both her thoughts and the thoughts of Professor King. She knew he made a great deal of sense. She also knew however that no matter what choice she made there was going to be an immense amount of pain involved.

After going into the closet to retrieve her coat she began to head back to her dorm room. The steady raindrops that fell equaled the many possibilities that may result from the choices that would eventually have to be made.

"Harold, you better to be the father because I'm done with Chase for good," Camara said for anyone to hear. Enjoying the rain, she walked slowly back to her room to call Harold and tell him the wonderful news.

56   April 17, 1993

April is the moodiest of all months in Rochester, New York. Severe shifts in the weather can range from warm sunny summer-like days, too late winter storms, or torrential downpours. God must have been in a lovely mood when he ordered a serene 72 degrees the for Camara's baby shower. It looked as if he finger painted the sky with wispy child-like clouds that resembled freshly spun cotton candy to compliment his powder blue backdrop. Although the clouds appeared to be arranged in a haphazard pattern all across the sky, they could not quite dull the luminous sun.

To get over the pain of her breakup with Chase, Camara decided to rekindle and start a new full blown relationship with Harold. In an effort to acclimate herself to the rigors of shared parenting, Camara would stay at his two bedroom apartment for one weekend a month. Moving in full-time was not in their immediate future although it was not completely ruled out.

There were two things about Harold that made him conveniently perfect for Camara in her current situation. The first was that she knew that Harold's love for her was genuine. There was zero doubt that he wanted Camara for his lady. In some ways, this turned Camara on. The joy that he exuded when he found out that Camara was pregnant with *his* baby was undeniable. He wanted to be a part of her life forever and a child together virtually ensured that fact. The fact that he was a family man also appealed to her.

The other thing that made Harold perfect for her situation was that there was safety in the known. Camara was convinced that Harold would never cheat on her because he could not see past her. She wanted nothing else to do with the pain of betrayal. Harold was a known and predictable commodity that Camara could invest in without undue risk of loss. Slow and steady was going to help her and her new family win the race.

Harold and Camara sat in his car down the street from Camara's mother's house. The usually quiet suburban street was lined with cars because of Camara's baby shower.

"Ok, so your next doctor's appointment is at 10:45 on Wednesday right baby?" Harold asked politely.

"Yeah," Camara said plainly.

Shifting and turning towards her as the leather seats squeaked softly Harold said, "I know you said no, but I really want to know if we are having a boy or a girl. Can we please find out then?"

Camara exhaled annoyingly and replied. "Harold, I told you before, I am old fashioned. I want to be surprised. Knowing what I'm having is like telling the birthday girl what she is getting for her birthday months in advance. It spoils the surprise. So no I'm not finding out what my baby is going to be until he or she decides to enter this world. We can wait. We got a little less than two months to go. Relax…"

"Ok, honey, you're right. You know me…I just like to plan and prepare. Have fun at the shower ok? What time should I pick you up?" Harold said still sounding upbeat.

"I can't stay the whole weekend. I have two ten-page papers that both have to be done by Monday. I'm going to ride back to school with Rhonda after the shower. Thanks for dropping me off. See you on Wednesday," Camara said as she kissed Harold quickly and maneuvered herself out his luxury mid-sized BMW.

With a pink, yellow, and white over-sized sundress, white flip flops, dark sunglasses and a floppy yellow beach hat, Camara appeared to be attending a fun in the sun beach party than her own baby shower. Walking down the street with her flowery mesh off-white purse over her right shoulder and her left hand both holding and rubbing her very pregnant belly, Camara took the short walk to her mother's house.

Sprawled from one indoor column to the other, leading into the family room was a huge 'It's A Baby' party sign with the letters alternating from pink and blue respectively. In front of the sofa were about two dozen neatly wrapped gifts of all shapes and sizes. About thirty or so of Camara's close friends and family were also sporadically scattered throughout the house.

"Hey, yall! The mommy to be is in the house!" yelled Camara's 17-year-old cousin Tynisha as loud as she could over the music. It was hard for Camara to distinguish one word from the other as her female guests came rushing to her with kisses and well wishes.

After her mother gave her a quick but tight hug, Rhonda who was hosting the party also hugged and kissed Camara and then pulled her to the side and said, "On the way back to school I really need to talk to you about something important, ok?"

"Sure, is everything cool?" Camara asked.

"Yup, I just want to talk that's all," Rhonda said.

Camara stepped into the dining room to see a side table that had bowls of potato chips, pretzels, fruit punch, Jordan almonds, Ritz crackers, pepperonis and hot pepper cheese on it. The main table was reserved for a beautifully decorated pink and baby blue diaper bag cake. Camara was truly taken back and humbled by the superfluity of genuine love.

"Can I please have everyone's attention? Can I have everyone please come to the family room please," Rhonda asked.

Camara gathered herself and went back into the family room and sat down on the lone E-Z chair. All of her family and friends quickly made their way to the room, surrounding her.

Rhonda stood beside Camara and said, "Hello everyone. For those of you who don't know me, I'm Rhonda Wheatley and it is truly my honor to be the hostess today for my best friend Camara Truth's baby shower! I'd like to thank everybody here who came to show your love and support. I still haven't decided whether or not I'm going to be Aunty Rhonda or god-mommy but regardless I am going to love and treat Camara's bundle of joy like it was my very own. I just wish she would step into the ninety's and find out if she is having a girl or a boy. Inquiring minds need to know!"

Everyone laughed and seemed to agree.

Camara laughed back and said, "I am an old soul. Patience is a virtue. So we are all going to have to wait and see."

Surprisingly, the very reserved Mama Truth decided to take center stage, "I told my daughter the first day she went to college to keep them books open and her legs closed! Well, one out of two isn't bad because my baby will be graduating next month with a 4.0 or close to it. Shortly after that, she will be delivering my first grandchild. All I can say is this, Camara. I love you and I'm so very proud of you." Immediately Mama Truth began to cry and left the room.

Almost everyone in the room seemed to follow suit, except Camara who kept her authentic smile but did not shed a tear. The speech from the usually tight-lipped and very business-like Mama Truth meant so much to Camara. She began to think of the hard work that Rhonda did in putting together the beautiful celebration of her unborn child's life and the smile grew even wider.

I am not alone. I am not raising my baby alone. Thank you God for blessing me and my baby with such beautiful people.

■

"Girl, I am so tired. I don't feel like doing anything but I got to finish these papers. I'm going to talk to somebody Monday at NYU about taking a year off and beginning in the fall of 94. I want to spend at least a solid year bonding with my baby. I'm almost certain with my grades the graduate program will understand and delay my entry into the program for a year. It's just so much stuff sometimes. I can't wait for this baby to be born so I can celebrate with a bottle of gin, no juice!" Camara said riding shotgun in Rhonda's brand new teal Hyundai Scoupe.

There were plenty of things on Rhonda's mind that she wanted to talk to Camara about regarding her choice to move forward with Harold come hell or high water. Rhonda did not want to cause any undue stress to Camara during her pregnancy by voicing too much displeasure with the decision she made, however, she found it nearly impossible to hold her tongue anymore, "Camara, can I ask you a question?"

"Of course. You said you wanted to talk to me about something anyway right?" Camara asked.

"Do you in your heart of hearts believe that you are doing the right thing with respect to you, your baby, Harold, and Chase?" Rhonda asked earnestly.

Camara looked out of the moving window and remained silent. Rhonda could not figure if her silence was linked to a measure of shame she felt for her deception. Rhonda thought it could have been the pure anger Camara felt for getting herself in such a precarious position. The other possibility that occurred to her was that Camara was searching her heart and mind for the answer that eluded her. Rhonda waited patiently.

After about five full minutes of quiet contemplation, Camara gained her composure and said, "I don't know if what I'm doing is right, Rhonda. I truly do not know. What I do know is that my baby has to come first. I want my baby to have a good man as his or her father. Harold will be a good man for my baby and my baby deserves and needs that."

"I agree with you, Camara. I think Harold will make an excellent father. He seems like he's real cool. But you know what Camara? Through all of his faults and fuck-ups, I think Chase would make an excellent father too. I can't be sure, though. But more importantly, I truly believe he has the right to know that you may be carrying his child. I swear Camara, I am not trying to put more worries on your lap than you already have but as your friend—as your best friend—it would be criminal of me to keep quiet and act like everything is copasetic. I love you and that baby in your belly way too much for that," Rhonda said with big tears in her eyes just waiting to drop.

"And I agree with you, Rhonda. Although I can't say I believe that Chase would make an excellent daddy right now. I tried to talk to Chase. I tried to let Chase know that I had forgiven him. I had every intention of telling Chase everything including the possibility that the baby could be another man's. Even though I know that fact would have destroyed any chance of us getting back together, I was still going to tell him. But he told me that he had moved on, that our relationship was just too complicated for him and hung up on me. I am woman enough to admit that I played a role in whatever you wanna call this messed up situation. But I am woman enough to get out of it with flying colors. Fuck Chase and the horse he rode in on," Camara said.

As Rhonda pulled into the campus main parking lot she turned the car off and asked Camara, "Do you still love Chase? Do you still want Chase? If Chase was to be at our dorm room door and he asked you to become his girl again would you?"

"Ok, I am also woman enough to admit that yes I still love Chase and I'm still in love with Chase. I will always love him and if as soon as we walked up those stairs and he was waiting for me and asked me to be his again...I don't know," Camara said.

"But that's my point, Camara. You'd at least entertain Chase and the horse he rode in on. This is why it will never work with Harold...because of what you just said. You are going to try and build a family with a man that you don't love? And on top of that, the baby that he believes is his may not even be his at all? Has this thought ever crossed your mind, *What if the baby comes out and is the spitting image of Chase?* Camara, I love you but this is wrong, and somebody is going to pay a heavy price for this," Rhonda said sadly.

Camara knew that she could not debate any of Rhonda's points. Liking Harold for her child and loving Chase for herself simply would not mesh or co-exist. Whenever she thought about Chase hard, she simply overwhelmed her brain with thoughts of her baby. Putting all of her focus on her unborn child helped to clarify in her mind whose well-being was most important.

"Rhonda, I can't argue with you. Even if I could I don't have the energy to. All I can ask you is this. First, please keep everything that we have discussed between us. And lastly please respect the fact that I am doing what I feel is best for my child first and myself second. So even if I'm wrong I swear before God I'm doing it for the right reasons," Camara said as Rhonda nodded her head slightly in tepid agreement.

For the first time in their nearly four-year history as roommates and best friends, they spent a quiet and slightly uncomfortable, wordless night together.

57   April 30, 1993

Trying to forget his ex-girlfriend Camara Truth and the indelible mark she left on his very being was like trying to forget his name. However, his pig-headed nature suggested that ultimately he could achieve amnesia. Whenever the strong urge to write her a letter or pick up the phone to call Chase simply ignored it and acted as if Camara never existed.

Tiring of his grandparent's attic, Chase was ready to move into his own apartment. He counted up his re-up money and placed $2500 inside of a Nike shoebox which slid nicely underneath his bed. Soon he'd be able to buy a house.

Thanks to an uncle of a childhood friend, Chase was finding his way slowly but surely through the ultra-competitive cocaine market. The uncle who was on his way to do a small bid in the clink gave a few of his clients to Chase for him to keep happy while he was locked down. Most of these clients were white, well to do, and functional, thus elevating them to platinum level status in the wide world of cocaine. If they wanted to party after a long day at the office all they had to do was give Chase a page and he would deliver it to their door like pizza. And, Chase had the best blow this side of New York State.

Because he could get a page at any time day or night, Chase never left home without three things; plenty of sacks of cocaine, condoms, and his nickel-plated pistol. All of which he kept handy in the glove compartment. With a burgeoning new career, plenty of money in his pocket and in his shoebox, and released from the shackles of a relationship Chase was hyped and ready for whatever situation blew his way.

■

Every time that Chase's cream colored pager vibrated so did he with exhilaration. The vibration of the pager meant one of two things to Chase; sex or money. Money meant driving out to suburbs like Penfield or Chili, or swanky city neighborhoods like Corn Hill, Park Avenue or Monroe. All Chase had to do was to bring that magic white elixir into some of the very special folks of those fine communities. With just under a thousand dollars in his pocket already, Chase had been casting spells all day long.

Having recently waged a war against love and lost in remarkable fashion, Chase wanted to reacclimatize himself with the peace and ecstasies of lust. With his battery solar-charged by the Sun all day, Chase was fully energized and on attack mode driving down Genesee Street.

Both sides of the street were filled with soldiers of all ages, shapes, and sizes. Some were on solo missions wearing tight jeans, lipstick, and a bad attitude. Others went into battle arm in arm with their band of sisters. There was safety in numbers. So a ragtag brigade across the neighborhoods would assemble in a matter of minutes with their only mission to complete was to have as much fun as humanly possible on this warm and friendly Friday night.

Chase soon spotted a combatant pushing precious cargo east on Genesee Street. She was average looking and sported a short ponytail that poked out of the top middle of her head. Her dingy yellow mini skirt looked as if had been through a couple of tours of duty. She made up somewhat for the fashion faux pas with a cute white halter top, and five-inch white pumps. The precious cargo that she was pushing was a crusty baby carriage. Inside, around, and atop of the carriage was her hollering one-year-old son riding shotgun with pampers, Newport cigarettes and a baby bottle housing a mixture of Sprite and red Kool-Aid.

"Hey, Miss Lady? Do you need a ride?" Chase asked as he slowed down and pulled over just before reaching West High Terrace.

Smiling once she got a decent look at Chase's handsome face and welcoming grin, the young mother began to walk towards his car leaving her stroller and the baby in it unattended.

"What side of town do you live on, sweetie?" Chase asked smoothly as she put both of her hands firmly in the middle of the driver's side window tossing her head slightly back and to the left an attempt to appear sexy as possible.

"I guess the west side. I don't really know what side it's called but I live on Saratoga off Lyell. Why? You gonna to give me a ride or something?" The young lady asked.

"I can do that," he said as he smiled hard showing off his one dimple.

Chase's hormones began to rage like a trapped tiger injected with steroids. There was nothing remotely spectacular about the young woman but that had no bearing on his rising libido which smelled woman flesh and was hungry for more than a taste.

"You drink or smoke?" she asked hopefully.

"I don't but I don't mind if you do. Hop in. We can go up on Conkey Ave and I'll get you nickel bag," Chase said as he got out of the car to get a better look at his makeshift date for the evening. Having a pocketful of money lent to his overall feeling of invincibility.

"I only smoke if I'm drinking. We can either go to the Bootlegger's on Clifford or just get me a Crazy Horse. We can go to my crib and chill."

The unknown variables of the hunt were invigorating to Chase. He was about ninety percent sure that this hunt was going to end with a fresh kill. Butterflies fluttered their beautiful wings just outside of his cerebral cortex and the breeze was getting Chase hornier by the minute. After the young woman grabbed the baby out of the stroller, Chase quickly stashed it in the backseat. She hopped into the front seat with the baby.

The young woman made herself at home inside Chase's car. Without asking she pulled her last cigarette out of the box and lit it up. It took for Chase to cough a few times before she rolled down the window.

"That's cool. Let me help you put your baby in the backseat. I don't have a booster seat or nothing like that but I'll make sure his seatbelt is on, though," he said before he drove off.

"Don't worry about that. Only white people wear seatbelts. His ass can ride up here with me. If you don't mind do you think you could grab me a couple of loosies too? Make sure they're Newport's. Thank you, daddy," the young woman said in a whiny irritating tone. Chase was oblivious to her request as they drove off into the night.

■

The woman's apartment looked like something out of welfare weekly. The floors from the kitchen to the bathroom were begrimed so heavily it was hard to tell whether the original floor color was grey or white. The living room couch was the color of an ancient evil backgammon game gone astray. The couch pillows were dank and filled with the stale smell of cigarettes. The television with no knobs and a putrid green tint to the screen made a lame attempt to broadcast an old Hogan's Heroes episode.

Sitting on the couch trying his best to get comfortable as he waited for the young woman to put the baby to sleep, Chase felt something run across his Nike's. His reflex betrayed him and forced him to look down only to see a rat the size of growing kitten scamper methodically away into the bathroom.

Revulsion forced him to quickly go into the bedroom while hoping not to run into anymore of the rat's family or friends on the way.

Immediately upon entering the room the smell of old urine hit his nose hard. Scanning the room for more possible rodents the only thing Chase could see in the semi-dark room was a dresser drawer, two mattresses on the floor, a clock radio, an ashtray on top of a beat-up old wooden TV dinner tray, and a tan waste basket.

The young woman was doing her best to smoke a Phillies Blunt filled with marijuana and rock her son to sleep at the same time. The baby was having none of it as he cried and cried. Grabbing the pacifier that was tied around his neck with a shoestring, she stuffed into his mouth briefly stopping his cries.

Chase took this as an opportunity to slide in bed behind her. He could hardly contain himself. Still fully clothed the young woman barely moved as she felt Chase rub up against her. Starting to grind on her he did his best to keep out of view from the baby. He rubbed on her making sure to not touch the bottom of the baby's dirty feet. To Chase's surprise, she matched his rhythm grinding with him in nearly perfect sequence.

As Chase went for the gold and tried to remove her panties from her body, it seemed to Chase as if the baby sensed what was about to happen and began to cry louder than ever.

"Damn, DaQuan! I wish you would shut your mouth and take ya ass to sleep!" the young woman said as she smacked her teeth.

With her back to him, Chase stopped fidgeting and went for the gusto pulling her panties down to her ankles and then onto the floor with zero resistance. The young woman then tooted her backside out even more in anticipation for the incoming penetration. Making sure his billfold was still intact, Chase unbuttoned his pants and pushed them down to his ankles. He pushed it deep inside the wet but loose walls of the young woman like an animal.

The baby now was screaming at the top of his lungs as his head bounced up against his mother's breasts due to Chase's powerful thrusts. Making sure that he did not see the baby Chase leaned back and closed his eyes while gripping her right shoulder. The young woman remained quiet as Chase screamed in ecstasy and her baby screamed in frustration.

After Chase reached his orgasm he pulled out of her exhausted. It took him several minutes to finally catch his breath. Once he did, he realized exactly where his sex drive had dropped him off. He was beyond disgusted with himself. *I gotta get the fuck outta here* he thought as he frantically tried to hatch an escape plan.

"Bae, you got a couple dollars?" The young woman seemed to say out of nowhere. Chase pulled up his pants and quickly turned his body so that the young lady could not see exactly how much money he was holding.

"I got twenty bucks on me now but I got a couple more bucks in my car. I'll go to the store and give it to you when I get back. You want something?" Chase asked earnestly as he could pretend. He walked around to her and put the money on top of the TV tray.

"Umm, yea. Get me a pickle, some skins, and another Crazy Horse. You're coming back, right? Don't lie," she asked suspiciously.

Smoothing out his clothes and getting his keys out of his pocket Chase assured her he was coming back in a matter of minutes. Relatively convinced of his sincerity the young woman said "Alight leave the door unlocked then so I don't have to get up. This little nigga will definitely be sleep by then or I'm a put his nappy headed ass to sleep for good."

Relieved that he was free Chase strutted out of the apartment knowing he was not ever going back there ever for any reason. When he got inside of his car and turned on the ignition a funny thought rolled through his head. *Damn! I never even told her my name. And I don't think she told me hers...*

■

Hunger pains were running suicide sprints from one side of Chase's stomach lining to the other like they just caught their second wind. Chase never slept on an empty stomach and tonight would be no different. He made his way to Eddie's Chicken Coop.

Chase popped in a cassette tape featuring a montage of the newest Hip Hop hits by A Tribe Called Quest, Black Moon, Snoop Dogg, and Digable Planets, among others. 'Throw Ya Gunz' by Onyx, the mesmerizing ode to firearms surrounded Chase's imagination and threatened to shoot to kill unless he gave in and nodded his head rhythmically over and over in full accordance. Chase was so lost in the music that he lost track of how fast he was driving across the Upper Falls Boulevard Bridge.

As he passed by the old Bausch and Lomb factory flashing red and blue sirens screamed at him to slow down and pull over, breaking him out of his sonically induced trance. When he looked at the speedometer of his Cutlass Oldsmobile it read 44 in the 30 miles per hour zone. Chase acquiesced to the police car's request and pulled over.

This was the first time Chase had ever been pulled over by the police. Vivid flashes of Rodney King and the pummeling he took at the hands, batons, and wicked mindset of the four Caucasian Los Angeles police officers had Chase on edge and ready to jump. His inner voice did its best to calm him down but Chase's heart and pulse rate were racing like Mario Andretti and A.J. Foyt. He was able to focus enough to reach into his pocket to grab his license. It was not there. Panic- stricken and scrambling through his billfold in hopes that it was tucked between Mr. Benjamin and Mr. Grant, Chase came up empty.

With the police officer still inside of his patrol car, Chase went into the glove compartment to see if his license was hiding out there. As soon as he opened it to his he remembered what was seeking refuge inside. Ten sacks, each filled with a half of gram of cocaine, and his loaded pistol. Instincts told him to grab his McNair University ID along with his insurance card and registration while quickly closing the glove compartment door afterward.

Chase looked to his left as a white police officer wrapped hard on his car window with a huge black flashlight. Rolling down the window Chase said in a voice that sounded as if it was going through puberty, "Hello, officer."

"I'm going to need your license and registration. I clocked you going 45 in a 30," said the officer plainly.

Well, officer, I apologize for speeding. I'll be honest with you. I have my registration and I even have my insurance card but I left my license in my other pants at home," Chase said.

"Well, sir, I'll be honest with you. You just might be fucked. It is against the law to operate a vehicle without your driver's license. On top of that, you were speeding. That means I can give you two tickets, tow your car, and have you spend the rest of the weekend in jail," he said while moving the flashlight closer to Chase's eyes to keep him somewhat disoriented.

"Well, officer, I do have my college ID," Chase said as he handed the policeman his ID along with his registration. He hoped the officer did not notice how hard he was shaking.

"Do you have any warrants or any arrests? And is your driver's license valid? " The officer said looking stone-faced at Chase.

"Not that I know of, sir, and yes, my license is valid."

"I hate liars. When I run your name through the computer everything you just said is going to come back like you just told me right? You're cleaner than a bar of soap right?" The officer asked.

"Yes, sir—to my knowledge," Chase said nervously.

The officer slowly walked back to his car, closed the door, and started to gather information on Mr. Chase Douglass. Chase's whole life flashed in front of him. The relative ease and relaxed flow of college seemed as if it happened in a past life. What he would not give right now for the ability to be able to transport back in time and do-over every mistake that led him out of school to this moment. Chase was looking at a good stretch of time in prison if the police officer decided to search his vehicle.

So badly he wanted to hide the cocaine sacks in a better place and toss the gun. With the searchlights of the policeman's staring at Chase and his Oldsmobile, he knew that was a near impossibility. For a split second, he thought about swallowing the bags and then praying to God for safe digestion. Before he could act on any of his thoughts the officer was back standing in front of his driver's side window.

"Well, young man I got some good news and some bad news. Which one you want first?" the officer asked still stoic giving away nothing.

Chase rubbed his hands up and down his thighs before reaching his knees to help to release the nervous build-up of energy. "I'll take the bad news first sir."

"Well before I give you the bad news let me ask you a question. Do you have any illegal drugs or firearms in your vehicle? Remember, I hate a liar."

Chase was horrified as he debated the pros and cons of honesty in this situation. Asking himself as fast as he could about the legality of a searching his car under these circumstances. "No, officer, I don't have anything illegal in my car. I'm a college student and I graduate in a couple weeks," he lied.

"Fair enough. The bad news is that your license expired last month. That gives me the legal right to fuck you in every hole—no Vaseline if I so desired," the officer said. 'Officer Friendly' loved the power he wielded over the timid motorist.

Chase went numb. He forgot to renew his license last month and it was looking like it could be the biggest mistake of his life.

"That said, I'm going to write you three tickets, one for speeding, one for operating a moving vehicle without your license on your person, and one for driving on an expired license. I am also going to impound your car. That's the bad news," he said.

"So, you did say something about some good news right, officer? I'd love to hear it please," Chase said pathetically.

"The good news is that I graduated from McNair University and I'm proud alum. Therefore, I am going to assume that my beloved Alma Mater would never let into its hallowed halls a violent drug dealer. So, I'm not going to search your vehicle. You have no warrants or no arrest record so that also played in your favor. Bottom line is I could take you to jail but I'm not. Consider this your lucky night. You have five minutes to grab your personal belongings before the tow truck comes."

No words ever sounded sweeter in the English language to Chase. He patiently waited for the officer to go back to his patrol car after writing him the three tickets. Once he was inside, Chase went the trunk and grabbed his black leather book bag which gave credence to his college student defense. He went to the passenger side and as fast as he could with one swipe pushed all of the contents inside the glove compartment into his book bag. He took all of the keys off of his keychain leaving the ignition key only. Chase slung the book bag on his shoulders and waved a thankful goodbye to the officer. Because darkness is the absence of light, they cannot exist at the same time. Chase needed to choose one or the other. He walked south into the darkness.

58 May 22, 1993

Stretched out naked on her bed among her legion of teddy bears, Camara fresh out of the shower was doing her best to take it all in. The hope was that a hot shower would help to alleviate the slightly dull ache in her back and lower abdomen. Rubbing her belly as usual with her index finger in a circular motion, Camara sense of nostalgia began to take over.

Her college life at McNair University was about to come to an end in a mere few hours. The new friends and enemies along with the growing life inside of her made Camara marvel at how just unexpected life can be. Nearly all of her bags, boxes, and suitcases were packed. The only items that remained were spread neatly across Rhonda's newly bare bed. A black bra, a mauve silk maternity dress, and her deep forest green cap and gown proudly waited to be adorned by the soon to be graduate. *I never thought in a million years I'd be walking across the stage to get my degree pregnant. I am so proud of myself for making it this far at least.*

Rhonda had decided to go home to be with family from out of town who came to witness her grand walk across the stage. Rhonda did, however, promise Camara that she would come pick her up from the dorm room once she returned. Their last names being Truth and Wheatley respectively ensured they would be seated close to each other in the graduation line.

For Camara, staying on campus alone was a welcome respite. The quiet time helped to calm and focus her soul on her unborn child. The baby was the only thing that kept her sane and quite functional despite the circumstances surrounding its conception. The quiet was broken by the ring of the telephone. Sitting up slowly Camara picked up the telephone on her nightstand. "Hello."

"Hey sweetheart, how are you feeling?" Harold asked politely.

"Hold on, Harold. I gotta go pee all of a sudden. You can hold on or I can call you right back. Are you at work?" Camara asked quickly.

"I'm at work and I'll hold on," Harold said.

Camara walked as fast as she could to the bathroom. Luckily for her, she was already naked because if she was not she may not have made it to the toilet safely. Lightheaded with the pleasure of relieving herself, Camara nearly forgot that Harold was waiting on the phone for her. She wiped herself, washed up and slowly walked back to her bedroom.

"What's up, Harold?"

"So your big day is here! All the books, the numbers, the papers, the studying, the professors have come down to today. Are you ready to walk across the stage sweetheart?" Harold asked excitingly.

"Yes to all of the above. How is work so far today?" Camara asked.

"It sucks because I'm here instead of being there with my beautiful lady on one of the most important days of her life. But I had no choice. This job is going to make sure that you and our baby is well taken care of. Sometimes sacrifices have to be made. But in any event I just wanted to call you to tell you congrats on your day and that we are going to celebrate tonight. I love you," Harold said passionately.

"Thank you so much, Harold. I'll see you this evening," Camara said sounding as pleasant as she could.

Whenever Harold would tell Camara 'I love you' she would secretly cringe. On one hand, she did honestly love Harold, just not the way in which he loved her. So whenever he would say it in a tone that suggested he wanted to hear it said back to him, she would focus on other aspects of their conversation and be overboard positive about that. Rarely would she say it back to Harold and never did she say it first.

The graduation ceremony was slated to begin at 1:00. Looking at her clear jellyfish colored Swatch, Camara calculated that she had a little over three and a half hours until the big walk. Rhonda promised her she would be there by 11:30 which gave her two solid hours that she had no idea what to do with. Putting on her clothes all except for her cap and gown, Camara settled down on the suite couch and opened up the novel *Whispers* by her favorite author Dean Koontz. The novel made time pass quickly.

From outside the door, Camara heard keys jingling. Then the door slowly opened revealing Rhonda with a huge smile.

"Happy Graduation Day, girl!" Rhonda said as she walked in open armed.

"Ah, happy Graduation Day to you too, Rhonda," Camara exclaimed as she and Rhonda did their very best to embrace despite Camara's stomach.

"I am so proud of you, Camara," Rhonda said choked up through tears.

"Not more proud than I am of you. You are the best sister I never had," Camara said.

They hugged again and sat down beside each other on the sofa clasping hands. Rhonda wiped away a few tears and said, "Camara, I still don't agree with how you're handling this but I am going to do my best and help you handle it in any way I can. I've also decided that I'm going to be a godmother instead of an auntie. You're Mommy and I'm Gommy."

"Gommy? What the hell is a Gommy?" Camara said laughing hard.

"It's God and mommy all smashed up," Rhonda quickly retorted.

"I ought to smash you up for coming up with that dumb ass name," Camara said as the two of them laughed hard. "Damn girl you done made me laugh so hard I gotta go pee again. My lower back has been bothering me since last night. I'll be so glad when this baby comes out of me."

Rhonda stood up and went into her bedroom and marveled at how lifeless it appeared. No posters, pictures of loved ones, clothes scattered everywhere, textbooks or lecture notes. It saddened her that her life at McNair University had indeed come to an end.

"Almost four years ago we met. We've been through an awful lot. I do believe it was fate that christened our sisterhood. I mean we instantly hit it off. We could have hated each other. And now we are about to walk that stage together. What a blessing," Rhonda said to Camara as soon as she re-entered the bedroom.

"I could not have said it any better. Now stop with all that mushy stuff! I promised myself I wasn't going to cry anymore. But I did mean to ask you why you came here so early? Didn't you tell me you were coming around 11:30?" Camara asked.

"Well, you know, I got a pretty big family. We came about four carloads deep. Everybody was real anxious to get outta Buffalo so we came up early. I dropped them off at the Perkins in town. I'm too nervous to eat. But really I wanted to come up here and talk to you and clear the air. I wanted to reiterate that I am here for you and my god baby. The decision is not my decision to make. Your decision is here for me to respect. I vocalized my concern and after that, all I can do is respect it. The bottom line is you are my best friend and sister and I love you dearly, period," Rhonda said as she once again wiped away tears flowing from her eyes.

This was the best that Camara had felt since finding out that she was with child. To have a friend the caliber of Rhonda Wheatley in her corner, Camara felt beyond blessed. She tried to imagine how much darker her pregnancy would have been without Rhonda there by her side helping her walk through the foothills and mountains and it frightened her.

■

Exhilaration, excitement, and bitter-sweetness filled the Tuttle North Ice Rink. A little less than 800 students were about to receive their Bachelors of Science or Bachelors of Arts degrees in majors ranging from Accounting to Women and Gender Studies. A forest of graduates who were donned in green caps and gowns were smiling, laughing and taking pictures of treasured friends who made lasting impacts on their lives.

Professors from each department were assigned to walk out with the graduates and lead them to their appointed seating. The graduates stood in line alphabetically. They each held in their hand a prompt card that had their major, the type of degree they were receiving, and their name phonetically spelled out.

A silver haired older gentleman dressed in a dark blue suit with a red tie grabbed the microphone and said, "Graduating class of 1993 may I please have your attention? I am President Robert Van Dees and I'd like to have the honor of being the first person to say to you all congratulations on a job well done!"

Applause and boisterous cheers rang out inside the 2500 seat arena as the graduates hi-fived and hugged each other enthusiastically. President Van Dees continued, "The weather outside is not ideal but there is no rain in the forecast. I know everyone has plenty of family and friends that have come from great distances to watch you all receive your degrees. So, we want to make sure the show goes off without a hitch. I'd like to first introduce you to a man that will be helping me on stage today. I'm quite sure more than a few of you have had the pleasure of sitting in his class, please welcome Dr. Archibald King!"

The graduates once again clapped and cheered. No one cheered louder than Camara Truth and Rhonda Wheatley. Camara was surprised at first to see Professor King on stage. When she thought about how dedicated he was to each and every student that crossed his path, it all made sense.

"Esteemed graduates I cannot begin to tell you the supreme honor it is to be involved in this graduation ceremony. Like a lot of you, I too started at McNair University in 1989. So in a sense, I'm graduating with you, although I'll still be here God-willing for many years to come. I hope that you have learned as much from me as I have from you. Now that we got that out of the way, it is time to get down to brass tax. I will be reading off your names and achievements. As I read your name you will walk across the stage to the Honorable President Robert Van Dees to receive your replica degree. The official degree with all the trimmings will be mailed to you in the next two to three weeks. I am just as excited and anxious as all of you are to get this show on the road. Congratulations once again to all of you and I will see you on that graduation stage!" Professor King yelled as he exited stage left.

The cheers were even louder as the graduates began to realize that the moment of truth was almost at hand. Making his way from the stage, Professor King made it his business to visit with both Camara and Rhonda.

"Miss Truth and Miss Wheatley, two of my most beloved and respected students please tell me, how does it feel to accomplish greatness?" Professor King asked smiling from ear to ear.

"Greatness? I don't know if I'm willing to go that far, Professor King. However it does feel great to know that I finished what I started," Rhonda said.

"Greatness is what I said and greatness is what I meant, Miss Wheatley. Do I have to quote the bleak numbers associated with African American high school dropout rates in either of your respective cities? Not to mention New York State or the United States of America for that matter. I happen to know for a fact that both of you overcame tremendous personal obstacles and still shined! If I'm not mistaken, Miss Wheatley, your grade point average is somewhere north of 3.5. And your partner over here standing to your left is only graduating summa cum laude and third in a graduating class of nearly 800 pretty smart young folks. Both of you are off to one of the finest graduate schools in the country. Greatness! I rest my case and I will see both of you lovely young ladies later. I love you both!" Professor King said as both ladies rushed to hug and kiss him.

"We love you too, Professor King!" they said in nearly perfect unison.

"Ok everyone it is show time! Please make sure you are in the right line. There are ten lines with about 80 of you in each. Please under no circumstances switch with someone or leave the line for any reason. Also, make sure that there is enough space between you and the persons both in front of and behind you. The last thing we want is a repeat of the class of '87 which we don't have the time to get into. Once you reach outside all talking is to cease. It will take approximately eight minutes to walk to the stadium and another ten minutes seating everyone. Dr. Zarcone, if you and your line will lead the way we can get this show on the road!" President Van Dees said as he made his way outside.

■

Although there were little chances of rain there were also little chances of the sun making an appearance at McNair University for the graduating class of 1993. Clouds ruled the sky all around Ed Meath Stadium.

The stage extended from the touchdown to just short of the ten-yard line. The president of the college, distinguished alum, and local dignitaries filled the grandly decorated stage complete with a red carpet, flags and flowers of many different seeds.

Almost the entire football field from the twenty-yard line west to the twenty-yard line east was filled with sitting graduates impatiently waiting. The rest of the stadium stands was filled to near capacity with family, friends, and well-wishers.

The former governor of New York State's commencement discussed seizing the future by holding on to, and implementing, tried and true morals from years past. For the first time since he lectured his first class, Professor King was nervous. Wearing a black suit with a white button-up shirt and a silver tie, Professor King kept wiping away the sweat from his forehead with his silk pocket square. He could not figure if it was because he had never spoke in front of an audience of this size or if it was because the magnitude of his own personal accomplishment. He went from prison to being a professor. Having sway over impressionable but intelligent young people was a gift from God, Professor King believed. As he sat on stage surrounded by highly educated and successful people very much like him, Professor King did his best to control both his nerves and his emotions.

Camara Truth, on the other hand, was trying her best to control the ever growing pain that was visiting her lower abdomen every forty to seventy seconds. Camara was also dealing with the fact that she had to urinate again even though she went to the bathroom less than an hour ago. A wave of pain traveled from the top to bottom of her uterus.

Please let this be false labor. Not now. Please God, not today. Don't make my baby come yet. Please let me walk across the stage first…

"Camara, are you all right?" Rhonda asked in a loud whisper sitting three seats from Camara.

"Girl they better start calling people up now. I might not make it. This baby is acting like it's ready for the world!" Camara said as quietly as she could.

The thunderous applause answered Camara's question as Sir Edward Elgar's popular 'Pomp and Circumstance' began to play softly underneath. The first row of students on both sides of the football field stood up. The group of students seated to the left, starting from the inside isle walked first towards the middle of the football field, then towards the stage, and then turned left to the side of the stage where four steel steps greeted them on their way to glory. After the last person on the left side of the aisle reached safely in line, the graduates from the right side of the aisle followed suit.

Camara breathed in deeply to try and focus on gaining her strength. She looked towards the stage and imagined herself with a degree in hand to try and block out the sharp pain that seemed to want nothing for Camara except the discomfort that it was dispensing. This time, she used her whole hand to rub in a circular motion on her stomach.

"Excuse me, I promise I will get back to my assigned seat but I have to check on my best friend. She is pregnant and I have a feeling that she's in duress. Do you mind if I switch seats with you?" Rhonda asked the red haired white young white woman who was seated next to Camara.

"Absolutely—no problem," the young woman said. Rhonda exchanged places with her rather smoothly.

"Camara, are you about to have this baby? I know you're in pain. If you are we can leave now or have the ambulance meet us here."

"We can leave? Rhonda, I wouldn't dare take away from you what you rightfully earned. You are going to walk across that stage for your family and your friends and for yourself! Even if I was to give birth right now promise me that you will walk across that stage first! I mean it! I love you and I appreciate you but you worked hard for your moment and I'll be damned if I take it away from you!"

"You can't take away what I freely give to you, Camara. My moment is your moment. My moment is my god baby's moment. The health of both of you is my moment. I'm staying right by your side. When you give birth we give birth! I could care less about a piece of paper some man that I don't know is going to give me compared to what you are about to give the world. I love you but at this point, I could give a damn what you say because it is about you and my god-baby," Rhonda said sternly.

"Ok, Gommy. I hear you loud and clear. I love you and I truly appreciate it. I think I'm ok but I don't know because I've never given birth before. So please keep your eye on me because my sole intention is to have both of us walk across this stage without a hitch," Camara said as she sat back and tried to get comfortable.

Three more rows! God, I know you are with me. I don't want to ruin anybody's graduation day. We are almost to the stage. Please hold my baby up just a little longer.

The time had come for Camara's and Rhonda's row to stand up to take their walk across the stage. Putting on her bravest of faces, Camara grabbed the back of the chair in front of her with both hands and stood up. The clinching and pinching inside her was nearly too much to bear as she almost collapsed. However, Rhonda was there. She grabbed Camara from behind and stabilized her until she was strong enough to begin walking.

There were so many people in the audience and Camara had no idea where her mother was. She had hoped that her mother was not close enough to see the painful expressions on her face. Suddenly the pain stopped altogether and Camara thought she was out of the woods. With Rhonda, monitoring close behind Camara finally reached the left side of the stage near the metal stairs. There were seven students ahead of her as she patiently waited for their time to shine.

"Ryan Sutter...BS in Accounting," Professor King said with a huge smile and congratulatory handshake.

"Rhonda, please make sure I make it to the top of the steps. I know I'm about to have my...oh, God!" Camara moaned as she held her belly and nearly collapsed again.

"I got you! We are walking across this stage together!" Rhonda reassured her.

"Elonda Thistle...Political Science," Professor King said as he looked and noticed the distressed look on both Camara's and Rhonda's faces.

He instinctually knew Camara was close to labor. The strength that it took to stand in the wake of an impending birth was amazing and stubborn at the same time Professor King thought. But he admired her tenacity to fully complete what she started four years ago regardless of her condition.

It took every ounce of muscle in the fiber of Camara's being to get up those four steps. Once she scaled that mountain, she stood proudly there atop of it for a few seconds to soak it all in. Camara was so focused on getting on stage that she nearly forgot everything else.

"Card, Miss Truth," Professor King whispered with his hand extended.

As she handed Professor King her card he stepped away from the podium and asked, "Miss Truth, are you all right?"

Then the most intense pain that she ever experienced came crashing down. Remarkably enough she withstood it. Rhonda now standing on stage with her was close enough to her to hear Camara's courageously quiet yelp.

Camara had wanted to cry for months. The pain of betrayal and subsequent breakup with the love of her life, the joys of having good friends by her side, confusion about the father, and her complicated yet loving relationship with her mother all hit Camara as soon as she looked out onto the crowd.

"Camara Truth…Business with a minor in Economics…summa cum laude. Phi Beta Kappa!" Professor King said with a cracking voice.

Camara looked to her belly and then to the crowd again to see nearly everyone standing and applauding as she walked across the stage. The pain ratcheted up again, this time even more severe. She made it to President Van Dees, shook his hand and received her replica degree. Camara then fell to her knees just short of the stage landing. It was clear her water broke.

"Camara!" Professor King yelled as he ran over to her and scooped her up wedding night style and carried her down the stairs. Rhonda never ran as fast in her life toward Professor King. Boldly, Rhonda stopped mid-stage and grabbed the microphone, "Rhonda Wheatley, Sociology and Political Science…double major…magna cum laude."

The crowd roared with laughter tempered by concern for her friend Camara. From the audience, several members of Camara's family came rushing to her aide.

Professor King figured there was not enough time to take her to the hospital or even the campus clinic. He knew this baby was coming now. He carried Camara just to the right and slightly behind the stage.

He held her tightly in his right hand as he instructed a fellow professor to pull off his suit jacket from the left side. Once that was accomplished he then switched Camara to his left hand and off came the suit jacket.

"Ok everybody listen. Camara and her baby are going to be all right. I need three or four of you ladies to make sure that someone has called the ambulance and be on the look-out for them so you can properly direct them to our location. Gentlemen, I need you to take off your shirts and suit coats. Childbirth is a messy thing. I also need you to run as fast as you can and find me a huge bowl for one of the dining halls, rubbing alcohol and as much bottled water as you can find. The rest of you gentlemen I need you to ensure Miss Truth's privacy by turning around and standing post."

With about twenty-five members of both Camara's and Rhonda's family surrounding Camara, they created an impromptu circle of privacy.

The Professor King continued, "I need Camara's mother and Miss Wheatley. I need you on both sides of Camara to hold her hands and to give the strength that she sorely needs at this time."

To the letter, everyone followed instructions and sprang into action. Professor King rolled his sleeves, got to his knees, and positioned himself and his large hands to be the chariot bringing Camara's baby into this realm. Camara's cousin Louis came back quickly with several bottles of water, two of which Professor King instructed him to pour all over his hands. He wiped his hands with a t-shirt and swallowed the rest of the water. Quickly he sanitized his hands with the alcohol.

Although he appeared as if he was in control and knew exactly what he was doing, Professor King had never been more afraid in his life. He amazed himself by how he was able to remember the emergency childbirth lessons from old television shows and what he could muster up mentally from his aunt who was a midwife.

He checked Camara and found her fully dilated and could feel that the baby's head had engaged the pelvis. Camara was strong and beautiful. Mama Truth made sure her daughter was as comfortable as possible.

"Camara, honey, you are seriously dilated. I need you to focus on your breathing and not your pain. On your next contraction, I want you to take a deep breath and push with everything you got, ok? Here we go…Mama Truth, Miss Wheatley make sure she gives us a nice push on her next contraction. As the pain hit a crescendo and washed over her body, Camara screamed and pushed as hard as she could.

"Oh, that was productive! Oh, you are so strong. Take a deep breath and get ready to go again. You're in control now. Push when you're ready," Professor King said looking directly at Camara.

The push seemed to ease the pain and she wanted to do it again. Using her womanly instincts, she patiently waited for the next opportunity for a productive push. When the time was right she showed God the only thing greater than himself.

"I see the head! I see the head!" Professor King yelled like an excited schoolboy.

"That's it," Mama Truth whispered in her daughter's ear. "I'm so proud of you. Now push for Mama Truth. Bring my granddaughter home."

Bravely and without reservation Camara continued to push with an even louder yell as the baby was a little more than halfway out of her. Professor King was amazed at what he was witnessing. A few seconds later, Camara powered her first born child into Professor King's waiting hands.

Professor King held it in his hands as it let out a small cry which ushered in tears of joy from Mama Truth and everyone else. The graduation crowd began to sing happy birthday.

"It's a girl! A beautiful baby girl like her mother!" Rhonda said happily over the now raucous crowd.

Camara was on the brink of exhaustion. She so badly wanted to pass out but maternal instincts provided her the strength she needed to remain alert.

"Please, can I see my baby?"

Professor King wrapped her up in a blue dress shirt and handed the baby to its mother. Camara had never seen anything so beautiful. She looked to Camara like a plump juicy sun-soaked raisin with the most gorgeous eyes ever. She was the spitting image of her mother. Finally, Camara cried. She knew what it felt like to bring life to the earth.

"Nisa Rhonda Truth is my baby's name. Thank you all so much for helping me to bring her to life," Camara said as she cried even harder. Rhonda completely lost it. She had to be comforted by her mother as if she had just given birth.

Camara looked Professor King and mouthed thank you. She loved the man and was blessed their lives had collided in such a beautiful way at McNair University. *I don't know if this is Harold's baby or if it is Chase's baby. What I am 100 percent sure of is that this is my baby and I will dedicate my life to her,* Camara thought before she drifted into a well-deserved and extremely peaceful sleep.

LEG
Lady Esquire Group, LLC
Publishing & Management Firm

SILVER
BACC
BROS

Made in the USA
Lexington, KY
15 December 2019